A TALENT
FOR
MURDER

ANDREW WILSON

A Talent for Murder is not authorised
by Agatha Christie Ltd

**SIMON &
SCHUSTER**

London · New York · Sydney · Toronto · New Delhi

A CBS COMPANY

First published in Great Britain by Simon & Schuster UK Ltd, 2017
This paperback edition published 2018
A CBS COMPANY

3 5 7 9 10 8 6 4 2

Simon & Schuster UK Ltd
1st Floor
222 Gray's Inn Road
London WC1X 8HB

www.simonandschuster.co.uk

Simon & Schuster Australia, Sydney
Simon & Schuster India, New Delhi

A CIP catalogue record for this book
is available from the British Library

Paperback ISBN: 978-1-4711-4824-8
eBook ISBN: 978-1-4711-4823-1

This book is a work of fiction. Names, characters,
places and incidents are either a product of the
author's imagination or are used fictitiously.

Typeset in Sabon by M Rules
Printed and bound by CPI Group (UK) Ltd, Croydon, CR0 4YY

Simon & Schuster UK Ltd are committed to sourcing paper
that is made from wood grown in sustainable forests and support the Forest
Stewardship Council, the leading international forest certification organisation.
Our books displaying the FSC logo are printed on FSC certified paper.

To fans of Agatha Christie everywhere,
and one in particular

Editor's Note

Agatha Christie never spoke of her disappearance in the winter of 1926. As a result it has remained one of the great mysteries of modern times.

When I first mentioned the idea of this book to her, she was understandably reluctant. However, she agreed to be interviewed on condition that the resulting volume should not be published until at least forty years after her death. I too served my solicitors with notice to the same effect.

I must admit it is odd to see my own name as a character in these pages. I played a very minor part in this narrative and I have tried to keep my role to the bare minimum. It really is Mrs Christie's story and as such a great deal of it is told from her point of view, rather than my own.

In addition to Mrs Christie, I tried to speak to as many of the protagonists as possible to get an overview of the main events. Neither I, nor Mrs Christie, witnessed all the ensuing action and so, rather than leave out essential pieces of information, I decided to call upon the power of the imagination to reconstruct certain scenes.

This book is dedicated to those who did not survive the eleven dark days in December 1926. May they rest in peace.

– John Davison

Chapter One

Wherever I turned my head I thought I saw her, a woman people described as striking, beautiful even. That would never have been my choice of words.

Of course, when I looked again across the glove counter or perfume display it was never her, just another dark-haired woman trying to make the best of herself. But each of these imagined glimpses left a piece of scar tissue across my heart. I told myself to stop thinking of her – I would simply pretend the situation did not exist – but then I caught sight of another pale-faced brunette and the dull ache in my chest would flare up again and leave me feeling nauseous.

When I had first fallen in love with Archie, I had likened the feeling to a white dove trying to escape from my chest. Now that Archie's head had been turned by this creature I imagined the dove being strangled with a necklace of barbed wire and slowly rotting away inside me.

The distant sound of a brass band playing carols lightened my mood for a moment. I had always adored Christmas and I was determined that this year was going to seem just as festive and jolly as normal, at least for Rosalind's sake.

I walked over to the doll counter and a bank of china-white faces with blank blue eyes stared back at me. I picked up a doll with straw-yellow hair and ran my fingers down its smooth pale cheek. How funny that I had named my own daughter after my childhood doll, a toy that I had admired but rarely played with. Even then I had preferred to make up my own stories. Rosalind had not inherited my imagination, which was probably for the best as sometimes my fancy, although it had its benefits, left me feeling wrung-out and close to wretched.

As I put the doll back down on the counter and was about to pick up its black-haired twin with eyes like plump blackberries, I felt a pricking at the base of my skull. The hairs on the back of my neck bristled and a shiver went through me. I turned round, certain that someone was studying me, but met only the kindly eyes of elderly ladies dressed in their smart tweeds. I comforted myself with the knowledge that the Army & Navy Stores in Victoria was the kind of place where nothing dreadful could ever happen.

I had been coming here since I was a girl, when Granny B. would take me shopping to buy lengths of ribbon and bags of buttons. Afterwards my grandmother would always treat me to a delicious strawberry ice. And yet now, there was something terribly wrong. The feeling of dread was physical. My mouth was dry and my throat tightened. My breathing had quickened. I raised my hand to my neck to try to loosen the collar of my blouse, but that didn't help. I still felt as though someone was watching me and they wanted to do me harm.

When I was a small girl I had suffered from nightmares in which the character of a gunman had appeared to me. He had looked, so I had told my mother and sister, Madge, like a French soldier carrying a musket. But it had not been the sight of the gun that had frightened me. Rather, there had been something else that had disturbed me, something about his nature, his character. He was a personification of evil, a force I knew even then was only too real. Sometimes I would have dreams in which I would be sitting at the dining table at Ashfield, the family house in Torquay, and I would look up to see that his spirit had stolen into the body of my dear mother or Madge. Now I could almost feel the Gunman's hot, sour breath on the back of my neck.

I gathered my things together and, with the kind of slow, deliberate pace of a cat sensing the approach of danger, walked towards the exit onto Victoria Street. The sharp slap of the cold December air came as something of a relief. I had to stop myself from looking around nervously. My hands were trembling, my mouth still dry.

Surely the sense of danger I had felt in the Stores and on the street could not have been merely a product of my imagination. Yet I felt my cheeks redden as I remembered the incident of the cheque. I had been down at Ashfield, clearing out the house after my mother's death. What with the ten- or eleven-hour days, the boxes full of family mementoes, the moth-eaten clothes, the piles of Grannie's dresses, and the crowd of memories from my childhood that threatened to transport me back to the past, I must have lost my senses for a moment. I had been asked to write a cheque and I had signed not my own name but that of Blanche Amory, a character from a Thackeray novel. What had come over me? Was the same thing happening to me now? Was I losing touch with reality? It was a terrifying feeling.

I tried to take a couple of deep breaths, but my chest felt tight. I could not shake off the sense that at any moment something awful would happen. I wanted to rush back to the safety and comforts of the Forum, my club on Hyde Park Corner. But I didn't want the Gunman to follow me there. With a deliberately slow pace I set off down Victoria Street in the direction of the Underground. As I approached the entrance to the station the crowd began to swell. Even though my legs felt as though they might give way at any moment, fear propelled me forwards. Luckily, the station was busy and I disappeared amongst the throng. I pushed my way through the crowd, looking around as I did so. I bought myself a ticket and descended into the dark bowels of London. I felt sure I had shaken off whoever it was who had been following me. As I breathed in the sooty air I felt, for a moment, happy and safe again.

Some of my smart Sunningdale friends always thought it was rather quaint that I loved travelling on the Underground. But it was such a rich source of material: all those intriguing faces, those curious characters, not to mention the delicious possibilities it presented when it came to plot. *The Man in the Brown Suit* was a perfect example. It was a bit of a silly story, but it had proved popular with the readers, no doubt because of its dramatic opening which I had chosen to set on the platform at Hyde Park Corner.

That had been such a fun novel to write and I had dashed it off relatively quickly, not like the turgid stuff I had been churning out lately. Perhaps I needed a holiday. I hoped the short break in Beverley would do me – do both of us – the world of good. I certainly wasn't a subscriber to the theory that unhappiness bred creativity. This last year had been the most miserable of my life and look what I had produced: the Frankenstein's monster that was *The Big Four*, a novel that had been stitched together from a series of short stories, and a few lacklustre scenes for a book, *The Mystery of the Blue Train*, that would not flow.

A blast of hot air signalled the imminent arrival of the train. I grasped my hat and stepped closer to the edge of the platform so I could have a better chance of securing a seat. Another step and I could easily lose my balance and fall onto the tracks. Everything, all the pain that I had suffered over the course of the year, would come to an end. Archie would be free to marry, there would be none of the shame that always came with a divorce, and Rosalind would learn to love her new mother. What was it my daughter had said to me? 'I know Daddy likes me and would like to be with me. It's you he doesn't seem to like.' Only a child, in all her innocence, could utter such a thing. And yet while this was an accurate description of the state of our marriage, the observation had felt like another dagger to the heart.

As the train emerged from the blackness and started to hurtle towards us I took a step back. The noise of the engine vibrated in my ears, deafening me for a moment. Just then, I felt a light touch on the base of my spine. I turned to look round, but in that split second the pressure on my back intensified. I felt myself being shunted, pushed forwards towards the tracks. I opened my mouth to scream, but my throat had turned to sandpaper.

My hands reached out at awkward angles in a bid to hold on to something, anything, but I clasped at nothing but hot air. I could feel the skin on my cheeks begin to burn from a ferocious all-consuming heat that seemed to be sucking the liquid from my eyes. Just as I was tipping forwards, my head lolling like the doll's I had handled in the Stores, I felt an almighty wrench pull me back, a strength that I had hardly thought possible. I gasped at the force of it. It was then I felt myself melting away as I fainted and collapsed onto the platform.

I became aware of someone breathing into my ear. At first, I thought I was in bed, with Rosalind beside me. But then I became aware of a sourness, an unpleasant ferric odour that forced me to open my eyes. I woke up to a world of fragments and disjointed faces.

'I'm a doctor, stand clear, please stand clear,' a voice said.

I tried to speak, but could not. Again, there was that foul stream of air on my face. I felt someone cradling my head. The touch was soft and delicate, but my body, instead of relaxing, began to tense up. I attempted to sit, but the long fingers with their silky touch eased me back down again.

'Now, now, lie there for a moment or two. You nearly had a nasty accident. It seems that you fainted just as the train was approaching.'

'No, I felt someone—'

'Yes, you felt someone pull you back. That was me. I'm a doctor.'

Although the words should have been comforting, for some reason they sent a chill through me.

'Thank you, that's very kind. But I'm feeling much better now. If you could just let me get on my way I would be most grateful.'

The people who had gathered around me had started to disperse now that they thought they understood the situation: a lady had fainted, a doctor who had behaved like a hero was in attendance and had stopped her from falling onto the tracks.

'I think it would be wise if you took a couple of deep breaths,' he said, before leaning towards me. The stench of his metallic breath forced me to take out my handkerchief and place it over my nose.

'Now listen to me very carefully,' he said in a whisper. 'I think I have something to say to you that you will very much want to hear.'

At the moment I removed my handkerchief from my mouth, again in a voice only I could hear, he said, 'I wouldn't scream if I were you. Unless you want the whole world to learn about your husband and his mistress.'

I couldn't take in what he was saying. What did he know of Archie and that woman?

'Yes, I thought that would get your interest. Now, what I suggest is that you let me help you up and we can go and have a cup of tea.'

I felt the spider-like touch of his fingers begin to encircle my wrist.

'Sweet tea, that's what I would prescribe,' he said in a louder voice. 'Wouldn't you agree? That's the best thing for shock.'

I did not know what to do. Should I make a dash for it? Obviously the man had some information that he thought he could use against me, against us. No doubt he was a dirty little blackmailer, keen to extort money from me. How was he to know that our resources were stretched? On the face of it, it looked as though we lived a gilded existence. Yes, I had written six novels, and a collection of Poirot stories, but the earnings had not been that high because of the awful contract with my first publisher, The Bodley Head, which had tied me to five books on a low royalty rate. Thank goodness my agent had managed to extract me from that. In addition, the house cost a fortune to run and there had been a great many unforeseen expenses.

I could refuse point blank, but what if he took his nasty story to the newspapers? That would destroy Archie, I knew. Even after everything Archie had told me I still loved him and I would do anything in my power to protect him.

'I know a nice little café just around the corner,' he said, pressing my wrist with his fingers. 'Shall I help you stand?'

'I think I can manage by myself, thank you,' I said, easing myself up off the ground. I brushed my skirt of the dust and grime, quickly adjusted my hat and assessed the man standing in front of me. The first thing I noticed was the contrast between his creamy pale skin and his black beard. He had eyes the shade of sloes and full, fleshy lips the colour of blood. He was of medium height, nicely-dressed and seemingly well-educated, not your typical grubby blackmailer.

As we walked out of the Underground and back down Victoria Street, unperceptive strangers might have assumed that we were a married couple. But if those passers-by had taken the trouble to look into my face, I'm sure they would have seen the uncertainty and anxiety in my eyes.

'What is it that you want?' I asked.

'Let's wait until we are settled with a cup of tea,' he said. 'That way it will be much more civilised.'

I searched the street for a policeman, but there were none to be found. But perhaps it would be better if I dealt with this myself.

'First of all I must congratulate you on the success of *The Murder of Roger Ackroyd*,' he said. 'Absolutely first-rate. How you pulled it off, it's really quite extraordinary. I'm sure you've had a great number of people tell you so, but you can add my name to your growing list of admirers. You must have quite a mind inside that pretty head of yours.'

'Surely the last thing you want to do is talk about books,' I said stiffly as we walked into the café and sat down at a table some distance from the other customers.

'Oh, but it is. But first let me introduce myself. My name is Patrick Kurs. I'm a general practitioner from Rickmansworth. I have a small practice, mostly full of neurotic wives and husbands who drink too much. I suppose you could draw a parallel between Dr James Sheppard in *Roger Ackroyd* and me. Quite a fascinating character. You see, Mrs Christie, I believe you and I are remarkably similar in many ways.'

'I'm not sure what you mean,' I said, before a girl in a

black-and-white uniform came to our table to take our order. Dr Kurs ordered a pot of tea for two.

'As I was saying, I have made a great study of your work, Mrs Christie, and I am certain that you have a first-class criminal mind. You seem to know how a murderer's brain works. It's almost as if you have some kind of inner knowledge of how a killer feels. It's most uncanny.'

'Thank you,' I said, before I realised that what the doctor was saying was, in most people's eyes, far from a compliment. 'I mean – yes, that may be so, but what has this got to do with my husband? I would much rather you address the business at hand.'

When the girl returned with our tea we fell into silence, but as soon as she retreated, Dr Kurs shifted in his seat and cleared his throat.

'Very well,' he said. 'You see, it's come to my attention that your husband has been having a – how shall I put this? – an intimate relationship with another woman. That's correct, isn't it?'

I simply nodded my head, but I could feel my eyes blaze with hatred.

'And I take it you would rather this fact and the details be kept out of the newspapers?'

'So it is money. That's what you want?'

Dr Kurs blinked and looked slightly taken aback. 'No, not at all,' he said, laughing. 'I think you've underestimated me, Mrs Christie. What I propose is something far more than mere financial gain. I have, I

11

suppose one could describe it, a certain scheme for you. You may think it unconventional, but it is something that I am sure you will find of interest.'

'What are you talking about?'

'It's a plan that you alone can execute. You, Mrs Christie, are going to commit a murder. But before then you are going to disappear.'

Chapter Two

'You must be insane, absolutely insane,' I said as I started to get up from my seat. 'I'm afraid, Doctor – if that's indeed what you are – that you need to seek some medical attention.'

'I'm far from mad, Mrs Christie. After all, I haven't told you what I know about your husband and Nancy Neele.'

The mention of that name took what little strength I had left out of me and I dropped back into my chair. In that instant, a memory came back to me from my childhood. I had been picking primroses with dear Nursie. The air smelt of spring, the sky was cornflower blue and the flowers were the same shade of yellow as the sun. We had left Ashfield, crossed the railway and had walked up Shiphay Lane before turning into a field through an open gate. One moment I had been crouching down to examine a particularly beautiful primrose and the next I heard someone shouting. The violence in the man's voice was unmistakable. The farmer asked Nursie what she thought she was doing. 'Just primrosing,' Nursie had said. His face turned beetroot red, his eyes popped out of his face and he ordered us to get off his property. He said that if we were not off his land in under a minute he would boil us alive. I remember that I interpreted his words so literally I thought I could feel the lick of the flames begin to burn my toes. Beads of sweat broke out over my forehead and I felt so frightened that I thought I was going to be sick.

That was exactly how I felt now when I heard the name Nancy Neele.

'Would you care for some more tea? You look a little pale, which is not surprising in the circumstances.'

'No, I'm sorry, I have a train to catch. I have to meet my husband.'

'Really? I doubt very much that your husband will be coming home. Or if he does I don't believe he will stay for very long.'

'And what gives you that idea?'

'I suppose one could say I have a source. A good one. You see, one of my patients is the same Nancy Neele that I just mentioned.'

'Indeed?' I tried to make myself sound confident, but I could hear my voice breaking with fear.

'She first came to me with a problem with her digestion, I think it was. But it soon became obvious that the real issue was her nerves. She couldn't sleep, felt terribly anxious and so on. And then, when we started talking, she told me everything. I've become quite her confidant.'

Although I felt like fleeing I steeled myself to carry on with the conversation. 'And what, may I ask, did she tell you?'

'That she has been having an affair with your husband. That they are in love and that they plan to marry. That Archie would like to seek a divorce from you, but that he is worried about how you might react. I think they are concerned that, when faced with the news, you might do something stupid.'

I had to force the words out of my throat, which was still dry. I knew I dare not take a sip of tea in case Kurs saw my hands shake. 'And what have you advised her?'

'I have, you will be pleased to hear, maintained a strict policy of impartiality. I serve as a mere sounding board, if you will.'

'Does she know you were looking for me? Did she send you?'

'Oh, my Lord, no. Not at all. She knows nothing about why I am here – or my intentions.'

This last word sent a chill through me. Surely he could not possibly think I was going to take him seriously?

'This is all quite absurd. All you've told me is what I already know for myself. That my husband has, temporarily, had relations with another woman who is not his wife. And that, Dr Kurs, is the end of the matter. It is an entirely private affair and I have every intention of keeping it that way. Also I think you will find that there is something called a doctor's code of ethics. I am certain that breaking a patient's confidentiality must be against such a code and if you insist on—'

'Please do go ahead. Only I must warn you that I have in my possession a certain number of letters written by Miss Neele to your husband. I think you might find it highly embarrassing if any of these were extracted by some of the less savoury publications.'

Was he telling the truth? It was difficult to know. I stared into his dark eyes and felt something I could only describe as evil. I knew it would be unwise to underestimate him or cross him. But I couldn't let him get away with this.

'Well, I will certainly need some kind of proof of what you say.'

'Very well, expect something to arrive at your house shortly.'

'My house? You know where I live?'

'I know everything about you, Mrs Christie. It's been an enjoyable process, watching you, following your every move. As I have said I've made quite a study of you. Not only your books, but your whole life. If you doubt me simply ask me a question.'

I could not think of a single thing to say. I felt my throat closing up.

'Very well, let me expand on that point,' Dr Kurs continued, stroking his carefully trimmed beard. 'Let's just take something at random, shall we? I know, for instance, that you have an expert knowledge of poisons because of the work you did as a nurse and in the dispensary in the VAD during the war.'

'Such work was extremely common, Dr Kurs, and I am sure such an insight can be gleaned from sources in the public domain.'

'Indeed, Mrs Christie. But what is perhaps not in the view of the common man is your work with Dr and Mrs Ellis. I believe you learnt a great deal from them, particularly Mrs Ellis, did you not?'

The revelation left me speechless. 'And what about another chemist of your acquaintance? The one who used to carry around a sample of curare in his pocket. As you no doubt know, *Strychnos toxifera* is a rather pretty vine originating in South America. The natives there soon discovered it to be an effective poison and dipped their blowgun darts or arrows in the paste made from the plant. Once shot, a victim died from asphyxiation in a matter of minutes. What would you say, Mrs Christie, if I told you that, like that chemist of your youth, I too carry around curare in my pocket?'

I was tempted to tell him once more that he was mad, but something told me to keep my suspicions to myself. When I left the café I would go to the nearest police station and inform the authorities that there was a man who claimed to be a doctor in Rickmansworth who had lost his power of reason. The police would haul him off to the asylum and that would be the end of it.

'Let's just say I have my ways and means. Working

as a general practitioner for the last twenty years does have its rewards. Many of my patients, you see, commute into London and some of them hold positions of power and influence. One can, if one puts one's mind to it, find out almost anything about practically anyone.'

'I see,' I said weakly.

'For instance, I also know a great deal about your dear unfortunate brother, Louis Montant Miller, whom you call Monty, and his experience after the war, his overindulgence of spirits, whisky particularly, and his abuse of opiates. I think the newspapers would be very interested to hear about the crimes and misdemeanours of a mystery novelist's family. Their readers, I am sure, would come to the conclusion that you don't have to look very far for your inspiration. One never knows, the publicity may do you the world of good. That is, if you decide to go down that particular route, which somehow I very much doubt.'

I could stand it no longer.

'I'm afraid that I really must go. I have a train to catch,' I said, standing up.

'Very well, Mrs Christie. It seems a shame to cut our meeting short, as there were so many other things I would have liked to have talked to you about. But we will have another conversation soon.'

'We will?' I said, as I caught another whiff of his metallic breath.

'Oh yes, most definitely. In the meantime, go about your life as if nothing has happened. For instance, you must go with your secretary to Ascot tomorrow night as you normally would.' How did he know about that? 'And when you leave here I wouldn't contact the police if I were you. I have left instructions that, on my arrest or detention, certain documents and information be released to selected editors of various journals.'

'Goodbye then,' I said, turning from him.

'One more thing,' he said. 'Those plans I talked about. All that has yet to be set in motion. A great deal of thought, as I am sure you must be becoming aware, has gone into the plotting of this.'

Even though I loathed the very sight of him, I found it difficult to break away from his gaze.

'And by the way, you didn't faint. Rather, it was I who pushed you. But it was I who also saved you. One could say that I have the power to kill and the power to cure – an extension of my vocation as a doctor, I suppose. Expect a letter to arrive at your home on Friday. You may think you have a mind for murder, Mrs Christie, but you will soon find that you are not the only one.'

I made it to the Ladies' room just in time. I ran into the cubicle and just managed to shut and lock the door behind me before I fell onto my knees and was sick into the lavatory bowl. After pulling the chain, I stayed in the cubicle for longer than I needed as the nightmarish events of the morning continued to swirl around in my head. I knew I should go straight to the police, of course, but what if the horrible things Dr Kurs had said to me were true. The man had the power to ruin not only my life, but also the lives and reputations of my husband and my brother. Any gossip or scandal in the newspapers would almost certainly encourage Archie to break all contact with me. As for poor Monty, my brother's dependence on opiates was already dangerous; any more worry could result in even higher doses and almost certainly an early death. Could this man Kurs be nothing more than a lunatic, a fantasist? He was, without a doubt, mentally unhinged, but everything he said had been true, and there was a coldness and a heartlessness to him that frightened me.

But then an awful thought occurred to me. What if none of it had really happened? Could I have imagined the whole dreadful scene? I recalled the incident with the cheque when my mind had been disturbed. Was I suffering from another, more serious, attack? I had to try to pull myself together.

I took out my handkerchief and wiped my mouth. I dabbed some cold water on my face and contemplated myself in the looking glass. What a sight. My pale skin had turned an unnatural hue, almost like a ghost's, my blue eyes were bloodshot and my hair quite unkempt. I pinched my cheeks to give me a little more colour and tidied myself as best I could. When I came out of the café, it took me a while to get my bearings – the encounter with Kurs, real or imagined, had left me as unsteadied and imbalanced as a compass out of kilter. I started to walk down Grosvenor Gardens, past a building that always reminded me of Paris, and then Grosvenor Place in the direction of the Forum. I still felt nauseous and weak, but I willed myself forward.

As I caught a glimpse of Hyde Park Corner, I stopped for a moment. I unzipped my large handbag, took out a white handkerchief and pressed it to my mouth. The clean smell of the freshly laundered square of starched fabric reminded me of Ashfield and my mother. Instantly, I was a child again, safe in her arms. If only Kurs had pushed me down onto the tracks; at least then I would be with her.

The memory of my encounter with him – which had felt so horribly real – coursed through me like quick-acting poison. I held out my hand to grasp hold of a non-existent support as my legs threatened to give way. Hot tears flowed down my cheeks and I heard the sound of myself sobbing. I was conscious of people walking past me, but I could not bear to look up to meet their gaze. Was I going insane?

'Excuse me, is there anything I can do to help?' The man's voice was distinctly upper class and clipped, but carried with it an undernote of kindness.

I looked up through my tears and saw a couple staring at me. The man was tall with a good head of blond hair swept back from a high forehead and fine features, and he was wearing a smart black suit and expensive shoes. The girl, who also had blonde hair, was much younger, pretty and as slim as a reed.

'Sorry, I-I just had something in my eye, but I'm sure

it's cleared itself now,' I said. 'For a moment I felt completely blinded.'

'Oh, how dreadful, would you like me to check?' said the girl.

'No, I'm sure I will be all right,' I said. As I tried to move, my legs weakened and I fell back towards the wall that guarded Buckingham Palace.

The girl cast a concerned glance at her male companion – was it her brother? – and reached out to steady me. 'Here, please allow me,' she said.

'I'm so sorry to be a burden,' I said as I blinked back the last of the tears. 'I don't know what came over me. I'm on my way to the Forum, it's not far.'

'Please, you must let us accompany you,' said the man.

'Oh no, I couldn't possibly trouble you,' I said.

'It's no trouble at all,' said the girl. 'Sorry, my name is Una Crowe, and this is my friend John Davison.'

As I introduced myself, Davison's intelligent grey eyes sparkled with acknowledgement and curiosity.

'Surely not the famous author?'

'An author, yes,' I said. 'Famous, no.'

He told me how much he had enjoyed *The Murder of Roger Ackroyd*, which had been recommended to him by one of his colleagues at work, a man by the name of Hartford. Normally, I would have been delighted to hear his thoughts on the subject and enjoy the praise, but Kurs's recent mention of the novel had left a sour taste.

'I can't believe you haven't read it, Una,' he continued. 'It really is wonderful. It's got the most extraordinary ending, quite surprising, but I won't spoil it for you. But I must ask, with the *Roger Ackroyd* book, I wonder how—'

'And what is that you do, Mr Davison?' I said, trying to change the subject.

'The Civil Service, Whitehall, terribly boring,' he said.

'Not that boring,' said Una, smiling.

He cast her a slightly cross look.

'How long have you worked for your – your particular department?' I asked.

'Since Cambridge. It's been my life ever since.' It was obvious he did not want to elaborate.

'I've always thought that being a writer must be the most thrilling thing in the world,' said Una, filling the silence. 'Sitting around all day dreaming up plots. I'd love to try my hand at it. Of course, I realise I need some experience first.' Una continued to talk about her family, her brothers and sisters, her mother Clema and the loss of her father. Although he had died eighteen months previously she still missed him terribly, she said.

Una's voice seemed to melt away, almost as if I were hearing her from underwater. I remembered the time that I had first gone surfboarding with Archie. What fun that had been. How we had adored South Africa. I recalled that day when I had launched myself onto the board a little too enthusiastically. I had felt the energy of the wave die away but then had been completely unprepared for the enormous tidal swell that had swallowed me up and pulled me down beneath the surface. I had taken in a great deal of water, and heard Archie's voice from beneath the waves. What had he been saying? I could not make out the exact words, but I knew that his voice was full of concern and worry. I had been sure then, on that holiday, that he had loved me. And that had only been four years ago.

'Mrs Christie? Mrs Christie?'

It was Una. I felt a light touch on my arm, a touch that brought me back from my reverie. I focused on her superficially pretty face, but then noticed the semicircles of shadows that lay beneath her eyes. Grief even left its mark on the young. She was another version of me – of course, she was much more beautiful, far younger, but she carried around with her an open raw wound that would not heal. Did she also sense that I had suffered the recent loss of a parent too? Certainly, I felt some kind of strange, irrational connection with her; perhaps one day we would be friends.

'I'm sorry, you must forgive me,' I said, smiling at her. 'I was daydreaming. A terrible habit of mine.'

'Dreaming up one of your ticklish plots, no doubt,' said Davison, smiling. 'Bluff and double bluff, red herrings and the like.'

'I'm afraid I was rather,' I lied, as we continued to walk towards the Forum.

'I know you must be terribly busy, but if at some

24

point you could spare the time to talk to me, I would be grateful,' said Una. 'I've tried my hand at a few short stories, and a batch of poems, mostly about my—' A look of utter desperation clouded her eyes and Davison placed a hand on her shoulder.

'Of course, my dear,' I said. 'You are welcome to ask me anything you like, but I'm afraid I may not be the best person. I still think of myself as very much an amateur.'

'I doubt that very much,' she said as we came to a stop outside the Forum. 'And I really cannot wait to read *The Murder of Roger Ackroyd.*'

I gave Miss Crowe the address for Styles, my house in Sunningdale, and thanked her and Davison for their small, but important, act of kindness. We said our goodbyes and as I started to walk up the steps to the club I heard footsteps. I turned to see Davison, who pressed a thick cream-coloured business card into my hands.

'Don't be alarmed,' he said before I could respond. 'If you need to contact me please do not hesitate.' He paused and looked around him. 'I know Hartford, the man who mentioned your book to me, would be very interested in meeting you too.'

'Whatever for?'

'He believes, and I am sure he is right, that you have a first-rate brain.'

'I hardly went to school,' I said. 'My education is patchy to say the least.'

'Nevertheless,' he said, lowering his voice, 'I think that you may be a valuable asset for the department. Perhaps you could come in and meet him. We could talk some things over in private. There are certain delicate cases that you may be able to help us with.'

'What sort of cases?'

'I can't really say any more here, but I think you would make an excellent addition to the service,' he said, glancing over at Una, who was waiting for him on the street. Everything clicked into place. Davison worked for some kind of secret department. 'If you could write or telephone we could talk about it a little more.'

I was almost tempted, but of course the timing could not have been worse. 'I'm afraid I wouldn't be much use, especially at the moment.'

'Writer's block?'

'Something like that,' I said. As I looked into his intelligent eyes I thought about telling him something of my ghastly encounter with Kurs. But I still could not be quite certain whether it had not been more than the product of a frenzied, overactive brain. I opened my mouth to say something more, but then Una shouted over to him – if he didn't hurry up she was going to freeze to death, she said.

'Well, please bear us in mind when you feel you have a little more time. Goodbye.'

As I entered the lobby I caught a glimpse of Mrs de Silva walking into the library. I was quite fond of my Sunningdale friend with whom I had travelled to London that morning, but I knew I could not face her and so I took the stairs up to my room at the top of the building. I quickly shed my clothes, changed into a kimono that had once belonged to my mother and walked down the corridor to the bathroom. As I waited for a bath to run I brought the sleeve of the silky blue fabric to my face and breathed in the comforting smell of lavender. If only my mother were still here; she would have known what to do.

Since her death, in April, I had often felt my mother's spirit close to me. She had regarded herself as something of a clairvoyant. What was it my sister Madge had once said? That, if she didn't want Mother to know a certain something, she was careful not to stand in the same room as her. I willed my mother to come to me to give me a clue about what I should do, but there was an unassailable barrier between us: death.

I slipped off the kimono and lowered myself into the hot water. If I could just relax a little I might be able to figure a way out of this dreadful situation. I tried to think of happier times: of the feel of the water and the sunshine on my back in South Africa and Honolulu; of the giddy delights I had felt when I had first met Archie at the dance in Chudleigh; of the news that my first novel had been accepted for publication. The memories drifted over my consciousness like ripples in water, but I could not let go of the overwhelming sense that I was being poisoned. Of course, this wasn't a physical poison that would result in organ failure or respiratory problems or a heart attack. This toxin was seeping into my soul, staining everything that was good and honourable in my life. If I allowed it to spread I would be left as lifeless as one of the cadavers I had seen spread out on the mortuary slab during the war. The poison would have to be cut out before it infected the whole. There was, I knew, a risk that part of me would have to be sacrificed, like that amputated leg that I had once thrown into the hospital furnace, but I could see no other way.

After easing myself out of the water and drying myself, I dressed in the kimono again and went back to my room. I sat on the bed with an exercise book, half of which I had already used for the plotting of *The Murder of Roger Ackroyd*, and began to note down the events of the day, including the names Dr Patrick Kurs, Archie Christie, Nancy Neele, John Davison, Una Crowe and, at the bottom of the list, my own initials: A.C. As I did so I felt distinctly uncomfortable. This was one story I did not want to write.

Chapter Three

When I awoke from a night of fitful sleep my head was in a complete fug. I could still recall the stench of his breath, a smell that had left me with a near permanent nausea. When I sat down for breakfast the sight of the congealed scrambled eggs turned my stomach. I decided it would be best if I went hungry. Although I had doubted my sanity, I knew now that my encounter with Kurs had been all too real.

As I walked out of the Forum I half expected him to be waiting for me, standing over by the Royal Artillery Memorial like a harbinger of ill fortune, a sentinel of death. The recurring nightmare of my childhood, the sinister figure of the Gunman, had become a reality. Had I had a premonition of him since girlhood? Or had I somehow conjured his appearance? And how would it ever be possible to free myself of him? I recalled the conversation with Kurs of the day before. I was certain I could disappear for a few days, but there was no possibility that I could commit an offence, never mind one so heinous as murder. Writing about crime was one thing, but doing it oneself? It was quite out of the question.

I had considered telephoning that nice man Davison and asking his advice about what to do. But what if – as I suspected – Davison contacted the police? Could I risk that? Would it not be better if I tried to handle this myself?

The thought of Kurs's touch on the base of my spine sent a chill through me and turning up the collar on my coat against the cold did little to comfort me. I was due to see my agent at his office on Fleet Street, and although I had thought of cancelling the appointment, I remembered that Kurs had told me to go about my business as usual. Normally I would have taken the Underground, but the nasty incident at Victoria was still fresh in my mind, and so I took a taxi. The car stopped outside number 40 Fleet Street, a tall, imposing building, and after taking a couple of deep breaths I made my way up to the office. Of course, there was no question of telling Mr Cork about my troubles; ours was a purely professional relationship and I could not bear it if I were to break down in front of him.

As I entered the office a tall young man with an enigmatic smile greeted me. Edmund Cork had taken over the agency from the fearsome Hughes Massie after the old man's death, and he seemed to be making rather a success of it. I feared, however, that his expectations for me were higher than the poor reality.

'Good m-morning, Mrs Christie, p-please sit down,' he said with his slight stutter.

'Thank you,' I said.

'Now, h-how is the writing progressing? Well, I hope?'

'I'm afraid I haven't made as much progress as I had wished. Ever since the death of my mother I have found it rather difficult to concentrate.' There was no need to mention the recent upheaval in my personal life.

'Of course, of course,' he said. 'Take your time by all means. But I am pleased to inform you that there do seem to be a good many people waiting for your next book. The *Evening News* will almost certainly want to buy the serial rights. Perhaps we could ask for an increase on the £500 they paid you for *The Man in the Brown Suit*.'

At the time, I had been astounded by the amount of money the newspaper had been prepared to pay for the opportunity to serialise my novel, even if they did run it under that ridiculously silly name, *Anna the Adventuress*. I had considered complaining about that, but then I thought of the £500 and decided to keep my mouth firmly shut. I used the money to buy my darling Morris Cowley motor car.

'And we are, of c-course, looking forward to the publication of *The Big Four*.'

I certainly wasn't; in fact, I wished I could have strangled the thing at birth. Had it not been for the help of dear Campbell, Archie's brother, I doubted whether I could have pulled the thing off.

'I wish I could have come up with something a little more original. After *Roger Ackroyd*, I feel that my readers, such as they are, will be more than a trifle disappointed.'

'That c-cannot be helped now,' said Mr Cork, running his long, elegant fingers across a pile of papers on the desk in front of him. 'How do you like the cover design? Rather striking, I thought.'

The artwork, in tones of blue and black, showing a giant number 4 towering over the silhouette of the London skyline at night, was probably the best thing about the whole book. Again, this was something I thought best not expressed at this point.

'I'm rather dreading the reviews,' I said.

'Oh, don't mind those. However, I have heard that we are likely to get what I hope is a positive one from *The Times Literary Supplement*. By the way, I have heard that publication is scheduled for the autumn in America.'

There was a slight pause.

'I'm sure you have your head full of ideas for the next book, and you wouldn't want to give anything away, b-but you couldn't possibly g-give me a—'

'I'm afraid I'd rather not say,' I said. 'I'm rather superstitious on that score, as you know.'

'Of course, I understand,' he replied.

I let him continue to talk business – contracts, percentages, serial negotiations – for the next twenty minutes, but I could not concentrate. 'I must return home so I can get back to my desk,' I said, standing up.

'Thank you once again for calling in to see me, Mrs Christie.' Mr Cork led me towards the door. 'And I look forward to receiving your new book whenever you are ready. I won't hear the last of it from my wife until you do. She does rather hope it will feature your funny little Belgian detective with that curious moustache. Can you put her out of her misery?'

'I am giving nothing away, Mr Cork,' I said. 'I would have thought you knew me better than to ask.' The words formed themselves in a rather harsher fashion than I had intended.

'Of c-course, g-goodbye,' he said, blinking and looking a little startled. 'Until next t-time.'

As soon as I was out of the door I felt the sting of shame eating away inside me. Why had I been so rude to dear Mr Cork? The taxi driver who took me from Fleet Street to Waterloo Station also tried to engage me in polite conversation, but I was so full of anger and anxiety that I cut him short too, which in turn resulted in me feeling even more at odds with myself.

Normally, I loved travelling by train and would usually savour every moment of the journey home to Sunningdale, but today I felt I could not enjoy even the simplest, most joyful of sights. Kurs was turning my soul black.

From the station I walked the ten minutes home with my overnight bag, again without noticing my surroundings. With each step the feeling of dread increased, as if I were walking towards my death. Apart from Rosalind and Charlotte, my secretary and good friend, and of course Peter, my wire-haired terrier, I had this past year come to associate the house with nothing but misery and despair.

When I had first looked around the rather grand and absurd house, with its gabled bay front and tall chimneys, I knew that it would cost too much money to run, but Archie had declared that it was just what we had been looking for, and so I had agreed. Later, I had learnt that the house had a reputation for being if not exactly cursed, then certainly unlucky; its first owner had apparently lost a great deal of money and its next had experienced marital difficulties – I had heard that the mistress of the house had run off with another man. And whatever had possessed Archie to name it Styles, after the house featured in my first novel, a building steeped in deception, deceit, and murder?

Kitty the maid took my hat, coat and overnight bag and told me that Miss Fisher – Charlotte – had taken Rosalind and Peter out for a walk. Thank goodness, as I knew it would be hard for me to stop myself from telling Charlotte everything. If she saw the distress in my eyes I would have to lie and say that I had had yet another argument with Archie. She knew all about my marital problems, I'm sure the whole household did, including the servants; one would have to be deaf to be ignorant of them.

Upstairs, in my bedroom, I took out the set of three golf balls and tees in a leather case that I had bought for

Archie for Christmas. I opened the case and breathed in the heady smell of new leather. A silly present, really, in the face of it all. Who was I fooling? Archie was most probably lost to me now. Another woman had captured his heart. But I knew that, if tomorrow he were to say to me that he had thrown over Miss Neele, I would be ready to embrace him. A line from one of my books came back to me: 'The heart of a woman who loves will forgive many blows.' It was certainly true enough for me.

I knew that he was too handsome for me the first time we met at that dance given by the Cliffords at Ugbrooke House. He was tall, fair-haired, blue-eyed, with a classic profile and a dimple in his chin that made me swoon. I had been much younger then, only twenty-two, but I had always considered myself plain, despite what some of my previous suitors had said. What on earth had Archie ever seen in me, I wondered. I was hardly the world's best conversationalist. But there had been something, some spark, some connection, that both of us felt on that first meeting fourteen years ago.

He had, I remembered, persuaded me to disappoint a good number of dance partners that night; he wanted, it seemed, to monopolise me. And I had been swept away by him. At the end of the evening I told myself to be content with the mere thrill of the occasion; I was sure that I would never see him again. I would make do with good, kind-hearted Reg, who one day would return from Hong Kong. He had sent me nice letters and although I realised that he would make a decent husband I knew he was not the sort of man who would thrill me every time he walked into the room. Looking back, I acknowledged that I had been a fool to expect anything more than the Reggies of this world. I should not have aimed higher. I should not have sought out or accepted the attentions of a man like Archie. How I wished that I had listened to my mother who had warned me of his character. How had she put it? He had, she had said, a ruthless streak. And Archie's mother, Peg, had never liked me and, quite ridiculously, had branded me as a 'modern' woman, no better than I should be. All because I had been rather fond of wearing those Peter Pan collars. How funny, I thought. Nothing could be further from the truth.

The opposition of both our mothers, together with the advent of the war, had made us all the more determined to forge a future together. And so, when Archie had been given three days' leave in the Christmas holidays of 1914, we ignored the protestations of his mother, with whom we were staying, and married on Christmas Eve. It had all been done in such a rush that I had not had the time to get ready properly. I must have looked quite a fright in that funny little purple velvet hat. It did not matter, of course, because we were happy.

'Mummy! Mummy!' I heard as the front door opened. 'We're back!'

I dabbed my eyes with a handkerchief, checked myself in the glass and came down the stairs to greet Rosalind, my little angel.

'Oh, you should have seen Peter, he was so funny,' she said, taking off her coat. 'He made a little friend, a little sausage dog called Freddie, while we were walking on the edge of the golf course. The two of them started chasing each other around. And then all of a sudden this golf ball came whizzing past them and they shot off in the direction of—'

'That's enough now, Rosalind, dear,' said Charlotte in her singsong Scottish lilt, putting a hand on the girl's shoulder to quieten her. 'You can tell your mother all about it after you've had your bath.'

Rosalind opened her mouth to protest, but Charlotte shot her one of her faux-stern looks that always did the trick. When my daughter was upstairs and the maid had retreated to the kitchen Charlotte took my arm and, as I suspected, began to question me about what was wrong. I looked awfully pale, she said. Had I been crying? I told her that I was suffering from another attack of nervous tension, brought on by the ongoing situation with Archie. She offered to postpone her trip to London the next day – she had been so looking forward to her day off – but I told her that on no account must she do such a thing. Unknown to her, I had my own motives for getting her out of the house.

Yet I don't know how I would have coped without her support, the sight of her kind grey eyes, the soft touch of her hand on mine. Charlotte sometimes said things that were difficult for me to hear. After the initial revelation about his affair with Miss Neele, Archie had left me, only to return a few weeks later. He had admitted that he had made a mistake, and he thought that it was worth trying to keep our marriage going for the sake of Rosalind. We shared a bed for a time, but that had all stopped months ago and now he slept in another room. 'He won't stay,' Charlotte had said to me, a remark that had made me furious at the time. I related that conversation back to her now and told her that she had been right all along.

'Well, it sounds as though you could do with some cheering up,' she said.

'I think you're right, Carlo,' I said, using the name that Rosalind had given her.

'Dancing it is then – doctor's orders.'

I gasped, as I immediately thought of Kurs and what he had said to me.

'No, I'm being selfish. You're tired, I can tell.'

'Nonsense,' I lied. 'I'm sure it will do me the world of good.'

Chapter Four

I had hoped that the dancing would do something to calm me, but as I lay in bed my nerves felt frazzled. When sleep eventually came it was disturbed and, at dawn, I was relieved to see the weak December sunlight begin to leak through the edges of the curtains. I got up and walked across the bedroom to the chest of drawers in the corner. In the third drawer down, amongst a selection of ribbons and buttons, souvenirs and postcards, I pulled out an envelope and from it I selected a letter. It was the letter my father had written to my mother a few days before his death. 'You have made all the difference in my life,' he had written. 'No man ever had a wife like you. I thank you for your affection and love and sympathy. God bless you, my dearest, we shall soon be together again.' At times, over this last year, I had taken out the letter and pretended that Archie had written it to me. It was silly and foolish, but it made me feel better; now I knew that it would be impossible to make that imaginative leap.

As I sat at my dressing table, brushing my hair, I heard Charlotte telling the maid that she would be back later that evening, soon followed by the slam of the front door. Now all I needed to do was deal with Archie. I knew I couldn't tell him the truth. I couldn't risk Archie being at Styles when something arrived from Kurs. No, I would need to behave in such a way as to alienate him even more so as to drive him out of the house. That shouldn't be too difficult. Archie was a supremely selfish being and hated feeling guilty just as much as he hated the thought of not being happy. If I could try to make him feel both guilty and unhappy I would have brought about the desired effect.

I dressed for breakfast and went in to see Rosalind, who was playing with her teddies on her bed. She told me that she had already had breakfast, and she wanted to know what the day held in store for her. I too could have asked the same question.

'If you are a good girl and stay in your room for the next half an hour or so, I promise to take you to see your grandmother later,' I said, hoping that I would be able to keep my word.

'Can Peter come too?' she asked.

'Very well,' I replied.

Archie had already finished a plate of bacon and eggs by the time I arrived in the breakfast room.

'Good morning,' he said, barely looking up from *The Times*.

'Good morning, dear.'

Archie grimaced at this term of endearment, but said nothing more.

'Oh, it will be lovely to see some real countryside,' I said. 'Berkshire – it's all very well and good in its own way, but it's a little too clean-cut and organised for it to be remotely like real countryside, don't you find? How I long for some open space and fresh air. I don't feel I can even breathe properly in this county. To be near the sea or the wilds of Dartmoor. Don't you think that would be wonderful, Archie?'

'I hardly think it practicable,' he said.

'I'm sure you could get a position in Exeter or Plymouth. Or you could set up your own business and come up to London and stay in your club for a few days when need be. I do think we would be happier, don't you, Archie?'

'Well, I—'

'And we could put whatever has happened behind us and start again. We might even be lucky enough to buy one of those houses on a cliff overlooking the sea. Do you remember when we were first married and we took that jaunt along the coastal road from Dartmouth to Strete and Torcross? And do you remember me pointing out that rather wonderful house that seemed to hover over the bay just outside Blackpool Sands? St Michael's Manor, I think it was called. I'm sure I would be able to write there, in a room overlooking the sea. We could take Peter for such lovely walks and Rosalind, well, imagine how much she would adore it. I'm sure she would just come alive, all of us would. And we both know so many people down there, people we really like, not the superficial set that you get up here. And just imagine the—'

'I'm really not at all sure that would be a wise decision.'

'What do you mean? How could it not be? After all, you've seen how difficult it has been here for me to write of late. I think a change of scene would do us all the world of good.'

'Perhaps you're right, but I'm afraid it's not going to happen. My job is just not the kind one gives up. I doubt I'd find another position that easily and—'

'And?'

'Well, there are certain things I would miss, if you want me to be honest.'

'I don't doubt it,' I said sharply. I knew the tone of my voice would anger him.

'And what is that supposed to mean?'

'You know very well, Archie.'

'I think this discussion is over. I've got work to do.'

'And while we're talking of things you would miss, what about Miss Neele? Surely she would be one of them, or do you have no intention of missing her at all because you have no intention of giving her up?'

'Do you really want to hear the truth?'

I remained silent as I bit the inside of my cheek so hard that I began to taste blood. Although I had manufactured the argument there was no denying that the emotions I felt now were deep and all too real.

'Do you?' Archie repeated. I could see a vein throbbing in his forehead.

I nodded.

'Well, the truth is this. I've got no intention of moving to Devon with you because I'm no longer in love with you, Agatha. I'm sorry – I've told you I am sorry a thousand times – but our marriage is over. You know we've tried. You know how I tried, how I came back. But it's impossible – I can't pretend any longer. I love Nancy, Miss Neele. We want to get married and start a new life for ourselves. You know it will be for the best in the long run.'

'I know nothing of the kind,' I said, tears beginning to stream down my face. 'You've always been selfish. My mother was right when she said—'

'When she said what? Your mother was nothing but a—'

'Don't you dare say a word more. Not a word, I tell you. She always said how ruthless you could be. Don't trust him, she told me. He's only got his own interests at heart, not yours. And here you are fighting for your right to be happy. But what about my right to be happy?'

'At this stage, I'm afraid I couldn't care one jot whether you are happy or not. All I know is that it's become impossible for me to carry on being with you. You've become quite unbearable.'

He paused. A nasty silence lingered in the air like a poisonous gas.

'Did you go and see that doctor?'

The word made my heart miss a beat. 'Doctor? Who do you mean?'

'The one I mentioned to you a while ago. The one who has had great success with women and their nervous problems.'

'No, no, I didn't. And I keep telling you I don't have a problem.'

'So when you signed that cheque and you didn't know who you were, that behaviour was quite normal, was it?'

I did not answer him.

'I am only trying to help. You know I will always care for you,' he said, placing his hand on my arm. His touch felt as lifeless as a dead fish.

'Take your hand off me,' I said. 'You don't care for me. You only care for yourself. I doubt if you really care for that simpering little creature of yours. She may have good looks now, but one day they will fade and you will pass her over too.'

'Don't you dare—'

'And if I do dare to talk about her in such a way? What then?'

'You are simply being hysterical again. And you know how I can't bear it. You really are your own worst enemy, Agatha, don't you realise that?'

'So I suppose the weekend is quite out of the question?'

He looked appalled. 'The weekend?'

'In Beverley.'

'Oh that.' It was obvious he had forgotten about it. 'I think it's for the best if I stay with the Jameses tonight and for the weekend, don't you?'

'And I suppose Miss Neele will be a guest?'

'I don't see how—'

'Will she or won't she be a guest at Hurtmore?' The appropriateness of the name of the Jameses' cottage was not lost on me.

'She will.'

'Yes, so I think you're right. I will cancel the rooms.'

As Archie opened the door, his frame filling the space, I wondered whether I would ever see him again.

'I do love you, Archie,' I said. 'Whatever happens, remember that, please.'

He turned away from me and walked from the room. A moment or so later I heard the front door slam. I covered my mouth with my fist to stifle the sound of my sobs. I had succeeded in driving him away for the weekend, I had achieved exactly what I had set out to do, and yet I felt absolutely wretched. I wiped my eyes as the maid came into the room carrying a tray.

'Have you finished, ma'am?'

'Yes, thank you. I'm going upstairs to write.'

'The morning post is here, ma'am. Shall I put the letters down on the table?'

I nearly snatched the post out of the poor girl's hand. By the time I had reached my bedroom I had shuffled through the letters and selected the one I knew was from Kurs. The handwriting, in black ink, was measured and precise. I sat down on my bed before I tore open the envelope.

The first letter I took out left me momentarily confused. Disjointed fragments of sentences and odd words jumped out at me: 'cream complexion', 'intensity of feeling', 'that very special place which we can call our own', and 'many ecstasies to come'. Then, with a sickening feeling, I realised that the handwriting was Archie's and that this was a love letter that he had written to Nancy. There were other words, other phrases, that left me blushing. He had never addressed me in such intimate terms; in fact, I had not been aware that Archie had even possessed such words in his vocabulary. No wonder that woman had such a hold over him.

I dropped the letter on the bed and took out another thin sheaf of paper.

Dear Mrs Christie

    I hope this finds you in good spirits. It was a pleasure to meet you on Wednesday and I am looking forward to becoming better acquainted with you in the next few days.

    In case you are having any doubts about the plan that I proposed to you I am enclosing one of the many letters that your husband sent to Miss Neele.

*Over the course of the last couple of months Miss
Neele has regularly brought in such protestations
of love so as to seek out my advice. She regards me
very much as her guardian, I believe, who is able to
dispense not only medicines for her delicate health
but also supply her with guidance. She also told me
that she was worried that her parents, with whom
she still lives, would find these letters and so, when
I offered to keep them for her at my practice, she
was more than grateful. I am sure you will agree
that the correspondence makes for illuminating
reading.*

*I suggest we meet this Friday morning, at 11.30,
at the Silent Pool near Newlands Corner, Surrey.
I will issue you with more instructions then. All I
will say for now is that today you are going to step
away from your life.*

Yours most sincerely
Dr Patrick Kurs

By the time I had driven the twenty or so miles from
Sunningdale, past Newlands Corner to the patch of
rough ground near the Silent Pool, I had decided on my
course of action. I tried to convince myself that, once
it was all over, and I related to Archie everything I had
done to keep his name out of the newspapers, he might
learn to love me again.

As I got out of the car I drew the collar of my fur
coat around my neck. I listened for signs of another

car approaching but all I could hear was the sound of the wind in the trees and the lonely cry of a distant bird. I walked past Sherbourne Pond, along the path to the Silent Pool. I had heard it said that the pool might have been an old chalk quarry fed by underground springs. The water was as clear as a looking glass, but I had no desire to see myself reflected on its still surface.

I had always believed that past tragedies often left their mark on a place like a stubborn bloodstain that could never be removed. Here, it was no different, and the trees seemed to whisper a tale of sadness. Apparently in days gone by a girl had come to bathe in the pool. But no sooner had she taken off her clothes than she had been shocked to see a man on horseback approach out of the mist. The nobleman had tried to entice her out of the water but the further the man proceeded into the pool the further the girl swam away until she got out of her depth and drowned. Later, when the man's hat had been found at the scene, he had been identified as King John. The story, I knew, was likely to be apocryphal, but it still made me shiver and as I walked I fancied I could still hear the muffled cries of the girl gasping for air.

As I passed through a tunnel of trees I saw a figure with his back to me.

'Hello, Mrs Christie,' said Kurs, without moving. 'Come and admire the water. It is looking particularly enchanting today.'

I had to force myself to walk towards him.

'I have always been drawn to this spot,' he said. 'Not only because of its rather morbid history of which I am sure you are aware. The Silent Pool holds a rather special place in my heart. Do you know why?'

'No,' I said in a whisper.

'It is here that I first proposed to my wife.'

'You're married?' I tried to stop myself from sounding astonished, but it was too late.

'I am indeed. Even though that may come as something of a shock to you. Do you think it odd, Mrs Christie, that any woman would want to marry me?'

'No, it's just that—'

'It doesn't matter to me in the slightest. And actually what is rather amusing is that although my wife no longer finds me appealing she will not grant me a divorce.'

'And why is that?'

'Look at your own situation, Mrs Christie. I think it's safe to say that you would rather hang on to your husband, even after what he's done to you.'

'Well, I—'

'Imagine if you never let him go. Imagine how he would feel if you refused to free him from the ties that bind you together. Certainly, whatever kind feeling he ever had for you would evaporate. That love would surely turn to resentment and the resentment would mutate into a poisonous, festering hatred. You never know what he might be tempted to do if he felt he was given no choice. One day he might not be able to contain his feelings any longer. He might start to fantasise about what it would be like without you. If you could just disappear then his life would be so much simpler. He could start afresh, perhaps even one day, when everything had blown over, marry again.'

'What are you saying?' I said, suddenly so terrified that I could hardly speak.

'Don't worry. I'm not here on Mr Christie's behalf. Oh, my dear me, no,' he said, laughing. 'Did you really think—'

I smelt his breath again. Perhaps Kurs saw me wince because a moment later he took out his handkerchief and placed it over his mouth for a second or two. I noticed the white fabric rising and falling with each breath. I imagined him dead, with the handkerchief placed over his face, the cotton no longer moving.

'What I have in mind is much more ingenious than that. As I said to you when we first met, you and I have a great deal in common. We both have rather inventive minds. In fact, I have always rather fancied myself as a writer of detective novels. Like you, I am a great fan. Edgar Allan Poe, Wilkie Collins, Conan Doyle, and a whole host of imitators. I've tried my hand at writing them, too. Fiendishly difficult, but I think I do have, if I may say so, an extraordinary aptitude for plotting, which is, as you know, the chief skill of any detective-fiction writer worth his, or indeed her, salt. I haven't sent the manuscripts off to a publisher just yet. They need a little polishing but perhaps that is something you could help me with.'

'Perhaps,' I said in a non-committal fashion. He really was quite insane.

'Sorry, I've rather wandered off the central point. Getting back to my wife, Flora. She won't give me a divorce – a Catholic, you see – and so I am afraid I am going to have to resort to more drastic measures. I am going to have to kill her. Or rather not me, Mrs Christie, for you are going to kill her.'

'Me?'

'Yes. If she dies, if she is killed, then of course the police will suspect me and quite rightly so. If she dies I will not only sidestep the question of divorce but also inherit quite a large sum of money. I will be the number one suspect. But, you see, if she is killed by a stranger – and I have an alibi – then there will be nothing linking me to the crime.'

'But it's impossible.'

'You of all people, of all writers, should know that nothing is impossible in the world of the detective novel.'

'But this is not a novel, I'm afraid. This is—'

'I know,' sneered Kurs. 'And it's so unbearably messy, isn't it? I often wish that life was more like the stuff of fiction.'

'But don't you think it rather dangerous to confuse the two?'

'I'm not here to have a philosophical debate with you,

Mrs Christie. I am here to tell you about what is going to happen next.'

'Next?'

'Yes, next. From now on I think it will be easier for you to think of yourself as a character controlled by me. I will issue you with a set of instructions, a list of things to do at certain times. If you follow them to the letter you will have nothing to worry about. If you don't then I'm afraid your husband's unpleasant little secret will be published in the press.'

'You don't think I'm going to go along with this – this charade.'

'I don't see what choice you have.'

'But I could very easily report this whole thing to the police. I don't think they take kindly to blackmailers.'

'Yes, you could. But I am assuming that you value the health of your husband.'

'I do, yes.'

'I'm sure you wouldn't want him to come to any harm. And then there is, of course, your daughter. Seven is such a vulnerable age, don't you think? During my career I've been called out to the bedsides of several young children who I am afraid did not survive. Terribly tragic. It often spells the end for the parents too, of course. And by the way, if you think you could just call the police and have me arrested, please reconsider. I have an associate, a degenerate character who takes pleasure in this sort of thing, who will set in motion certain procedures on my arrest. I think he is looking forward to being given the chance to act out his perverse desires. And by the way, his appetite for this sort of thing is much stronger than mine.'

I could feel the hatred emanating from my eyes.

'I can understand your reluctance to speak. Also, you know as well as I do that there are certain poisons that cannot be traced in the body after death.'

If I had had a gun at that point I would most likely have shot him in the head. Indeed, I had to dig my nails sharply into the palms of my hands to stop myself from clawing his eyes out.

'And so I suggest you start listening to me.'

The afternoon passed in a – what was it? A blur, a daze, a fog? No matter how hard I thought I couldn't find the right word to describe the strange feeling that possessed me. I supposed that was because I felt as if the events were not happening to me but to some other person entirely.

After leaving Kurs at the Silent Pool, I returned to Styles. The housemaid told me that I had missed a telephone call from Mrs de Silva, who wanted to know whether I would like to play bridge. I sat through lunch, not really tasting the chops placed in front of me, and I paid little attention to Rosalind's prattle until I felt a tug at my sleeve. Rosalind was saying something about a trip to see her grandmother. Apparently I had promised her, and said that Peter could come too.

I had to do something to fill up the day and, after

what Kurs had told me, writing was out of the question. I ushered Rosalind and the dog into the Morris Cowley and drove to my mother-in-law's house in Dorking. I could never relax with her at the best of times. Peggy observed every little thing I did and I got the feeling that she was always ready to judge me. Today I was even more on edge than usual. I couldn't any longer blame my nerves, as I had previously, on the great loss I had felt following my mother's death. And I couldn't tell her what was really on my mind.

As I turned off the engine I looked at my hands gripping the steering wheel and saw my wedding band glinting in the pale sunshine. I ran my fingers around the smooth metal and with tears stinging my eyes I wrenched off the ring and placed it inside a pocket in my handbag. I knew Peggy would notice; hopefully she would blame my nervousness on marriage troubles. After all, this was, I told myself, not so far from the truth.

I felt the older woman's keen eyes on me as soon as I stepped through the door. We exchanged pleasantries, Peggy offered me some tea and a piece of her over-cooked fruit cake and, as we sat in her small sitting room, awkward silences were filled by talk of Peter and Rosalind.

'You are looking well,' said Peggy, raising an eye-brow. From the tone of her voice, and her quizzical facial expression, she obviously meant the opposite.

'Yes, I am,' I said, trying not to sound strained.

Another silence. 'Darling,' I said, turning to Rosalind, 'why don't you sing that song you've been practising. I'm sure Granny would love to hear it.'

Rosalind was a little shy to begin with and so I started the song for her. '"I know a fat old policeman, he's always on our street/A fat old jolly red-faced man, he really is a treat."' Rosalind joined in with the chorus and by the time we had reached the last line, '"But once he did arrest a man and laughed until he died,"' she was in her element, belting out the lyrics with glee. After finishing the song, I caught Peggy's eyes fixed on the place where my wedding ring normally sat. Our eyes met and she looked away, shiftily, as if she had just caught a glimpse of something she wished she had not seen.

'Dear,' she said, addressing Rosalind, 'why don't you go and take Peter into the garden. I found a new stick for him to play with the other day. Just by the back door.'

The girl ran off in a tornado of excitement, accompanied by a series of excited barks.

'My dear child,' said Peggy as she got out of the armchair and walked over to me. 'I know this must be extremely trying for you, but you must keep strong if only for the sake of your daughter.'

I took out a handkerchief and dabbed my eyes. How could I begin to explain?

'The truth of the matter is that Beverley's off, the weekend is cancelled,' I said. 'And I was so looking forward to it. Archie has decided to spend the weekend with, with ... I'm sorry, I cannot bring myself to utter her name. I've been feeling so wretched.'

'I know it must be terribly upsetting for you, my dear, but I am sure that after Archie has had his little fling he will come back to you and he will love you all the more for having forgiven him this minor indiscretion.'

I tried to respond, but Peggy silenced me by placing a hand on my shoulder.

'Just give him time. I know it's terribly fashionable for women to assert their own rights and whatnot, but that sort of independence is not always the best thing for a marriage. Give him freedom now and he will repay you with love for the rest of your life.'

I didn't believe a word of it, and I doubt Peggy did either. It was obvious that she was on his side. Of course she was – she was his mother and she had never forgiven me for stealing her son away from her. She never liked the fact that I earned my own living, quite a respectable living at that. She would much rather have a daughter-in-law who was a placid housewife instead of one who wrote about crime and murder. Instinctively, I knew that she also yearned after a grandson, something I had failed to provide and now would never do so. Most probably Miss Neele could give her that. Perhaps it would be best if I were to disappear after all.

At that moment, Rosalind came in from the garden screaming with joy, her cheeks as red and plump as overripe apples. Her entrance brought our superficially intimate conversation to a close. I stood up and promised her that I would do everything in my power to make Archie happy. I left the house as the sun was fading from the sky. I drove back to Styles to find that, as I had expected, Archie had not returned home. I bathed Rosalind, watched as she ate a supper of some sausages and put her to bed. Then I sat at my desk to write a series of letters.

First, I wrote a vague and equivocal letter to Archie outlining how I felt the need to get away. Our marriage, I said, had reached such a point of crisis that I needed time to think. I would be going away for a few days, he was not to worry and I assured him that my love for him would endure. Then I wrote a letter to Archie's brother, Campbell, a man of common sense and utter reliability. Of course, I could not tell him the truth of the matter – no, that would put my family at risk – but perhaps I could give him a clue to where to find me. All Kurs had told me earlier that day was that I was to travel to a northern spa town – how many of those could there be? Just as was signing my name I heard the telephone ring and so I pushed the letter into an envelope and placed it inside my bag. Perhaps it was Kurs calling with more information. As I rushed to answer the telephone I felt a mixture of relief and a strange disappointment when I realised it was Charlotte.

'Hello, dear,' I said. 'I hope you are having a splendid time.'

'Yes, it's been a lovely day. I won't bore you with the details. I was just calling to ask whether you would like me to come home.'

'Why? Is anything the matter?'

'Oh no, just I thought in case you might need me.'

'No, don't be silly. I'm looking forward to a quiet evening by the fire. And I've got Peter to keep me company.'

'Only if you are sure. I'd hate to think – well, think that you were lonely or unhappy in any way. I really could not enjoy myself if I knew you were feeling—'

'What nonsense. I'm absolutely fine. Now, you carry on and I will see you when you get back.'

I returned to my desk, feeling a little guilty for deceiving Charlotte in this way, and so to her I wrote a rather more fulsome letter, explaining how I could not make my real feelings known to her over the telephone. I told her that I needed to leave the house as my head felt like it was fit to bursting. The implication, I knew, was that I was leaving because of Archie. As a postscript I asked Charlotte to send a telegram to the boarding house in Beverley cancelling the rooms for the weekend.

I listened for signs of movement. When I was certain all was quiet and I was unlikely to be disturbed I walked over to the corner of my room. The sound of my heartbeat pulsed through me as I lifted up the chest of drawers and with my weight shunted it forwards. I ran my hand over the rough surface of the floorboards until I felt the sharp edge of a loose nail. From my bag

I took out my nail file and prised it into the gap by the floorboard and as it came loose I pushed my right hand inwards. My fingers brushed past wood shavings, dust balls, detritus and dirt until they came to rest on a grey metal box. I gently eased it forwards – I was careful not to disturb its contents – and brought it out of the hiding place. I dusted it down and then, using a small key that I had hidden at the back of one of the drawers, opened the box. From there, I took out a leather pouch, unfastened its brass buckles, unrolled it and checked the series of labelled vials inside. All was in order. I placed the pouch inside my handbag, which I zipped up, and put the box back under the floor, resealed the floorboard and shifted the chest of drawers into its original position.

Was there anything else I had to do? Ultimately it was difficult to imagine my immediate future as Kurs had provided me with only the bare bones of his plan: that I was going to stage my disappearance and then travel north. As I walked around the house, a house that I had once so disliked, I began to feel a certain nostalgia for its excessive vulgarity. It was, I thought, like the sense of sudden fondness one feels towards a distant, unlikeable relative who announces that they have an incurable illness and do not have very much time left. I wandered into Rosalind's room to see my daughter sleeping. I sat on the edge of the bed and stroked my little girl's hair. I watched her breathe as softly as the flutter of a moth's wings.

Would I ever see my daughter again? I knew that if I stayed in the room for a moment longer I would never leave. I lightly kissed Rosalind on the cheek and after stealing one backward glance I gently closed the door. I placed the letters to Archie and Charlotte on the hall table so that they would see them when they came in, listened for the servants to make sure that I could slip out without any fuss, patted Peter – dear Peter – on the head and bent down and kissed him. Again, I could not allow myself to indulge my natural feelings for the dog too long as the emotion would, I knew, consume me to the point of complete collapse.

It was all so tempting, at this instant, to allow myself to fall back on the mat and let the maid or Charlotte find me in an unresponsive heap. I had seen men in the war in a similar condition, empty shells, mere husks of personalities, remnants of the selves that they had left behind somewhere on the battlefields of northern France or Belgium. How could I even compare myself to those brave young men who had sacrificed themselves for their country? The analogy was inappropriate and unpatriotic. I stood up, slipped on my fur coat, took a deep breath and stepped out into the dark night.

Chapter Five

I saw the four flashes from his torch and pulled over to the side of the road. Kurs then got back into his car and I followed him up a desolate track that looked like it led nowhere. Perhaps it was Kurs's intention to lead me to an isolated spot where he would kill me. The thought actually reassured me; at least if he did slaughter me then I wouldn't have to go along with his devilish plan. Of course, it would be awful for Rosalind, for Charlotte, for Madge, but who else would really miss me? Peter, undoubtedly, I could be sure of his love. But my death, after all, might be for the best.

The track ended in what looked like a clearing. Kurs stopped his car and turned off his headlights. As he walked towards my car he used his torch to illuminate his way. His beard and his eyes seemed to disappear into the enveloping blackness and, as he approached, he looked like an unholy apparition, a mere collection of fragmentary and floating body parts. The wind in the trees sounded like a silenced scream, a noise that made me think of a woman with a bag over her head, a rope around her neck, slowly being asphyxiated.

'Good evening, Mrs Christie,' said Kurs as he opened the door of the car. 'Such a delight to see you again.'

I did not say anything.

'I hope you haven't forgotten your manners? That would never do.'

I felt as though I had something stuck in my throat.

'G-good evening,' was all I could manage.

'Now I think you know what we have planned. Do you have any questions?'

I shook my head.

'As I outlined earlier, think of me as the author of these events. And I mean that literally. For too long you have been able to control your characters, killing them off on nothing more than a whim. Now it's my turn. And now you are my character. So, could you please get out of the car.'

I remained where I was.

'Get out of the car,' he said. 'I do hope I don't have to repeat everything twice. That would be most tiresome.'

I eased myself off the seat and stepped out into the darkness. The cold snaked its way down my back, making me shiver.

'Yes, it is rather chilly tonight, don't you find? Which is why I am going to ask you to leave your fur in the car.'

'What on earth do you mean?'

'Just as I said. You are to leave the fur coat in the car. You can keep your handbag, as I'm assuming that contains some of the necessary supplies you will need to commit the crime. That's right, isn't it?'

I thought about the poisons inside my handbag and how I would like to use one right now on the monster standing in front of me. 'Y-yes.'

'Very well, but leave your dressing case and your driving licence.'

'But—'

'I do wish you would stop worrying about minor details.'

'I wouldn't call leaving my coat behind a minor detail. I will catch my death of cold in this weather.'

'Precisely. That's what we want people to think, don't we? Or rather it can be one of the lines of enquiry. As I told you, we want to create a scenario that will deliberately confuse the authorities. And don't worry about the cold, I have thought about that.'

'And what about the things I may need? The things in my case?'

'Your stockings and suchlike? I'm not an expert, but I am sure those can easily be purchased elsewhere, can they not?'

I nodded my head.

'Very well then.'

As I began to take off my coat I felt the wind begin to whip my skin. I felt as cold as if I were standing there naked. I looked for signs of a house in the distance. There was nothing for miles around.

'Where are we?'

'On the plateau, Newlands Corner.'

The two of us were absolutely alone. Even God seemed absent from this desolate place. Or was he? Perhaps there was a way out of this hellish situation after all.

'Could I ask you a question, Mr Kurs?'

'Please do.'

'Do you believe you are a good doctor? I mean do you feel that it is your job to heal?'

'Some of my patients have said that I do possess some sort of power.'

'But you want to make people better? That is your goal as a doctor, is it not?'

'At one point I suppose you could say it was.'

'But not any longer?'

'No, I'm afraid not.'

'And what, may I ask, made you change your mind?'

'You would have to say that I felt rather out of sorts.'

'Because?'

'This and that,' he said dismissively. 'But mostly because of my wife, Mrs Christie, whom you are going to kill. I wonder how you are going to kill her. Poison, I would imagine. That would be my best guess. You don't think I am naive enough not to know what you are trying to do? I wouldn't try to appeal to my conscience, Mrs Christie, because I don't believe I have one.'

'I was just—'

'Now, before I lose patience. Could you move away from your car.'

I remained fixed to the spot, terrified. He pushed past me, breathing a cloud of halitosis into my face, and calmly got into the driver's seat. He checked the inside of the car to make sure that I had left nothing incriminating in the vehicle. He turned on the headlights and the bright white beam blinded me. I tried to walk forwards but I stumbled. I stretched out my hands to break my fall, and felt the sharp scratch of a piece of flint cutting through my glove and into my wrist.

Kurs started the car, slowly drove it near to what looked like an expanse of nothingness and then jumped from the vehicle.

'Stop!' I cried, as the car that meant everything to me – independence, success, a symbol of my writing career – began to disappear. I reached out, stretching my hands into the dark night, but it was too late. 'No!' I screamed, stumbling once more. The dank smell of the earth hit my nose. I scrambled to my feet and ran on into the darkness. I made noises I had never dreamed possible, primitive grunts and screams. 'No!' I shouted, my voice rasping and broken. 'No!'

The incline was far from steep, but as soon as the car picked up speed its descent was inevitable. Darkness sucked it down and away from me. I listened as the Morris Cowley careered down the hill, blasting through brambles and saplings, bracken and clumps of dead wood. It was terrifying, like the sound of an animal being hunted to its death. The noise possessed me, vibrated within me. It felt as though the very earth beneath my feet was moving, splitting apart.

And when it was over – when the car had finally crashed at the bottom of the hill – it was even worse. The silence sounded so bleak, empty and final.

Kurs walked over towards me and took my hand. There was no point resisting. He could do with me what he wished.

'How does it feel to be a ghost, Mrs Christie?' he said.

Chapter Six

It was a quiet morning at Surrey Constabulary head-quarters on Woodbridge Road, Guildford. Superintendent William Kenward, Deputy Chief Constable, had enjoyed a large cooked breakfast, perhaps a little too indulgent even for him, he thought, as he eased himself up out of his chair. Naomi, his wife, had tried to tell him not to eat quite so much and although he had attempted to diet it did not seem to be working. For some reason, his waist-line, already the diameter of a fairly sturdy oak tree, seemed to be expanding. He had tried to resist, so far successfully, his wife's demands to go and see the family doctor, a man he did not like.

Just before eleven o'clock, Kenward was glancing through the week's paperwork when a call came through from one of the sergeants. Apparently, a man had telephoned the police to report that he had spotted an abandoned car, a Morris Cowley, near Water Lane, Newlands Corner. Not such an out-of-the-ordinary occurrence. What appeared to be very queer indeed was that inside the car he had found a woman's fur coat, a small case and a driving licence. There was no sign of a body near by and neither were there any traces of blood. The circumstances intrigued Kenward and he set off to the scene with a certain spring in his step.

He had learnt to recognise the feeling, a sensation of anticipation and excitement twinned with an almost physical reaction that ran through to the very tips of his fingers. His wife knew when something had attracted his attention in this way and would often comment, in that rather dry manner of hers, 'By the pricking of my thumbs ...' a phrase which Kenward would complete, '... something wicked this way comes.' His wife said that when he was in this frame of mind he often reminded her of a bloodhound.

With his rotund face, neatly clipped moustache and generously proportioned figure he looked nothing like the dogs he had once overseen at the police station in Camberley – the dogs had been used to sniff out prisoners of war who had escaped from Frith Hill during the war – but like them he had a nose for crime. He was still basking in the glory of his success in bringing the Byfleet poisoner to justice, an investigation that had inevitably attracted the attention of the national press. This new case had all the hallmarks of a similarly high-profile investigation as the abandoned car belonged to a writer of detective fiction, a Mrs Agatha Christie of Sunningdale – or so he had been informed.

On arrival at the scene, Kenward first examined the vehicle. There were, it seemed, no signs of a struggle or violence of any kind. The brakes were off, the car was in neutral gear and it looked as though it had started its journey at the top of the hill. The sergeant then led Kenward over to meet Frederick Dore, the man who had first reported the car to the police. After thanking Dore for alerting the authorities to the matter Kenward asked him what time he had made the discovery.

'Eight o'clock this morning or thereabouts,' said Dore. 'I was on the way to work when I stopped for a cup of tea at the kiosk opposite. While I was there I got chatting to a girl, a gypsy girl she was, I think from the camp near by, and she said that a friend of hers had seen a car that looked like it had crashed or something. She pointed out the spot and told me she had heard a car crossing the top of the hill at about midnight last night.'

'And what did you do then?'

'I went to examine the car and I found it in its present condition, just as you've seen it yourself. The lights were off and the battery had run right down. I'm a car tester, you see, so naturally I had an interest.'

'Go on,' said Kenward.

'The lamp had evidently been left on until the current became exhausted. I looked around at the surrounding area and gathered that if anyone had accidentally run off the road at the top the car would have pulled up earlier. There was no sign that the brakes had been applied.

I looked for skid marks – the ground is still soft, see – but I couldn't find any.'

'So your assumption is that the car was—'

'Yes, been given a push at the top of the hill and sent down deliberately. I thought it was all a bit strange and knew it was a matter for the police and so I asked Alf, Alfred Luland who has the refreshment kiosk on the other side of the road, to look after the car while I went to the hotel, the Newlands Corner Hotel, on Clandon Road, to telephone the police.'

Kenward thanked Mr Dore for his help and instructed his men to contact the Christie household to find out if she had made her way home yet. Perhaps, he surmised, she had merely staggered from the car in a daze and wandered down to the road where some Good Samaritan had taken pity on her and driven her back to Sunningdale. Yet he doubted it somehow. No, there was a great deal more to this case than that, a great deal more indeed.

Chapter Seven

Charlotte was at a loss to know what to do. She picked up the letter once more and tried to focus on the words. A sleepless night had left her with red, stinging eyes. She had interpreted every creak of the house or distant bark of a dog as a sign of her mistress's arrival. In the weak grey light of dawn she had taken herself off to the kitchen and made herself a cup of tea. Perhaps she should call the police, she thought. After all, Mrs Christie had said that she had had to leave Styles because she felt somehow unsafe. It was obviously something to do with that wretched husband of hers, but even if he was a heartless devil, surely Archie would never do anything to hurt his wife?

She walked into the hallway and picked up the letter Agatha had left for her husband. She even thought of steaming it open and had taken it into the kitchen for that very purpose before coming to her senses and returning it back to its original position.

If only she had taken an earlier train, thought Charlotte. Why hadn't she picked up the fact that Agatha had been feeling upset during that telephone call? To be honest, she had known all too well, but the truth of the matter was that she had been having too much of a good time in London to return. She was nothing but a selfish, superficial creature, she said to herself. It would serve her right if her mistress had done something stupid. No, she wouldn't allow herself to think such a thing. What utter nonsense.

At that moment, Charlotte heard a knock at the door. She rushed towards it – it would be Agatha, she had returned, she had simply mislaid her key – but she was shocked to discover a policeman standing there.

'Is this the home of Mrs Agatha Christie?' asked the young man.

'Yes, yes, it is,' said Charlotte.

'Is Mrs Christie at home?'

'No, I'm afraid not,' she said. 'I'm her secretary, Charlotte Fisher. Why?' Suddenly she feared the worst.

'Her car was found abandoned early this morning, near Newlands Corner in Surrey. But there doesn't seem to be any sign of her.'

'Oh, no,' said Charlotte. She was too shocked to say anything more.

'Is Mr Christie at home?'

'No, I'm afraid not. He is staying with friends.'

'Could you provide me with an address for him?'

'Very well,' said Charlotte, feeling a mix of guilt and

satisfaction. Mr Christie would, she knew, not thank her for giving the police the details of the Jameses' cottage, where he was staying with Miss Neele, but perhaps it served him right. Maybe now he would come to his senses.

'He is with Mr and Mrs Sam James, Hurtmore Cottage, near Godalming.'

As soon as the policeman left, Charlotte picked up the telephone. She supposed she had better warn him. She asked the operator to connect her and a moment later Mrs James answered the telephone. She asked to speak to Colonel Christie.

'Hello? Charlotte? Whatever is the matter? Is it Rosalind?'

'No, no, it's Mrs Christie. A policeman has just called at Styles. She didn't return to the house last night – I know I should have telephoned you earlier – but apparently the police have found her car, abandoned, in Surrey, near Newlands Corner.'

'Oh, how frightful – did Mrs Christie say anything to you before she left?'

'No, and you see I didn't return from London until after eleven, or perhaps nearly twelve. By that time she had gone. She did leave me a note. She left a letter for you too.'

'Very well,' he said. 'I'll be back at Styles within the next hour or so.'

He sounded nervous and on edge. Quite right too, thought Charlotte. If her mistress – her friend – had done something stupid she would never forgive him, the brute. What on earth did he see in that silly young girl? If only she could give him a piece of her mind. But from the nasty arguments that she had heard over the course of the last few months the marriage, it seemed, was doomed. But surely it wasn't worth this? Perhaps Agatha had stayed out all night to give him a taste of his own medicine. Yes, she was sure that was it. She was trying to make Archie jealous.

But then a series of hellish tableaux flashed through her mind: a body floating in water, a woman's broken corpse at the bottom of a cliff face, a swollen-faced cadaver hanging from a tree. She told herself that Agatha would never do such a thing. But there was one method of death that her mistress might consider: poisoning. Oh please, God, no, she thought. Please not that.

Chapter Eight

Kenward did not like the look of this Colonel Christie. He could not yet tell exactly why that was, but he was sure that the man was hiding something. Whatever it was the Colonel was keeping back, Kenward was confident that he would draw it out of him.

He had arranged for Christie, together with the secretary, Miss Charlotte Fisher, to accompany him to the scene of the disappearance. Perhaps if they were forced to see the abandoned car their memories might be jogged a little. At the moment neither of them was providing him with much information that was of use. Miss Fisher had hinted at marital difficulties between the couple, but when pressed on the matter she had side-stepped the issue. She had, however, shown him a letter in which Mrs Christie had used a telling phrase: having to leave the house because her head was fit to bursting or some such expression, a line which he interpreted as suggestive of the husband's guilt in the matter. But when he had asked Christie about their marriage, the Colonel had looked at him with distaste, as if Kenward had just uttered an obscenity. Christie had maintained that, while the couple had experienced some difficulties in their marriage, these issues were minor ones. He had been worried about his wife, it was true, but not because of any marital problems. He feared that the death of his wife's mother had affected the balance of her mind. There was, Kenward suspected, some truth in this, but by no means the whole truth. And as Christie was relating this information, Kenward noticed a certain shiftiness around the Colonel's eyes.

The driver stopped the car and Kenward directed Miss Fisher and Christie towards the abandoned Morris Cowley. Already the news of the incident had spread about the neighbourhood and a ragbag of curious sensation-seekers had gathered around the vehicle. Each of them no doubt had his or her theory, but as he passed them he saw a certain gleam in their eyes, an appetite for murder.

'Here, as you can see, is the vehicle,' said Kenward. 'First of all, Colonel, can you identify this car as your wife's?'

'Yes, indeed it is.'

'Not yours then?'

'No, she bought it with the money she earned from selling one of her books to a newspaper.'

'So, it's a profitable line of work, this writing business?'

'It has its rewards, but it's also rather a precarious way of making money. I know my wife was worried that she would not be able to repeat the success of her earlier books.'

'Is that so?'

'Indeed. She was also suffering from lack of inspiration. Ever since her mother died.'

'Miss Fisher, you can confirm that?'

'Yes, I can. On both points. I know that she was having trouble writing her next book, *The Mystery of the Blue Train*.'

Kenward led them nearer to the car and opened the door of the driver's seat. He noticed that Charlotte Fisher gasped as she saw the fur coat and the dressing case, an object she said she had last seen laid open and empty on her mistress's bed a day or so before.

'As you are aware last night was quite cold,' said Kenward. 'I'm told the temperature around midnight was only thirty-six degrees – and like you I'm curious to know why Mrs Christie would leave the car without her fur.'

Both Charlotte and the Colonel remained silent. Kenward then held up the driving licence.

'This was also found in the vehicle. A strange gesture, don't you think? Again, I must ask you why Mrs Christie might do such a thing.'

'I'm at a loss to explain it,' said the Colonel.

'It's all so baffling,' said Charlotte. 'I find the whole situation so upsetting. To think of her out here at night and in the cold. What was she doing? I do hope she is all right. I mean, anything could have happened.'

'I'm sure we will get to the bottom of it,' said Kenward, casting a quick glance at the Colonel. 'Well, thank you for coming out here. I will get one of my men to drive you back to Sunningdale. This afternoon I am going to organise a search of the immediate area. I have asked for the help of our special constables. As soon as I have any information I will, of course, let you know.'

Kenward himself took part in the search, with a team of eight special constables overseen by Captain Tuckwell and his deputy, Colonel Bethall. He had instructed the men to look out for anything that might strike them as unusual – a lady's handkerchief, scraps of paper, personal possessions, items of clothing, money and, of course, a murder weapon or a body. As the men beat their way through the undergrowth, they did indeed come across items of potential interest – the occasional empty bottle, an old towel, a child's teddy bear missing one arm – but nothing that looked like it had any bearing on the case. He doubted the Colonel had murdered his wife, but one could never tell. In his career Kenward had learnt one very sad fact about human nature: the majority of people were driven by entirely selfish motives and there were those who when in a corner or a fix would resort to murder. Greed was always a motive, of course, and then there was jealousy or lust or vengeance, or a combination of all four. But he had to remind himself that, as yet, no evidence of a crime had come to light. A lady, suffering from a nervous condition, had disappeared in strange circumstances. The question was: would she be found dead or alive?

Chapter Nine

As the train pulled out of King's Cross and started its journey north, I experienced an odd feeling, one of liberation. I was, after all, no longer Mrs Christie or even dull old Agatha Miller. I was now somebody else.

The night before, in the gloom of Kurs's car, I had been given a new identity. At first I had been horrified, appalled even. I had thought his suggestion too cruel, but when I had tried to complain – I told him that taking that name was simply out of the question – he refused to listen to my entreaties. As I sat there, with the wind rattling around the car, I felt as though I was being sucked down into a vortex.

'I don't mind what Christian name you use,' Kurs had continued, 'but yes, that is to be the surname you use to register at the hotel.'

I could hardly bring myself to say it. 'N-Neele. But why? Surely any name would serve as well.'

'True. But I think it might do you good.'

'Good?' The word stuck in my throat. 'How on earth could it possibly do me good?'

'In an imaginative sort of way, but you know all about that. I just think that if you take on the mantle of Miss Neele you might find certain things easier to act out.'

I had, I must confess, fantasised about what it would be like if Archie's mistress were to die. I had even toyed with the idea – in a purely hypothetical way, of course – of how I might go about killing her. Poison was the most logical solution. Some kind of infusion or tincture which would cause a quick, but probably not painless, death and one that could not be traced in the body. Yes, I could imagine Nancy Neele as a victim of murder all too well. But as a murderer herself?

'Do you mean to say that you want me to try and implicate Miss Neele in a murder? To raise suspicions that she is a killer?'

As Kurs laughed the car filled with the stench of his breath. 'My – your mind is much more wicked than I expected. I hadn't thought of that.'

'What do you mean?'

'I only meant that by taking on her name it might lend a certain – I don't know – a certain allure which perhaps you have lacked recently.'

I felt full of anger for this devil of a man sitting next to me. What did he presume to know about me? Unfortunately, his assessment was true enough. I had neglected Archie, turning away from him when he needed me, brushing him off with a polite peck on the cheek or the forehead when he desired something more. Yet those things were private, certainly not to be discussed with a complete stranger, let alone one such as this.

'You are full of poison, Mr Kurs,' I said.

'We are kindred spirits then, aren't we?'

'What on earth—'

'I know how your mind works, Mrs Christie. You may pretend to be all sweet and innocent, the hurt and wronged wife. But don't tell me you haven't wished Miss Neele a slow and painful death.'

I felt myself blushing in the dark. I wanted to tell him that, while that may have been so, it was merely a game that I had played in my head to make myself feel better, certainly nothing I would ever have acted upon.

'As I suspected. In fact, I have a pet theory, Mrs Christie. I would wager a considerable amount of money on something.'

'What is that?'

'This: that I am quite convinced that, had you not had the outlet of your books, books that are full of murder, poisonings, betrayals of the worst kind, you yourself may even have been tempted to commit a heinous crime.'

'That is the most ridiculous thing I've ever heard. Quite preposterous. Just because I make a small living out of writing about crime and its detection doesn't in the slightest mean I could possibly do it myself.'

'We will see about that, won't we?' Kurs smiled. 'I think it will be quite the experiment, something I may have to write a paper about one day.'

'The only reason I am sitting in this car with you, listening to your nonsense, is because of your threats to harm my family. There is, Mr Kurs, no other reason. If you suspect that I am of the criminal fraternity I must, I'm afraid, disappoint you. I hold life to be sacred and I believe there can be nothing worse than snuffing out the existence of another person.'

'A very noble sentiment, I'm sure.'

'And true, Mr Kurs. True.'

As Kurs ran his fingers through his beard the whisper of his whiskers unsettled me. At any moment I thought I might let out an unholy scream.

'I think it's time for us to leave now,' said Kurs. 'But before we do let me just sort out your wrist. It seems you are bleeding a little.'

'No, don't worry,' I said, but he ignored my protestations.

I closed my eyes as I felt the surprisingly soft touch of his fingers on my hand. I heard the opening and closing of his medical bag, the sound of scissors cutting into a bandage.

'Now, this may hurt a little,' he said as he started to clean my wrist with a piece of cotton wool and hydrogen peroxide. 'Only a surface wound, but we wouldn't want you getting an infection.'

The sting came as something of a relief. 'Where are you going to take me?' I said through gritted teeth.

'London,' he said as he finished working on my hand. 'I have some rooms there where you can rest. Don't worry, you will be quite safe. There, that feels better, doesn't it?'

Kurs had driven me to Victoria, or rather Pimlico, to a rather shabby block of flats just off the Vauxhall Bridge Road. I knew it was only a ten-minute walk to the Stores, but the area felt run-down and squalid, not at all like Ealing where my dear grandmother had lived. As Kurs showed me into the dank little mansion-block flat, into that cold bedroom with a horrid iron-frame bed, I tried to comfort myself with memories from my childhood. Oh, how I had loved to crawl into Grannie's huge mahogany four-poster in the early morning. Whenever I thought of my grandmother I always pictured her in the summer, the elderly woman proudly tending her roses. The secret to the glorious flowers had been a regular dose of the bedroom slops, she had said. That had made me laugh. And what was that game I had adored? A chicken from Mr Whiteley's, it was called. I had pretended to be a chicken and my grandmother would converse with the shopkeeper about how best the bird should be prepared. How I had squealed that time Grannie had said that she rather fancied a skewered chicken and pretended to sharpen her carving knife so that she could cut me up into tasty little pieces. It hardly seemed so funny now.

Unsurprisingly my sleep was fitful, my dreams haunted by awful visions of Archie and Miss Neele. But curiously, in the morning I did wake up feeling like a different person, as if I no longer had to carry around the heavy burden of myself. Somebody, even if that somebody was as vile and twisted a human being as Kurs, had given me permission to step away from my life. As I awoke I had mouthed the words to myself. 'Neele,' I said. 'My name is Neele.'

The thought invigorated me, pleasured me even, an emotion immediately followed by the shadow of guilt. I had always believed that shame was a force for good. After all, what kind of state would the world be in if people simply did as they wished without the confines and constrictions of proper social behaviour? But I knew that the normal rules and restrictions that existed would not help me. Guilt would only get in the way. I knew that if I were to do half the things Kurs had suggested – *if* – then it would be better to pretend to be someone else. And who could be better than a woman I hated?

After leaving the flat we made our way to the car. As I passed a post box, I realised that I still had the letter that I had written to Campbell in my bag. I cast a quick glance at Kurs to see if he was looking – fortunately his attention was directed towards a policeman who had been flagged down by a passing motorist. I slowly took out the letter addressed to my brother-in-law and although I dared not actually post it – I could not risk inciting Kurs's fury – I let it slip down behind me onto the ground in the hope that a kind stranger would spot it and place it in the box for me. If it got to Campbell then at least Archie and Carlo and Madge wouldn't think that I had done myself in; if they had half a brain between them they might be able to work out where I was going.

Kurs stopped by his car and glanced in my direction. For a moment his eyes narrowed as he looked back towards the block of flats and the post box, but then as he became aware that the policeman was beginning to walk in our direction he opened the door for me and told me to get in.

'We don't want any fuss now, do we?' he said, as if he were talking to a patient with a history of mental instability.

'No, I suppose we don't,' I said, meeting his gaze. Just then I saw a middle-aged man in a suit, a clerk of some sort, stop by the post box and look down to the ground. He picked up the letter, studied it for a moment, and then placed it in the box.

At Harrogate Station, we alighted from our separate carriages and took two taxis to two different hotels: I to the Swan Hydropathic Hotel and the doctor to a guest house a few streets from the Pump Room. Kurs had told me that he would come over to the Hydro later that evening, but from this point it was important for us not to be seen talking in public together. He would, however, communicate with me by letter, documents which he insisted be destroyed. He also told me that while I had the freedom to explore the area during the day, it was essential that I return to the hotel in Harrogate each night. He didn't need to remind me of how much hurt he could inflict upon those closest to me if I did not follow his every instruction.

After paying for the taxi, I stood for a moment and admired the rather splendid four-storey hotel set back from the road and fronted by a large expanse of lawn. With its ivy-covered façade and series of imposing chimneys and attic rooms it looked more like a country house than a hotel. I walked through a covered portico and up towards the desk.

'Good evening, ma'am,' said the lady.

Next to her I felt very shabby and poorly dressed. I still wore the grey skirt, green jumper and dark grey cardigan that I had on from the day before, as Kurs had given me no opportunity to buy any new garments. He had, however, given me a small attaché case that had once belonged to his wife. Everything else, he said, could be purchased in Harrogate.

'Do you have any rooms available?' I asked.

The lady wrinkled her nose as she looked down at the guest book. I needed a long, hot bath, as Kurs's flat in London had had no facilities beyond a lavatory and a basin. He had given me a bowl of hot water that morning, but how I longed for a proper soak.

'Yes, we do. How long are you staying?'

'For at least a week, I should imagine,' I said.

'The rate is seven guineas a week for board and lodging.'

'That seems very reasonable,' I said. Kurs had provided me with a certain amount of information – information that I should follow to the letter – but it was curious that he had allowed me some freedom as to imagining where I had come from. 'I've just arrived – from South Africa, from Cape Town,' I said. I remembered how I had enjoyed that trip there with Archie. 'I'm so looking forward to spending some time relaxing here in Harrogate after the rather busy three weeks I have had since arriving in England.'

'Well, I am certain we can promise you that. The weather won't be quite as nice as you are used to back home, but Harrogate is, as I am sure you will discover for yourself, rather famous for its top-class service. I'm not sure if you are aware but in the hotel we have a range of superior facilities such as a Turkish Bath and the Vichy Bath, if you are interested. Could I take your name?'

'Neele. Mrs Teresa Neele,' I said. I decided to change my imaginary status to that of a married woman, as I didn't want to attract the wrong sort of attention from the male guests at the hotel.

'Very good, Mrs Neele. Do you have any luggage that the porter can help you with?'

'No, my luggage is arriving separately,' I said. The ease with which I lied gave me something of a thrill.

'But I am looking forward to doing a spot of shopping. I've heard there are some rather good shops here.'

'Indeed. If you need a list of names please let me know. Now, here is your key, Room 105.'

I turned away and started to make my way to the stairs when I heard the receptionist's voice.

'Oh, Mrs Neele, Mrs Neele?'

I returned to the desk.

'I'm sorry, I forgot to give you this. There's a letter for you that just arrived.'

'Thank you,' I said.

As soon as I entered the comfortable room, with its pink rose-print wallpaper, I felt myself relaxing. I savoured the silence. I walked over to stand by the armchair next to the window and look out at the lawns and the fine specimen trees at the front. I spotted a couple of young blonde-haired children, accompanied by their governess, playing with a spinning top and squealing in delight. The sight of the young girl reminded me of my little Rosalind. How I missed her already. I tried to picture what she might be doing. Had she asked for me? I hated to think of her waking up and me not being there. But then the alternative was so much worse. I was not here to take the waters or recover my health, although I was in desperate need of such a course of treatment. The letter I held in my hand was a testament to my real purpose. I couldn't avoid opening it any longer. I sat down on my bed and started to read.

Dear Mrs Christie, or should that be Neele?

I do hope you have an enjoyable stay at the Hydro. They say it is one of Harrogate's finest hotels.

To prepare yourself for your role I think it only right that you try and get into character. Think of yourself of one of the great actresses of the London stage and lose your inhibitions. From now on, you can discard the sensible Mrs Christie and have a little fun. Your first task is to go down to the Palm Court tonight and, when the band strike up, as I am sure they will, 'Yes! We Have No Bananas', take to the dance floor and dance the Charleston. If you don't do this I'll think you a terrible sport. Not only that, but I will take your rejection of this simple task as a refusal to accept your future challenges.

I will be watching you, but please do not try to talk to me, even though I know you may find it difficult to resist.

Yours most sincerely
Dr Patrick Kurs

The man was an utter sadist. I could just picture him sitting in the bar as he watched me humiliate myself on the dance floor. The whole thing was ridiculous. I was not in the mood, I did not have any evening clothes and I hardly had the figure for it anyway. But did I have a choice? Was it too late to go to the police? Of course,

I could show the authorities the letters, but what if Kurs then did something awful out of spite? Even if the police caught him and locked him up, would my family be safe? One day, he said, when I was least expecting it, he would do something terrible. The things he had suggested were too awful to recall, but one of the less obscene scenarios was the blinding of my child. How could I live with myself if that came about? It was too ghastly to contemplate.

I looked at myself in the bathroom mirror and tried to make myself a little more presentable. I took out a small, framed photograph of Rosalind from my handbag, and placed it on the bedside table. As I did so, tears came into my eyes. I bit my lip, but the tears continued. I returned to the bathroom to splash water on my face, but I looked even worse than before. From my bag I took out some powder and applied a little to my nose and face. At least I managed to cover up those unsightly blotches. I splashed some eau de Cologne over my green jumper and dark grey cardigan and left the room.

In the dining room I toyed with a supper of lamb chops and boiled potatoes before abandoning it and moving into the Palm Court. The music jarred my nerves, each note a form of torture. The band, comprising six men and a female singer, seemed like they were having a simply wonderful time, as did the handful of guests on the dance floor. As I took a sip of water I spotted Kurs walking into the room. He chose a seat near the band and ordered himself a drink, something non-alcoholic – the hotel was strictly teetotal – but I couldn't make out what. He cast his eyes across the room, took in the fact that I was there, but did not allow his gaze to rest on me. He pulled something out of his briefcase, a notebook of some kind, and waited. Then he walked up to the female singer and whispered something in her ear.

The band finished 'You Forgot To Remember' before they started up the melody for that ridiculous 'Bananas' song. I was somebody else, I told myself. I could do this. I took a deep breath, walked over to the dance floor and, with a rather theatrical flourish, started to twist my feet, before breaking out into a fast-kicking and tapping movement. As I heard the words, 'Yes! We have no bananas/We have-a no bananas today,' I started to swing my arms backwards and forwards to the rhythm. I couldn't bear to look in Kurs's direction, and mostly danced with my back to him. In fact, I tried not to look at anyone as I sensed that some people, the women in particular, thought my behaviour and my dress most peculiar. When I did swing round in Kurs's direction I could not help but notice him. His eyes were lowered in a slightly embarrassed fashion, almost as if he had walked into a room to find me changing, and a suppressed smile snaked across his lips.

The song continued its hellish progression, its lyrics – 'He, he, he, he, ha, ha, ha, whatta you laugh at?' – taunting and tormenting me until it was finally over. As the last strains from the tinny-sounding banjo faded away, my arms came to a rest at my sides, my feet slowed their pace and all the energy seemed to drain from my body. The band immediately struck up the ballad 'All Alone'. 'Just like a melody that lingers on/ You seem to haunt me night and day . . .'

Blushing, I lowered my eyes as I returned to my seat. There I finished my glass of water and, without looking towards or even acknowledging Kurs, returned to my room. As soon as I was inside, I burst into tears. I felt not only humiliated but dirtied too, as if someone had stolen a part of my innocence. I undressed and crawled into bed, the lyrics of 'All Alone' playing in my head.

Chapter Ten

Kenward read and reread the notice in front of him:

> Missing from her home, Styles, Sunningdale, Berkshire, Mrs Agatha Mary Clarissa Christie, age 35; height 5 feet 7 inches; hair, red, shingled part grey; complexion fair, build slight; dressed in grey stockinette skirt, green jumper, grey and dark grey cardigan and small velour hat; wearing a platinum ring with one pearl; no wedding ring; black handbag with purse containing perhaps £5 or £10. Left home by car at 9.45 p.m. Friday, leaving note saying that she was going for a drive.

Yes, that would do. He would arrange for the notice, which had been compiled from what Charlotte Fisher and the servants had told him, to be released later that day, together with a photograph. He and his men had taken a number of statements and had started to build up a picture, although a far from complete one, of the missing woman. How queer that she should write mysteries, he thought. From his enquiries he had gathered that Mrs Christie was something of an enigma, even to those close to her. Or was that because they weren't revealing the whole truth? He had, after interviewing the servants at Styles, discovered that Colonel Christie and his wife had exchanged cross words on the morning of the disappearance. He had also heard gossip about the Colonel's private life, an allegation that could have some bearing on the case. It was a rather delicate matter regarding the Colonel's dalliance with a younger woman, and it would have to be raised at some point.

The day's main event, of which Kenward had high hopes, was a longer and more detailed search of the countryside around Newlands Corner. He was sure that the men would unearth something. There had been various reports relating to the disappearance, testimonies which he had in front of him at his desk. The abandoned car had apparently been spotted by a cattleman from Chilworth by the name of Harry Green. He had seen the headlights in the early morning gloom but he had decided to do nothing about it as he was on his way to work. An hour later, at about eight o'clock on Saturday morning, a gypsy boy called Jack Best had also noticed the car. Then Frederick Dore, the man who had first alerted the police, came onto the scene. He hoped that the new description would prompt more people to come forward.

He didn't understand how any man could betray his wife. That poor Mrs Christie, he thought. She must have been in a truly desperate state to leave her husband and drive to the top of that bleak hill. Or had she? Kenward took out the statements and laid them in front of them, noting down the important times and places. It was true that the evidence at the scene of the disappearance – the abandoned car, the fur coat, the driving licence – suggested that the balance of her mind had been disturbed. But if Mrs Christie had wanted to commit suicide would she have taken her handbag from the car? And why was there no trace of her body? Perhaps they would find something in the course of the next search, but he had a niggling suspicion that she had not done herself in.

Miss Fisher had told him that Mrs Christie had left a letter for her husband, a document that the Colonel said he had burnt. When pressed on the issue, Colonel Christie maintained that its contents were private. It sounded odd to him.

Colonel Christie maintained that on the night of Friday, 3 December, he had been staying with the Jameses at their house near Godalming. Statements from Mr and Mrs Sam James corroborated this. But could the Colonel have left the house while the other occupants were sleeping? After all, it wasn't that far a drive between Godalming and Newlands Corner. What if the Colonel had lured his wife to the spot with the promise of some kind of reconciliation? Could he have killed her, disposed of her body and then pushed the car down the hill? Although he had no proof at the moment, he had a sneaking suspicion that the investigation might soon become a murder inquiry.

Kenward checked his watch. It was time for him to meet his men at the scene. He had given orders for the constables to enlist the services of locals as the area that needed to be combed for clues was enormous. By the time he arrived at Newlands Corner, he was pleased to see that the civilians numbered a couple of dozen. As he got out of the car he immediately recognised one of the young men, Jack Boxall, who worked as a gardener in Guildford. Kenward regarded the fresh-faced man as something of a younger self as he himself had trained as a gardener before he had entered the police force. Boxall often dropped by his home to talk bonemeal, roses and manure, conversations that made Naomi laugh. If only the public could see the great detective talking horticulture, she would say. Since Mrs Christie's disappearance Kenward had taken it upon himself to start reading some of her novels in case any of them contained clues. Was there not a line in one of the books about her detective, a rather silly, effeminate man who went by a foreign name, growing vegetable marrows? He rather hoped that was all they had in common.

'Good morning, Boxall, thank you for volunteering,' he said. He noticed that the boy's father, a painter and decorator, stood some distance away in the crowd.

He removed his hat, cleared his throat and addressed the men.

'First of all, I must thank you for coming out on a Sunday. One of the reasons why we have enlisted your help is because many of you know the area around Newlands Corner much better than we do. Some of you, I have been told, play golf on the Roughs while others regularly walk your dogs. I am asking those of you who know the terrain to keep an eye out for anything that looks unusual. If a bush or a tree or a patch of ground seems like it has been disturbed please alert one of the sergeants. Or if you see car tracks please let us know. Obviously, if you come across any garments or personal items, please do not handle these, and report them to an officer straight away. I don't need to say how grateful we are for your help today. Let's see what we can find.'

Kenward then set about dividing the men into groups. He told Boxall, his father and his friends from Guildford to concentrate on the area north-west of Newlands Corner and the village of Merrow while the police and another group of locals would work on the section of land that bordered the Silent Pool. He strongly suspected that the land around the pool, if not the water itself, would throw up some clues. Using a long stick he started to beat his way through the grass and brambles. He was not young any more and, with his bulky frame, he could not move as quickly as he once did – was it really true that he had once competed in, and won, that tug of war at the London Road Rec? – but he had not lost his steely determination.

'Do you think we'll find her, sir? Mrs Christie?' asked Tom Roberts, one of the force's probationary constables.

'I'm not sure, Roberts,' he replied. 'As you know, in most cases of disappearance the person involved is usually found within the first day. I don't get a good feeling about this case, I'm afraid to say.'

'Do you think the lady is – is dead, sir?'

'I think it's too early to say for certain,' he lied.

'It's mighty queer though, isn't it? What with the fur coat and that driving licence. You don't think there's foul play involved, sir?'

'I wouldn't be surprised, but keep that to yourself for now, son.'

'Right you are, sir,' said the lad, his eyes brightening at the knowledge that he had been made privy to a piece of secret information. 'Do you know who did it?'

'It's too early to say,' said Kenward, thwacking a bramble. 'Now keep your eyes on the ground and move down towards that slope on the left.' It was best not to say too much at this stage. 'And not a word to anyone, mind.'

Kenward concentrated on the job in hand, examining fallen branches, badger and fox holes, and expanses of damp grass. He was proud of his reputation as a thorough and meticulous detective. What was it one of his lads had said about him? That he had a very sharp, penetrating gaze? How that had made Naomi laugh. He had worked his way up the Surrey force, but he would never describe himself as an ambitious man as each promotion had happened naturally. There was something unbecoming about ambition, he had always thought. And look at the number of crimes people committed because the silly fools wanted more – a more attractive husband or wife, the spoils of an inheritance, a grander house, or the means to buy jewels or dinners in fancy restaurants.

One only had to look at the Christie case. He would not be at all surprised to find that the Colonel was as base as they come. For all his airs and graces, Colonel Christie, thought Kenward, was nothing more than an animal, a beast unable to control his desires. He had wanted to ditch his rather plain wife for a younger, sexier version. Perhaps Mrs Christie had found out about his plan, refused to give him a divorce, at which point the Colonel had lost his temper and, in a fit of anger, murdered her. Kenward bashed the ground again with his stick and swore to himself that he would get to the bottom of this case if it were the last thing he did. That stuck- up Colonel would not get the better of him. If he did discover evidence of foul play, Kenward would not rest until he had witnessed the hangman placing a noose around the man's head and listened as the Colonel's neck snapped. The sound, he thought, would be a most satisfying one.

Chapter Eleven

The two friends had enjoyed a long and delicious lunch at the Savoy before retiring to John Davison's flat in the Albany. John took Una's coat from her and asked if she would care for another drink. As he began to pour out a small brandy for the pretty, blonde-haired young woman he noticed a fresh pile of papers that his secretary had left for him. As he flicked through them, checking to see if there was anything of an urgent nature, his eye fixed on a familiar name.

'Good God,' said Davison under his breath. 'Sorry, Una, frightfully rude of me. It's just—'

'What is it?' she asked. 'What's wrong?' She jumped up from the sofa and walked across the drawing room to stand by his side.

'It's Mrs Christie – you remember her?' he said, passing the brandy to her.

'Yes, of course. What is it?'

'It looks like she's gone missing.'

'What do you mean? Let me see.'

She took hold of a piece of paper, an official report from the Home Office sent to Davison. 'It does seem very odd,' said Una. 'I wonder what is behind it all? Husband trouble, most likely.'

'Perhaps. But that day we met her she did behave quite oddly, I thought. It was obvious there was something wrong.'

'Is that why you went to talk to her on the steps?'

'Yes, I got the feeling that she thought that she might be in danger. She never said as much, of course, but she had a frightened look about her.'

'So you slipped her one of your cards?'

'You don't miss a trick, do you? Just a spot of business, that's all.'

'Oh, come on now, Davison. You can tell me. You know I won't say anything.'

'I don't know anything of the kind. I know how your mind works. Actually, I'm not entirely sure I do.'

'What on earth do you mean?' she asked.

'Well, I know you have a first-class brain, but some of the conclusions you come to seem to defy logic, and yet—'

'They are often right?'

'I wouldn't go so far as to say that, but yes, you do seem to have a knack for hitting things spot on. If it wasn't for your fondness for gossip, I might have recommended you for a position.'

'That is very sweet of you, Davison. But you know I

couldn't bear to be cooped up all day in a stuffy office. All those bureaucrats would drive me mad. It was hard enough dealing with some of Daddy's colleagues. Gosh, those Foreign Office dinners. Do you remember them?'

Davison laughed, but then realised that Una had tears in her eyes. It had only been, what, eighteen months since she had lost her father, a man she adored beyond measure. Davison had often worried that Una would never find a man clever or witty or handsome enough to compete with the colossal figure of Sir Eyre Crowe. Davison knew that Una was extremely fond of him, but he also knew that he would never be right for her.

'Yes, I do, but I think you were always a little too young to enjoy them properly,' he said. He could see that Una's face had frozen, as if her father's ghost had suddenly enveloped and paralysed her. It would be better to try and change the subject. 'But, yes, this is all very odd about the disappearance of Mrs Christie. I wonder what really went on. I will have to put some feelers out.'

'Well, I think you may need some help. I wouldn't have thought the stuffed shirts would be much use investigating that. What do they know of the intricacies and mysteries of the female heart?'

'You may have a point there, Una, but apart from a few secretaries we have precious few people who could help. Miss Richardson is over in Berlin and then we have another lady in Turkey and, yes, one in the

Balkans. So I'm afraid the stuffed shirts, as you call them, will just have to do their best.'

'I know, Davison,' she said, her eyes as bright as crushed diamonds. 'Why don't I help?'

'You?'

'Don't sound so appalled. You said yourself I have a talent for this sort of thing. You know how much I wanted to be a journalist, until Daddy forced me to put it aside. Out of respect for him I had to agree ...' Her voice started to break. 'I could simply make a few discreet enquiries for you, see what I could find out. It might be such fun. Just what I need after the horrors of the last couple of years.'

Anything he could do to try to cheer Una up would be looked upon most favourably by her mother, Clema, a woman who had very close ties with his boss. But on second thoughts it would be inappropriate to let Una, whom he had met through her father and had known since she was a girl, get mixed up with his work. There were certain things that would have to be kept from her.

'No, I'm afraid it's a no-go,' he said. He watched her face drop and the old unhappiness begin to possess her once more. 'But I know, why don't you try and follow the case for one of the newspapers?'

'Do you think I could?'

'I don't see why not. You are naturally curious and you do have a talent for wheedling things out of people.'

'How thrilling! I can see my name on the front page now.'

'Let's not get ahead of ourselves. Of course, you know you will have to keep certain things to yourself – you don't want any of your society friends to know what you are up to and tip off the papers before you get your scoop. No gossiping over tea with your sisters. And absolutely no indiscreet whispers while your head is lying on the pillow.'

'You beast!' she said, laughing. 'I could take you to the highest court in the land for suggesting such a thing. Seriously, Davison, do you think you could give me any help to get me started?'

'Perhaps,' he said, suddenly heartened that he had done something to take her mind off her father's death. 'I'll see what I can do. But you must promise me not to go off on any of your wild goose chases.'

'Very well,' she said. 'Do you have a file on her?'

Davison tried not to look startled.

'For goodness' sake, don't pretend I don't know about your files. Daddy used to bring them home all the time. So do you?'

He nodded his head. 'But there is nothing in it at all incriminating, I can assure you. Hartford commissioned it after I told him that I had met her. Standard procedure in the circumstances, considering the possibility that she might one day work for us. She seems completely above board, apart from her eccentric brother, who returned from the war with a few battle scars, not quite right in the head by all accounts.'

'Well, we all have our crosses to bear, don't we?' she

said. 'And remind me again of the name of the novel that you and Hartford think so highly of?'

'*The Murder of Roger Ackroyd.*'

'And is it really as clever as all that?'

'Oh yes, most terribly. I won't spoil it for you, but you simply must read it.' He got up and walked over to his bookshelf. 'Here – see what you think.'

Una opened the book and read out the dedication: '"To Punkie, who likes an orthodox detective story, murder, inquest, and suspicion falling on everyone in turn!"'

'How funny. Who's Punkie?'

'A nickname for her sister, Margaret.'

'And who is this – how do you pronounce it – this Poirot?' asked Una as she flicked through the book.

'Oh, a most peculiar, but intriguing detective. Belgian. Works by the power of his little grey cells. An unusual character. In fact, a most unusual writer. Although Mrs Christie may present herself as a normal wife and mother, nothing out of the ordinary, dig under the surface and I guarantee you will find someone much darker and altogether more interesting.'

Chapter Twelve

I was awake before I heard the knock on the door. A moment later Rosie, the pretty little chambermaid, entered with the breakfast tray. I couldn't bring myself to talk to her and so I pretended to be asleep, only stirring when I heard the click of the door shutting behind her. I poured myself a cup of tea and retired back to bed with the *Daily Mail*. I turned the pages idly until I got to page 9. The sight of my name in print made me feel ill, but I felt compelled to read the report even though they had got my age wrong by a year. Apparently, my car had been found at around eight o'clock on the Saturday morning. 'It is believed that it was allowed deliberately to run down from Newlands Corner with its brakes off,' it said.

The police had been looking for traces of me all weekend and they had dredged the Silent Pool for my body. There was even a quote from Archie who told the readers of the newspaper that I was a 'nervous case' and it was most likely that I had suffered some form of nervous breakdown. I wondered if he really believed that. And what on earth had he told dear Rosalind? There was also a bad photograph of me. Although it did not look anything like me, I would still have to keep a low profile.

I threw the newspaper across the bed and began to dress quickly. I had decided that I would walk down to reception and ask the manager to call the police. I would bring this farce to a close. Kurs had no power over me. He was nothing but a megalomaniac with a warped mind. I wouldn't let him control me. I rushed to the door, but just before I opened it I caught a glance of myself in the looking glass. What a fright! Like a madwoman. Who would believe me? What happened if I was carted off to the asylum and locked away? Kurs could deny everything. But I had the letters. I seized my handbag containing all of Kurs's instructions. Yes, all I had to do was to show the police the evidence and the whole sordid story would come out. But what if Kurs had the audacity to follow through with his plans? If he so much as touched a hair on Rosalind's head I knew that I would not be answerable for my actions. I would be prepared to hang to protect my daughter. But would I be too late? Could Kurs really do those unutterable things to my dear, innocent child? And what of his associate? That degenerate? Did he really exist? How on earth could I ever be sure?

I had to calm down and think clearly. I forced myself to drink another cup of tea and have a crust of a roll with butter and jam. I took out my notebook and read through the sequence of events since Wednesday when Kurs had first appeared in my life. Surely there was another way? I had always rather doubted my intelligence, but recently people had praised me for my methodical mind and what they said was a certain ruthlessness with which I could manipulate a reader. That Davison man had even tried to recruit me to be some sort of secret agent or spy. Quite absurd. But was there a way in which I could try to outwit Kurs? Even if there was, I doubted that I would have the courage to do so.

He had told me to regard myself as a different person, a character. What if I applied his advice to Kurs himself? What if I began to think of Kurs not as a twisted, deeply dangerous individual but as someone I had created in my imagination? I tried to think of some of the villains in my books. There was the enigmatic Mr Brown in *The Secret Adversary* and Dr James Sheppard in *The Murder of Roger Ackroyd*, but surely there was no one I had invented who was quite as base as Dr Patrick Kurs? I jotted down some more possibilities, in a similar way I might begin to plot out a novel, feeling slightly unnerved that I was one of the protagonists in the drama.

After bathing and dressing I left the hotel and spent the morning in town. I bought some necessities for my toilet, a couple of notebooks and a selection of pencils, and then just as I was passing the W.H. Smith Library in Parliament Street, I felt a few drops of rain on my face. The sky was dark and ominous and I had left the hotel without an umbrella. I darted inside just as the shower intensified.

I took my time to enjoy the library and its bounty. If only I could spend the next few days reading at leisure, what a delicious prospect that would be. Yet it was impossible. Nevertheless, I went through the motion of selecting some books as if I were a normal, respectable lady with a little too much time on her hands.

As I did so I stole glances at the people around me. What was the mousy librarian with the half-moon spectacles hiding? As she stamped the books of the old lady in the smart tweeds was she thinking of a child she had borne out of wedlock and given away? And what of the elderly lady herself, so very prim and proper, with her soft skin and apple cheeks – could she be slowly poisoning her invalid husband, slipping a few grains of arsenic into his tea each day to bring about an early death? I imagined her sense of moral superiority, her assertion that she was on the side of righteousness, her belief that she was justified in putting her husband out of his misery, that he was going to a better place. And who was I to say that she was wrong? Each of us had our secrets. Some of them were small, insubstantial things: no one knew, for instance, of my nickname for Mr and Mrs de Silva – Mr and

Mrs Silver Plate, a name I had given the couple because I suspected my Sunningdale neighbours to be more than a little insincere. Archie did not even know of that.

Then there were the bigger, fatter, juicier secrets, secrets that had the power to ruin lives. For instance, how long had Archie been seeing Miss Neele without my knowledge? Had he been carrying on with her while making love to me? Had there been other women besides her? The thought sickened me. I tried to think of the last time we had shared a bed. Months ago now, almost a year. No doubt I was to blame. It was true I had neglected him after my mother's death. I had thought that lovemaking would be disrespectful to my mother's memory; not only that, but I had felt as frozen as the wilds of Siberia. Those kind of feelings – that dizziness, that lightness in my head and in my body, that need – had dried up. I blushed when I thought of the number of times Archie had touched me on the back of the neck or pressed his fingers to my shoulder, often a precursor of intimacy, only for me to turn my head and walk away from him. If only I had shown him a little more tenderness perhaps none of this would have happened. If we had continued to enjoy a full and happy married life, then perhaps Archie would have remained faithful, he would have had no need to seek out other women, younger, more attractive women like Miss Neele. She, in turn, would not have run to her doctor for advice and Kurs would not have come up with his wretched plan. Was it all my fault?

By the time I emerged from the library the rain seemed to have stopped, although the sky was still dark. But as I walked down Parliament Street the heavens suddenly opened once more. The rain was even fiercer this time and in a matter of minutes I felt sodden to the skin. I ran and took shelter underneath an awning of Louis Cope. I was in desperate need of some new clothes, but did I really want to offer up my poor and neglected self to the harsh light of a looking glass? Yet the task could be avoided no longer. Brushing the drops of water from me I entered the shop. When I saw a young, elegant woman wearing a plaid V-neck sweater – I really could not understand this fad for sportswear – and then another beautiful creature parading around in a rose-coloured chenille-crêpe dress I turned and started to make my way towards the door again. I felt old and frumpy next to these dazzling girls. But then, just as I was about leave, I thought of Miss Neele in her navy-blue blouson dress that tied around the hips into a beguiling front bow. I imagined Archie's hands touching her, reaching out to place his fingers on her, lifting the hem of her dress a little higher so he could feel her stockings underneath. Tears of frustration, jealousy and rage pricked my eyes. That woman! How had she seduced him? What wiles had she used to lure him to her bed?

'Excuse me, madam. Can I help you?'

I turned to see a woman around my age with kind brown eyes and prematurely greying hair.

'Terrible weather, isn't it?' she continued. 'And I can see you've stepped out without an umbrella. If that's what you would like I can—'

'That's very kind,' I said, cutting her off. 'But in fact I'm going to need more than just an umbrella. I've just arrived from South Africa, and it seems my luggage has gone astray.'

'Of course, madam. If you would follow me.'

She led me towards a section of the shop devoted to ladies' fashion and told a stern-faced, skeletally thin woman of my need of a whole new wardrobe. When she heard this, the shop assistant's face softened and she immediately began to fuss about me, taking my measurements and asking my thoughts on everything from pleated skirts to jabot blouses.

'Would you mind taking off those wet clothes and I'll bring over a few things for you to try on,' she said as she led me towards a changing room.

'I don't want to look too fashionable,' I warned her, worried that she was going to dress me in clothes that would make me look foolish.

'Don't worry,' she said. 'I think I understand just the kind of things that would suit you.'

As I closed the door behind me, a cartoon I had seen in a magazine sprang to mind, in which a short-sighted old lady asked a young woman dressed in mannish clothes, 'Did you say you were going up to Trinity or

Girton next term?' I quickly opened the door and called out to her, 'Or too like a man.'

A few minutes later the assistant returned with a brown silk dress and a red bolero blouse, together with a pair of brown heels. After slipping into the dress and tying up the bow at the front I stepped back and took a look at myself in the glass. The effect was so pleasing I felt confident enough to open the door and stand in front of the assistant.

'Oh yes, that does suit you very well indeed,' she said. 'Don't you think?'

'Yes, I think it does,' I said, smiling.

'Now, I've spotted a couple of other things too, a rather gay dress with a pattern – don't worry, it's not too gaudy – a flower silk-crêpe dress, a lovely coat with a fur trim and a nice salmon-pink evening gown. Should I bring them over?'

When I first saw the rather futuristic design – all red triangles, yellow squares and black oblongs – that graced the top section of the blue crêpe dress I wanted to send the assistant away with it. But I was persuaded to try it on. The delicious feel of the crêpe against my skin brought colour to my pale cheeks and the cut of the dress – with its inverted shoulder tucks, swagger tie-collar and button-trimmed hip band – showed off my figure to its best advantage. As I examined myself in the glass I could hardly believe it was me. I looked like the kind of woman I stared at with astonishment if not also a touch of envy.

'Would you like to try the coat with that?'

The assistant passed me an oatmeal-coloured coat, trimmed with lynx on the collar, cuffs and around its bottom edge.

'Yes, I think that works very well indeed,' she said.

I had to agree. I felt enveloped if not by love then certainly by luxury. The effect was quite extraordinary. As I stood in front of the glass I noticed that my posture had changed. I was standing tall and confident, like a woman of the world. In this guise, I could walk down the street and no one would ever guess the kind of difficulties I had suffered. I probably couldn't afford it, but I pushed thoughts of expense out of my mind.

'You look like a new woman,' she said.

'Indeed?' I replied as I admired my back view.

'And here's the flower silk-crêpe dress,' said the assistant, whose thin face was now beaming with delight.

Back in the changing room I slipped on the dress – a subtle orange colour printed with blue flowers and bands of blue that circled the low waistline – and I felt the transformation continuing. I gave the assistant a shy smile as I stepped out to show her.

'Just beautiful,' she said. 'And finally the salmon-pink evening gown.'

The lightness of the georgette fabric took my breath away; in fact the dress was so flimsy that I felt almost naked. I remembered my wedding night, the first time Archie had seen me without clothes. The thought of that night brought a blush to my cheeks.

'How do you find it?' said the assistant from the other side of the door.

'It's – lovely,' was all I could manage. I felt too indecent to step outside to show her, but I knew that I would have to buy it. I was certain that I would find the perfect occasion on which to wear it.

Chapter Thirteen

'I've told you, Miss Crowe, we have no further information relating to this case. You will have to wait for a statement, I'm afraid. There have been no further developments and I cannot be seen to be favouring one journalist over another. Goodbye.'

As Kenward put the telephone down, he swore under his breath. Damn reporters. He didn't think highly of the new breed of female journalist. A most unsuitable job for a young lady. And fancy the girl saying that she was the daughter of the diplomat Sir Eyre Crowe. Extraordinary what some reporters were willing to invent in order to make an impression or curry favour. He wasn't having any of it. The more she had tried to charm him the more resistant he had become until finally he had brought the telephone conversation to a close. He had better things to be doing than chatting on the telephone to some lady reporter who obviously had no morals. Mrs Christie had been missing for two days now and still they had found no trace of her.

The search had resumed at dawn earlier that day. Three dozen local men had been recruited and a charabanc had taken them from the police station to Newlands Corner. Kenward himself had supervised the operation. He had told the men to search the area as if their lives depended on it. It was important, he had said, to carry on walking in a straight line. There should no deviation: bushes had to be searched thoroughly and the men were told to look up into trees for anything suspicious. When he had been a young constable he had been called out to cut down a young woman who had hanged herself from a big ash tree in the family's garden. She had got herself pregnant and the man, an older chap, had left the country and apparently she could not bear the shame of it. Kenward would never be able to forget the girl's face, her eyes full of torture and pain, the skin ghostly but still beautiful, the red necklace of death that circled her throat.

'Sir?'

It was Hughes, one of the young constables.

'Yes?'

'Colonel Christie would like to talk to you on the telephone.'

'Well, let's hear what he's got to say for himself, shall we?'

'Very well, sir.'

A moment later, Kenward heard the Colonel's clipped tones.

'Kenward, I thought you'd like to hear it first, as it may put the situation in a new light. It could even show—'

Kenward wanted to interrupt, but years of experience had taught him it was always better to let people take as long as they needed to get to the point. In fact, often the point was not the point after all; what relatives and witnesses said as they perambulated and expostulated gave more away than they realised.

'It seems to show that my wife was in London in the early hours of Saturday,' said the Colonel.

'And what is the "it" you are referring to, Colonel Christie?'

'A letter. A letter that my wife wrote to my brother, Campbell. She wrote it, I presume, on the night she disappeared, Friday evening. But it seems she addressed the letter to my brother's place of work, in Woolwich. He only just discovered today that Mrs Christie had gone missing and as soon as he learnt of that fact he telephoned me.'

'And the letter? What did it say?'

'Nothing more than that she was planning to spend a few days in a northern spa town.'

'Northern spa town, eh? Can't be too many of those. I'll get my men on to it straight away. Of course, we will have to see the letter in question.'

'I'm afraid that's not going to be possible.'

'And why not?'

'My brother told me he burnt it after reading it or misplaced it.'

'Which is it, Colonel?'

'Misplaced it, yes. I'm certain that's what he said. But the envelope survived, apparently.'

'Did it now?' It all sounded mighty queer to him. 'Then we will want to question your brother and see the envelope to examine its postmark.'

'Of course. I think you'll agree it is a piece of good news.'

'Good news?'

'Yes,' said the Colonel, his voice tinged with irritation. 'It shows that – that she didn't do something stupid.'

'Stupid?'

'For God's sake, Kenward, you know what I'm saying. The letter shows that my wife must have been alive in the early hours of Saturday morning. And that the letter was posted in London shows that she must have left the scene of the car accident or whatever it was and made her way to town.'

'But Mrs Christie is still missing.'

'Yes, but – somehow she made her way to London, where perhaps she is now. Look here, Kenward, I'm sure you are doing a splendid job, but it's obvious that these searches of the countryside are not going to turn up any clues to my wife's whereabouts. I must thank you for all your help, but I think it's time I called in the help of Scotland Yard.'

'The Yard? Whatever for?'

'If she's in London they may be able to help. And surely it's a better bet than dealing with—'

'Yes, Colonel?'

'Dealing with the force down here.'

'By all means, please contact the Yard, but I doubt they will be of much use.' Did the Colonel know that Scotland Yard would only intervene on the request of a force? Probably not. Let him find that out for himself.

'Well, I intend to pay them a visit this morning,' said the Colonel.

'Very well. Goodbye.'

The Colonel's behaviour reminded him of another case, a Surrey banker by the name of Ledbury. One day Ledbury stormed into the police station to report his wife missing. He suspected that she had run off with a writer, a bohemian type by all accounts, who lived in the same village. Kenward had informed him that unfortunately the police could not act unless they had evidence that a crime had been committed. Had Mrs Ledbury acted of her own free will, he had asked. That was not the point, Mr Ledbury had replied. His wife hardly knew her own mind, he had said before storming out of the station, uttering a froth of profanities under his breath. The next thing Kenward knew was that the body of a woman had been found in a patch of woodland. The woman was indeed Mrs Ledbury and she had been strangled. Kenward took his car to Mr Ledbury's red-brick palace just outside Guildford only to find that the banker had blasted his brains out in the garage.

Colonel Christie might not be a jealous husband, like Mr Ledbury, but he was that other dangerous type of man: a guilty husband. Kenward knew that guilty husbands, like rats, reacted badly when cornered. No one knew who they might bite.

Chapter Fourteen

'That damn policeman,' said Una, slamming down the telephone. 'Wouldn't tell me a thing. And he talked to me as if I were a child – no, not even a child, more like an imbecilic child.'

'What do you expect?' asked Davison.

'I thought at least he'd show me a little common courtesy,' she said as she ran her hands through her blonde hair. 'Hardly reacted when I mentioned Daddy's name.'

'Sometimes these things can work against one,' he said.

The two friends were taking tea in Davison's Albany flat. It was a ritual as essential to his day as shaving and reading *The Times*.

'But if he thinks he's going to put me off the scent, he's wrong,' she said.

'Little does he know who he is dealing with,' said Davison archly.

'Oh, shush, you beast. Now let's see what we know.'

She outlined how Mrs Christie had disappeared near Newlands Corner at some point on Friday evening or in the early hours of Saturday morning. It was claimed that Mrs Christie still felt bereft at the death of her mother – something which Una said she could understand – but she doubted whether the writer would have committed suicide.

'You know only too well how the loss of Daddy nearly proved too much for me, and I would have done something silly had it not been, well, for the thought of all the people I would have left behind,' she said. 'I couldn't bear the idea of hurting Mama so, and then there was Eric and Asta and dear young Sybil. And then you too . . .'

'Me?' Davison sounded genuinely surprised.

'Yes. You know what a good friend you've been to me. And I hope I've been one to you, too.'

'Yes, you have.' He didn't want to talk about how Una had supported him. In fact, he felt uncomfortable with Una's new spirit of honesty which had from time to time possessed her since her breakdown. 'But let's talk about what needs to be talked about – Mrs Christie.'

'Yes, the mysterious Mrs Christie. We need to find out who she was close to. Is there anyone in your office who could help?'

'There may be. I can check, but I would say it's best not to rely on any more information coming our way from that direction.'

'Why is that?'

'It's not something that need concern you, my dear.'

'You sound exactly like that dreadful Superintendent Kenward. The old stuffed shirt.'

'Stuffed shirt now, am I?'

'Oh, I didn't mean it like that. It's just that I was hoping for some little titbit of information from him, some snippet of gossip.'

'You know very well that men don't gossip. You need to get a woman on your side.'

'I suppose you're right. But who? I expect Miss Fisher, the secretary, has tightened up like a clam. Too busy worrying about her job to engage in idle chit-chat.'

'Yes, I suspect you are right.'

'The first thing I'm going to do is approach the servants. They always have the loosest of tongues, don't you think? Mama's maid was always the person who knew best what was going on in our house. She pretended to be all high and mighty, but if you buttered her up the right way she would tell you everything. You should have heard some of the things she told me about some of Daddy's guests. She even knew something of the bedroom habits of the Cabinet ministers.'

'Now you're making me blush, Una.'

'Oh, come off it, Davison. You know as well as I do that—'

'I know no such thing. Now, back to the matter in hand. If you try and talk to the servants, I will make a few enquiries at the office and see what I can find out about Colonel Christie.'

'Do you suspect he's a brute?'

'I expect so. Must husbands are, aren't they?'

Una laughed, a sound Davison had not heard in such a long time. He had missed the spontaneous expression of joy, the chaotic guffawing and unladylike snorting that had once defined Una's personality. For a long time he had assumed that part of her had been lost, gone to the same grave as her father in that lonely churchyard in Swanage. If this little game could help restore something of her joy for living then he would do everything in his power to help her.

'I don't think I will ever marry,' said Una, breaking the silence between the two friends.

'Why ever not?' said Davison, feeling quite shocked.

'Oh, I don't know. It's like you say, husbands can be terrible bores. I've never met one yet who I thought I could imagine marrying myself.'

'I hope not,' said Davison, laughing.

'You know what I mean – even Daddy. Even though I loved him deeply, he could be awfully annoying to Mama sometimes.'

'Really?'

'Yes. And the bohemian types you see nowadays are no better than the traditional ones. They pretend to believe in freedom, but they control their wives or girl-friends just as fiercely as the stick-in-the-muds.'

'I'm sure you'll find some suitable gentleman. One day you'll fall in love and look back on what you've said today as silly nonsense.'

'I doubt it somehow. I wish I could marry a man who just let me be myself, without any kind of restrictions or expectations. I doubt I'll meet anyone like that.'

Again, the two fell into silence. Should he say anything? wondered Davison. Was now the moment? Was she trying to force him to speak? He opened his mouth to ask her a question, a question only half formed and opaque, when Una patted him on the knee and jumped up from the sofa.

'Listen to me, prattling on like a schoolgirl. We've got a case to crack. I'm determined to beat that dimwitted Kenward to it. That will show him.' She paused. 'Oh, sorry, Davison, were you about to say something?'

He shook his head and smiled. 'No, nothing, nothing at all.'

Chapter Fifteen

What had possessed Kurs to choose this particular place? I couldn't imagine him stepping foot on sacred ground. But then was I any better?

He had arranged to meet me here, at Christ Church on the Stray, to talk about the worst crime imaginable: murder. I felt relieved that there was no one else in the churchyard; I could not bring myself to look another Christian in the eye. I glanced at the clock on the church tower: I had a quarter of an hour to spare. The east wind was harsh and bitter and had begun to freeze my lips, but I did not feel comfortable taking shelter inside the church. I pushed my hands deep into the pockets of my new coat and started to walk around the graveyard.

As the clock struck the half-hour I noticed a figure clad in black open the gate and walk towards me. It was Kurs, but it could so easily have been the spectre of death himself. Non-existence seemed like an attractive option; I would rather perish than carry out Kurs's orders.

'How are you settling in? I hope you are quite comfortable?' he said as he approached and stood by my side at a gravestone.

A perfectly respectable question, yes, and in most situations it would have been a highly appropriate one, but now the enquiry seemed sick and perverse. What could I say? That I found the hotel to my satisfaction? That I enjoyed the band? And that I was looking forward to a massage? I merely nodded my head.

'Good. I was worried that you would find it, I don't know, a little too unsophisticated for your tastes. I'm sure some of the guests are a little provincial, but it won't be for long.'

'I wanted to ask you – when—'

Kurs lowered his voice to a whisper, though there was no need to do so as the churchyard was, apart from us, empty.

'When you should commit the murder?'

'I wish you wouldn't put it like that.'

'I'm afraid that is what it is. You are, I know, rather a fan of straightforward sentences. I've read your books, Mrs Christie.'

'Indeed,' I replied.

'So I thought by the end of the week might do very well.'

I was taken aback not only by the proximity of the deed in question, but also by the use of language; it was as if his request was as innocent and easy to achieve as the submission of a sponge cake or a pot of strawberry jam to the village show.

'By the end of this week? No, that's impossible, it's just too soon,' I said.

'Well, I'm afraid you have no choice. It should all be quite manageable.'

'But—'

'Let me outline what I think might work best. I want you to leave your hotel and travel to Leeds, where my wife, Flora, has been living for some time, ever since the breakdown of our marriage. I want you to travel to her house and there I want you to kill her. As I said, I don't care what method you employ, but I would advise you to choose one that makes it easy for you to slip away unnoticed. I don't see why you should get caught for the crime any more than I should. And perhaps, I would have thought, you might enjoy the experience. It might even lend your books a greater degree of, how shall I put it, authenticity?'

Kurs took off one of his black leather gloves as he opened his briefcase. From this he withdrew a large brown envelope, which he held in his hands as he continued to talk.

'Of course, after killing her you need to make sure you travel back to Harrogate, as we agreed. On notice of her death – which, of course, should be verified by a doctor – I will travel up to see her body, to confirm it for myself.' He took a deep breath and as he exhaled he puffed out his chest in satisfaction. 'I can't tell you how wonderful this makes me feel. I do believe that there is divine providence at work, don't you?'

'I'm sorry?'

'It seems appropriate that we are meeting here, in one of God's holy places. It seems so fitting somehow. If all goes to plan it is as if God himself had overseen the whole thing.'

'I think your view of God is rather different to mine.' I spat the words out as if I had tasted something fetid in my mouth. I suddenly felt nauseous and weak. I stretched out a hand to steady myself on a gravestone.

'Here, please let me help,' said Kurs, moving towards me.

'Please – no. I'm quite all right, thank you,' I said.

His free hand hovered above my wrist; although my cut had begun to heal, I could not bear him to touch me. He let his hand remain there for a moment too long – it was obvious Kurs enjoyed my sense of discomfort – before he withdrew.

'Perhaps a walk around the churchyard may help you feel a little better? Did you get a chance to study some of the gravestones?'

He started to lead the way along the grassy pathway, while I trailed behind him like an obedient, dead-eyed child.

'I must admit I am something of a hobbyist when it comes to graveyards. It's the first thing I do when I visit a new town or city. The things one can find out from a headstone – simply fascinating. And then there are the things that one can never know. I often play a game when I arrive at a graveyard for the first time. I take a walk around, just as we are doing now, and I like to imagine the lives of some of the people who are lying below. Take this grave here, for example. The grave of Marmaduke Lupton, born in 1799 and died in 1849. Who was he? His name – a rather lovely name, don't you agree? – gives him the air of a burgher of the town. I imagine him as a rather solid character, as solid as the stone of Harrogate, a man with a set of fine whiskers and a strong moral character and an unflinching belief in God. But you see, written on the grave as plain as anything, is the fact that his daughter, Christana, died in 1828 when she was only one year old. How do you think Marmaduke coped with that? Do you think the death of the child shook his belief in God? Maybe he coped by telling himself that the everlasting Lord took only the best, the most innocent. You've gone very quiet. What do you think, Mrs Christie?'

'I – I'm not sure.'

'You are looking a little pale. I hope you are not coming down with influenza. Perhaps you should try the waters while you are here. They are said to be miraculous, but I don't care for them myself. Have you tried them?'

'No, no, I haven't.'

He stopped and turned to me. I felt a blast of that breath on my face.

'Before I forget, here are all the details for the arrangement on Friday. Everything you need should be inside: there is the address, a physical description of Flora, a few photographs and an outline of her daily routine.'

He stretched out his hand to pass me the envelope. I did not move. Kurs looked coldly at me, a gaze as heartless and deathly as that of a cobra I had once seen studying a lizard it was about to bite and devour. Kurs continued, keeping the envelope in his hand, but then a moment or so later, by a mound of fresh earth, he stopped. I followed his gaze to the headstone, newly engraved, which read: ELIZA REID, 1919–1926. A girl born in the same year as Rosalind.

'Are you not curious to discover why the girl died?' His dark eyes shone like jet stones. 'No? That's not like you, Mrs Christie. One who has always taken such a keen interest in death. Well, let me enlighten you. One day – I think it was September of this year – she was playing out with two friends here on the Stray. But the two friends, nasty little girls, Susan Potter and Jemima Pargeter, ganged up on her and ran off, leaving her all alone. I suppose a man found her crying and took pity on her. Perhaps he offered to take her home to her mama and papa, but instead of doing that he led her down to an outbuilding on the edge of town, where he—'

'Stop,' I said quietly. 'I can't hear any more. Please stop.'

'Do you not want to hear the end of the story? Again, that is most out of character. I'm sure you will understand when you do.'

I felt so drained and empty that I let the words flow over me. I would not listen to the details of this depravity, nor give Kurs the satisfaction of indulging his sadistic pleasure in the retelling of the incident.

'Have you finished?' I said, finally meeting his eye.

'Now, please take the envelope.'

I did not move my arm.

'I do hope you are not having second thoughts. Remember what happened to poor Eliza Reid. By the way, the police still haven't caught the man. And if you are wondering, no, I had nothing to do with it – as I have said it is not my thing at all – but I wouldn't be surprised if an acquaintance of mine, one I have mentioned, knew something or other about the crime.'

I felt my legs collapse beneath me and I fell back onto a patch of damp earth. Again, Kurs reached out to help me but I refused to take his hand.

'I'm just feeling rather faint. Sorry,' I said. I did not want to admit to him that his nasty little story had affected me so badly. Without looking at him, I took the envelope.

'Goodbye, Mrs Christie.' He started to walk away, but turned to face me for a moment. 'Oh, and please, you are very welcome to take notes. In fact, I would recommend it. You never know, one day you might even thank me for this. It might inspire you to write your greatest novel yet.'

By the time I had regained my composure and looked up, Kurs had gone.

Chapter Sixteen

Una stood outside Styles and wondered what to do next. What a horrible house, she thought to herself – flashy and vulgar, not at all the kind of place Mrs Christie would choose. Perhaps it had been her husband's idea, thought Una. Her own mother and father's taste had always been so, how could she put it, restrained. One took it for granted that one's friends had money; there was no need to boast about it or go about buying houses or cars that screamed wealth. The family home in Elm Park Road was a case in point, packed as it was with threadbare Persian rugs, tatty leather armchairs and ancient tables bearing generations of scratches, marks and stains.

Una knew that Mrs Christie belonged to the middle classes. There had been, she had learnt in the course of her research on her, a certain amount of family money, but Frederick Miller, the father, had got through it quickly enough. The Millers were respectable, but certainly not bohemian or intellectual, and she supposed little Agatha had grown up with particularly suburban taste. Of course, one could see this in her writing, thought Una. There was, after all, no attempt to experiment with form or do anything challenging or daring. Mrs Christie was no Virginia Woolf – that much was certain. And yet there was something about the plotting that was – how could she put it – rather subversive. She had never read a novel quite like *The Murder of Roger Ackroyd*.

There was, as Davison had said, a great deal more to Mrs Christie than the image she chose to present to the world. After all, not many middle-class girls grew up to write clever crime novels like Mrs Christie. She obviously had a side to her character that was – well, definitely not middle class, and so she'd be unlikely to feel at home in this kind of house. No wonder she had run away, thought Una.

She had waited outside for twenty minutes or so and she knew she would have to act soon before Colonel Christie returned. His car was not outside and she had telephoned earlier to ensure that he was out. The girl had said that the Colonel would return at 6.30. It was nearly six already. Una took a deep breath of cold air and walked down the driveway and knocked on the door. There was no sign of movement from inside and so she knocked again, louder this time. A shadow approached the door and then stopped.

'Sorry – no reporters. I've been told not to open the door to you,' said a girl from inside.

Una had to think quickly. Luckily, she knew how to treat servants.

'I'm certainly not a reporter. Now please open the door immediately.'

The door opened to reveal a nervous young woman with anxious eyes and fingers that twisted together like the bucketful of eels Una had seen on that fishing trip with her father to Scotland.

'I'm from Collins, Mrs Christie's publisher,' said Una grandly.

'Oh dear, please come in, ma'am.'

'I will, thank you. It's terribly cold outside.'

Una stepped into the hall and looked around her. Yes, just as she had expected – it looked like a compressed, and far newer and cleaner, version of a country house. The people who lived here wanted to ape the life of the upper classes, but while they had a certain amount of money, they had precious little confidence to decide on a style of their own. And yet it was called Styles! Simply incredible.

'I'm afraid the Colonel is not at home, m'lady. But he will be back shortly, I'm sure.'

'But it's you that I've really come to talk to.'

'Me, miss? I've got nothing I can help you with, I know nothing about the mistress's books and the like.'

'Well, why don't we have a little chat?'

Una smiled, knowing that the deployment of that smile seldom failed when she wanted to get her own way. What was it Davison called it? Her secret weapon.

Anyway, its deployment on this occasion seemed to work and the girl's face softened and she immediately relaxed.

'You really do have the sweetest face, don't you know? In fact, I'm surprised nobody has approached you to be a model for the illustrated magazines. A great deal of money can be made, I've heard.'

'Really? I've never thought of it.' The girl blushed and started to giggle stupidly.

'Is there anywhere we could talk?'

'Talk, ma'am?'

'Yes, as her publisher there are a couple of delicate issues I'd like to try and clear up.'

'Oh, I'm not sure, miss. I think you should talk to the Colonel about that.'

'Well, to be honest – what's your name?'

'Kathleen, or Kitty to my friends.'

'To be honest, Kitty, it's something rather delicate. Something best talked about away from the company of men, if you see what I mean.'

Kitty looked startled and confused, but she tried her best to disguise her sense of discomfort.

'I see, well, perhaps you should come into the lounge, sorry, the—'

'Indeed,' said Una, smiling.

Even though Una was in a stranger's house the innate superiority of her class meant that she assumed the role of mistress with ease.

'Please sit down, Kitty,' she said.

'Oh, thank you, ma'am.'

Una looked the girl directly in the eyes and lowered her voice.

'It must be a terribly distressing situation for you, what with all the attention from the press. A pack of jackals, the lot of them.'

'Awful it is, ma'am. You wouldn't believe how some of them carry on.'

'I can quite imagine. As you know, as her publisher, I only have Mrs Christie's interests at heart. I am sure once all this nonsense has been settled and the where-abouts of Mrs Christie come to light – as I am sure they will – there will be an appetite for what the newspapers call a follow-up story. You know the type of thing they do – full picture spreads of all the parties involved, along with detailed write-ups. All very well and enjoy-able if you are a reader, not so pleasurable if you are one of the unfortunate people caught up in the drama. Am I right, Kitty?'

'Yes, m'lady.'

'The situation is this. The newspapers will be desper-ate for anything they can get their hands on. And these things – letters, diaries and suchlike – suddenly take on a value. Do you understand what I am saying?'

Kitty's face darkened. 'If you think that me or anyone else in the house would dream of selling such things to the paper, you are very much mistaken, I'm sure.' The girl looked cross, her face as crumpled as a dry dishcloth.

'I wouldn't dream of suggesting such a thing.' Una leant closer towards the girl. 'But it's come to my attention that a certain policeman, who shall for the moment remain nameless, is in the business of making a tidy little profit by selling certain things to the newspapers.'

'Really? Well, I said to Rose, the girl who works for the Sandwich family across the road, that one of the policemen who came here the other day was a rum 'un. Was the one with the slightly gammy eye and the—'

Una nodded confidentially and gave a slight wink of encouragement.

'I see that you're a very clever girl, Kitty. Nothing passes you by.'

'I like to think so, ma'am. My mother used to say that—'

'I suppose you didn't notice anything unusual in the behaviour of Mrs Christie recently?'

'I'm sure I couldn't really say.'

'Nothing out of character?'

'Not that I can think of.'

'And relations between Mrs Christie and the Colonel. How were they?'

'Just as to be expected.'

Una could see that questioning along these lines would get her nowhere. She needed to see inside the desk of Mrs Christie. She was sure her private papers might offer some kind of clue to her disappearance.

'Quite so,' said Una. 'As I was saying, it would be helpful, as her publisher, if I could protect the reputation of Mrs Christie. Some damage has of course been done, there's nothing we can do about that, but we can certainly try to prevent certain aspects of Mrs Christie's life from reaching the clutches of the popular press.'

'I think the Colonel ought to—'

'As a woman I am sure you will agree that there are certain things a husband would rather not see published in the pages of a less reputable Sunday newspaper.'

Kitty bit her lip and her face reddened.

'If you could tell me where your mistress kept her writing things I will go and have a look so as to spare the blushes of the Colonel. Heaven knows, the policeman in question may have got his hands on some compromising material already. Let us hope he has not. And when the Colonel comes back I can have a conversation with him about the sensitive material and put his mind at rest that none of it will ever see the light of day.'

'Very well, ma'am. Her desk is in her bedroom. By the window. I don't look inside, but I know that's where she sits sometimes when she does the writing of her books.'

'Thank you, Kitty. You are doing your mistress a great service. I am sure she would be very proud of you.'

Una had to restrain herself from running out of the drawing room and bolting up the stairs. She glanced at the clock on the wall. It was a quarter past six. She would have loved to have taken her time, examining the room and its decor, but she knew she would have to be quick. She walked straight to the desk and began to rifle through the papers. There were bills for household expenses, sheets of paper with columns detailing incoming and outgoing expenditure, figures for sales of certain novels and some correspondence from her agent, Edmund Cork. Gosh – if that was how much a woman could earn from dashing off a short story Una thought she should pursue her dream of being a writer. There was a file of newspaper cuttings relating to her novels, reviews and the like, and a couple of notebooks full of scribbles. Una opened one at random; she could hardly make out the scrawl of the handwriting.

There was nothing of use here. She was wasting her time. Then, as she picked up another notebook, a letter fell out onto the desk. Again, the handwriting was difficult to decipher, but she could just about make out the signature, 'Madge'. She started to read the letter. It was obvious, from even the briefest of glances, that the matter of the letter was delicate. Words jumped out at Una like poisonous little bullets: 'marriage', 'difficulties', 'affair', 'liaison', 'crisis', 'Archie', 'divorce', 'that girl' and 'Nancy'.

Before she could read the whole thing she heard the sound of a car engine outside. It must be the Colonel. He had returned early. She quickly ran her shaking hands over the desk as if the action itself were enough to bring forth the materialisation of more intimate letters. The noise of the engine stopped. She heard a car door slam. She stuffed the letter inside her handbag and left the bedroom. What should she do? How could she explain herself? She would have to take a gamble. She wanted to run, run as fast as she could, but she could not be seen to panic. With a stately gait – wouldn't Miss Temple at the Academy be proud of her posture now – Una walked down the staircase. She could hear the tread of the Colonel's shoes approach the door. As she stood at the bottom of the stairs she saw, through a panel of glass, his shadow at the door. He was opening his briefcase to take out a set of keys. She turned to make her way to the back of the house, where she supposed the kitchen was located. Kitty looked up from the table where she sat, wide-eyed and terrified.

'Don't get up,' said Una, grandly. 'I really must be going.'

'But, the – the Colonel—'

'Don't bother him,' she said, striding across the kitchen to the back door. She tried the handle and pushed. The door did not move.

'We locked it because of the reporters and the like,' said Kitty.

Una spun round on her heels and flashed her eyes at the girl.

'The keys,' she said plainly, without a note of fear in her voice. 'Could you pass me the keys?'

Una heard the Colonel began to turn the lock of the front door.

'But what about the Colonel?'

'I'm afraid I can't talk to him now,' she whispered.

'You see, I have just discovered something upstairs in Mrs Christie's desk that would upset the Colonel a great deal. Trust me, he really doesn't want to have to deal with this at the moment. I am sure he has enough to endure, don't you think?'

The front door opened.

'But?' Kitty looked like she had been struck by a form of paralysis.

'After all, you wouldn't want to be blamed for the discovery of something that casts your mistress in a bad light, would you?'

'No.'

The front door slammed. Una heard the Colonel walking across the hall towards the staircase. She felt a moment's relief when she heard his feet on the stairs but then there was silence, before she realised that the Colonel had started to retrace his steps.

'Kitty?' he called out.

The sound of her name roused the girl from her state of unresponsiveness. She opened her mouth to speak, but Una stopped her.

'Give me the keys now,' she said in an imperious whisper.

Kitty turned her head slightly towards the kitchen door and then quickly took out a set of keys from her apron pocket and pressed them into Una's hands. Una sprang towards the door like the cat she had once seen outside the back of Elm Park Road about to do its business when the cook had thrown a bucket of scalding water over it. She forced the keys into the door, turned the lock and ran out into the cold night leaving the door wide open. She heard the sound of the Colonel behind her – 'Who on earth?' – and then the incoherent babbling of Kitty and snatches of the interrogation that followed: 'A lady publisher', 'No, never seen her before', 'Did she give her name – what was her name, you stupid girl?', 'No, sorry, sir', 'Did you not think to wait for me?' and the final sound of sobbing.

She ran down the side of the house and out into the road just as the Colonel opened the front door. Una crouched behind a neighbour's hedge and as the Colonel approached she pushed her face deep into the fur trim of her coat to stifle the sound of her heavy breathing. She heard the Colonel getting nearer and then saw the glint of his chestnut-brown brogues in a gap in the hedge.

'Damn reporters,' he swore under his breath. 'Next one I see I swear I will throttle – even if it is a woman.'

He turned on his heels, but Una remained in her secret pocket of darkness behind the hedge until she was sure he had retreated back inside the house. When she stood up she felt dizzy from the danger, the fear, and the unmistakable thrill of having stolen something from inside the house. Was this how Davison had felt when, in his early days, he had worked – what was that silly phrase he had once used? – 'in the field'? How exciting it all was. She knew she didn't want to be a spy as she didn't want to run the risk of getting knocked off. Davison had told her some awful stories of people getting garrotted and poisoned and pushed off cliffs. But if she could get this sort of feeling from working in journalism then surely this was just the job for her. She couldn't wait to tell Davison of her little scrape – but on second thoughts perhaps it was better if she kept this to herself for the time being.

She took out the letter, but it was too dark to see anything more than the few phrases she had read earlier. That Colonel was a sly one. And who was this Nancy he had been bothering with? Una hurried along the dark street, towards a lamp-post that she had seen earlier and under the glare of its light she started to read. As she did so she noticed that her hands were still trembling.

Chapter Seventeen

I took another sip of morning tea and suddenly felt happier than I had in days. I had, at some point during the night, decided to go to the police and tell them all about Kurs. My dreams had been haunted by visions of dead children: a terrible nightmare about Eliza Reid, whose grave I had seen, in which the little girl, screaming at the hands of her torturer, suddenly changed into Rosalind.

On the way back to the hotel from the cemetery the day before, I had paused outside Harrogate Police Station. I had taken a couple of steps up towards the front door and stopped while I thought about my actions. I just wished the ordeal was over. Perhaps if I went into the station and told the police all about it they would bring the whole sorry episode to an end. I would show the officers the letters that Kurs had written and they could just telephone Scotland Yard and issue a warrant for the doctor's arrest. I could return from

Harrogate and be with dear Rosalind, Charlotte, and Peter within a day. Then I thought of what Kurs said his associate would do to Rosalind and I had turned away from the welcoming glow of the police station and walked into the darkness back towards the Hydro. I had dined alone, but at some point during the meal, when no doubt I had been looking especially bleak, I looked up to find a middle-aged woman standing by my table.

'I'm so terribly sorry to disturb you,' said the lady. 'But my husband and I were just wondering whether you would like to join us. We've been watching you since you arrived. It can't be much fun eating alone.'

I didn't know quite what to say. I was certainly not in the mood for socialising, and of course I couldn't tell the nice, slightly overweight lady the truth.

'That's extremely kind of you,' I said. 'Most kind. But I'm afraid I'm not the best company at present.'

'Why, we can cheer you up. Well, Arthur certainly will.' She pointed over to a neighbouring table where a red-faced man was gesturing in a rather over-expressive manner. 'You should hear some of his jokes. Some of them are so terrible one simply has to laugh.'

'Perhaps some other time,' I said.

The lady moved a step towards me and placed a hand on my sleeve. She really had the most beautiful blue eyes, full of kindness.

'I understand. Are you here for the waters? They do say they work wonders. I'm sure they will make you feel like a new person.'

'Not really,' I said. 'I've just lost a child, a daughter.'

'Oh, my dear,' said the lady. 'Do you mind if—'

I did rather, but the woman proceeded to sit down next to me.

'I'm so sorry. That must have been awful for you.'

'Yes, it was rather. I can't imagine how I will ever get over it.' I imagined standing by a dank, dark hole and the undertakers lowering a small coffin into the ground. Tears began to sting my eyes. 'But I suppose one has to go on, even though one doesn't feel like it.'

'These things are sent to test us, don't you think?'

'Perhaps,' I said, wiping an all too real tear from my face. 'I'm sorry, what's your name?'

'Mrs Robson. Janet Robson.'

'Hello – I'm Mrs Neele. Mrs Teresa Neele.'

As we shook hands I noticed the warmth emanating from the lady's skin.

'Well, if at any time you want to dine with us, just let me know. Or if you would like to take a walk around the town one day?'

I didn't know what to say. There was an awkward pause that lingered over the table.

'Oh, I'm terribly sorry,' I said. 'You must think me very rude. It's just that the – the loss has affected me rather badly, as I said. Sometimes I am not sure where I am at times. And my memory is shot to pieces. Please don't think me rude.'

'Not at all, dear, not at all.' She stood up, smiling kindly. 'I must get back to Arthur before he starts trying to talk to one of the poor waitresses. Sometimes he can be terribly overfamiliar. And please don't forget – if you ever need dining companions, here we are.' Again she touched me lightly on the sleeve and walked back across the dining room to her husband.

For the rest of that evening I had felt absolutely wretched. Why had I said that about a dead child to Mrs Robson? I pushed my plate of food away from me uneaten and returned to my room. I wished that I had come up with another excuse for my strange behaviour – a physical illness that affected my mind, a melancholy that had descended upon me for no reason, withdrawal from an over-dependency on alcohol. The voicing of my greatest fear – the death of my daughter – had somehow made it more real.

I had gone to bed feeling despondent, and the night-mares had plagued me all through the early hours of the morning. I had woken up clammy and afraid, but as I reconstructed the fragments of the dream I felt pos-sessed by a wave of anger. How dare Kurs inveigle his way into my life in this way? What right did he have to dictate what I should do? As if I could ever go through with what he suggested. By the time I had risen from my bed I had made up my mind. It was time to free myself from this ongoing psychological torture. I would have to take a risk, that much was certain, but it was, I rea-soned, a risk worth taking. Otherwise, I feared that I would go quite insane. I knew that I was not one drawn to introspection – all that self-indulgence, and to what end? – and anything that bothered me I tended to let find expression in my novels.

As I stepped into the breakfast room I saw Mrs Robson seated at the couple's usual table. I made a point of going over to talk to her.

'Good morning,' I said, trying to smile.

'Good morning, my dear,' said Mrs Robson. 'My, you are looking much brighter this morning, if you don't mind me saying.'

'Yes, I am feeling much better. Please forgive me for my gloomy spirits last night.'

'Not at all, dear. Would you care to join me for breakfast? I'm afraid Mr Robson is rather the worse for wear this morning. Dyspepsia.'

'That's very kind, but I have some letters I really must deal with. I've been rather negligent of my correspondence these last few days.'

'Of course. Well, perhaps we will see you later for dinner?'

'Yes, perhaps.'

I walked over to my table and ordered two boiled eggs and toast, with a pot of tea. I extracted my notebook from my handbag and looked at the series of scribbles I had made since Kurs had entered my life. How extraordinary, I thought. Surely I would, at least, be able to use some of this in a novel. Obviously, it would have to be much, much darker than the neat stories that I had written so far in my career, books which always tied up the loose ends and ended on a note of resolution

152

and the restoration of order. Evil had been successfully expelled from the book and from the reader's mind and goodness ruled once more. But someone like Kurs upset the normal order of things.

I wondered what lay at the root of him. Had he been born evil or had something – some awful experience like cruelty or loss or wickedness – twisted his mind? One day, when all this was over – and how much I prayed it would be over soon – I would like to ask him a few questions. How on earth would he react when a policeman knocked on his door, I wondered. I knew he thought of me as a mere woman whom he believed he could manipulate at will. I had gone along with him out of fear, out of a terror that he, or one of his degenerates, would harm firstly Archie's reputation and then, and this was much more frightening, my daughter. But really he would never get the chance. After breakfast was over I would simply walk down to the police station and inform them of everything that had happened. Then I would place a telephone call to Charlotte and tell her to make sure that Rosalind was safe in the house. I would instruct her to lock the doors and let no one, absolutely no one, into Styles.

I took another sip of tea and tried to imagine my future. If my marriage to Archie was over – and I had to face up to the probability that it was – I would have to resolve to make a new kind of life, with just Rosalind and Charlotte. And then, of course, I would always have my writing. I felt now that I could begin to write again. Perhaps it had been good for me to have this break, this crisis, in my creative life. Indeed, this experience, this dark episode, may well have helped. It had certainly not been wasted, I thought. I drank the last of the tea, gathered my coat and handbag and started to walk out of the hotel. But as I passed the reception desk I heard a voice calling out a familiar name.

'Mrs Neele. Mrs Neele?'

Of course, that was my name now. I turned to face the nice Scottish girl who I had talked to the day before. What was her name? Moira, that was it. Such a lovely name. But did it not also mean something in Ancient Greek?

'A parcel has just arrived for you, from London, I think,' said the girl.

'That sounds exciting,' I said, approaching the desk. What on earth could it be?

But as soon as Moira handed the small package to me I froze. The handwriting was Kurs's.

'Is everything all right, Mrs Neele?'

'Yes, everything is – is.' I didn't know what to say, but then the words started to flow out of my mouth. 'I think it must be a ring from London. A ring that I thought I had dropped in Harrods.' Why was it that I was always much more articulate when I made things up?

'That is very fortunate,' said Moira, casting a slightly suspicious glance towards me. The girl suspected that the package contained something a little heavier than a ring.

'Yes, I suppose it is rather. Thank you.'

With a feeling of dread, I carried the parcel up to my room. I closed and locked the door behind me. I sat on the bed and carefully began to tear the top edge of the package. A whiff of something earthy and unpleasant hit me.

I tipped the parcel on its side, but whatever was inside refused to move. I opened the edge again and peered inside. There was something the size of a small child's fist wrapped in tissue paper.

I took a deep breath and eased my hand inside. Almost as soon as the tips of my fingers touched something soft and fleshy they recoiled. Blood had started to ooze out, spreading a sinister bloom across the tissue paper.

I dropped the disgusting thing onto the bed, but as I didn't want to stain the bedspread I picked it up and threw it into the basin in the corner of the room. Feeling weak and nauseous, I stood over the basin for a minute or so as I contemplated what to do next. What the devil had Kurs done?

I checked the inside of the parcel again, but there was no note or letter. Kurs must have been assuming that the object – whatever it was – would be enough to get his message across. I approached the basin again.

Traces of blood had started to leak out onto the white porcelain. Slowly and delicately I began to pick back the blood-red tissue paper. As soon as I did so I saw a tuft of something brown. Was it hair? I peeled back another layer and saw a couple of claws, four small pink pads and a larger, darker metacarpal pad. It was a dog's paw – oh no, it was Peter's paw – the end of which had been severed and showed a mass of bloody gristle and tendon. I let out not a scream, but a howl of pain. How could Kurs do this to me? The poor creature had not deserved to suffer.

To begin with I thought it was the fault of my tears that blurred my vision. Peter, my darling Peter, had the same colouring, but there was something not quite right. I was sure that the bottom of Peter's legs – the same legs I would often clasp together and raise up to my face, proclaiming them to be darling little rabbit's feet – had more white in the fur than this.

I touched the brown-and-white fur which was as smooth as silk. I steadied myself on the basin as I forced myself to continue looking at the grisly sight. My stomach heaved, but I swallowed back the bile and made myself examine the creature's forepaw.

No, this was not the paw of Peter, thank goodness, but it still belonged, or had belonged, to some poor unsuspecting dog. It was a message from Kurs to show me just the kind of brutality that he was capable of inflicting. How had he done it? I couldn't bear to think of what had happened and the pain the dog must have suffered. I only hoped that he had had the decency to put the creature out of its misery afterwards.

I wrapped the paw back in the bloodied paper and then took out a handkerchief from my handbag and covered the paper in that for more protection. I placed the severed limb back in the envelope and started to walk across the room towards the door. But as I passed the bed my legs went from under me. I clasped hold of the edge of the bed and started to sob again. I imagined Peter, always so friendly, wagging his stubby tail as a stranger stopped by to stroke him. Then the sudden terror and panic as he felt himself being held down. And the horror of what happened next.

I saw my daughter playing in the garden and then the shadow of Kurs casting a darkness across her face. I had to stop myself imagining what awful things might happen next.

Chapter Eighteen

Superintendent William Kenward stood by the side of Albury Mill Pond with a sense of anticipation rising inside him. He was sure his latest operation would net results – literally. He smiled to himself as he thought of the pun. And to think some people accused him of not having a sense of humour. He had ordered his men to rig up a series of enormous nets – the kind he had seen draping beneath the high wire in that travelling circus that had visited his town when he was a boy – and on his instruction the gates would be opened and the water would spill through the nets. Any large objects – the body of a missing lady novelist, for instance – would get caught in the nets as the water drained through the sluice.

He had agreed for Jim Sykes, a reporter from the *Express*, to watch every stage of the operation. He and Sykes went back a long way – a friendship of sorts that had started when Kenward was a constable and

Sykes a cub reporter on the local paper. Now both men were older, substantially heavier and a great deal more cynical about human nature. Over the years they had come to a mutual, unspoken understanding that bene-fited both of them: Kenward gave the reporter tip-offs and snippets of information, while Sykes would often highlight the policeman's success at solving particularly tricky cases and, in so doing, would portray him in an especially attractive light.

'What do you hope you might find today, Bill?' asked Sykes, his notebook at the ready.

'The draining is merely a normal procedure under these circumstances. We are looking for anything that might help us locate Mrs Christie. Items of clothing, personal possessions, shoes and suchlike.'

'Come off it, Bill. That's not what you said earlier.'

Kenward looked around him and lowered his voice. 'I know, I know. Look – and this is off the record, of course – if I'm right about this I expect something rather nasty to be caught in those nets.'

'What do you mean?'

'I think Mrs Christie lies at the bottom of this water. How she ended up there we will have to wait and see. But the body, when we find it, should give us some clues.'

'Do you think she's dead?'

'Of course, there is no other explanation.'

'And what about Superintendent Goddard's theory? The Superintendent from the Berkshire Police believes that she is merely playing an elaborate game of cat and mouse with her husband.'

'What wife in her right mind would do that?'

'That's just it, she might not be – in her right mind, I mean.'

'Perhaps not. But there's something not right about the Colonel's story. Very fishy, if you ask me.'

'He might be a cad. What do you think he did?'

Kenward looked around him again. 'I know I can't prove it yet, but I think the only thing that makes sense is that the Colonel and his wife had some kind of row. We know that he was seeing some girl on the side. Perhaps she found out, threatened to cause a scene, there was a struggle, a fight. Maybe Mrs Christie fell or she was pushed. Either way, I'm convinced that she is no longer alive. You know just as well as I do what people are capable of. Especially husbands who find themselves in hot water. At the very least, discounting the Colonel, perhaps she wandered away from the car in a daze and slipped. Anyway, all this is strictly off the record, right?'

Sykes was silent.

'Right, Jim?'

'Very well. But you promise to give me the story first. An exclusive? Agreed?'

'Agreed. Look, the men are ready.'

Kenward and Sykes walked towards the sluice gate. He acknowledged the officials from the Surrey Water Board and a couple of other reporters he was on nodding terms with. But there was one figure who hovered at the edge of the group, a pretty young girl in a smart suit and coat. As he met her gaze she stepped forward and introduced herself as Miss Crowe. It was the same girl who had tried to prise information from him on the telephone.

'Superintendent, I wondered if you could tell me what you are doing here.'

'What does it look like I'm doing, fishing?'

The comment drew laughs from the crowd of men. But Sykes was looking like he wanted to push the young girl into the pond.

'I haven't seen you before. Are you new?' said Sykes.

'Yes, sort of,' said the girl.

'Who are you working for?'

'Well, I suppose one could say that I'm working for myself.'

'I see. So you're the one that is doing a spot of fishing.'

'I'm sorry?' she said.

'Fishing for information. Without having a commission or a job.'

The girl blushed slightly, but Kenward could tell that she had what he liked to call spark. Even though she spoke like a proper little miss, her eyes were full of fire.

'Look, if you want to stay, you can,' said Kenward. 'Just make sure you keep out of the way. And make sure you don't fall in.'

Again a comment of his prompted laughter all round.

'Yes, thank you,' said the girl. 'But you really don't think you'll find her here, do you?'

'Excuse me?' said Kenward.

'Well, it seems quite obvious, I would have thought. If Mrs Christie had wanted to do herself in, she would not have chosen to drown.'

'And how do you know that, may I ask?'

'Oh, just by reading her novels. No, if Mrs Christie had wanted to kill herself she would surely have chosen a less dramatic way.'

'So let me see if I have got this right. You are making your assumption purely on what you've read in her books?'

'Well, yes, I suppose I am. You see, Mrs Christie is an expert in poisons and poisonous substances. She used to work in the dispensary as a VAD during the war.'

'Did she now?' said Kenward in a patronising tone. He wished he had sent this girl away when he had first seen her.

'Yes,' said Una, immune to the sarcasm. 'If you read her novels you will see that she has, oh I don't know, a kind of affinity with poison. I'm sure if she did want to kill herself – which I very much doubt, by the way – then she would have chosen a substance that would simply have allowed her to slip away to sleep with very little pain or fuss.'

'Well, thank you, miss, for that insight. Yet I'm afraid, if you don't mind me saying, it sounds as though you would be more suited to book reviewing than the nitty-gritty of crime reporting.' He turned away from her. 'Now, if we can get back to the job in hand. Grimes? Are you ready?'

Kenward signalled for the gates to be opened and, almost immediately, a great groan was emitted from deep within the pond. The water gushed forth in a surge so strong it had the power to crush a man. Spray clouded the surrounding area and the occasional globule of water landed on the faces of the group that stood by the sluice. When he spotted a dark form flow through the gates, Kenward strained his head to try to see beneath the surface of froth and foam, but the constant churning of the water made it impossible for him to identify the object. It was only when the water had reduced to a trickle, and the bottom of the pond had been exposed, that he saw a dark brown shoe. Kenward nodded for a constable, dressed in fishing waders, to retrieve the shoe from the net.

'What size is it?' shouted Kenward.

'A ten. Looks like a man's,' responded the young constable.

'Damn it,' he said, turning away. 'And there's nothing else in the net? Any other items of interest?'

'It doesn't look like it,' said the young man, his fingers working through the net.

'Well, let's make sure there is nothing on the bottom of the pond. Something could have been weighted down and could be sitting in the mud.'

He turned round, unwilling to let the rest of the group see the anger and frustration in his face. How could there be no trace of her? He did not understand. It just didn't make sense. He smelt a trace of sweetness in the air, a welcome relief from the stench of methane that emanated from the depths of the pond. He looked up. It was that damn woman reporter again.

'What does this mean?' asked Una.

'Mean?'

'Yes, I wondered if you had a response. Or what your next course of action might be.'

'It's a routine search. This one did not throw up anything of particular interest. But the elimination is part of the process. If you think this is a quick or instant operation, then, Miss Crowe, you really do have a great deal to learn.'

'And your next step?'

'To carry on looking. I have every confidence that if we continue with the search of the area then we will unearth some clue to the whereabouts of Mrs Christie. It's logical.'

'And what if you don't?'

Kenward blinked in disbelief. 'That is not a possibility I can contemplate,' he said.

'But what's your theory?'

'My theory?' He looked over towards Sykes who was glaring at him with barely suppressed anger. He would have to mind his own counsel if only to keep Sykes on board. After all, he had promised to give him the exclusive when the body was found. 'I don't have one. I don't work by theories, I work by evidence.'

'But if you'll forgive me, Superintendent, the evidence suggests that Mrs Christie is still very much alive.'

'Says who? I know there are those who believe that, but that's just pie in the sky.'

'And the sightings? What of them? The ones reported in *The Times* this morning?' Una rustled her newspaper and started to read from page 18. '"A man has come forward who says that about an hour before dawn on Saturday morning he was approached by a woman at Newlands Corner, who asked him to start her car. The car had evidently been out in the frost all night, and the woman's hair – she was hatless – was covered with hoar-frost. She appeared to be strange in her manner. With considerable difficulty the man started the engine of the car, and the woman drove off in the direction of Chandon. It was about two hours later that the car was discovered abandoned near the spot from which she was seen to drive away."'

'Have you finished?" asked Kenward in an ironic tone.

'No, not quite,' replied Una. 'There's something else from the newspaper in the same story. Listen. '"Early on Saturday morning a porter, who was the only railway-man on duty at Milford Station, a few miles south of Godalming, was approached by a woman, who enquired about the trains going in the direction of Portsmouth. He was lighting the station lamps at the time, and did not pay much attention to the woman's appearance, but he noticed that there was frost on her hat and that she seemed somewhat strange in her manner. He went on with his work, after replying to her question, and does not know in which direction she went."'

'And that's quite all?'

'Yes, but don't you agree—'

'The only thing I agree with is that a couple of people have come forward and offered their opinion. No doubt you know about the reward offered by the *Daily News*?'

Una nodded.

'Well, can I put it to you that there may be a connection between the reward of £100 and the fact that certain people have passed on their so-called evidence? It happens every time a rag offers a reward. The amount of extra work we are bogged down with you simply would not believe. I imagine you are quite new to this kind of work, Miss Crowe, but please give me the benefit of the doubt. I've been in the police force for nearly thirty years now so I know the tricks – and the treachery – of the press.'

'Come off it, Bill, we're not as bad as that,' said Sykes.

Kenward's colour darkened. There was no disguising his anger now.

'Why is the *Daily News* offering £100 to the person or persons that would provide them with the "first information leading to the whereabouts, if alive, of Mrs Christie",' said Kenward. 'Why only alive? What happens if the poor woman is dead – did they ever think of that?'

There was silence. 'No, they didn't,' he continued. 'The stupid, ignorant swines. Sorry, Miss Crowe, but you see how it gets me going.' He raised a hand to his temples. He could feel that pain in his head coming on again. He took a deep breath. 'Now, if you will forgive me I have to continue the search of the area. Goodbye.'

Kenward walked off in the direction of the empty pond, cursing under his breath. If it wasn't for him and men like him the jackals would have nothing to report on. He would have to remember that. He couldn't allow his vision to be contaminated by their constant carping and questioning. He had half a mind to ban the lot of them from the operation, but he knew that, at some point, he would need their help.

As he approached the pond he felt even more depressed in spirits. The draining had exposed not a smooth muddy surface as he had hoped, but a hollow almost completely full of thick green weed. It would, he knew, be difficult to search the whole area thoroughly, but they would have to try.

'It's full of weeds, sir,' called another of the constables from the pond. 'Can hardly make out a thing.'

'I can see that, Jones,' said Kenward. 'Start from the edge nearest me and you and Lyons can work towards the sluice gates.'

'But—'

'But nothing. Now please carry on with your instructions. If you find anything suspicious or of interest, let me know.'

'Very well, sir.'

Half of him wished he could pull on the set of waders that he still kept in the back of the police station and get down into the pond with his men. He was sure that, given the opportunity to search the mud and the weed, he would unearth something that might offer a clue. But he knew he was past engaging in that kind of physical activity now. After all, it took all his energy to walk up a flight of stairs. Naomi had been constantly at him to go and see the doctor. One day he supposed he would, but he was afraid of what the doctor might tell him. He knew it was unlikely to be good news.

Chapter Nineteen

Una left Albury Mill Pond in a state of fury. What an annoying little man! How dare he try to humiliate her in front of those other reporters. She was new to this game, that was fair, but what she did not want to tell him was that she knew a lot more than she was letting on. If she had so wished she could have given Kenward a vital piece of information that might have helped his inquiry. Had he been a little more polite perhaps she might have told him some of the contents of the letter she had picked up at Styles. But after the way he had treated her, well, now that was quite out of the question.

What a blockhead that man was. Why did he insist on thinking that Mrs Christie was dead when all the evidence pointed to the contrary? And he really did not look in the best of health. Perhaps it would be better if another man led the investigation.

When she reached the car that she had borrowed

from her brother, Eric – she had told her family she was going to visit a friend in the country and would be away for a couple of days – she took out the folder of information that she had compiled on the case. At the top of the stash of documents was the letter from Madge to her sister, Agatha, which gave her not only the name of the woman Colonel Christie had been having an affair with – Miss Nancy Neele – but also the fact that she came from Rickmansworth. Una's next task was to try to see if she could find her. So far the woman's name had been kept out of the papers, but she would not be surprised if it did not appear in the next few days. Obviously, she could not expect a friendly greeting if she turned up at Miss Neele's door asking for an interview. She would have to think of some other excuse to get into the house. But what?

Una took out the road map from the glove compartment and studied how best to get from Newlands Corner to Rickmansworth. She assumed that when she arrived at the town in Hertfordshire she would be able to find a public library. They carried telephone directories and gazetteers and suchlike and it shouldn't be hard to find Miss Neele's address. By then she should have worked out what to say to make sure she got her foot through the door. She started the engine and as she drove northwards through Surrey and Berkshire she felt full of excitement and enthusiasm for what lay ahead. If only her father could see her now: independent, happy and full of energy. Surely if he were alive he would have to give his blessing to her new career. Of course, she knew that in the circles in which she mixed the men who worked for the press, unless one were the editor of *The Times* ('and even then' her father would say), were considered rather common. Stuffed shirts, the lot of them.

If she were in charge – say, if she were ever to go into Parliament like Mrs Astor – then she would try to break down these kinds of silly divisions. Oh, she knew she could be an awful snob at times, but these old-fashioned attitudes really had to change. There were some other things that she would like to change too, but she knew people were rather stuck in their ways. The nasty comments she had heard about men such as Davison, and indeed Mrs Astor's own son, Bobbie. What right did anyone have to nose around in another person's bedroom? She laughed when she considered that she had done exactly that less than twenty-four hours previously. What a terrible hypocrite she was!

She arrived in Rickmansworth in high spirits and parked the car on Church Street, just outside the Feathers public house. She walked up and down the pretty provincial street, found the police station and the fire station, but there did not seem to be a library. Then, next to a little café, she spotted a dress shop, quite a smart one too. Perhaps she could just chance her luck. Una bent down a little and, out of sight of the dress-shop window, pulled on the hem of her pleated black crepella skirt. Nothing happened. Opening her handbag she took out a metal nail file and used it to cut into the fabric. With a hard pull the silk lining began to tear. She adored the skirt, but nevertheless the ripping sound was most terrifically satisfying. When she was convinced she had completed the little act of destruction she opened the door to the sound of a tinkling bell and stepped inside.

'Good morning,' said the red-faced, rather comfortably shaped lady behind the wooden counter.

Una could feel the woman's eyes on her as she assessed the quality, and expense, of her attire. Her style was understated – it did not scream wealth – but anyone with any education or knowledge of fashion would immediately realise that, while some of her clothes were far from new, they had cost a good deal of money.

'How can I help?' she added.

'Oh, yes,' said Una, smiling. 'I do hope you can help me. I seem to have ripped the hem of my skirt. Can you see?'

'Let's have a look, shall we?' said the lady, lifting up the counter and then kneeling down for a closer inspection.

'A quiet day for you?' asked Una.

'Yes, thank goodness. I've been rushed off my feet these last couple of weeks. Trying to get the ladies ready for Christmas. Only a few weeks away now.'

'Yes, it is a terribly busy time of year for all of us.'

'Are you from around here?'

'No, I'm just up from London visiting friends for a

few days, and today, just as I was leaving, I would go and trip over one of their blasted Labradors.'

'Never mind, I'm sure we can mend it. It's beautifully made.'

'Oh yes, I picked it up in Paris the last time I was there.'

'Jean Patou?'

'Chanel,' replied Una. 'I don't know whether you can do it so it looks natural. What do I mean? Oh yes, invisible mending.'

'There is an elderly lady we use who did spend some time in the French ateliers. Wonderful little hands, she has. But I am afraid you would have to leave it with us.'

'Oh, I see. I haven't got anything else really very suitable, apart from a white-lace evening dress, hardly appropriate for daytime. There's nothing you could do now?'

'Well, I could try and patch it myself, but I'm afraid I couldn't guarantee that the stitches would be invisible.'

'I see,' said Una, frowning. 'My friends have left for London already so I can't borrow anything from them. But I'm sure there is a friend of my cousin who lives near here. I'm sure you won't know her. A Miss Neele?'

'Nancy Neele? Oh, yes, Miss Neele is a regular customer.'

'The blasted thing is I've left my address book in London. I don't suppose you have her address to hand?'

'Let's see,' said the dressmaker, standing up. She walked behind the counter and opened up the lid of a wooden card index. 'Neele. Here we are. Yes, Miss Neele lives in Croxley Green. With her parents, I believe.'

'Of course. Do you know the name of the house?'

'Rheola.'

'Yes, what a strange name. Sounds Welsh to me. Are the family Welsh?'

'No, as far as I know. Her father, I think, is from Hampstead.'

'How curious. Anyway, that is splendid. What I will do is call in and see if she can lend me something. Then I will come back and drop in the skirt.'

'So you will be spending a few more days in the area?'

'I'm sorry?'

'You won't be going back to London?'

'Yes, that's right. I intend to visit some more friends in the country.'

'And please give my best regards to Miss Neele,' said the woman. 'She's a lovely girl, isn't she?'

'Yes, simply gorgeous.'

'And those twin brothers of hers, what are they called?'

'Oh, I've never met them, I'm afraid. I hardly know her, to be honest.'

'And the friends of yours in the country – where are they?' The dressmaker's chattiness – natural in someone of her profession – was becoming more like an interrogation.

'Oh, out in the sticks somewhere,' said Una, trying to sound deliberately vague. 'The country – it's like the universe, don't you find? Simply stretches on and on.'

'And it's too far for you to call on them for assistance?' Una did not like the tone of the woman's voice.

'Oh, them, oh no. My friends' sisters Juliet and Baba have simply the worst possible dress sense. If I put myself in their hands I'd look like an old dowager duchess from the last century.'

This made the dressmaker smile and any trace of suspicion melted away. 'Well, good luck. And just call in again when you are ready.'

'Thank you, goodbye.'

Una breathed a great sigh of relief when she left the shop. She hadn't been prepared for the Spanish Inquisition, but she thought she had performed quite well under the circumstances. Back in the car she studied the road map once more and plotted her route to Croxley Green. She still had not thought of a way of getting inside the Neele household apart from stealing through the back door like a common burglar. She took out her mother-of-pearl compact from her handbag and studied her reflection in the mirrored surface. She was, she thought, getting quite good at this lying game. She applied a spot of lipstick and a sheen of powder before setting off for Croxley Green, just outside Rickmansworth. She passed the village green with its quaint windmill and drove around the village straining her neck in search of the house. She drove by a number of large Victorian and Edwardian houses that, as far as she could see, did not seem to bear any names – that or their identities had been covered by the vigorous growth of laurel bushes or yew trees. As she turned a corner she spotted a postman and she slammed on the brakes.

'Excuse me, excuse me,' shouted Una as she wound down her window.

The man touched his hat. 'How can I help you, miss?'

'I'm looking for the Neele house. Rheola, is that what it's called?'

'Indeed it is. Let's see – if you take the second left and then the first right you should see the house straight in front of you.'

She followed the postman's directions which, as promised, led her to the front of the house. She turned off the engine and as she did so she noticed that her fingers were shaking. She ran her tongue over her dry lips, stepped out of the car and walked up the driveway. She paused for a moment before she rang the bell. The door opened and a maid said, 'Can I help you, ma'am?'

'Yes, I'm here to see Miss Neele. Is she at home?'

'Can I say who is calling?' asked the maid, her eyes hardening.

'Yes. Can you say it's Clara Miller. I'm a cousin of Mrs Christie's.'

The girl blinked, uncertain what to do or say, but Una's smile seemed to help calm her nerves a little.

'I'll see if she is receiving visitors today. Would you mind waiting?'

'No, not at all.'

'This way, please.'

The girl showed Una into a glasshouse that was crowded with exotic pot plants, ferns with unruly tendrils, and succulents with sharp green and red spikes that rose into the air like sinister, blood-tipped daggers. The air seemed clouded as if someone had recently sprayed the room with a fine warm mist. As she waited, Una dug the nails of her right hand into the palm of her left. Would she have the nerve to go through with this? She felt a bead of sweat break out on her forehead. She loosened the collar of her coat. From one of the rooms at the back of the house, perhaps a kitchen or a scullery, Una heard some frenzied whispering – a suppressed argument between two women – followed by the words, 'Very well, I'll deal with her.' A moment later, a striking, dark-haired young woman entered the glasshouse. Her eyes were black and full of resentments and unspoken accusations.

'How may I help?' she said flatly.

'Miss Neele?'

'Yes.'

'I know this must be terribly awkward for you.' Una could still hear the sound of the servants talking through one of the doors. 'Is there anywhere we could talk? In private?'

Una smiled, but the smile froze on her lips when Miss Neele replied, 'I think whatever you have to say can be said here.'

'Very well,' said Una, clearing her throat. 'As you know, Mrs Christie has disappeared. And as a family we are all, quite naturally, worried about her welfare.'

The comment was met with a look of indifference bordering on disdain.

'I just wondered if there was anything at all you knew that might help. The sooner we find her the sooner we can clear up this mess. It's been terribly stressful for all of us, as you can imagine. Thank goodness Cousin Agatha's mother passed away some months back.'

'I would have thought that was part of the problem,' answered Nancy.

'Excuse me?'

'Archie – the Colonel – has always insisted that Mrs Christie has never been the same since her mother's death,' said Nancy.

'Perhaps, but I am sure there are other factors involved, don't you think?'

Una observed Miss Neele wince slightly as if she were trying to suppress a cry of pain.

'I'm afraid I can't see how I can help you. I only know the couple on a very superficial level. So I am afraid you will have to excuse me, Miss—'

'Miss Miller.'

'I really am terribly busy, but I thank you for your visit.'

As Nancy started to turn from her, Una felt the opportunity slipping away. She would have to say something.

'As I am sure you are aware, the situation is very

delicate. I know the newspapers have been camping outside the family home. Awful beasts, these journalists, don't you find? I mean imagine if they got hold of a piece of evidence that really showed things how they were.'

Nancy remained fixed to the spot. She turned her head and looked at Una.

'What exactly do you mean?'

'Oh, there is so much gossip and nonsense printed in the press. But I suppose often these silly journalists have to resort to making things up because they don't have the hard evidence to back up their stories. Now, if they did have something certain to go on, showing Mrs Christie's state of mind and the reason behind her disappearance, well that might be exactly what they were looking for.'

Una opened her handbag and pulled out the letter she had taken from Agatha's desk.

'What is that?'

'This? Oh, it's a letter written by Madge – Margaret, Mrs Christie's sister, I am sure you know – describing the situation and offering advice about how best to proceed.'

Miss Neele took a step closer to her.

'It makes for fascinating reading because it is, how shall I put it, extraordinarily intimate. Oh, you know what sisters are like. Do you have any?'

'No, no sisters. Only brothers, twins.'

'Well, if you had had a sister you would know the kind of thing. Affairs of the heart.'

'I see,' said Miss Neele, suddenly alert to the fact she was discussing a private matter within earshot of the servants. 'I'm sorry, I should have asked you into the sitting room. Please, follow me.'

As soon as she walked out of the glasshouse Una felt she could breathe once more.

'You've got an extraordinary collection of plants,' said Una, trying to make the atmosphere a little less tense between them.

'Oh yes, my mother's little hobby,' said Miss Neele as she led the way through the house to the sitting room. 'She has some peculiar specimens. She has one that lives off flies, can you imagine? Just ingests them, dissolves them, if you see what I mean.'

The attempt at small talk had done nothing to soothe the tension in the air. If anything it had only left Una feeling even more uncomfortable. Miss Neele showed her into a dark green sitting room and quietly shut the door.

'Would you like to sit down?'

'Yes, thank you.'

Una took her seat on a black velvet sofa, Miss Neele choosing to sit opposite her in a high-backed brown leather chair.

'And you were saying?' said Miss Neele, glancing at the letter that Una still held in her hand.

'Oh yes, this. Well, what I'm looking for is some answers so the family can find Agatha. The police seem to be convinced she is dead, which is ridiculous. We've appealed to the Colonel, but like many men in this situation he seems to have turned in on himself rather. I hoped that you might be able to help.'

'I see. And there is no question of going to the newspapers?' The dark-haired woman suddenly looked like a bewildered, frightened little girl.

'Oh no, don't worry about that. It's just information – that is all we're looking for. Information that we can use to good effect to finally bring this sorry saga to a close.'

'Very well. I probably don't know a great deal, but anything I do know I am willing to share with you.'

'Thank you.'

'Obviously you know about the Colonel and me. Please don't think badly of me. I'm not the kind of woman you think I am. You see, Archie and I are in love and we do intend to get married. We hoped that Mrs Christie would see sense and let the Colonel go. We, well, Archie knew that his wife could be a little – well, he knew that she had a vivid imagination – but neither of us expected this, not this scandal. My parents are furious, as you can imagine. They are on the point of sending me away. It means that Archie and I will be separated for a while, but I only hope that when this has all blown over I can return and we can be together at last.'

Una saw the tears begin to form in Miss Neele's dark eyes. She stood up and walked over to the chair and offered the girl a freshly starched handkerchief from her handbag.

'Thank you,' said Nancy. Una watched as Nancy, through her tears, focused on the corner of the handkerchief, which had a set of small initials embroidered in light blue cotton.

'"U.C." Who is that?'

'I'm sorry?'

'These initials here. Who do they belong to?'

Una realised her mistake immediately, but tried to make light of it.

'Oh, that's one of my friends I was staying with in the country this weekend. Darling girl, Unity Crawford. Do you know the Crawfords? They are all mad as hatters, the lot of them.'

'No, I don't believe I do. Please, you must think I'm terribly silly. I have been trying to keep everything in. But all this – this nonsense – has really been too much. And now it looks like I am going to have to leave the country for a while.'

'I know. And I'm sorry to have to force my way in like this,' said Una. 'You must think me extremely ill-mannered.'

'Well, I must admit when I first saw you I did think it a bit rich.'

As the two women laughed Nancy finally wiped away the last of her tears.

'But, honestly, I really don't see how much more I can help you. Archie knew nothing of this beforehand. Of course, he thought Agatha was even more anxious than normal – he told me that they had a row on that Friday morning. But there was no indication that she would behave like this.'

'And what do you think has happened?'

'Well, my theory, which Archie simply cannot understand, is that she probably disappeared so as to get her petty revenge on him. She wants to make him suffer. To make him feel a little of the pain that she is going through. I can sympathise to a degree. But to go so far as to involve the police? And now I've heard that this stupid man who is heading the investigation – what's he called?'

'Superintendent William Kenward, Deputy Chief Constable.'

'Yes, that's the fellow. There are rumours flying around that he suspects Archie of murder. Can you imagine? It's just outrageous.'

'Awful,' said Una sitting back down on the sofa. 'So you've got no idea where Mrs Christie might have gone?'

'No, none at all, I'm afraid. But I am convinced she is not dead. She's probably having a whale of a time somewhere enjoying watching Archie squirm.'

'Well, I'm not sure about that,' said Una. 'I can't imagine she is enjoying this any more than the rest of us.'

'Perhaps not.'

'And the Colonel? He hasn't told you anything that might lead you to suspect where she is?'

'No, I mean we all know how much she was attached to Ashfield, the house where she lived when she was a girl. But apparently there has been no trace of her down in Torquay. But surely you must know that?'

'Yes, of course.' Una looked down at the letter. 'Can I ask, does anybody else know about your relationship with the Colonel?'

A flash of fire returned to Miss Neele's eyes. 'Well, just our dear friends, Mr and Mrs Sam James, with whom we stayed on Friday night. Or I should say with whom we were supposed to be staying until Archie got that blasted telephone call on Saturday morning. Since then it's been absolute hell.'

'Your parents?'

'Well, yes, of course. They knew Archie and I were good friends, but they didn't realise the true nature of our friendship until a few days ago. It's been hell for them too.'

'Yes, I can imagine. But none of your other friends?'

'No, I have tried to keep it secret. Not out of any sense of guilt – even though I know it looks bad, and most probably is bad, but you must believe me, the Colonel's intentions were – are – truly honourable.'

'Yes, I believe you. And no one else?'

'No, no one, apart from my doctor. I have been suffering from an attack of nerves for the last couple of months. I went to the doctor one day and simply broke down. I had to tell him everything. He could see what a mess I was in. He has been the greatest support. I really could not have lived through this if it hadn't been for Dr Kurs.'

Her train of thought was interrupted by the sound of

the telephone in the hall. The two women listened as a servant lifted the receiver. A moment later the door opened.

'Excuse me, ma'am. There is a telephone call for you.'

'Davies, can't you see I am having a private conversation?'

'I'm ever so sorry, ma'am. But the lady says it is most urgent.'

'Who is it?'

'Mrs Peabody, ma'am. The lady from the dress shop in Rickmansworth.'

Una felt nauseous and weak. If she had not been sitting down, she thought, her legs might have collapsed beneath her.

'What can she want? I was only in her shop the other day. Surely it can't be that important?'

'I'm sorry, ma'am. I did say you were busy, but she said that it was of the highest importance. She asked about the lady's skirt. Something about it being ripped. I don't know what she was talking about.'

'How ridiculous. Sorry, Miss Miller, would you excuse me for a moment?'

Una watched as Miss Neele rose from the chair and her eyes settled on the piece of loose thread hanging from her skirt.

'I'm sorry, I've taken up more of your time than I should have,' said Una, trying to keep the growing sense of panic from her voice. 'Thank you so much. And let's hope life gets back to normal soon.'

'Indeed.'

'I wish you all the luck in the world, I truly mean that.'

'Thank you,' said Nancy. 'Are you sure you can't wait until I've answered this telephone call? I'm sure it will only take a moment.'

'No, I really must be going,' said Una, moving towards the door.

'Very well – but what about your handkerchief?' she said.

'Oh, please keep it. I'm sure Unity won't mind.'

By the time the two women stood by the front door Davies had returned to the telephone. The servant girl had started to frown.

'Ma'am?' she said suddenly.

'Well, thank you once again,' said Una, opening the door herself and stepping outside.

'Ma'am?' hissed Davies.

'Honestly,' said Nancy. 'Just tell Mrs Peabody to wait.'

'But—'

'So sorry, Miss Miller.'

'Goodbye.'

As soon as the door closed Una ran towards her car. She opened the door and tried to start the engine. It spluttered. The damn thing. Eric had told her that it could be temperamental, but why did this have to happen now? Just as she tried again, the door opened and Nancy appeared outside.

'Just a moment!' she shouted.

Una attempted to start the car again. The engine was still dead. Una dared not look up, but she could sense Miss Neele getting closer.

Una forced herself to let the car rest for a moment, but in those few seconds Miss Neele had run down the driveway. The crunch of gravel grew ever louder. She was close enough now for Una to see panic and confusion in her eyes. Una tried once more and finally the car started. Just as she put her foot down on the pedal Miss Neele banged on the window, the handkerchief still clutched in her hand. As Una sped away down the lane she heard the cries of 'Who are you? Who ...?' echoing behind her.

Chapter Twenty

After disposing of the nasty package containing the bloody paw in a rubbish bin behind the hotel, I walked to the station and took the first train to Leeds. In my notebook I wrote a series of points, listing them all under the letter 'M', for murder. I clutched my handbag closer to me. Inside was the leather pouch containing the vials of poison which I had taken from under the floor at Styles. I started to make a list of the deadly substances in my possession.

I had always been fond of belladonna. What a wonderful name, or rather, names: deadly nightshade, death cherries or devil's berries. I had always thought it interesting that, like many poisons, in addition to its sinister purposes – it was thought that the Emperor Augustus had used it to kill unsuspecting enemies – it could be used for the benefit of mankind. Women had dropped it into their eyes to make them look more seductive, while it had also been used as an anaesthetic during surgery.

The little chocolate-coloured Calabar bean was such an innocent-looking thing; it didn't taste, smell or look particularly deadly but if ingested it would result in excess salivation, loss of bowel and bladder and respiratory control, and finally death by asphyxiation. Interestingly, the two poisons, atropine in belladonna and physostigmine in the Calabar bean, had, if administered correctly, the ability to cancel each other out, but one had to be extremely careful of the quantities involved, as I had learnt from Sir Thomas Fraser's very useful paper on the subject. Atropine could save a life if three and a half times the fatal dose of physostigmine had been taken, but would actually quicken a death if four or more times the fatal dose had been ingested.

But how could I think such a thing? Neither of them would have the desired effect. What I needed was a poison that would mimic death itself. I ran through the list of fatal toxins and their particular qualities. I realised that there was only one that would serve the purpose: tetrodotoxin.

I had first heard about its use from a strange little man in South Africa. One night, on our grand tour in 1922, Belcher – the official leader of our group – had been boasting at dinner about my interest in poisons. At the time, I had found it most annoying that he made me out to be some kind of ghoul. I had tried to change the subject, but there had been one guest, the normally very dull Mr Bowes, whose eyes had suddenly come alive at the mention of the topic. At the end of the dinner, he had shuffled over to me and told me about his interest in chemistry, particularly the branch that concentrated on substances that could kill. By a roundabout fashion he had offered to introduce me to a man, Boreng, professor of biology at the local university who collected snake toxins and other poisons from the natural world.

And so it was that one morning I had found myself being treated to a tour of the man's laboratory. Of course, I found the visit absolutely fascinating: shelf after shelf was lined with bottles and vials of colourless liquids, as innocent looking as water. But I knew that the room contained enough poison to kill each and every inhabitant of an average town. Boreng, a small man whose face was lined with a series of curious scars, obviously liked my enthusiasm and knowledge of the subject because at the end of the tour he asked for me to stay behind, opened up a drawer with a gold key and produced a small vial.

'What's that?' I asked.

'This is one of the most deadly substances you will ever come across,' he said. He lingered over the letter 'S', pronouncing it as if he were something of a snake himself.

'Is it from a serpent?'

Boreng shook his head. 'Have you heard of the Lazarus poison?'

'No, I don't believe I have.'

'A toxin that induces a state of death, from which, if you are skilful enough, you can bring a person back to life?'

I shook my head. 'That's surely not possible.'

'You may believe that. But I have seen it done with my own eyes. The poison comes from the puffer fish. I've seen the same effect in a number of other species, certain toads, angelfish, sea stars, even a blue-ringed octopus. But this is the most lethal, the most deadly, the most effective. A colleague gave me a quantity of it after he returned from Haiti. Depending on the dose it can bring about a true death or it can lull someone into a death-like state. It's my gift to you in case you need it. In case you need to rise from the dead one day.'

What an odd thing to say, I thought to myself at the time. But nonetheless I thanked him, accepted the vial, and added it to my growing collection. Since then I had read up on tetrodotoxin and had learnt all about its history, its mention in the log of Captain James Cook, and its isolation by a Japanese scientist in 1909.

As with all poisons, the secret was in the dosage. My plan was to administer just the right amount of poison to reduce Flora's pulse to a level where it seemed non-existent. I would call a doctor, get him to witness the death and inform him of Flora's next of kin. The doctor would then send a telegram to Kurs and he would be satisfied that I had completed the task. I knew what would have to happen after that, but I hardly dared admit it to myself.

The question was, would I be able to bring Flora back from the dead? What if I couldn't? What if Flora actually died and I was found guilty of murder? How would Rosalind cope knowing that her mother had gone to the gallows for committing the most heinous of crimes? I knew that, in the eyes of God, any act of evil was wrong, but if I committed murder to prevent another murder would I then be judged as harshly? I had done so much thinking; now I had to act.

At Leeds railway station I stepped into the Ladies' room. As I examined myself in the glass I looked the image of a respectable middle-aged lady. Wearing the brown canton crepe dress, red bolero blouse and smart oatmeal coat that I had bought in Harrogate, I did not look like a person who was about to commit a crime. But criminals – murderers – came in many guises.

Following Kurs's instructions, I took a taxi from the station to Calverley Lane, a leafy suburb to the west of the city. I paid the driver and took a moment to observe the house, a huge Victorian affair set in its own grounds. It was a dark oppressive day: grey clouds sat low in the sky, there was only a mere suggestion of muted sunlight and, even at midday, a light burnt in the room at the front of the house. I walked up the stone steps and rang the bell. I told the maid that I was an acquaintance of Dr Kurs, who had sent me to see his wife with an important message. The half-lie worked and I found myself being led down a tiled hallway to a sitting room. Inside there was a pale-skinned auburn-haired woman who was lying on a chaise longue by the fire. She looked frail and her frame reminded me of a sick bird that I had once tried to rescue when I was a girl. If memory served me right I don't think that I had been successful.

'I'm so sorry I cannot get up, please forgive me,' said the woman. 'I'm feeling a little tired today. Sorry, I didn't hear your name.'

Would Flora recognise me from some of the photographs that had appeared in the newspapers? The images that had been reproduced in the press did not look anything like me; even I had to admit that in real life I was much more attractive.

'I'm Mrs Price-Ridley,' I replied. I didn't know where the name came from, but it seemed appropriate somehow.

'How do you do,' said Flora, smiling. 'Please, do come over and sit by me. It's dreadfully chilly outside, isn't it?'

'Thank you,' I said as I sat in an armchair directly opposite the chaise longue.

'And you have a message for me. From my husband?' She said the last word almost as if she didn't quite believe that she still had a husband.

'Yes, yes, a message of sorts.'

'Oh – how very rude of me. I haven't offered you tea. Would you like tea?'

'That's very kind, thank you.'

Flora picked up a small china bell that lay by her side and shook it a couple of times before the maid appeared at the door.

'Curston, could we have tea? Thank you. Now where have you travelled from today?'

'From Harrogate.'

'One of my favourite places in the world,' said Flora. 'And what brought you to Harrogate, may I ask? Your health?'

'In a roundabout sort of way.'

'My, how mysterious you're being. But don't worry. We will have our tea and then you can tell me what's worrying you. Because I can see that you are worried, my dear, and that will never do. They say it can take years off one's life.'

I smiled nervously as the girl entered the room with the tea tray.

'Thank you, Curston.' Flora waited for the maid to leave the room before she turned to me. 'I do hope my husband hasn't been a nuisance in any way, Mrs Price-Ridley. It's been a while since I've seen him and he has changed a great deal.'

I took hold of my handbag and placed it on my lap.

'No, it's just that he wanted me to deliver a message in person. He said he didn't want to write in case the letter fell into the wrong hands.'

'Indeed? The mystery deepens,' she said as she poured the tea. 'My husband, as I am sure you are aware, is a most peculiar character. He is very intelligent, I grant you that, perhaps too intelligent, but lately he's been suffering from what I can only describe as, as—'

I watched as Flora began to cry, quiet sobs that

gently rocked her slim, wasted body. I was unlikely to get a more opportune moment. I felt my breath quicken and my heart begin to race. I opened my handbag and slowly removed the small vial.

'I must apologise,' said Flora, taking out her handkerchief from the sleeve of her dress. 'I have been ill of late, an illness that I am afraid has been brought about, to a large extent, by my husband.' She blinked and turned her focus once more to me. 'Now, dear, to your message. I hope Patrick hasn't been cruel to you like he has to me. I can't see him, no, it would be too much for me. He says he wants a divorce, but I cannot allow it. Even though my mother and father have passed away I still feel it would be wrong, an insult to their memory. But listen to me going on like this. I'm sure you don't want to know any of this nonsense. It's my burden, a burden to be borne privately.'

I hid the tiny vial in the grip of my fist.

'Oh yes, the m-message,' I said.

'Do you have it there? In your handbag?'

'Yes, yes, I do.'

'You look very pale, my dear. Is there something wrong?'

An image of myself standing on the very edge of a cliff flashed into my mind. I could not see over the edge of the precipice. All I knew was that down below lay an infinite darkness and if I were to step forwards I would fall into a terrible abyss.

My grip tightened around the vial – I was in danger

of crushing it in my hand – and I felt a bead of cold sweat trickle between my shoulder blades. In that instant Flora dropped her handkerchief on the floor and bent down to pick it up. Just then, at the very moment when I knew that I should reach across and drop the poison into the woman's cup of tea, I froze. I could not go through with it.

'I'm sorry, I just can't do it,' I said.

'Excuse me?' said Flora, looking up, slightly bewildered.

'I can't do it.'

'What – you can't deliver the message?'

'No – this,' I said, opening my fist to reveal the vial of poison.

'Oh my,' said Flora, her eyes widening.

'Please, I understand if you want to call the police. It's unspeakable what I considered doing. I think the police will have to be brought in.'

'Now, let's not be quite so hasty. I suspect that Patrick has something to do with this. I'm right, aren't I?'

As I nodded tears began to flow down my cheeks. All the horrors that I had had to endure over the course of the last few days found expression in my crying. Flora raised herself up and came to stand by me.

'In your own time, tell me what that brute has asked you to do,' she said, placing a hand on my shoulder. 'And don't hold anything back for my sake.'

'My daughter – he said that, that he would—' I said. I could not continue.

'The depths to which he will stoop have long since ceased to surprise me, Mrs Price-Ridley.'

'But I'm – I'm not—'

'Not?'

'No, that's not my name. My name is Mrs Christie. Mrs Agatha Christie.'

Flora walked around the chair, sat down on the chaise longue facing me and studied my face.

'The writer? Of course, I see it now. I knew there was something familiar about your face. How extraordinary. Well, you must tell me the whole story. Here, have your tea.' She passed over a cup and then took up the other one, which she drank from in a self-consciously theatrical, overly enthusiastic gulp. 'And look – I'm still alive. Just,' she said, laughing.

The gesture made me smile and I managed to swallow a sip or two of tea myself before I started to recount the story of the last few days.

'But you see, I never actually intended to kill you. I just thought I could pass you off as dead and then a doctor would wire your husband who would then release me from this awful nightmare.'

'And did you think you really would be able to pull it off?' said Flora.

'I don't know. But you see I had no choice, no real choice at all. It was either this or my daughter would suffer in a way I found quite unimaginable.'

'Yes, quite. But what will you do now?'

'Now?'

'Yes.'

'I'm still very much unsure of that, I'm afraid,' I said. 'The whole thing is wretched, simply wretched.'

'And the police are quite out of the question?'

'Well, Dr Kurs – your husband – said that if I breathed a word of his plan to the authorities he would let this associate of his, some degenerate type—'

'That would be Tanner. Alfred Tanner?'

'He never mentioned a name to me. But he does exist then?'

'I'm afraid he does. When I was feeling especially low and vulnerable Patrick would relate to me certain aspects of this man's life. It was far from pleasant.'

'And he's never gone to prison? Never been sentenced?'

'I don't know how he has managed to escape the attention of the authorities, but there you are.'

'Well, the doctor said he would let this man carry out his evil wishes, do what he wanted with my daughter. And the things that he suggested, I simply could not—'

'Yes, well, don't dwell on that. Please. I am sure we can think of something.'

'Really?'

'Yes, now, will you have another cup of tea? You know, Patrick used not to be like this,' she said as she poured. 'No. To begin with he was actually normal, nice even.'

'How did you meet?'

'At a dance.'

'Oh, the same as me. That's how I met Archie, my husband. Only I'm afraid our marriage has not been happy for some time.'

'I'm sorry.'

'Yes, it's unlikely to survive, especially now. Archie wants a divorce, too.'

'And you'll give him one.'

I thought for a moment. 'If I come out of this alive, yes, I suppose I will. But it might be more convenient for him if I died.'

'Now, don't talk such nonsense.'

'I know I shouldn't, but this last week or so has been so dreadful, you can't imagine.'

'I'm sure I can. You forget that I am the one married to him.'

'How do you stand it?'

'Well, when he was living here in Leeds he was seemingly quite well-balanced. We had a normal life. Of course, Patrick has always been extremely ambitious. I am sure that is one of the reasons why he chose me. He knew my parents were wealthy and that one day I would come into a great deal of money.'

'I see.'

'But then when we moved down south and he started to mix with a different class of person he became even more fixated on what we did and did not have. He persuaded me to ask my father for a lump-sum of money so we could buy a bigger house in Guildford. Then that house was not big or luxurious enough and so he wanted more. I loved him then – or at least thought I did – and so I would try and do everything in my power to keep him happy. But then it all got much, much worse after the accident.'

'What accident?'

'He was involved in a collision with another motor car. He had been to deliver a baby in the middle of the night when a car spun out of control and hit him. The woman was maimed for life, terribly disfigured, and her male friend was killed outright. Patrick was left unconscious – the doctors thought that he must have hit his head on the steering wheel. Although it seemed as though he made a full recovery, I noticed that a few months after the accident his behaviour started to change. His breath began to smell quite foul, he was quick to lose his temper and his black moods were terrifying. Thank goodness we didn't have any children. Of course, he wanted them, well, a son. But we couldn't have them. After the accident, that's when he really began to punish me.'

'In what way?'

'He could not understand how God or nature or I, or a combination of all three, could deny him what he considered to be his right. The right to have a son. His image on this earth. He became obsessed with the idea, and made me undergo some awful treatments. The things he put me through. I'll spare you the details, my dear, but let me just say this: the reason I am how I am today is because of what he did to me.'

The room fell silent. I could hear the wind in the trees outside. In the distance a dog began to howl.

'Are you really very ill?'

'Yes, I am afraid so.' She ran her bony hand across her forehead. 'I haven't told anyone in case the news gets back to Patrick, but there is no hope.'

'What do you mean?'

'I have a growth, a tumour. In my womb. It's too late, there is nothing anyone can do.'

Flora tried to smile bravely, but I could see the pain, both physical and psychological, biting into her face.

'So you see, you can make use of me after all,' said Flora.

'I'm sorry, I don't understand.'

'Your original plan. I don't see why you can't go through with it.'

'On you? No, that's out of the question.'

'But, my dear, let's face facts. I've got less than a few months to live. If I can help you save the life of your daughter then you must let me. It's the only sensible thing to do.'

I looked into Flora's green eyes, eyes which seemed to possess infinite depths of kindness. 'And if there is only a slight risk of it going wrong,' she said.

'I wouldn't be confident of having the necessary skills to guarantee saving your life, I'm afraid.'

'But you were prepared to risk it when you first came in here. Am I right?'

'Yes, but—'

'But nothing. You know yourself there is little other option. Answer this question: do you want your daughter to suffer at the hands of—'

'Excuse me,' I said, feeling the anger rise within me. 'I don't see how—'

'You don't see how that monster could possibly hurt your daughter? As you know, my husband has at his disposal a number of rather unsavoury individuals. I could never prove it, but I've always believed that he, or one of his associates, was in some way responsible for the death of my parents. Of course, everyone including the police thought it was a straightforward car accident. Indeed, the coroner recorded a verdict of accidental death. But I've always had my suspicions that Patrick, or one of his men in the criminal underworld, had something to do with it.'

'What happened?'

'My mother and father had been to the theatre in Leeds, and then out to dinner. My father, who did like a drink, I must admit, well, he was driving back here when he supposedly lost control of the car and they hit a tree.'

'Oh my goodness. The poor things. And what makes you think—'

'That it wasn't an accident? I just feel that it might have been Patrick's twisted form of revenge. Perhaps he realised that his own accident had stolen something from him. He could not have a child and blamed me even though he must have known it was not my fault, and so he wanted to punish me. Of course, I couldn't prove anything. And he might well have had nothing to do with it. But I learnt not to underestimate Patrick.'

I felt a shiver play down my back.

'Oh my, you're shaking,' said Flora, taking my hand. 'And you are frozen. Here, just a moment.'

She walked over to the other side of the room and, from the back of a chair, retrieved a dark-red-and-purple Paisley shawl.

'Please, put this on,' she said, draping it around my shoulders.

'Thank you,' I said. 'I am feeling rather cold.'

When I told her that I thought it was lovely she insisted that I keep it. But I couldn't, I told her, shaking my head.

'You seem to be making a habit of refusing my requests,' said Flora with a sparkle in her eyes. 'I would be deeply offended if you refused – on both counts.'

I did not know what to say. I was reminded of a time when I was a little girl – I must have been only five – when my parents gave me a Yorkshire terrier for my birthday and I was so overwhelmed that I had to go and lock myself in the lavatory because I didn't know what to say.

'It suits you very well,' said Flora. 'Now, I think it's about time you started to tell me exactly what you had in mind, don't you?'

Chapter Twenty-one

Una put that morning's copy of *The Times* back on the dining table and opened her notebook. She underlined Dr Kurs's address and added him to her list of things to do that day. Yesterday, after fleeing the home of Nancy Neele in Croxley Green, she had finally located a public library in Watford where she found out a little more about the doctor. He had, she learnt, studied at London University; after graduation he had worked in Leeds before moving down south, first to Guildford and later he established a practice in Rickmansworth; and he had published a couple of papers relating to pain relief and palliative care. Surely there could be no harm in paying him a visit?

When she had telephoned Davison last night from her comfortable but quite simple hotel in Guildford she had filled him in on some of her findings. She had not wanted to tell him everything because she knew that he would disapprove of her methods. Imagine him knowing that she had stolen into Colonel Christie's house under an assumed name. That she had deliberately pulled at the hem of her skirt and then gossiped with a local dressmaker to find out the address of Miss Neele, the Colonel's mistress. And that she had called on Miss Neele's home under the guise of one of Mrs Christie's relatives. No, it was best to try to keep certain things secret. When she had finally won her scoop and the story had made a real splash then she could inform Davison of some of the less than honest means she had employed along the way. But not until then.

After breakfast she left her hotel and drove from Guildford back to Rickmansworth, careful not to take the route through the centre of the town in case she was spotted by the dreadful Mrs Peabody. She parked at the top end of Rectory Lane and walked until she located the house that Dr Kurs used as both his surgery and his home. The Scottish lady who worked as his receptionist told her that the doctor would be back at around midday. Una did not leave her name but said that she would come back later. Instead of returning to the centre of the town she walked down towards the canal, where she spent an hour or so thinking over the case. She was sure she was on to something, something that could change her life.

Back at the surgery, Una gave her name to the receptionist. As she waited for the doctor to return, Una looked around the bay-fronted room. Its overall feel was one of order. Everything here was in its right place.

A large bookcase behind the reception desk was filled with medical textbooks and journals. There was a shelf with a vase of flowers and another one used to display a selection of what looked like old-fashioned examination instruments. There was a glass-fronted cabinet, inside of which stood a number of blue ridged bottles. As Una squinted to make out the indented lettering on one particular bottle a bearded man strode into the surgery.

'Good morning again, Mrs Johnston,' he said. His voice was deep and rich, just the right kind to inspire his patients to share all sorts of confidences.

'Nearly afternoon, Doctor.'

'So it is, so it is.'

'And who do we have here?' he said, looking at Una. 'I don't think I know you, do I?'

'No, no, you don't,' said Una, standing up. 'I am visiting from London, but I am staying with friends near by. There is a – a matter on which I would value your opinion.'

'Indeed?' said the doctor, raising an eyebrow.

'This way,' he said, ushering her into the consulting room at the back of the house. 'Please sit down. And how can I help?'

Una had recently discovered that her deceptions often worked best when they involved a nugget of truth. Perhaps it was better to apply the same strategy here.

'I – I have been having problems with my nerves, doctor.'

'In what regard?'

'Well – they have been bothering me since the death of my father eighteen months ago.'

'You were very close?'

'Yes, we were. I was his favourite child. Well, I always liked to think so. Perhaps it was my imagination, but I always thought we had a special bond. Anyway, since his death I feel I can never be happy. I just can't imagine smiling, never mind laughing, ever again.'

'That is a perfectly normal feeling, my dear,' said Kurs, walking around his desk and coming to stand by Una. As he started to talk Una smelt the awful stench of his breath. She wanted to reach into her handbag and pull out her handkerchief, but then she remembered she no longer possessed one. 'We all deal with loss in our own individual ways. Some of my patients have been floored by the death of a parent, while others regard it as an opportunity.'

'An opportunity?' said Una.

'Yes, peculiar as it may sound, some people seem to flourish after the death of a mother or father. Perhaps they feel that they never got the chance to be quite themselves while their parent was still alive. And now that they are dead, well, they feel a new sense of freedom.'

'What a strange idea. I really can't imagine it. No, the feeling I have is, I don't know quite how to describe it, but it's an awful sense of impending doom. Like there is a blackness, a hollowness, within me that will never go away. Is there any way you could possibly help me?'

'Well, there are certain tonics I could prescribe. Certain sedatives that can help calm the nerves. But may I ask you a few questions first?'

'Yes, of course.'

Kurs took hold of Una's fine wrist and felt her pulse. 'Your heart is beating a little faster than I would have expected.'

'Really?'

'Yes. Can I ask, are you experiencing any other kind of difficulty in your life? Apart from your feelings of loss relating to your father?'

'No, not that I can think of,' said Una. 'Well, one of my friends is going through the most beastly time of it at the moment, so I could be feeling the effects of that, I suppose.'

'What kind of situation is that?'

'Oh, simply terrible. She's the one who recommended you to me, actually, so perhaps you know something of the case?'

'Yes?'

'Yes. Miss Neele. Nancy Neele.'

Una observed a spark burn in Kurs's dark eyes.

'I presume she told you something of the difficulties she is in,' she continued. 'I feel so terribly sorry for her. I am sure she never envisaged anything like this might happen when she embarked on her, her friendship, with Colonel Christie.'

'I am sure you realise that what my patients tell me within the confines of these four walls remains completely confidential. I know nothing of the case apart from the little I have read in the newspapers. Mostly tittle-tattle, I must say.'

'And Miss Neele has said nothing to you?'

Kurs took out a stethoscope from his black leather bag, slowly placed it in his ears and gestured towards her chest. She bit her lip as she became enveloped by a poisonous cloud of halitosis.

'May I?'

'Yes, of course,' said Una, beginning to loosen her blouse. The shock of the cold metal on her skin took her breath away.

'Yes, your heart is showing a certain tendency to race. Perhaps it is best if I give you a little something to calm your nerves.'

'A tonic?'

'Yes. Would you excuse me for a moment?' Kurs opened the door and started to talk to his receptionist. Una heard the sound of a bunch of keys being taken out of a drawer, followed by a muffled conversation.

'Now, what I am going to give you should do the trick,' said Kurs, walking towards her with a small colourless bottle and a glass of water.

'Oh yes,' said Una. 'What is it?'

'There is no need to worry about that. It seems from what you have told me that you have had too much on your mind recently. It's time you had a rest. All those thoughts rushing around in your head, no wonder your pulse is racing and your heart is speeding.'

From one of his desk drawers, Kurs took out a pipette and used it to draw up a few drops of colourless liquid which he then deposited into the glass of water. As the two solutions merged the liquid turned a cloudy white.

'You mean to give it to me now?' said Una. She could not help sounding more than a little terrified. She wished she had never brought up the subject of her anxiety now.

'Yes, from what you've told me, I think there is a danger that your nerves could be all shot to pieces if you carry on as you have been.'

'And I couldn't take this – this tonic when I get home?'

'I think it's best that it is taken under medical supervision,' said Kurs, smiling.

Una did not like that smile. In fact, she didn't like this doctor one little bit.

'Now, if you just drink it,' he said, passing the glass to Una. 'It may not be to your taste, but I can guarantee that you will start to feel better within minutes.'

'It sounds like a miracle cure,' said Una, putting the glass down on the desk. 'Almost too good to be true.'

'Some of my patients have told me that this particular remedy has helped them in ways they could never imagine. It not only calms the nerves, but it also forces the body to relax. It breaks the vicious circle of anxiety that can be so debilitating.'

'I think Miss Neele told me something of the sort,'

said Una. 'She said that you gave her something that really helped her nerves. Perhaps this was the same sort of tonic?'

'It may well have been, Miss Crowe,' said Kurs, passing the glass to her. 'Now if you take a few sips you will begin to feel for yourself the effects of the medicine.'

Una lifted the glass to her lips. Although she did not like the doctor, surely, she reasoned, he could do her no real harm? He was a general practitioner, after all, whose job it was to safeguard the health of his patients. And he knew nothing about her real intentions, after all. Perhaps it would be best if she were to swallow a little of the draught? It might actually do her a spot of good. And in taking the dose she would gain the doctor's trust.

'She said that after taking the medicine you prepared for her she felt like she was, how did she put it, like she was floating on air. Sounds heavenly to me. Really, what with the death of my father and then the troubles surrounding Miss Neele, I could do with that kind of release.'

Una placed her lips around the edge of the glass and raised the beaker a little more. She could feel the cool liquid begin to bathe her lips in its soporific wash.

'She told me she wished she had never got involved with that man, the Colonel,' she said, lowering the glass to her side. 'What a scandal it is. What do you think of it all, Doctor?'

'Think of it?'

'Yes, of this awful case,' said Una, placing the glass back on the desk. 'This disappearance of Mrs Christie.'

'Oh, not very much.'

'You don't have any professional insight?'

'Professional insight?' said Kurs, taking hold of the glass and passing it back to his patient.

'Yes, I wondered whether, as an expert, you might be able to offer something that could help explain it.'

'I'm afraid I wouldn't know,' said Kurs. 'Now, I really must insist you drink this. It will be for your own good. Your mind, by your own admission, is under the most terrible stress. And these thoughts about this case are doing nothing to help. It would be best if you tried to forget the whole thing.'

'Yes, I am sure you are right.'

With trembling hands Una raised the glass to her lips once again.

'You will feel lethargic and a little sleepy, but within the hour, after a period of rest, you should be back to normal. You should be able to go about your life without being gripped by that awful sense of doom and gloom. That blackness should have lifted, for the time being at least. And that is what you came to see me for, isn't that right?'

'Yes, thank you,' she said. 'You are very kind.'

What could she do? The doctor's eyes were fixed on Una's hands and her mouth.

'Now, take a sip or two,' he said. 'Please.'

The muscles in Una's throat tightened and constricted.

'I just feel—'

The doctor placed his hand under the glass and moved it closer to her mouth. Una tasted the bitter liquid.

'Very good, and now swallow,' said Kurs. 'That's right. And another sip. Yes, and one more.' Kurs took the glass from her hand and placed it on the desk. 'Can you feel the drug beginning to do its work?'

Una immediately felt the tension drain away from her body. But then she felt awfully tired, as if she wanted to go to sleep. She observed herself as if from the other side of the room: what a silly fool she had been. She saw Kurs's beard come closer. She could smell his metallic breath, but she could no longer react. She felt her eyes closing and imagined being enveloped by a shroud of black velvet.

Twenty minutes later she began to stir. 'Where? What?' she said, her hand rising to her head.

'Now don't worry, Miss Crowe. Do you remember? You came to see me? I'm the doctor that you asked to see.'

'Oh my,' said Una, suddenly feeling like she wanted to be sick. 'Please.'

'Yes, here,' said Kurs, passing her a bowl and a cloth. 'You may feel some signs of nausea.'

'Thank you,' said Una. 'But I can't—'

'You can't remember. That's totally normal. It's one of the immediate side effects of the treatment. But I am sure you will begin to feel the benefits.'

'I will?' said Una, her eyes darting around the room.

'I just feel so terribly sick. And I can't remember talking to you.' She started to raise herself from the chair, but immediately had to sit down again. 'My head. It's pounding.'

What on earth had happened? She could remember walking into the doctor's surgery. She could recall having a conversation with his receptionist. She could picture that cabinet in the room next door.

'When the nausea and the headache have worn off your spirits will be lifted. Many patients compare it to opening the curtains and seeing the sunshine in their lives for the first time. You will, of course, continue to feel sad about the loss of your father, but it will no longer affect you in quite the same way.'

'My father?'

'Yes, you came here to ask for some help in coping with the loss of your father. Don't you remember?'

'Yes – no,' she said, feeling the tears on her cheeks. She opened her handbag to retrieve her handkerchief, but could not find it.

'Here, please permit me,' he said, taking a handkerchief from one of the drawers in his desk.

'Thank you,' said Una, pressing a corner of the freshly starched linen to her nose.

What on earth had she done with her handkerchief? She vaguely recalled giving it away to somebody, another lady. She felt a panic in her breast, the sense that she was in danger. She gripped the sides of the chair and steadied herself. Fragments of the last few days flashed into her mind: searching through Mrs Christie's desk and the discovery of the letter about Nancy Neele; the visit to the dressmaker's; the awful scene with Miss Neele herself. But she could not understand why she had made an appointment to see a doctor. It was true, she had been feeling very low about her father, but she had been certain that she had managed to put those feelings to one side.

'And the next time you see Miss Neele, please give her my very best wishes,' said Kurs. 'I am only pleased that she saw fit to recommend my services to you.'

'Miss Neele?'

'Yes, your friend?'

'Yes, yes, indeed,' said Una, suddenly remembering the reason she had paid the doctor a visit. But what on earth had passed between them?

'And please let me know how you progress with your career. A most interesting choice of profession for a modern young lady. I wish you every success.'

Una looked blankly at him. She could not remember telling him anything relating to her recent investigations, but she supposed she must have done. She suddenly felt so utterly stupid.

'You know, I am quite fascinated by the disappearance of the lady novelist,' he said. 'I may have very little to offer in terms of professional insight, but you would be most welcome to hear what I have to say.'

'Really? Yes, I would love to hear your thoughts on the subject,' said Una.

'Do you need any help? Should I call you a taxi? Or would you like to wait here for a while until the ill-effects of the drug have worn off?'

'No, no thank you,' said Una. 'I will sit in my car for a while, I think.'

As Una turned to go she heard the doctor begin to clear his throat.

'Have you spoken to many people?'

'Yes, a good deal,' said Una. It wasn't quite the truth – she had indeed spoken to a handful of people, but the only problem was she had been unable to speak to anyone of importance. Apart from Nancy Neele, that is, and she had not given much away. However, she must not lose heart. She was still ahead of most of the newspapers, she was sure.

'And of course, Nancy must have filled you in on a great many of the details?'

'Yes, indeed,' said Una nervously.

'Where do you think Mrs Christie is now? Or do you believe she's dead?'

'Oh, I'm not sure. But I don't believe she's dead. Perhaps she went away to try and punish her husband. To try and make him feel a little of the pain that she had suffered.'

'Yes, an interesting theory,' he said, pausing. 'Miss Neele mentioned a few details along those lines too.'

'Really?'

'Yes, looking back, I suppose she did suggest such a thing. Quite a lovely young woman, don't you think?'

'Yes, quite lovely.'

'Have you known her long?'

'A good few years.'

'Through your family?'

'Yes, a connection through my father.'

'And how do you feel about your father now? I noticed that when you came into the surgery the mention of his name brought tears to your eyes. I do hope you are much better now, after the treatment.'

'Yes, I am sure I will feel the benefits in time.'

'There is always the possibility that you may need another treatment, of course.'

'I see.'

'Perhaps we should make an appointment?' Kurs consulted a diary on his desk. 'I will check with Mrs Johnston, but what about Friday of this week? Eleven o'clock in the morning? Is that convenient?'

'So soon?'

'Yes, I find that the tonic works best when applied twice during the course of one week.'

Una looked uncertain.

'And of course we could always talk about the Mrs Christie case after that appointment. However, I'm afraid you wouldn't be able to use my name in connection with this. Anything I said you would have to use only for your own information and research. Would you agree to that?'

'Yes, of course, thank you.'

'I would like to continue the conversation now, but

I am afraid I am due to see another patient. I doubt if she will last the day, the poor thing. Only a girl – what, how old? Eight years. Sometimes life can be unbearably cruel, don't you find Miss Crowe?'

'Yes, indeed. Goodbye, Doctor.'

'If you see Mrs Johnston on the way out, please let her know that you will need that appointment on Friday morning.'

'Thank you.'

Una tried to walk as calmly as she could out of the building, but she feared that at any moment her legs would collapse from under her. She did not pause by the reception desk of Mrs Johnston, merely nodded her head as she passed, and then rushed out of the surgery into the leafy street. She gasped for air as though she had just surfaced from deep water.

Chapter Twenty-two

Kenward thought it was time to ask Colonel Christie a few questions, difficult ones. He had done all he could to be polite and treat him like the gentleman the Colonel thought he was; Kenward had had his doubts about the man's breeding and behaviour, but he had kept these mostly to himself. He had, however, employed a couple of men to follow the Colonel, but so far Christie had done nothing out of the ordinary: each day he left his house in Sunningdale and travelled to work at the Rio Tinto Company building in the City, returning home to Styles each evening. The scandal surrounding his wife's disappearance had obviously put the dampeners on his friendship with Miss Neele, as his men informed him that the two had not seen each other since the news broke.

The nice, well-mannered approach had obviously not worked, and so it was necessary to try a different tack. He had asked his men to pick up the Colonel from

Styles and bring him to the station for questioning. He had arrived half an hour ago, but Kenward thought it a good idea to make the Colonel wait for a while. He had often found that letting a man stew produced results. He stood up and asked the constable stationed outside to bring in the Colonel. A few moments later, Christie stormed into his office.

'What is the meaning of this?' he said, shaking his hat at Kenward.

'Please, Colonel, sit down.'

'No, I will not sit down unless you tell me what you think you are playing at. Sending a car to my house and bringing me here like this. The reporters will have a field day.'

'I am sure that if you've done nothing wrong you'll have nothing to worry about.'

'And what is that supposed to mean?'

'Look, Colonel, if you will sit down then perhaps I can ask you a few questions.'

'You don't seriously believe I have done anything to harm my wife in any way?'

'I'm afraid I really don't know, but perhaps after our conversation I might have a clearer idea. Now, please, sir.'

The Colonel took a seat and Kenward returned to the chair behind his desk. He slowly opened his file and read through a couple of statements.

'What I want to get clear is some of the chronology of the events on Friday night and Saturday morning.'

'I've told you everything already. You know where I was and what I was doing. I have a cast-iron alibi.'

'Yes, your alibi,' said Kenward, taking up a piece of paper. 'Supported by your friends.'

'You've spoken to them, I hear. Mr and Mrs James and—'

'Yes, the other guest at Hurtmore Cottage that weekend, Miss Neele.'

'I don't want her name being dragged into this,' said the Colonel. 'She's already been plagued by newspaper reporters – she telephoned me to tell me that one lady even pretended to be one of my wife's cousins and managed to talk her way into Miss Neele's home. Can you imagine? The whole experience has been most distressing for her and her parents are threatening to send her away, out of the country. Of course, I can't see her, as I am sure you are all too aware.' The Colonel said the last sentence in a particularly pointed manner, as if to draw attention to the fact that he knew that Kenward had been following his every move.

'Well, there is, I am afraid, very little I can do to control the appetites of the popular press. Now as to your movements on Friday night, perhaps you could tell me once more about what you did – and when?'

The Colonel glared at Kenward, but the Superintendent met his gaze with a cold stare. The eye-to-eye duel continued for a few moments, until the suspect swore under his breath and began to talk.

'As I have already told you, I arrived at Hurtmore

Cottage, near Godalming, straight after work, so it must have been around half past six. There I met my friends Mr and Mrs Sam James and later we were joined by Miss Neele, who was to stay for the weekend. All four of us had drinks and then dinner and then we retired to bed at about eleven o'clock. I had a good night's sleep and I knew nothing was out of the ordinary until the Saturday morning when I received a telephone call from Charlotte Fisher, my wife's secretary, who informed me of Mrs Christie's disappearance. But you know all of this, I've told you a thousand times. I really don't see the need to go over it all once more.'

'And you are certain you did not leave Hurtmore Cottage on the night of the third of December or during the early hours of the fourth of December?'

'No, I did not.'

'And your car – where was it?'

'It was in the garage, the garage at Hurtmore Cottage.'

'And you are quite sure you did not leave your friends?'

'Yes, quite sure,' said the Colonel with a heavy dose of sarcasm. 'Now, really, I think it's time you began to—'

'Please sit down, Colonel. I am the one who will decide when this interview is over.'

'And as to having men follow me day and night, it's humiliating. It's as good as being declared guilty.'

'I'm sorry you think so,' said Kenward. 'But it's a purely procedural matter.'

'I don't care. I feel I'm being treated like a common criminal.'

Kenward did not respond, letting the Colonel's words speak for themselves.

'Now, if I can ask you once again,' Kenward resumed. 'On the night of the 3rd of December – I can see here from these statements that Mr and Mrs James testify that they never heard you leave the house.'

'Yes, that's right.'

'But surely they would have been asleep?'

'Indeed. But the family's dog would have barked and raised the alarm if I had tried to leave the house and start the car.'

'The dog?'

'Yes, the dog. Handsome little thing. But noisy as hell.'

'And Miss Neele. Would she have been in a position to witness whether you left the house or not?'

'I am not sure what you are implying, but if you mean to insinuate—'

'I don't care what you do in your private life, Colonel. It's my job to gather the facts. If you won't answer the question I am afraid I may have to bring Miss Neele down to the station and ask her myself.'

'You will do nothing of the sort. Nancy – Miss Neele is, as I have suggested, feeling rather a nervous wreck as a result of all this nonsense. My blasted wife! I wish she—' The Colonel stopped himself.

'Were dead?'

'Don't be so ridiculous! I was about to say I wish she had never brought this scandal into our lives.'

'And perhaps she wouldn't have if you had been more of a devoted husband.'

'Poppycock. Mrs Christie is a highly intelligent woman, capable of the most intricate manipulations. I wish people would see my side of the story instead of jumping to these preposterous conclusions.'

'So you categorically deny you saw her on the night or the morning she disappeared?'

'How many times do I have to repeat myself?'

'You didn't steal out of the house that night and drive to Newlands Corner?'

'No.'

'Where you met your estranged wife?'

'No.'

'Where you then had an argument, an argument that became more tempestuous?'

'No, that's—'

'And during the argument you struck her violently? Perhaps so violently you worried about the consequences?'

'This is—'

'And then you killed her? What did you do? Did you strangle her, Colonel Christie?'

'No, honestly, I've said that—'

'And then dispose of her body? Where did you take her? Did you bury her somewhere?'

'No! I think you've lost your mind if you think that I would do such a thing. Really, I do think this is completely unacceptable.' The Colonel pushed his chair back and stood up suddenly. Whatever handsomeness he normally possessed had been disfigured by the demon of fury. His face had turned beetroot red and his eyes were wide and bulging. 'If you carry on like this I really must insist on bringing in my solicitor. In fact, I have every mind to contact him anyway. This is nothing less than intimidation. You know you have no evidence and the reason why you have no evidence is because I am innocent.'

Perhaps he had gone too far, Kenward thought. But what other explanation was there for the disappearance? Surely a woman could not simply vanish from the face of the earth without any trace? He sensed he was not going to get anywhere with this line of questioning – the Colonel was putting on too good a show – and so he would have to think of another approach.

'I'm sure everything will become clear in due course,' said Kenward, standing up. 'I don't mean to detain you, Colonel. But perhaps we can have another talk in the next few days?'

'I don't think so. If you want to arrest me, do so. Otherwise, I'm at a loss to see how I can help you with your enquiries. Good day.'

Kenward waited for the Colonel to leave the room before he took out the bottle from his desk drawer. He took a swift sip, then another, and then picked up the telephone. It was time to use more underhand measures. If the Colonel did not want to play fair then he would have to face the consequences. He dialled the number of the Press Association and asked to be put through to his contact on the crime desk, Alexander Massey.

'Massey? Yes, it's Kenward here. I think I may have something for you. Yes, it's relating to what we talked about the other day. Yes, the Christie case. I think we may be able to get the husband to crack.'

Chapter Twenty-three

Happy people have no history. Who said that? Probably one of those gloomy Russians. I had never quite grasped the full meaning of it before, but now I thought I understood. I looked back at my earlier self as rather like a blank page. The days when I had been content – the hours spent playing in the sunny garden at Ashfield, the idle chats with my mother, the endless roller-skating on the promenade in Torquay – seemed insubstantial somehow. The death of my mother, then Archie's betrayal, and now the shadowy presence of Dr Kurs had all crowded upon me, leaving their dark marks.

I recalled my mother talking of how each of us should meditate on death and live like a pilgrim or a stranger on the earth. We were merely passing through. 'Tomorrow is an uncertain day,' she would say, quoting from *The Imitation of Christ*, a book she always kept by her bed.

Perhaps this was Flora's attitude. I was astounded by

her resilience, and the fact that she seemed so carefree in the face of death. We had spent the best part of the day together and during that time I felt as though I had formed a special bond with her. Flora had, with a logic that defied argument, set out the reasons why it was right for her to sacrifice herself for the sake of my daughter. If the experiment did not work, and the dosage did not succeed in reviving her, then she would go to her death knowing that her passing was not in vain. She insisted, she said, in writing a suicide note so that, if she were to die during the procedure, I would not be blamed. She even stated that she was actually looking forward to the experiment; it might prepare her for her own inevitable demise, which was only a few months away. Despite this, I knew that even if the plan worked, Flora's 'death' would only buy me a little time: the real horror would come later when she woke up. What would I do then?

As I girl I had always been fascinated by the story of Lazarus of Bethany, the man Jesus had restored to life four days after his death. I remembered my mother reading to me from the Gospel of John and weeping when she related the part about the rolling back of the rock of Lazarus's tomb and the sight of the man still dressed in his grave clothes. I knew that to attempt something similar would be nothing short of sacrilege. And yet I had no choice. I just hoped I would not be cursed forever.

Chapter Twenty-four

'Come in, come in,' said Davison. 'Where on earth have you been?'

'Berkshire, Surrey and Hertfordshire,' said Una, entering the elegant first- floor flat of the Albany.

'Oh my, thank goodness you have returned to civilisation.'

'It wasn't quite as bad as that, but the worst thing is that I've got to go back to the country tomorrow.'

Davison led Una down the passage with its exquisite collection of engravings and portraits. Certainly, Davison had an eye for beauty; he also had a generous private income that enabled him to pursue and satisfy his interests.

'Come and sit down. Would you like some tea?'

'Yes, yes please.'

'Now, tell me what you've been doing. I was beginning to wonder whether you had run off with a rich suitor.'

'If only I could be so lucky. No, I've been on the trail of Mrs Christie.'

'What did you discover? Have you got your scoop yet? I see the story is all over the papers again this morning.'

'No, not yet. But I'm convinced I'm nearly there.'

'Well, I want to hear all about it. Excuse me for a moment, won't you,' said Davison as he disappeared into the kitchen to make the tea.

Una took her seat in a dark maroon leather chair by the fire. She always loved visiting Davison at his set and often called by unannounced in the hope of finding him with a close friend. She had never met any of his associates; she was sure she would like them, given half the chance. In the past she had taken the opportunity, when Davison had briefly left the flat to post a letter or been called to the telephone, to scour his home for clues. Bureaux were searched, desks opened, letters read, but to no avail. Today, her attention was drawn to the pile of journals and newspapers on the table, an eclectic mix to say the least.

'Interesting about the girl, isn't it?' called out Davison.

'The girl?'

'Yes, the one named as a "friend of the Jameses" this morning. Obviously, the one Colonel Christie has been involved with.' Any concerns about keeping certain details secret from Davison now melted away.

'Oh, you mean Miss Neele. I've been to see her already.'

A moment later, Davison appeared at the doorway. He was not carrying the tea tray.

'What do you mean, you've been to see her? I thought she would be off limits.'

'Oh yes, I expect she is. But I used a secret technique of mine.'

'Let me guess what that is,' said Davison, smirking.

'Don't be so underhand and beastly.' Una laughed. 'No, I simply pretended to be a cousin of Mrs Christie's. She let me in and gave me some vital information.'

'What's that?'

'I can't tell you now, you'll just have to wait for my scoop to appear. Now where's my tea?'

'Very well. But you're not going to get away without telling me a few prize titbits.'

Una picked up the *Express*, and read the story about how the Surrey and Berkshire police forces had been foolish not to call in Scotland Yard. *The Times* focused on yet another unsuccessful search of the area around Newlands Corner, mostly led by a group of local men and the Guildford and Shere Beagles Hunt who had been asked to keep a special lookout. However, at the end of the first paragraph there was a fact that jumped out of the page, something that surely would be worth following up: apparently, before Mrs Christie disappeared the novelist had written a letter to her brother-in-law Campbell Christie and the postmark on the envelope was clearly defined as the SW1 postal district. Perhaps Davison would have a contact inside the Post Office; certainly there was no harm in asking.

'So, tell me, where did you find Miss Neele?' asked Davison, returning with the tea.

'Just outside Rickmansworth, in Hertfordshire.'

'I'm not sure I've ever been to Hertfordshire. Oh yes, I remember. Once, I had to attend a dreary weekend party at some awful house, an old friend of Hartford's who had this enormous pile near St Albans. He told me that it would be worth meeting him, but it was one of the worst weekends of my life. One day I'll tell you more about it.'

'Well, once this is over I doubt if I'll ever want to go there again.'

'Really?'

'It's been a fascinating experience, not at all what I expected. But the most wonderful thing is I am sure that at last I have found my vocation.'

'I'm pleased to hear it.'

'I thought once I had given it a go I might tire of it rather, but it's the opposite. I find it absolutely thrilling. Especially the coverage of crime. All those beastly murders. So fascinating.'

'Are you sure? I had assumed you were just doing it as a way of finding a husband. Hardly territory where one would find a suitable man but as they say beggars can't be choosers.'

Una's laugh was loud and infectious and quite ridiculously high.

'Please, quieten down, you'll have my neighbours gossiping,' said Davison.

'It will be good to give them something to talk about. You need someone unsuitable in your life to make you a subject of idle chatter, don't you think?'

'The less said about that the better. Now, moving on. Tell me all about what you discovered.'

Una thought for a moment. She would, she decided, be quite selective in what she said; after all she didn't want Davison to become annoyingly protective. She had a job to do and she needed to be free to do it without any interference.

'Of course, the police were hopeless, totally unco-operative,' said Una. 'And so I had to find other ways to gather information.'

Davison looked doubtful. 'Such as?'

'Well, first of all I managed to talk my way into the Christies' house, when the Colonel was out, thank goodness. I found a letter written to Mrs Christie from her sister—'

'What do you mean you "found" a letter?'

'Well – when I was in the house, I saw a letter which gave me quite a good deal of background on the affair.'

There was no disguising Davison's horror. 'I think I must have misunderstood you. You pushed your way into Colonel and Mrs Christie's house? And then you stole a letter from them?'

'I know, I know,' she said, trying to make light of it. 'But please don't scold me. It was important. It was the only way. The letter gave me the name of Miss Neele. So you see I got that information a few days ago, and although I am sure I could have made a name for myself by selling that to the newspapers I decided to hold back in the hope that it might lead somewhere else.'

'You know I cannot condone this, Una. You know what you did was against the law?'

'The law! There are certain times when, well, when one has to be creative, don't you think? Surely you're not telling me your department has always acted within the confines of the law?'

'That is entirely different,' he said, his face reddening. 'It's done in the country's best interests, in the name of national security.'

'You can call it that if you like. But I know the kind of things that go on, the things the public never hear about. And, as you very well know, the morals do not always bear close inspection.'

Davison fell silent for a moment. 'But you must take care, Una. I don't want you to find yourself behind bars – or even worse no longer around to tell the tale. Promise me you'll be careful.'

Una hesitated. She had her own rules for what being careful meant, but she wasn't about to outline these to Davison. 'I promise,' she said.

'And what did you discover from the letter?'

'I found out that the Colonel had been having an affair with a Miss Nancy Neele. I thought she might be able to shed some light on the case and so I found my way, via a very chatty dressmaker, to the home of Miss Neele. That conversation led me to Miss Neele's doctor, who I am sure knows a thing or two about the disappearance.'

'What makes you so certain?'

'Oh, I don't know, let's just say feminine intuition. I've another appointment with him tomorrow. Although he says I won't be able to use his name, he promises to give me some background information on the case.'

'This is all very fascinating, but I am not keen on you gadding about the country talking your way into strangers' houses. You never know who you might meet.'

'What, like a suitable husband, you mean?'

'You may joke, Una, but I do feel protective of you. You do remember what I promised your father, don't you? The conversation I had with him before he died?'

The sparkle faded from Una's eyes and the smile disappeared from her face.

'You know what I'm trying to say. Your father gave me the task of making sure you didn't come to any harm. I would be failing in my duties if anything were to happen to you.'

'Yes, I can see that. Thank you, Davison, said Una, reaching out to touch him lightly on the leg. He really was the sweetest of men.

'So you must promise me not to do anything silly or foolhardy. No more rushing off to strange counties like Hertfordshire without so much as a word of warning.'

'Very well,' said Una, picking up *The Times*. 'Now, tell me. Do you have any useful contacts inside the Post Office?

'Why?'

Una filled him in on the story about the discovery of a letter that Mrs Christie was said to have posted to her brother-in-law, Campbell Christie, and which bore the postmark SW1.

'So you think Mrs Christie came to London after her disappearance?' said Davison.

'Yes, or she gave it to one of her friends to post for her. Perhaps she had a secret life that she didn't want her husband to know about?'

'Why does everyone have to have a secret life? Can't people be just decent and honest and straightforward?'

Una cast him a questioning glance. 'I'd like to hear your own answer to that.'

'Excuse me?' said Davison. There was laughter in his voice, but it was, thought Una, the kind of laughter one used when one wanted to cover something up.

'Your work, and all that goes with it,' she said. 'The deception, the lies, the deceit, the undercover nature of it all.'

'Oh, that,' said Davison, waving a hand in the air. 'For a moment I thought you were referring to something else entirely.'

'No, not at all,' said Una, smiling. 'I wouldn't dream of it. Anyway, I was wondering if you had any contacts with the central London Post Office system?'

'We do, of course. But I'm not sure how they might help you in this matter.'

'Neither am I,' said Una. 'That's the problem. I'm not sure what to do next. I have a few leads to follow up. As I said, I am going back to Rickmansworth tomorrow. But after that, I feel I've come to rather a dead end. The police aren't showing any signs that they will help me, and there is no way I can go back and see Miss Neele or Colonel Christie.'

'Well, I can make a few discreet enquiries at the Post Office about the letter. I can certainly find out when it was franked. That much should be quite straightforward.'

'That would be something, I suppose.'

'But of course, no one would know who posted the letter apart from Mrs Christie, or, according to your rather twisted and degenerate mind, her secret friend.'

'Talking of secret friends—'

'Enough,' said Davison, holding up his hand, his eyes sparkling. It was obvious that Una's revelations about her rather unconventional investigative methods had not damaged their friendship. 'I've warned you already not to approach this subject. No wonder you are suited to journalism: your mind is like ... like something one does not refer to in polite conversation.'

'Davison!'

The two burst into laughter, a laughter that rang out through the flat with such force that the delicate glass shards of Davison's beloved Napoleon III chandelier began to tinkle with delight.

Chapter Twenty-five

Surely it would only be a matter of time before he cracked the case, thought Kenward. If he could just turn the screw on the Colonel a little bit more then he might be able to wring a confession out of him. It was all about the delicate application of psychological pressure: too little and the murderer wouldn't feel the need to share any information, too much and he would shut like a limpet.

The last twenty-four hours had proved eventful for Kenward and his team at Surrey Constabulary headquarters. In the afternoon, two boys had reported that they had come across a tin under a bush near the place where Mrs Christie had abandoned her car. Inside the tin was a strange message: 'Ask Candle Lanche. He knows more about the Silent Pool than ...' He had asked his men to go through the local directories to check whether there was anyone of that name living in the vicinity, but they had drawn a blank. He had even passed it to one of the constables, Hughes, who he knew to be a crossword fiend. Could it be an anagram, he wondered?

After a couple of hours of playing about with the letters, Hughes had come up with a few half-baked suggestions, but finally Kenward had decided that the message was nothing more than a silly hoax. He suspected the two boys, Frederick Jones and Stanley Lane, who claimed they had found the tin, as being the perpetrators, but he couldn't prove it. No doubt he could have questioned them further, but he didn't want to waste any more time, because he had been called away from the station after the discovery of a shoe.

The item had been found by a member of the public out walking on the lower slopes of the Downs near Albury. Could it have belonged to Mrs Christie? If so, could there be other scraps of clothing near by? One of his men drove him to the site of the discovery, and although he had high hopes for the importance of this piece of potential evidence, when he arrived it was obvious that the shoe had been safely rotting away for some time. Then, later that night, just as he had been getting ready for bed, he heard a knock at the door. He opened it to see Hughes; he knew that the constable would not bother him at home unless it was important.

'What is it?' asked Kenward, eager to hear the news. 'Oh yes, I suppose you had better come in.'

Kenward led him into the kitchen.

'A call just came into the station. A body of a woman has been pulled out of the Basingstoke Canal.'

This was it. This was the breakthrough he had been waiting for.

'What does she look like? Can you tell me?'

'It's difficult to say, sir. I haven't seen the body yet, but I don't suppose she's the prettiest sight.'

'Was she wearing clothes?'

'Oh yes, indeed, sir,' he said, turning the page of his notebook.

'Can you say what kind of clothes she was wearing?'

'I'm no expert in that regard, sir, but the witness said that she was a well-dressed lady.'

'Where has the body been taken? The mortuary?'

'Yes, sir.'

'Well, what are we waiting for?'

Hughes squinted at Kenward's dark blue wool dressing gown, which strained itself to contain his rotund form, and his green-and-white-striped pyjamas beneath.

'Oh yes, of course,' said Kenward, coughing, 'I'll just change my clothes.'

The door to the mortuary was opened by Dr Anderson, an elderly man who looked like he was only a step or two away from death himself. His skin had yellowed and thinned to the point where it appeared to be as insubstantial as the parchment of an ancient book. His back had bent double so he had difficulty in lifting his neck and meeting the gaze of the two policemen.

'Come in, she's inside on the slab,' said the doctor in a matter-of-fact manner.

Kenward and Hughes followed him down a corridor to the back of the building. The bare room consisted of nothing more than a marble slab and a wooden shelf on which stood pieces of surgical equipment, metal dishes and glass jars of various sizes. The smell of preserving fluid hung in the air like some foul ghost.

'There was no identification on her body and I don't think a handbag of any description has been found near by,' said Dr Anderson, reading from his notes.

Kenward approached the slab with a certain degree of nervousness, not because he was afraid of seeing a dead body – the sight of a corpse, no matter how decomposed, no longer shocked him – but because of the anticipation that rose within him. For a moment, before he felt ready to look over to study the face of the dead woman on the slab, he had to steady himself. There was, he knew, a bare light bulb hanging over the body, casting everything in the room in a clinical glare, but to him it looked as though the bulb was dimming. The periphery of his vision darkened, obscuring and restricting his sight to nothing but a shadowed tunnel.

'Kenward, are you all right?' someone said.

He was conscious of Dr Anderson by his side. He turned his head, but the room looked as though it had been upturned, like something from the *Titanic*. He felt a person take his arm and lower him into a chair. His head, he was aware, had been placed between his knees, but he felt a great straining around his middle and a dull pain in his heart. He took a series of deep breaths and gradually the world righted itself before his eyes. Yet the sight that greeted him – Anderson, ochred, tortoise-like, and crawling towards death – did not offer a great source of comfort.

'Kenward? Kenward?' said Anderson, monitoring his pulse. 'You had us worried for a second.'

'Just a funny turn. Sorry about that.'

'Are you sure you want to do this now?' asked Anderson. 'Why not come back in the morning after you've had some rest?'

'No, no, I've fully recovered,' said Kenward, standing up from the chair. 'No need to worry about me. It's this lady here we are concerned with, who I very much hope—'

The sight of the woman lying on the marble slab stopped the words in his mouth. He blinked a few times, hoping the action would correct what he saw. The disappointment hit him like a fist in the chest and for a moment he thought he might suffer another attack. The woman lying before him was in her early twenties, short, only about five feet tall, with long black hair that trailed across her body like seaweed. Her skin was pale and translucent, on her left temple one could see a cluster of fine blue veins. She was also unmistakably pregnant.

'Damn, damn you,' said Kenward under his breath. He directed the curse not only towards the unfortunate drowned woman who had murdered her unborn child, but also to Colonel Christie and his missing wife.

By the time Kenward went to sleep that night his dreams were haunted by horrific images. The drowned woman on the slab took on the form of Mrs Christie. In his dreams he went over and over how the Colonel had murdered his wife: he had strangled her at Newlands Corner, carried her limp body to the boot of his car, then he had driven to the dark canal where he had dumped her body in the water. He then returned home to his friends' cottage near Godalming, to the warmth of his mistress's bed, and behaved as though nothing had happened. It all could have been achieved within the space of a few hours. How long would the drive have taken him? It was around ten miles between Hurtmore Cottage and Newlands Corner and then another twenty or so miles from there to the canal, depending on the place where the body had been dumped. The Colonel could have done the whole journey – and committed the murder – in under three hours. Yes, it was possible. He awoke early thinking he had solved it all, only to realise, in the cold light of dawn, that he had solved nothing: the body that had been found was not that of Mrs Christie. Breakfast was a dismal affair; he was grumpy and snapped at Naomi when she had tried to cheer him up, and he had pushed his plate of buttered toast and boiled eggs away from him, uneaten.

He arrived at his desk seething and full of anger, his resentment only softened slightly by the ingestion of a measure or two of whisky. He began the day by reading the newspapers on his desk. On the top of the pile was the *Daily Express*, where he read that his force was being criticised for not bringing in Scotland Yard. Was that the Colonel's doing? Had he some influence in Fleet Street? Another newspaper carried a story about a so-called sighting of Mrs Christie – there had been so many of them he had lost count – but this latest one, from a woman who claimed to have seen the novelist wearing a spotted sealskin coat and had reported the sighting to Wokingham Police Station, carried with it a quote from Superintendent Goddard of the Berkshire Constabulary: '"I'm afraid that not much importance can be attached to her statement," he said, "but personally I think Mrs Christie is still alive."' Damn that Goddard. Why couldn't he keep his mouth shut? He was only playing into the Colonel's hands.

His sourness of spirit only dissipated when, after taking another drink, he read that Miss Neele had been named as a friend of the Jameses. That should do the trick, Kenward thought, that should begin to irk the Colonel. And sure enough, as he sat at his desk, a call came through from Christie. Kenward repeated that he had nothing to do with the leak of the name to the press and no, he did not have a clue about how they could have got hold of it. 'Servants, most likely,' he lied. 'You know how they talk.'

He spent the morning talking to his men and arranging the volunteer force that would help with the search. An operation like this depended on the good-will of the public and it was extraordinary how many ordinary men, women and children were prepared to spend hours in windswept countryside, on a cold December's day, looking for clues. No doubt many of them were inspired by the kind of silly books Mrs Christie wrote for a living; perhaps they saw themselves as amateur detectives on the hunt for information that would help them solve a murder. If only they knew how laborious the work really was; there was nothing glamorous about solving crimes. Let them stand in front of a mortuary slab and look at the bloated body of a drowned woman. Give them a hundred contradictory witness statements to take and read through. Once this was over, once he had solved the mystery of Mrs Christie, and solve it he would, perhaps he would retire. But what would he do? Police work had been his life. He wasn't ready to go just yet. Not when he had Colonel Christie to deal with.

He asked one of his men to telephone the Colonel to ask him whether he could drop by Newlands Corner at some point during that afternoon; after their previous heated conversation he reasoned that it would be better if the request came from someone other than himself. If the Colonel asked any questions about the nature or purpose of the invitation, Kenward told his man, he should try to keep the response vague and say that the Superintendent wanted to show him something at the site of the disappearance.

Kenward then set off for Newlands Corner where he helped direct the search, which today would extend as far as the villages of Peaslake and Chilworth. During the morning the usual detritus was unearthed: a discarded piece of lady's underwear (which was discounted as having belonged to Mrs Christie because of its extreme girth); a boy's shoe; a couple of battered footballs; an old, moth-eaten tweed jacket that looked as though it had been worn by a tramp; and a batch of rain-stained love letters between a young servant girl and a local chauffeur. With each new cry from the crowd, with each new discovery, Kenward felt his heart expand and his breathing quicken; each inevitable disappointment manifested itself as a dull ache in the chest.

The Colonel arrived at Newlands Corner just after lunchtime. Kenward watched as Christie, petulant and haughty as ever, stepped from the car, accompanied by Charlotte Fisher, together with her sister, and the family dog.

'Thank you for coming, Colonel,' said Kenward, leading Christie away from the two women. 'I very much appreciate the trouble you've taken to come out this afternoon.'

Christie looked at him askew, unsettled by Kenward's friendly and polite manner.

'You may be wondering why I asked you here this afternoon, but I wanted to apologise. If you feel as though you have been intimidated in any way or placed under any undue pressure then the fault must rest with me.'

As Kenward extended his hand the Colonel nodded his head.

'You must be aware that during the investigation we have to look at all lines of enquiry and, at one point, we had to focus on you.'

'So you are saying that you no longer suspect me to be involved in the disappearance of my wife?'

Kenward looked over his shoulder.

'If it was up to me, I would issue a public statement announcing your innocence,' he whispered. 'But you know how things are.'

'Indeed,' said the Colonel, as the muscles in his face began to relax. 'And what made you change your mind, may I ask?'

'Certain evidence has come to light, which I cannot share with you just at this time, which seems to show that your wife is still alive.'

'Really? But where is she?'

'We are not sure. But I believe we are quite near to finding her.'

'My goodness. What a relief. You have no idea how pleased I am.'

Certainly the Colonel looked like he was genuinely happy to hear the news, but Kenward knew how men, and women too, could dissemble their features to suggest the opposite of what they really felt.

'Must have been a terrible business, what with

the newspapers and their horrible muckraking,' said Kenward.

'Just awful, you can't imagine. I feel like I've been a prisoner for these last few days. I can't go out without a newspaperman trying to get some quote or a snatched photograph. People looking at me as if I am a common murderer.'

'Have you thought about granting an interview? Perhaps that would settle things once and for all. You could get your point of view across to the general public. As I said, we have some information that suggests Mrs Christie is alive, but her whereabouts are unclear. An interview might help draw Mrs Christie out of hiding.'

'I don't know. The way the press twist one's words . . .'

'I know a very trustworthy chap at the *Daily Mail*. Your wife's favourite newspaper, is it not? If she were to read some words from you in that newspaper then perhaps it might help.'

'Perhaps.'

'Anyway, think it over. And as to this afternoon, I thought we might be able to take a walk around the site, see if we find anything.'

'Of course, I will certainly do anything to help.'

The two men started to walk across a ridge of heathland and down a gentle slope that led to a wood. Peter followed behind the Colonel, stopping to sniff at the occasional patch of ground. Apart from the cries of birds and the wind in the trees no sound interrupted the men's conversation. By the time the Superintendent and his suspect reached a stretch of woodland that bordered a chalk pit no one could see them.

'I can't imagine what it must be like out here at night,' said the Colonel. 'To think that my wife was alone here, it doesn't bear thinking about. Anything could have happened to her.'

'Yes, that is what we were worried about.'

'And what makes you think she is alive? I know you can't really say, but could you give me a clue?'

Kenward fell silent.

'Is it a letter? Has she written to you?'

The Superintendent held Christie's gaze and lowered his chin as if to confirm the question, but yet he was careful not to say any more.

'I can't understand what can have come over her. Obviously, I think the episode must be related somehow to her mother's death. As I have told you the loss did strike at the very heart of her. I was talking to a psychiatrist the other day and he told me how bereavement can sometimes bring about loss of memory, what he called total amnesia.'

'The scenario is certainly possible,' said Kenward. 'And if that were the case then perhaps an interview, if it was seen by Mrs Christie, could restore her memory.'

'Do you really think it might help?'

'Look, Christie. I know you hate the press, and I do too in my own way. Have you seen the coverage today? The criticism of our force? It's too much to bear sometimes. But in certain situations one has to face up to the fact that the press can be used to one's advantage.'

The Colonel looked uncertain.

'Look, why don't I put you in touch with this chap from the *Mail* and you can talk things over with him? I will tell him that you haven't made up your mind whether to consent to an interview, but you wanted to meet him first to talk things over.'

'Very well, you may be right.'

'I think so. When I get back to the station I'll make the call. Oh, and just one more thing, if you do decide to talk to the man from the *Mail* could you not mention what I have suggested today? The information about Mrs Christie being alive – it's best if that remains between us for the time being.'

'Yes, very well,' he said. 'Whatever you say.'

Kenward watched as Christie bit the inside of his cheek. He was obviously nervous at the prospect of the interview, and so he should be; his contact at the *Mail*, George Fox, was one of the toughest, most ruthless operators on Fleet Street. Not that he was going to tell the Colonel that.

'Don't worry, I am sure that the interview will bring some positive results,' said Kenward. There was a certain truth to that statement, he thought. He looked up and spotted a group of searchers moving slowly in a line across the brow of the hill. 'Why don't we join those men and see if they've uncovered anything of use?'

Chapter Twenty-six

Rosie knocked gently on my bedroom door and came in with the breakfast tray. I could feel her eyes watching me as I sat up in bed. Did she know my real identity?

'Thank you, dear,' I said, as I poured the tea and then opened that morning's *Daily Mail*.

The girl lingered a moment or so longer than she needed. 'That will be all,' I said and she left the room and closed the door. I turned the pages of the newspaper, but then stopped when I saw page 9. I felt my face redden and my breathing quicken. The silly, stupid fool. What on earth had he been thinking? I couldn't believe the words, nor the ridiculous headline, BELIEF IN VOLUNTARY DISAPPEARANCE, followed by 'Wife's boast that she could disappear'. I tried to read slowly, calmly, but I consumed the words greedily, a paragraph at a time.

'It is quite true that my wife had discussed the possibility of disappearing at will. Some time ago she told her sister, "I could disappear if I wished and set about it carefully."

'They were discussing something that appeared in the papers, I think. That shows the possibility of engineering a disappearance had been running through her mind, probably for the purpose of her work.'

Was he referring to that time Madge and I had been talking about a review of a detective novel that had as its central premise a staged disappearance? I think I had made some throwaway remark about this, of course never intending it to be taken seriously.

'Personally, I feel that is what happened. At any rate, I am buoying myself up with that belief. You see, there are three possible explanations of her disappearance: Voluntarily; Loss of memory; and Suicide.

'I am inclined to the first, although of course it may be loss of memory as a result of her highly nervous state.'

POISON

'I do not believe this is a case of suicide. She never threatened suicide, but if she did contemplate that, I am sure her mind would turn to poison. I do not mean that she has ever discussed the question of taking poison, but that she used poison very largely in her stories.

'I have remonstrated with her in regard to this form of death, but her mind always turned to it. If she wanted to get poison, I am sure she could have done so. She was very clever at getting anything she wanted.'

The damned cheek of it. After all the sacrifices that I had made: living in Styles, a house that he had chosen and which had depressed me ever since we moved there; the set of friends from the golf club, Archie's friends really, whom I had been forced to endure; and the news about the betrayal with a woman I had regarded as, if not a friend (no, certainly not that), part of our circle.

'But against the theory of suicide you have to remember this: if a person intends to end his life he does not take the trouble to go miles away and then remove a heavy coat and walk off into the blue before doing it.

'That is one reason why I do not think my wife has taken her life. She removed her fur coat and put it into the back of the car before she left it, and then I think she probably walked down the hill and off – God knows where. I suggest she walked down the hill because she always hated walking up hill.'

That last sentence made me laugh – how well Archie knew me – but then the laugh changed into a whimper and then a sob. Through a veil of tears I stared at Archie's photograph in the newspaper. That dimple in his chin, his square jaw, his handsome face. I had to admit to myself that I still loved him, still yearned for him even after all he had said, all he had done.

I allowed myself to cry for a couple more minutes, before I wiped my eyes and then splashed my face with cold water. I could not allow myself to be weak, especially not today. I proceeded to dress, gathered my things together and when I looked as presentable as possible – my pale skin was still red and blotchy around the eyes – I dressed and went downstairs for a light breakfast.

When I was eating my toast a member of staff walked over and gave me a letter that had just arrived. The sight of the familiar scrawl turned my stomach and I forced myself to take another sip of tea before opening the envelope.

Dear Mrs Christie

I do hope you are enjoying your stay at the Hydro and that you are finding it to your liking.

I'm afraid that your period of rest and relaxation must face an interruption as no doubt you are aware the week is coming to a close. I do hope everything goes to plan, as we discussed. As you know, if anything does go amiss then there will be consequences.

Once everything has been taken care of I want
you to let me know by placing a notice in The
Times. I thought a simple advertisement, stating
your name, Neele, would suffice; I will leave the
exact wording up to you. As I have stated before I
expect you to burn not only this letter, but also all
my previous correspondence as well as any notes
you may have made relating to this matter.
I wish you all the luck in the world. I doubt
after your task has been completed we will see each
other again. But I will be sure to follow your career
with interest, especially to see whether your recent
experiences influence your writing in any way.
Yours most sincerely
Dr Patrick Kurs

I stuffed the letter into my handbag and made my
way to the station. It was another blustery day and the
cold brought yet more tears to my eyes. I could hardly
comprehend what I was going to do.

As I stepped onto the train I felt as guilty as a
murderer – or at least a murderer cursed with a conscience – and I avoided the gaze of fellow travellers. I
pulled my hat a little further down over my forehead so
as to cast my face in shadow and, after selecting a car-
riage that was empty of people, took out my notebook
from my handbag. I knew that if I made the slightest
mistake I would be responsible for the death of another
human being. I would have committed murder. I wrote

down the procedure in my book once more, hoping that seeing the formula in black and white might make me feel a little better, or at least not so desperately anxious. I thought of the bottle of laudanum hidden in the drawer by my bed back at the hotel; that would offer a more comfortable death than any of the other poisons in my possession. The image of the bottle and its promise of eternal nothingness acted as a balm to calm my nerves. But then I felt a rush of panic: if I did believe in God then taking my own life would result in never-ending damnation.

I was procrastinating, trying to find reasons to stop myself from going ahead with the plan. As I approached the house in Leeds I felt like turning away and taking the train back to Harrogate, but I willed myself on. After all, Kurs could be watching me, or having one of his lackeys follow my every move. I stopped outside the door and forced myself to ring the bell. Flora herself answered the door.

'I've given the maid and the cook the rest of the week off as you suggested,' she said. 'Come in.'

As I stepped into the large, comfortable hallway I noticed that Flora seemed possessed of a new energy. Her eyes sparkled and she talked with an increased vitality. If I did not know otherwise I would have guessed, just by the bloom on her cheek and the carefree way in which she moved, that she had recently fallen in love. But I suspected that Flora's secret lover was none other than death itself.

'I can't wait to get started; I've managed to get the things you asked for. I've got salt to make a saline solution; I got that from my local chemist. He didn't ask a single question, not one. I've also got the various pieces of equipment that you said we would need, the length of tubing and a funnel, and of course we already had a bucket. It really was very straightforward. No trouble at all.'

I suddenly felt terribly depressed; the enthusiasm with which Flora greeted the experiment made me doubt the nature of the whole procedure.

'Flora, listen,' I said. 'I think we need to talk about a couple of things before – if – we start.'

'What do you mean? I don't understand – "if we start". Has anything changed? Has Patrick been in touch? What's happened?'

'Just take a deep breath and calm down for a moment.'

I took her by the hand and led her into the sitting room. Flora had got everything ready: there was a fire blazing at the far end of the room and, on one of the tables, she had arranged all the necessary equipment, a pile of starched white towels, a funnel, a bucket, a length of brown tubing and a bottle of ink, some sheets of white letter-writing paper, and a fountain pen.

'But everything is ready, can't you see? It's all been prepared. I am ready.'

'That's just what concerns me.'

'Excuse me?'

'Flora, I'm worried that you're rushing into this for all the wrong reasons. I know you want to help me, to help save my daughter, and I am eternally grateful for that. But I am distressed by your over-enthusiastic manner. I couldn't live with myself if I thought you were using this to, well, to hasten your own death. I would feel like I would be helping you to commit a sin.'

'I see,' said Flora, taking a deep breath and clasping my cold hands. She looked me directly in the eyes. 'I can promise you that I have every intention of waking up and greeting you as if it were the beginning of a new day. There are things I need to live for, mark my words, things I need to do before I die. I swear on my mother and father's graves, and you know how much I still value their memory, how much they mean to me.'

I believed her; it was impossible not to. 'Very well,' I said. 'But I want to ask you one last time if you are ready to do this. I won't mind in the slightest if you feel you can't go through with it for whatever reason.'

'Mrs Christie, Agatha. I trust you implicitly, you know that.'

'You do realise, as I said before, that there will be certain side effects of the drug, side effects that are likely to be most unpleasant.'

'Yes, I am aware of that and I am ready. But I wholly expect that, after all this is over, to be sitting up in bed and asking you to make me a nice cup of tea.'

I studied Flora's face; she looked much calmer now

and more relaxed and the frenzied mania had disappeared from her eyes.

'And the doctor?' I asked.

'Oh yes, like you said, I've dug up the most incompetent one I could find. A Dr Maxwell. His hands shake – a drink problem, I think. Here are his details.'

After reading the letter I took a couple of deep breaths and then reached into my handbag for the vial of tetrodotoxin. As I did so I was reminded again of that chemist I had known who had told me about carrying around a lump of curare. I had never wanted to find myself in a position where I could decide whether someone should live or die, but then I thought of dear Rosalind. I looked at my watch. It was already half past ten.

'Let's start the preparation,' I said. 'If I carry the tray with the tubing and the funnel would you mind bringing the bucket up to your bedroom? I think that would be the most appropriate place, don't you?'

Flora led me through the house and up the stairs to her bedroom on the first floor. The room was large and comfortable and overlooked the garden at the back of the house, a garden dominated by a large fir tree.

'When I was a girl my father had a swing attached to one of the larger branches of that tree,' said Flora. 'I used to adore it, swinging back and forth, the feeling of air on my face, a sense of weightlessness. That's how I like to think of it – death, I mean. A sense of liberation, freedom.'

I cast her a concerned look.

'But I'm not thinking about that today, I promise.'

'No, I hope not. I've told you a little about the drug that I am going to use, but you must remember that you will be completely conscious throughout.'

'So I will be aware of everything going on around me?'

'Yes, you will be paralysed, of course, and suffer a range of unpleasant side effects, but you will remain quite, quite lucid.'

As Flora sat on the edge of the bed and started to draft her suicide note I ran through the procedure once more, for my benefit as much as hers. As I talked I realised that I had started to detach myself slightly from the task in hand, rather like I had been forced to in my days as a VAD during the war. How little I had known when I had first turned up at the hospital, the old Town Hall in Torquay.

I remembered that drum of dirty dressings and bandages. My first instinct had been to burn the lot of them, but then the sister had told me that once the strips of fabric had been sterilised they could be used again. I recalled the four urns that were located at the end of the ward, pots that contained boiling water from which the nurses made the fomentations. The cry of the sister who continually derided the less able girls as 'only fit to go and see if the crock is boiling' echoed in my ears. I had always feared that one day I would be that very girl. And then there was the time when I had first witnessed an operation. The sight of the flayed flesh, the rancid smell of the open wound, the nasty red smile of the incision had been too much and I had nearly fainted; if it had not been for the swift action of a kind nurse I would have collapsed in theatre and disgraced myself entirely.

I had learnt quickly – I had been forced to – and I found that I had enjoyed the work. Perhaps it was something in my nature; I remember my mother telling me that one of my great-grandmothers had once been a hospital nurse. I realised very early on that I could not allow myself to be emotional; if I went to pieces then I would not be doing the men any favours. Even if my soul was crying out in pain I knew I could not show it; after a while I trained myself to be logical, even a little bit steely. That was what was called for today.

'I'm sure you won't need to use this, but just in case you do,' said Flora, handing me the letter.

'Thank you,' I said. 'Do you want to change into your night clothes? I think it would be for the best.'

I turned my head as Flora began to undress, but from the corner of my eye I caught a glimpse of the woman's shoulder, her smooth alabaster skin, her attractive figure. No one would ever know that her time was limited. How dreadful, what a terrible waste. When Flora had changed into her white lacework nightgown I watched her as she splashed her face with cold water, brushed her hair and climbed into bed.

'If you could make yourself as comfortable as possible. There, that's right. Shall I help you with the pillow?'

'That's very kind,' said Flora, shifting position slightly and loosening the collar of her nightgown.

I returned to the dressing table where I prepared the solution of tetrodotoxin. A little over 25 milligrams of the toxin taken orally was enough to kill a person; a seemingly insignificant drop would prove fatal. I knew that I would have to be able to interpret Flora's symptoms and be ready to act as soon as I thought the woman was in danger. Timing was everything.

I looked at my watch once more – it was now eleven o'clock exactly. I measured out the poison carefully, checked the dosage and checked it again, before I added the water.

'It may taste strange,' I said. 'Now before I pass it to you, are you sure you want to go through with this? There's still time to change your mind.'

'No, I've decided. I'm ready.'

'Very well,' I said. 'As I said, you may feel a number of very odd sensations, but try not to panic. I assure you I have everything under control.'

This last statement was not entirely true, but again it was the kind of thing I used to have to say to the wounded and butchered men I had seen during the war. The words acted as a comfort not only to the patient but to the nurse too.

Twenty minutes after I had administered the drug I started to notice the first symptoms. Flora's fingers rose up to her face as a quantity of saliva formed at the corners of her mouth. Beads of perspiration erupted all over her skin and her breathing had started to quicken.

'I know that although you can't talk you can most probably hear me. Flora, I'm here, it's Agatha. You might start to feel wretched – stomach cramps, nausea, headaches.'

Flora was about to endure a torture that I would not wish on my worst enemy, perhaps not even Kurs himself. And the process had only just begun: the stomach cramps would continue, her skin might take on a bluish tinge, her blood pressure would plunge to dangerously low levels, and she could suffer from seizures, excess sputum production, and respiratory distress. I monitored the woman's pulse and her breathing throughout the procedure, quick to pick up on any change.

'I know you can hear me, Flora,' I said as I wiped her brow. 'I'm not going to let you die.' I repeated the words softly.

As I sat by her, Flora's pulse slowed until it dropped to a level where it seemed non-existent. From my handbag I took out a little compact and placed it over her mouth: the mirror remained unchanged, a sign that would show that she was dead. It was time to call the doctor. I checked Flora once more before I left the room and walked down the stairs to telephone Dr Maxwell. A woman answered who told me that the doctor was with a patient, but would call at the house when he had finished. I gave the address and name of Flora Kurs, and told her that my friend seemed to have fainted. I returned to Flora's bedroom and sat by the bed, watching as the poor woman's body twitched and flapped on the bed like a dying fish on a sun-baked beach. By the time the doctor arrived, the spasms should have stopped and her body would look like that of a corpse.

I looked at my watch. It was now nearly twelve. I left her for a moment and went to the window at the front of the house to see if the doctor had arrived, but there was no sign. From my sleeve I took out a handkerchief and began to twist it over and over again in an effort to relieve the anxiety. I returned to Flora's bedroom to find her body still and lifeless. I knew that the next step in the inevitable progress of the drug was bronchospasm, followed by respiratory failure, coma and then death. I felt Flora's pulse once more. Still nothing. There was not much time left. Where was the fool of a doctor?

Just then there was a knock at the door. I checked the bedroom one last time for anything suspicious – I had safely hidden the tubing, the funnel, the bucket, and of course the vial of poison – and then quickly ran down the stairs. I opened the door to see a man in his sixties with thinning brown hair, reddened face and nose and dark shadows under his eyes.

'Hello – Dr Maxwell, I am here to see Mrs Kurs. Sorry I'm a little—'

'You must come at once. I think Mrs Kurs is – I think it may be too late.'

'What on earth—'

'Please, just hurry.'

'I was told that this was about a woman who had fainted.'

'Yes, she did, but then, oh I don't know. Please help.'

I rushed the doctor through the house and up the stairs to the bedroom. On seeing Flora's inert form lying on the bed Maxwell ran over and immediately took her pulse. With each passing moment the expression on Maxwell's face became graver and graver. Then, from his bag, the doctor took out his stethoscope and listened to the woman's chest.

'I'm afraid there is no hope,' he said finally. 'No, I'm sorry to tell you that she's gone.'

'Oh no, how awful!' I cried. The tears that began to flow down my cheeks were genuine, but their source was not the grief of Flora's passing. The tears were for myself, for what I might yet do.

'Can you tell me what happened? You say she fainted?'

'Yes, we were talking. She was in bed, as she is now. I went downstairs to make a cup of tea and when I returned she had slumped forwards in bed. I looked for some smelling salts, but I couldn't find any. That's when I called you.'

'And had Mrs Kurs been ill?'

'Yes, she had. She wrote me a strange letter asking me to visit. I took the train this morning and I let myself in – she had arranged to send me a key, you see. When I arrived I realised that the servants were not here, I presume she must have dismissed them for the day, and

I found Flora sitting up in bed. We talked for a while. I said she looked a little pale, and then thought a cup of sweet tea might help. And when I came back up from the kitchen she – she—'

'I see,' said Maxwell. 'And do you know anything about the nature of her illness?'

'No, but from the letter I got the impression that it was not good news. Of course, as soon as I received the letter I came at once.'

'Of course,' said Maxwell. 'And why didn't you contact her usual doctor, may I ask?'

'I'm afraid I had no clue who that was. I rang the first doctor I found in the directory, you see.'

'Yes, yes, I see. Well, of course I am going to have to telephone the police.'

I had prepared myself for this. 'Yes, yes, you must. I think the sooner they come the better.'

'Indeed. And do you happen to know who her next of kin is? They will need to be contacted.'

'Yes, her husband, a doctor also. Dr Patrick Kurs, of Rickmansworth, Hertfordshire.'

'Well, I will contact him and tell him the bad news, unless you would rather do that?'

'No, no,' I said, wiping a tear away with a corner of my handkerchief. 'I'm a very old friend of Flora's, but I am afraid I never met her husband. You see for the last few years I've been out of the country.'

'Yes, I see,' said Maxwell. I thought he looked a little strained, as if he were suffering from a particularly bad case of the drinkers' disease, gout. Then he raised his head and stared at me for a few seconds longer than necessary.

'I'm sorry to ask, but you remind me of someone. Have we met somewhere before?'

I felt weak-headed, as if I might faint. 'No, I don't believe we have.'

'Do you live in Leeds?'

'No, as I said, I've been living out of the country, in South Africa.'

'Indeed? That's a long way from Yorkshire.'

'Yes, it is. I've been there since my husband died in the war.'

'I'm sorry to hear that.'

'Perhaps I know a relative of yours, perhaps that is it, Mrs—'

'I doubt it. I don't have any family near here.'

'Is that so?' He stared into the distance, as if by doing so he hoped to reclaim a lost memory. 'And what did you say your name was?'

I knew that it would be unwise to give Maxwell the name I had been using at the Hydro. But what could I say? For a moment, my mind went blank. Then a word came to me, a word from my childhood, quickly followed by an image of a pretty village at the foot of a range of mountains. I was a girl again, on holiday with my parents in France, in the Pyrenees. The whole family was out walking one day when the guide, a kindly man, gave me a present of a butterfly that he had caught. It had been such a pretty little thing – oh the colours on its wings! – but then he had taken a pin and spiked the beautiful creature to my hat. I had been so upset that I had not known what to say or what to do and so I had fallen mute.

'Sorry, I didn't quite catch that.' Maxwell's voice jolted me back to the present.

'Cauterets,' I finally said. 'Mrs Jessica Cauterets.'

Maxwell turned from me and began to walk out of the room. I felt such a great sense of relief that I could have collapsed in a heap on the floor. But then, as Maxwell approached the door, he stopped and addressed me once more.

'I will need to contact Mrs Kurs's usual doctor, of course. Perhaps he might be able to shed some light on the nature of her death. I don't suppose you have the details or whether you might be able to find them for me?'

'I will see if Flora left any record.'

'I'll be downstairs in the sitting room.'

I listened at the door to make sure he had descended the staircase. I rushed across the room, opened my bag and brought out my compact; again the mirror remained clean. I ran my fingers across Flora's cold forehead and held her hands, which were now beginning to turn blue.

Chapter Twenty-seven

Una wondered whether it was wise to go back and see Dr Kurs. She thought about what Davison had said, how he had warned her about placing herself in danger and she certainly wasn't looking forward to the second dose of that tonic. But a doctor was a respectable member of the community. And he had told her that he could give her some background information relating to Mrs Christie and Nancy Neele. Of course, the doctor might not disclose anything of real importance, but, as she had learnt from reading Agatha Christie's novels, sometimes the small details made all the difference. When she arrived at Kurs's house in Rickmansworth she saw that two policemen were leaving.

'Sorry, miss,' said the older man, blocking her way with his outstretched hand. 'You may want to postpone your appointment with the doctor. We've just had to break some bad news to him, I'm afraid.'

'Oh dear,' said Una. 'I hope it's nothing too serious?'

'The worst news a man could get,' said the younger officer.

'Perhaps I should reconsider,' she said, turning away.

As Una started to walk with the constables down the path the figure of Kurs appeared at the door.

'Officers, would you let the lady pass?' he shouted.

What on earth had happened? wondered Una, as she brushed past the two policemen.

'Miss Crowe. Just the person I wanted to see,' he said. There was a certain desperation in his eyes.

'Dr Kurs. Are you all right? The police said you had received some bad news.'

'Yes, it's awful. Come inside and I'll tell you. When I heard the news I gave Mrs Johnston the day off. Of course, she wanted to stay to try and comfort me, but I didn't want her clucking around me like the mother hen she is. Oh, you must think me terribly cruel, Miss Crowe. I hope I don't come across as unkind, but when you hear news like this . . .'

'What happened?'

Kurs led her into his surgery and asked her to take a seat.

'It's my wife, Flora. I'm afraid I have just received news that she is dead.'

'Oh, how terrible. You must be feeling, well, like your world has fallen from under you.'

'Yes, I do rather. We had our difficulties, I must admit, and recently we had been leading rather separate lives due to our geographical differences. Flora lived in the north of England, where she grew up. She never liked living in the south, she said. And of course I had my patients here. I knew she had been ill for a while, but I didn't realise her condition had worsened to the extent that it had. The police told me that ... that she was found dead in her bed this morning.'

Any dislike Una had once felt for him melted away as a wave of sympathy washed over her. Her memory of losing her father was still so raw that the grief was just as painful as it had been when she had first heard the news.

'I'm so terribly, terribly sorry,' she said, tears forming in her eyes. The words were meant for herself just as much as for Kurs.

'Yes, poor Flora. She had a great deal to live for. Such a vital nature, always so happy. That is, until the disease started to eat her away. I will miss her so very much. But listen to me talking about myself. Sometimes I have to remind myself that I am the doctor.'

Kurs stood up and came round to comfort Una who now sat in her chair sobbing.

'I don't know what's come over me. I miss him – Father – so, so much,' she said, wiping her eyes. 'Please, you must forgive me. You must think that I am unbearably selfish. Here you are, you have lost your wife, and all I can do is go on about myself, about the loss of my father eighteen months ago.'

He placed a hand on her shoulder. 'There's nothing to forgive. And please don't try and restrain your emotions. What is that line from Shakespeare? "To weep is to make less the depth of grief."'

'*Henry VI, Part 3*?' said Una, sniffling.

'Yes, very good. I didn't know that—'

'That I have an education? At school they told me I was bright. I got a scholarship to Bedford College, but after Father died, I was so grief-stricken that it was thought best for me not to pursue my education. It did hit me rather hard, my father's death. In many ways, I don't think I will ever get over it. Sorry, you don't want to hear this. It's not an appropriate time.'

Una stood up to go, but Kurs pressed his hand down on her shoulder once more.

'I've got a little plan that might offer some comfort – as an alternative to the tonic.'

'Really?' Una had brightened a little now.

'It's something I have tried with a couple of my patients. They find it has helped them to some extent, it has lessened their grief. And they have been so very kind as to help me because it's something I am researching for a future paper. Perhaps – but no, I suppose this is the wrong time completely. No, please forget I ever mentioned it.'

'If there is anything I could do . . .?'

'In this country we survive on bottling things up, don't you think? Strength and endurance in the face of the utmost difficulty, that's what makes us British. That is all very well and good for those who are strong and can endure, but what about the ones who cannot face the thought of the dawn of the next day? At the moment, I have never been more sympathetic to their case. Poor Flora.'

'And how could I help?'

'As I said, I am in the process of testing a method to help treat those, like you, and now me, afflicted by bereavement. Instead of sweeping things under the carpet, so to speak, and not talking about one's feelings, I suggest that it may be better to focus on the loss, to acknowledge it and let one's emotions come to the fore. It is against the British way of doing things – in fact, I read about the technique and its development from some of my Continental colleagues – and I would be lying if I said some patients found the method too painful. But that is the very point – that is the reason why it is successful.'

'I'm afraid I don't quite understand. How would this involve me?'

'I wondered whether I might be able to test the method on you. I know you have been very badly afflicted by your father's death, but I hope that by exposure to your feelings you might feel better.'

'And how would it work? Is there a drug involved?'

'No, no drug at all. I would simply force you to confront certain things that perhaps you have been trying to avoid.'

'I haven't been able to visit my father's grave in Swanage since he died. Do you mean that?'

'Exactly. In fact, we could start with that very issue.

If you are amenable we could take a trip down to Dorset.'

'But what about your wife? What about—'

'The police say there's nothing I can do for the time being. There will be an autopsy, of course, and that won't be done until the middle of next week at the earliest.'

'I don't know, I'm not sure I am ready.'

'Of course, if you feel you can't help me at this time, then I totally understand. I know you've got that story to work on. I had assumed that I could fill you in on what I do know about the affair on the drive down there. But if you'd rather not, then—'

'I think it's a splendid idea,' said Una, although she had doubts and felt most unsure. 'Just what I need. I'm sure it will do me the world of good.'

'Excellent. I have a few things I need to do in the morning, but shall I see you back here tomorrow in the early afternoon?'

Chapter Twenty-eight

'Yes, thank you, goodbye,' I said as I shut the door on the last of the policemen. What an ordeal. I just hoped that I was still in time. I ran into the kitchen and retrieved the large pot that contained the several pints of saline solution that had now cooled. I carried the pot up the stairs as quickly as I could without spilling too much. I arrived in the bedroom short of breath, my hands shaking. If Flora wasn't dead then surely it was only a matter of minutes before she departed this world: her skin was as cold and white as the marble of an old tomb.

From my bag I wrenched out the length of brown rubber tubing. I dabbed a good knob of butter onto the end of the tube, opened Flora's mouth and quickly fed it down her throat; from experience I had learnt that eighteen inches of tubing was enough to reach the stomach. I arranged Flora in the prone position, so that her head lay over the side of the bed, and then, with the use of the funnel, started to pour the liquid down the tube. After the first pint had gone down I lowered the tube into the bucket that lay on the ground, and the water, together with some of the contents of Flora's stomach, gushed out. I repeated the procedure until I started to see that the liquid was clearing.

'Come on, Flora,' I urged under my breath. I held my friend's hand and squeezed it, willing life into her. But there was still no response. I said a prayer for Flora and then another for myself. It was hard to acknowledge, almost impossible to say the words to myself, but I had committed a murder. The enormity of it was too much to comprehend. How silly of me to think that murder could ever be a source of entertainment. I had made light of it in some of my books. Now I knew the true nature of murder, what it felt like, how its shadow could linger over a life and corrupt and destroy it. I felt like I had been the one to ingest a poison; I could feel a darkness beginning to seep through me, gradually eating away at my soul.

If only those policemen had not stayed so long. They had asked me all sorts of questions about my friendship with Flora, how we had first met, the nature of Flora's illness (of which I had had to plead ignorance), and of course the name of my friend's doctor. On this last point I had begun to panic. I could not allow a competent doctor anywhere near Flora in case they spotted not only signs of life, but also signs of poisoning. And so I had told them that Flora was under the care of her husband. If the police checked with him I was sure that Kurs would understand why I had had to lie. Fortunately both Dr Maxwell, who was looking like he needed his regular mid-afternoon drink, and the police seemed satisfied with my answers and said, on leaving, that they would return at some point over the weekend. They were sure, they said, that Mrs Kurs's husband would be in touch regarding the arrangements. Of course, they added, there would most likely be an autopsy.

As I looked down at Flora's lifeless but still beautiful body, I could not imagine it being defiled by the scalpel of the pathologist. What had I done? There wasn't much more saline solution left, only a pint or so, but I poured it down the tube and then lowered the pipe towards the ground once more. The water, now quite clear, gushed forth from the tube and spilled into the bucket. Then, just as she emitted a terrible groaning sound from deep within her, Flora's chest started to move. A moment later her eyelids began to flutter. I compressed the tubing, withdrew it quickly from her throat and, out of concern for Flora's feelings, hid it and the bucket out of view. Although Flora opened her mouth to speak, she could not utter a word.

'You're back,' I managed to gasp between sobs. 'I thought – that you'd gone. That it was too late. Oh, Flora.'

I wanted to embrace her, but I was conscious that Flora would be weak and probably still in pain. I did not have much time and there was still a great deal to be done.

'Is there anything you need? Water?'

Flora nodded her head weakly.

'Here you are,' I said, supporting the woman's head so she could take a sip. 'Why don't you rest for the next few hours while I get everything ready? Of course, normally I would nurse you here and stay with you. But do you remember I told you that I have to return to Harrogate? Don't worry, I'm not going to abandon you. You're coming with me. I am going to pack a small suitcase for you and tidy up the house.' I wiped the woman's brow. 'To think you went through all that just to help me. I will be eternally grateful, you know that. And one day I mean to repay my debt to you. Thank you.' I took hold of Flora's hand and rubbed some warmth into her fingers. 'I'll light the fire, I think. That should help. And maybe some sweet tea if you can swallow it? You will feel sore for the next few days, but that should wear off.' I watched as Flora opened and closed her mouth to try to say something.

'You want to know about Patrick? Well, the police were going to let him know the news of your death.'

'But, but – after?' she whispered. 'After?'

'You don't need to worry about that,' I said. But Flora was right. There was only so long we could keep this up. At some point, Kurs would discover what we – what I – had done. I did not want to dwell on the terrible revenge he would inflict on me and my family if I did not follow through with the next stage of my plan. In fact, I could hardly bear to contemplate what I knew I had to do.

Just after dusk I drew the dark green velvet curtains; although the house was set back from the road I did not want anyone, particularly any policemen who said they were 'passing' or 'concerned', to see inside. I emptied the contents of the bucket into the bath, making sure that I swilled it with a good quantity of water and bleach. I washed the rubber tubing and placed it back in my bag. I proceeded to pack some clothes for Flora, as well as a few pieces of her nicest, and most expensive, jewellery. At seven o'clock I tried to wake Flora, but I was met, as I knew I would be, by moans and grumbles.

'Flora, you need to wake up. Do you remember what we said? What we agreed?'

The words were met by a curse under her breath; it was obvious Flora was still suffering from the effects of the drug.

'I'm sorry, my dear, I know you want to sleep, and you will. But not here. Not just now. I need you to wake up. When we get to the hotel you can sleep then, you can rest for as long as you wish.'

'No, I need to ...' she said, the rest of the sentence degenerating into nonsense.

I reached into my bag and took out the bottle of smelling salts. I hesitated a moment before I held them under Flora's nose. The woman turned her head violently from side to side to avoid the pungent smell and then started to thrash around but I held the salts firm. Flora retched but there was nothing to bring forth.

'I'm sorry, my dear, but we really do have to get ready to go,' I said. 'Here, let me help.' I sponged my friend's face with a damp cloth and then combed her dank hair. She looked a fright but that hardly mattered. She was alive, a miracle in itself. I pulled off Flora's nightgown, a garment so stained it looked like it needed burning, and slowly I managed to ease her into a kimono. I placed a floppy hat on Flora's head and wrapped a long scarf around it, then slipped a pair of comfortable slippers onto her feet. That would have to do for now.

'Now, place all your weight on me,' I said. 'That's right, one step at a time. Slowly. That's it.'

I directed her out of the bedroom and down the stairs. There were times when the physical demands of the task were too much for me and I had to stop on the stairs and catch my breath.

By the time I had directed Flora into the drawing room and lowered her into a chair, sweat was pouring down my face. I took a moment to catch my breath before I went to use the telephone. I took up the directory and found the numbers that I was looking for. First, I ordered a taxi to take us to the railway station. It would have been more comfortable for Flora to travel all the way to Harrogate by taxi but I knew that that was too risky; when the police realised the 'dead' woman had disappeared they would check with all the taxi firms in Leeds and simply trace her back to the hotel. Although Flora was still incredibly weak, there was a possibility that the physical effort might help revive her.

Then I booked Flora into the Cairn Hotel, which was only a few minutes' walk from my own. I would have preferred her to take a room at the Hydro where I could keep a close eye on her but again this was far from sensible; it was bad enough that reporters were most likely snooping around after me. There was one other thing to do: a notice to be placed in *The Times* that would signal to Kurs that the plan had been carried out. I wrote the words in capital letters: 'FRIENDS AND RELATIVES OF TERESA NEELE, LATE OF SOUTH AFRICA, PLEASE COMMUNICATE. WRITE BOX R 702, THE TIMES, EC4.' I enclosed some money and sealed the letter, which I intended to post at the station.

As I waited for the taxi to arrive I went to make a pot of tea. Then, after helping her drink it – Flora could take no more than a couple of sips of the sweet liquid – I asked my friend if I could borrow a few items from her wardrobe. I selected a hat and a scarf and, standing in front of the glass, I shrouded myself in the same manner as I had disguised Flora. I waited by the front window unable to visualise anything beyond the end of that day. When I saw the lights of the car in the drive I eased Flora up from the chair and supported her to the car. I made sure she was comfortable and then returned to the house to fetch my handbag and Flora's suitcase. Shielding my face I told the driver to take us to the station; we were, I informed him, going to take a late train to London. My sister was not well and needed to be seen by a Harley Street specialist the next day; I hoped the misinformation would be fed to the police.

On the train I let Flora rest, but I kept an eye on her, occasionally testing her pulse to make sure that she wasn't about to retreat within herself again. At Harrogate I helped Flora into another taxi and accompanied her to the Cairn, where I registered my friend under the name of Daphne Flowers. I told the lady behind the desk that my friend had been taken ill on the train from London and that she would not like to be disturbed the next day; I said that I was local and would arrange for my friend to see a doctor. As she was rather sickly and off her food at present I said that I would take care of her dietary requirements. The lady from the hotel assured me that that would be acceptable.

In the room, I put Flora to bed and checked her pulse again; it was getting stronger. I made her drink a little water and told her that I would let her rest now and would return in the morning when I expected my friend to have recovered some of her strength.

'Thank you, my dear, for what you did for me today. It took enormous courage. I will never forget it.'

'I knew you could do it, I knew you could bring me back,' she said softly.

I was curious to ask her questions about what she had

experienced, if anything, but I would leave that until she regained her strength. Now wasn't the time to talk about the shadows of death.

'God bless,' I said, as Flora closed her eyes.

Chapter Twenty-nine

'Have there been any developments today in the press?' Kurs asked Una as they drove away from his house. 'Regarding Mrs Christie, I mean. I've only seen *The Times*, none of the other newspapers.'

'There's one extraordinary claim in the *Daily Mirror,* I think it was, not that I believe any of it. Sounds too far-fetched, I'm afraid.'

'Oh, really? What's that?'

Una related the story that she had read that morning as she had taken the train up from London. The newspaper claimed that the disappearance of Mrs Christie could be linked to the novelist's inability to finish her novel, *The Mystery of the Blue Train*. Surely it was ridiculous, said Una, to suggest that the writer's movements last Friday could be governed by a series of imaginary characters? How preposterous was that! Apparently the story had its roots in an interview with Mrs Hemsley, Colonel Christie's mother, who said that she believed her daughter-in-law was so worried about finishing the novel that she drove to Newlands Corner, where she deliberately ended her life or wandered around in a frenzy until she succumbed to the cold. When Una finished summarising the latest news she turned to the doctor and asked him what he thought.

'Yes, I agree with you, it sounds most unlikely. Most unlikely indeed.'

'So you believe that Mrs Christie is still alive?'

'Oh yes, in fact I know she is.'

The revelation hit Una in the breast with a suddenness that took her breath away. It was a few moments before she felt confident enough to speak without her voice breaking.

'And how do you know that she is alive?'

'Oh, I've seen her,' said Kurs as if it was the most natural thing in the world.

'You've seen Mrs Christie since she disappeared?'

'Oh yes, a number of times.'

The questions that fizzed in Una's brain threatened to spew forth in an unintelligible mess. She took a deep breath.

'And where is she now?'

'I'm going to take you to her.'

'What?' shrieked Una. 'I'm sorry, but I just don't understand.'

'Calm yourself, my dear. Perhaps I should have warned you sooner, but I've been watching you, you see. I suppose you could say I've been testing you.'

'Testing me?'

'Oh, yes. I wanted to see if you were prepared to help me with my little experiment. When you said yes then I realised that you were the one who could be trusted.'

'So we're not going down to Swanage? Down to see my father's grave?'

'Yes, we are. But I've arranged for Mrs Christie to meet us there.'

'Where has she been all week? How did she disappear? Did you help her? Why did she decide to leave her house? What's all behind this? Who—'

'One question at a time, my dear. It's quite simple. Mrs Christie, knowing of my special knowledge, my expertise, in treating those afflicted by grief, came to me when she felt she could no longer cope. I wasn't sure whether she knew that Miss Neele was already in my care, and of course I didn't mention that to her. We worked closely together, using many of the techniques I outlined to you, and she did seem to be improving until finally, when she learnt that her husband had been having an affair with Miss Neele, she experienced a total breakdown. She wanted to end it all, I'm afraid, and I learnt of her plan at the very last minute. Had it not been for my involvement I am sorry to say that she would have been successful. It was all very chaotic, and of course I didn't want to involve Mrs Christie in any kind of scandal, so I arranged for her to spend some time in the home of a colleague, a retired nurse I know who is very trustworthy, and lives in an isolated house on the south Dorset coast.'

'And how is Mrs Christie feeling now?'

'Oh, much better. She is, quite understandably, full of shame about her suicidal thoughts. She can't believe how close she was to ending it all. And, of course, she is embarrassed about the whole stink in the press. I've kept most of it from her, you see, but certain things slip out.'

'And why didn't you tell the police?'

'To begin with Mrs Christie didn't want me to, and then it seemed that too much time had passed. She was also concerned about the damage the revelation would do to her career. She has the highest ambitions, you see, and wants to create a profile as one of the best writers of detective fiction. For that to happen she realises that she needs the support of the public. So we thought that an interview with a sympathetic journalist might win people over.'

'And you chose me?' said Una, tears coming into her eyes.

'Yes, my dear, we chose you.'

'Does Mrs Christie know who I am? I mean how—'

'I've been her eyes and ears. I've filled her in on every detail of our conversations. And I presented her with an assessment of your personality that enabled her to see that you were the very best person for the job.'

'Even though I've never really written anything before? I'm a complete novice, a beginner. Really very much a nobody.'

'Mrs Christie warmed to that. She told me that she always loved an underdog. And she admired your spirit, your sense of adventure. In fact, she told me that she would very much like to meet you with the idea of using you as a heroine in one of her future books.'

'How extraordinary,' said Una, her eyes brightening. 'I don't know what to say.'

'You should be pleased with yourself, and quite rightly so. Many men would kill for what you are going to experience today.'

'I'm sure,' said Una. 'Well, thank you, Dr Kurs. Thank you.'

In the west the sun was already dropping down towards the horizon, casting bright shards of pink and orange light across the landscape. Una had not realised it was so late. What would she do for an hotel? She told herself not to worry, as she was sure that Dr Kurs would have organised something. Perhaps she would stay in the same house as Mrs Christie, and after their talk that evening she could continue the interview the next morning. But she would really have to let her mother know that she would not be returning to Chelsea that night. She asked Dr Kurs, when they reached the next town, whether he wouldn't mind stopping at a telephone box so she could inform her family of her plans. No, she wouldn't tell them exactly where or what she was doing; she would be suitably vague. She would just say she intended to pop round to a friend's house for tea, that she would not be back for supper and would most probably stay the night. The doctor assured her that this was a very good plan.

As the car passed through genteel suburbs into the wilder expanses of countryside, the two continued the drive in silence until Una, unable to contain herself any longer, began to talk. Her words were infused with a barely contained sense of girlish anticipation and excitement.

'This morning, when I awoke, I felt so low in spirits. I think it was the thought of seeing my father's grave. The idea did not sit well with me at all. At breakfast, Mother commented on it and asked why I was looking so miserable.'

'You didn't say?'

'No, I didn't tell them I was meeting you. Anyway, as I was saying, I really felt very depressed this morning, most down in the dumps, but now I feel, oh I don't know, I feel that life could not be better.'

'I'm very pleased to hear that, Miss Crowe.'

Una pictured Mrs Christie sitting on a verandah in a Bergère chaise longue, a tartan blanket over her legs. A rosy-cheeked, well-proportioned matron read to her from a novel of adventure or worked through that day's crossword with her. Occasionally, when the matron was not looking, Mrs Christie would take up a pen and paper and jot down a few thoughts regarding her next novel, before the nurse would gently remonstrate and tell her not to worry her head over such things. Overwork was one of the reasons why she had got herself into this state in the first place. She wondered what the novelist would say to her when they met again; would she even like her? What if she took against her and decided not to tell her anything? But then, she told herself, Mrs Christie needed her; Una was going to act as a conduit through which the novelist could tell her story and hopefully gain the sympathy of the public, a public who could very easily turn against her.

'And is Mrs Christie in a state of mind where she feels comfortable talking to me?' asked Una. 'I would hate to think that this interview brought about any additional stresses.'

'Oh yes. As her clinician I wouldn't do anything to threaten her well-being. Of course, I assessed the situation and actually came to the conclusion that she needed to make a clean breast of it. She needed to tell the truth to herself and to those well-meaning people out there who have been trying to find her.'

'And what about her husband? Should you not inform him?'

'I did indeed present that idea to Mrs Christie, but as soon as I mentioned the Colonel's name she became visibly agitated. It seems now she wants nothing more to do with him.'

'And her daughter?'

'Mrs Christie assumes that the child knows nothing of the matter and hopefully she can resume her relationship with her once all this is over. Once the article, your article, has appeared she intends to take her daughter away with her, somewhere out of the country.'

'I see. And what about you – would you want your name to be mentioned in all this?'

'In an ideal world, I think not.'

'That might prove rather difficult considering that you must have been closely involved in the disappearance. I wonder how we might be able to explain it. Did you push the car down the slope at Newlands Corner? I suppose you must have done. You must have arrived in two separate cars, of course. She stepped out of her car, released the handbrake, you pushed it down the hill then you both drove off in your car. Is that how it happened?'

'More or less. But I will let Mrs Christie give you the details. I think you will probably want to hear the whole incident told in her own words. That would make for much more gripping reading, don't you think?'

'Yes, I can see that. And where did you say we would meet her?'

'The house where she is staying is on the cliffs just outside Swanage. There is a most beautiful view from up there. But I suppose you know the area, don't you?'

'Yes, when we were children my parents always took a house in Studland Bay for the summer. And we had friends with a house in Worth Matravers. It will be odd to go back. Since Father died I have tended to seal all that off, contain it, and I have never felt like going back. I always thought it would be too distressing. In a way, I feared returning, partly because of certain dreams I used to have.'

'What kind of dreams?'

'Oh, the most terribly upsetting nightmares. I can't begin to tell you. But they always ended the same way, with me falling, falling off a cliff.' What she did not tell him was the name of the person who always caught her before she hit the ground: Davison. 'I would inevitably wake the whole house up with my screaming.'

'Well, you don't need to think of that now. You can concentrate on the questions you'd like to put to Mrs Christie.'

'Yes. You know, I am most grateful for this opportunity to prove myself.'

Kurs did not respond, he just turned to her and smiled. But Una noticed that while the muscles of his face moved, and his mouth stretched wide open, his eyes remained steely and cold, like a snake's. Doctors, she surmised, had to be quite unemotional for them to do their jobs. Yes, perhaps that was it.

She took out her notebook and began to scribble. She occasionally saw Dr Kurs cast a glance over at her writing, but she knew that her handwriting was so messy as to be almost indecipherable to anyone but her. Actually that wasn't quite true: Davison was the only other person she knew, apart from her brother, who could read it. She couldn't wait to tell Davison of her latest adventure. What a hoot they would have when she revealed to him that she had secured the scoop of the century!

As the car emerged from a road that cut through a dense forest the sky seemed to open and Una could see, in the distance, a sliver of grey-blue sea. The sense of excitement she'd felt as a girl, as the family travelled down to this same coastline, came back to her. How curious, she thought to herself, that Mrs Christie should have gone into hiding in a place situated so near the rugged cliffs and sandy beaches that she adored and remembered from her childhood. What were the odds of that, she wondered. Perhaps there was such a thing as destiny after all.

'We're not far off now,' said Kurs. 'Just a couple more miles and we will be there.'

The drive had been a long one and, before the meeting with Mrs Christie, Kurs suggested it might be a good idea if they both had clear heads. As long as she did not mind, he could do with a breath of fresh air, and perhaps she would like to join him for a brisk walk. Una, who had always loved walking, especially around the Dorset coast, told him she thought that this was a most splendid plan.

'What is she like, Mrs Christie?' asked Una. 'I mean, she must have the most extraordinary brain to think up the plots of those novels.'

'Oh yes. She is a most unusual woman in many ways. Quite a surprising character. You would never dream that she was capable of – of certain things.'

'Really? What sort of things?'

'I will tell you everything I know in a moment. Let's have that walk, shall we?'

Una waited by the car as Kurs gathered together his things, including his medical bag.

'Why are you bringing that? Is it in case we meet Mrs Christie? But I thought you said we would go for a walk first and then drive to the nurse's house.'

'Oh, this?' said Kurs, gesturing towards his case. 'I never go anywhere without it. It's like another limb to me, I'm afraid. And also it contains everything I need to save a life. One never knows.'

In the distance she could see the peculiarly low saddle roof of the church of St Nicholas; her father lay buried in the graveyard beyond. She wondered if her father's life could have been saved if a doctor had been present. Probably not, she concluded, as he had been suffering from kidney failure for some years. If only Daddy had rested as his doctors had told him he might have been able to enjoy a few more years. 'Indeed,' said Una, wrapping a scarf around her neck to protect her from the biting wind.

'Bracing, isn't it?'

They started to walk across the grassland in the direction of the sea. Una's eyes were drawn to the waves crashing on Old Harry Rocks, the chalk outcrops that lay isolated just off the coastline. She remembered the first time she had seen the enormous stone giants rising from the sea. Her father had pointed out the first stack and told her that it was called St Lucas's Leap, apparently after a greyhound had gone over the cliff while chasing a rabbit. She had imagined the terror of the poor dog as it careered over the edge of the cliff, its paws scrabbling in the air, and she had cried for the loss of the creature, but her father had cheered her up by taking her down to Studland to buy her an ice cream.

'Now, just a few things you should know about Mrs Christie.'

'Oh yes,' said Una, her mood brightening.

'I suppose I may as well tell you the whole story, start at the beginning, just as a novelist would.'

Una went to take out her notebook from her handbag, but Kurs gestured for her to put it away. 'Best if you don't write this down. This is just background information, so you know what's what.'

'I see,' said Una.

'I've been following Mrs Christie's career for a while, but my interest peaked on the publication of *The Murder of Roger Ackroyd*. I take it you've read the book.'

'Of course. I adored it.'

'Yes, I found her portrayal of the character of Dr Sheppard most interesting, and I enjoyed the audacious ending. And it set my mind to thinking what Mrs Christie might be able to do for me.'

'For you?'

'Yes, I could see that she had quite an unusual mind, a mind that was used to dwelling in the darker corners of the human experience. You see, Mrs Christie and I have quite a history.'

Una did not know what to make of that sentence. Surely he wasn't suggesting that they had enjoyed an intimate relationship? The story was getting juicier by the minute.

'I can see I have your interest now, Miss Crowe,' said Kurs.

The doctor and the aspiring journalist had reached the path that skirted the edge of the cliffs and the noise from the crashing waves below meant that both of them had to raise their voices in order to be heard.

'It's such an invigorating spot, don't you think? Standing on the very edge of the country like this. Whenever I come here, or places very much like it, I always feel I could do anything, achieve anything. Do you feel the same, Miss Crowe?'

Una was not quite sure what he meant, but she nodded.

'I feel as though you might have had – might have a very bright future ahead of you.'

It was difficult to hear, what with the roar of the wind and the turbulence of the waves below, but Una was sure that he had said something quite odd. He had spoken about her in the past tense. The realisation felt like a stab in the heart. She stopped and stared at him.

'What did you say?'

'Excuse me?'

'You said something about me, that I might have had a bright future ahead of me, before you corrected yourself.'

'Just a mere slip of the tongue, my dear. As I was saying, about Mrs Christie. You see, what I asked her to do was something quite unconventional and out of the ordinary. My wife Flora, whom I had grown to dislike by this time, had come into a great deal of money from her parents. It would work to my advantage to have Flora out of the picture. Obviously I could not get rid of her myself, as I would end up facing the hangman. And that's when I thought of Mrs Christie and her talent for murder.'

Una could not take in what Kurs was telling her. Surely it was some elaborate joke? 'I don't understand,' she said.

'I asked her to carry out a murder on my behalf. Of course, she put up some resistance, that was quite natural, but then I managed to talk her into it. Let's just say I applied a little gentle persuasion. Mrs Christie used her intimate knowledge of poisons to kill Flora, and did so, I am assuming, without bringing suspicion upon herself.'

'This – this can't be true,' said Una. Suddenly, she felt nauseous and giddy, as if she were out at sea on an unsteady boat. 'I don't believe you.'

'Oh, it's true all right. Do you not remember those policemen who called at my house yesterday to tell me the news of my wife's death? Do you not recall the sad look on their faces? I can assure you it is true. The news had been sent by telegram from Harrogate to the local force, who—'

'Harrogate? So Mrs Christie was in Yorkshire?'

'Oh, yes, all the time. Staying at the Swan Hydropathic Hotel. Do you know it? A first-class establishment, I believe. I'm sure the stay has done her the world of good. She will probably continue to enjoy their hospitality for a few more days before she returns home. Obviously, her marriage is in tatters, but—'

'So Mrs Christie is not here?'

Kurs looked at her as if she were speaking a foreign language that he did not understand.

'In the retired nurse's home outside Swanage?' she asked.

'Oh no. That was just a ruse to get you out here. I knew you wouldn't be able to resist. Curiosity, you see. That was your sin.'

The words of Miss Fromer from boarding school flashed through her mind. She had said something along the same lines to her once.

She focused on what Kurs was saying. Surely this couldn't be true? It must be one of those queer episodes where her mind was unbalanced, just like the one she had experienced after she had learnt of her father's death. She squeezed her eyes shut, but the terror she felt was all too real, and when she opened them again Kurs was standing before her, smiling.

'Curiosity and naivety,' Kurs continued. 'You can't remember, of course, but I discovered everything about you when you came to see me at the surgery. When you were asleep I searched your handbag. Everything I needed to know was there, in your notebook. I couldn't risk you ruining my plan, you see. So much work had gone into it. You do understand, don't you?'

She had to think quickly. No, it wasn't too late. She still had a chance to escape. She took a deep breath and with all her force launched herself forwards, intent on running across the grassland and back towards Swanage. But Kurs was too quick for her. He grabbed her arm and she stumbled, catching her face on a gorse bush.

'Look, you've hurt yourself,' said Kurs, bending down. 'Let's see. Nothing more than a scratch, but painful nevertheless, I should think.'

Una could not bear to look at him or listen to what she now knew to be his sickly compassionate tone of voice.

'Do you believe you are going to get away with this? I mean, the whole thing is quite ridiculous. The police will—'

'The police will do nothing,' snapped Kurs. 'You forget, Mrs Christie is highly unlikely to deliver herself to her local police station and confess to the murder. And there is nobody else who knows anything of the plan.'

'And what about me? Don't you think I—' The rest of her sentence dissolved inside her, the words eaten away by the fear that felt like acid burning from within.

She pushed herself up and bolted forwards again, but Kurs grabbed her ankle and tugged her back towards him with such force it felt as though her leg might be pulled out of the hip socket. From the corner of her eye she saw he had something in his hands. She felt something pull on her left leg, restricting the movement below her ankle. She kicked out with her other foot, hitting him in the face. She felt herself rise forwards once more, she was free to get up and run – she had escaped – but then something jolted her back down to the ground. The smell of the damp earth hit her nostrils.

She turned to see Kurs pulling on a line of green tape, binding her feet together. She kicked out again, but only hit Kurs in the shoulder. Using all the strength in her hands she clawed at his face, scratching his cheek. She struggled to stand up, even though her feet were bound, but a moment later she felt something slam into the side of her head. Kurs hit her again with a small rock just above her right eye. She felt a trickle of warm liquid run down her face and the taste of blood filling her mouth. She turned her head in panic as her vision distorted and blurred. The sound of her breathing – like an animal in a trap – made her scream out. But then something hard hit her around the head once more and she could not move.

As she lost consciousness she slumped back onto the ground. Kurs smoothed down her blue cloth dress that had gathered around her knees and pushed her note-book into his medical bag. He took her slight form in his arms and walked towards the cliff. Una regained her senses just as Kurs dropped her over the edge. She stretched out her arms in a desperate measure to claw herself back towards the side of the cliff. But it was too late. She felt nothing but a terrible emptiness.

She felt herself falling, twisting, tipping, falling further; she heard the fury of the approaching sea, terrifying as it crashed against the jagged rocks below. A series of images flashed through her mind. She thought of Miss Fromer, of that poor dog who had died chasing after a rabbit, of Mrs Christie, and of the taste of that strawberry ice her father had once bought her. Her last thought was for Davison. How would he ever manage without her?

Chapter Thirty

When I arrived at Flora's hotel I was surprised to see my friend in remarkably good spirits. A slight bloom of colour had returned to her cheeks and although she was still very weak Flora said that she felt extraordinarily well considering that she had very nearly died. The joke made her laugh, but I am afraid I could manage no more than a forced smile.

'But it worked!' said Flora. 'You should be pleased. Your trick fooled them all. It was amazing.'

'Yes, I know it did,' I said, flinging my handbag onto the bed.

'What now?' Flora's face darkened. 'Today an undertaker or that doctor will call at the house and they will be suspicious if no one is there. They will contact the police who will no doubt break down the front door to find – to find that what they thought was a dead body has gone missing. It's only a matter of time before Patrick will start to realise that something has gone wrong.'

'Don't worry about that,' I said, trying to sound calmer than I felt. 'You've been through a terrible ordeal. The last thing you need is more distress.'

'Yes, but Agatha, what on earth are we going to do? He's going to come looking for you, for us. Oh no, I can't bear the thought of it.'

I reached across and touched her arm; her skin had begun to feel warmer. I knew exactly what I must do, but I was loath to discuss it with Flora. 'I've got it all planned,' I said.

In that instant, Flora understood what I meant. She did not say anything, but the playfulness with which she had greeted me had disappeared. She swallowed, grasped my hand and nodded.

'You do understand I have no choice but to—' I did not need to complete the rest of the sentence.

'Yes, I do,' she whispered. 'I fear it's the only way.'

'It goes against everything I stand for, everything I believe in. I've tried to think of other possibilities, but there is no way out of this nightmare. I know I may very well suffer for all eternity, but if that is what it takes to save Rosalind then I am prepared.' Tears stung my eyes like little drops of acid. 'I'm sorry, Flora, for involving you in all of this.' I suddenly felt so tired. 'Sometimes I wish I had just killed myself right at the beginning, when Kurs first outlined his plan. It would all have been so much easier.' But would suicide make things better? No, taking my life would achieve nothing. Flora would be left alone having to face a vengeful, dangerous husband; Rosalind would be motherless and would have to live with the shame of it for the rest of her life; my sister Madge would be devastated and the news would probably send my poor brother Monty over the edge.

'Don't talk like that,' she said, closing her eyes. We sat in silence for a moment.

'Are you still feeling the effects of the drug?' I asked.

'I am rather. I'm feeling quite thirsty all of a sudden. Would you mind getting me a glass of water?'

'Oh, I'm sorry,' I said, standing. 'Will you ever be able to forgive me, Flora?'

'There's nothing to forgive,' she said. 'Apart from tardiness in fetching that glass of water.'

'Of course,' I said, trying to force a smile. 'And what about breakfast? Some toast?'

'No, just the water for now, thank you. I'm afraid both taps on the basin over there in the corner are only producing warm or hot water. I don't know what the problem is. Something must have happened to the plumbing. So you'll have to try the bathroom down the hall.'

'Very well, I'll be back in a few minutes,' I said, picking up a glass and leaving the room. I returned to find Flora still lying on the bed where I had left her, but a few red blotches had appeared on her neck and the upper part of her chest. 'Here you are, dear,' I said passing the water to her. 'I do hope you aren't having a reaction.' She looked at me oddly. 'You seem to have developed a little rash on your neck.'

'Oh, that's nothing,' she said, shaking her head. 'A sip of water or two and I will be much better. Actually, you know, I do feel a little tired. Would you forgive me if I went back to sleep?'

'Let me check your pulse.'

Flora held out her wrist as I counted the beats of my friend's heart.

'It is running a little quickly,' I said, looking at her with concern. 'Well, that's better than running too slowly, I suppose.'

'I think I will feel better after a rest.'

'Shall I come back at lunchtime? Perhaps you will feel hungry then? I could bring you something to eat.'

'Thank you. You are really very sweet.'

I was about to ask Flora what she would prefer – an egg sandwich, perhaps, or a plate of something more substantial – when she turned her head away from me and began to fall asleep. As I watched her, I envied her this moment of peace. I doubted that I would ever be able to feel comfortable or at ease with myself ever again.

As I stepped out of the hotel I saw a cluster of men standing around a car, passing a newspaper between them and gesturing towards it in an aggressive fashion. Fearing that the men were newspaper reporters, I pulled my hat down further over my head. I was certain that I heard one of them, a short fellow with a bald head and black moustache, say my name followed by the words, 'She's dead now, that's for certain.' I couldn't catch the rest of the sentence, but it seemed that the discussion centred on whether the death had been a result of suicide or murder. As I passed through the streets full of shoppers, many of them carrying Christmas presents and with faces glowing with joy, I felt as hollow and insubstantial as a shadow. But then, as I turned a corner, I nearly bumped into an old lady with silver hair and intelligent, china-blue eyes. The woman stopped as if she recognised me, but just as she opened her mouth to say something I turned away from her and hurried along, my chin buried in my coat, my eyes lowered. It was obvious that I wasn't as invisible as I felt; I would have to continue to be mindful.

As I entered my room, and took up my notebook once more, I thought about Kurs and how he would have reacted to his wife's 'death'. I imagined the policemen breaking the news to him, the insincere mask of grief that he donned, perhaps even a tear or two, and the sense of pleasure that would have flooded through his body after they had left. No doubt Kurs – who was due to arrive in Leeds to examine the body of his dead wife – thought that his master plan had worked, he had committed the perfect murder. Was there any way I could make him continue to believe that?

I had thought of all sorts of outlandish possibilities: could I go to the hospital in Leeds and steal the corpse of a woman of Flora's age and appearance? No, that would never work. Could I ask Flora to take the poison again and resume her position in her deathbed? I had been lucky in saving my friend once; I doubted whether Flora's body would be strong enough to endure a second dose. Or could I give her a sleeping draught and just hope the attending doctor or undertaker wouldn't look too closely? But what if Flora was carted away in a coffin? What then? I could hardly let my friend be buried alive. I had scored a line through the list of these imagined scenarios. No, none of these preposterous musings would do.

I had known it for some time, but I had been afraid to acknowledge the inevitability of my course of action.

I would have to kill Dr Kurs myself.

Chapter Thirty-one

It was, he already knew from his contacts in Fleet Street, being called 'The Great Sunday Hunt'. It was a snappy enough title, and if this didn't produce results, well, he didn't know what would. Kenward had spent the last two days preparing for yet another search for Mrs Christie. Later that day the press would print appeals for volunteers to come to Newlands Corner and help in the hunt for the missing novelist.

He had already amassed a huge force: if his calculations proved correct there would be fifty-three separate search parties, each headed by a police officer; an omnibus had been drafted in to ferry the volunteers from Guildford to Newlands Corner; search parties would also venture forth from the Clandon Water Works, Coal Kitchen Lane and One Tree Hill; a breeder of bloodhounds had contacted him offering his services in the hope that the dogs would sniff out a trace of Mrs Christie; and the men, thirty or so of them, from the

Duke of Northumberland's estate at Albury had promised to help again. It was their opinion that the novelist had committed suicide and they felt so protective of her body and reputation that they maintained they wanted to be the ones who found her so that they could deal with the situation with dignity and with as little scandal as possible.

Kenward, of course, had a different opinion. Frustratingly, the interview with Colonel Christie in the *Daily Mail* hadn't given him much to go on. Kenward had telephoned George Fox to ask if Christie had behaved suspiciously or said anything odd, but even Fox seemed to have been taken in by the man. If he could just arrest the Colonel and question him properly he was sure he would break. But in order to do that they needed to find a body.

There had been various offers to bring in mediums – he had heard that one newspaper was even running a stunt of this kind in the next day or so – but he didn't want to get involved with any of that nonsense. Some of the stories whizzing around in people's heads were quite extraordinary! He had even heard a suggestion that Mrs Christie had staged her disappearance in a bid to get publicity. There was no denying that all the attention boosted her public profile – he had seen an advertisement in that day's *Daily Mirror*, announcing that tomorrow's *Reynold's Illustrated News* would begin a serialisation of her mystery, *The Murder on the Links* – but surely, nobody, not even the most fame-hungry degenerate, would dream of wasting police time in such a manner.

As he planned the search, and organised the movements of the various interested parties, he was conscious that he did so with all the precision of a military operation. He had always liked detail and order. He would have been much happier if Mrs Christie had disappeared from her own home or a hotel room; in that way one could be methodical about the search and, with luck, one could find some evidence. The problem with the scene of this crime was that it was just so damned huge. Earlier in the day one of his constables, a lad who liked reading and fancied himself as something of an off-duty intellectual, had called the hunt for Mrs Christie an 'epic' feat of organisation. 'You should try your hand at reporting,' Kenward had joked. 'You are wasted in the police force, my boy.' That had got a few laughs in the station. But in truth Kenward did not feel like laughing, not one little bit. Although he would not admit it to anyone, he was beginning to feel like the hunt for Mrs Christie was perhaps a little too ambitious for him.

Not only that, but Captain Sant, the Chief Constable of Surrey Constabulary, had telephoned an hour or so ago and his tone was far from friendly. He was on his way, he said, and would be in Guildford within the hour. There were a few things that he wanted to discuss with Kenward about the direction of the operation. He would, Kenward told himself, have to stay confident; surely, if the men continued to search, they would find something, if not her body then at least some scrap of evidence, some trace, that would help explain the disappearance.

Kenward was on the telephone to one of the officers in the Berkshire force when Captain Sant came into his office; he hadn't expected him quite so soon. It was obvious from the impatient stare he gave him that he expected Kenward to draw the telephone conversation to a close.

'All in place for tomorrow?' said Sant.

'Yes, it's a devil of an operation, but it seems like everything is arranged.'

There was a pause, a pause that made Kenward feel distinctly uncomfortable. Sant cleared his throat.

'I won't lie to you, Kenward,' he said. 'I've had a telephone call from the Home Office. They are beginning to feel anxious about the distinct lack of results. They have also raised questions, justifiably so in my opinion, about the cost of all of this. They tell me that the sum involved is now hundreds and hundreds of pounds and—'

Kenward tried to interrupt, but Captain Sant raised a hand to quieten him. 'And while this is not an issue if the case comes to a satisfactory conclusion it would become a serious problem if we were not to find Mrs Christie. Do you get my drift?'

'Yes, sir,' said Kenward, feeling that all too familiar, uncomfortable pressure around his heart. 'I have every confidence that tomorrow we will find something. It's a matter of continuing, and deepening, the search. Mrs Christie, or some trace of her, is out there, I am sure of it.'

'You are totally confident in that regard?'

'Yes, yes, sir, I am.' Kenward felt anxiety begin to claw at the back of his neck.

'Very well. Let's talk again tomorrow,' said Sant, turning towards the door. 'But I don't need to warn you, Kenward, of the pressure that I am coming under. You've been a good man, you've done splendid work through the years, your work on the Blue Anchor Hotel murder was first rate, but I would hate to see this be your last case.'

Sant left the office before Kenward had a chance to reply. His immediate response was to open his desk drawer and take out the near-empty bottle of whisky. He hesitated for a moment, but then took a couple of swigs, draining the bottle. The peaty amber liquid began to soothe his nerves a little, but a question gnawed within him like some terrible parasite eating into his brain. What would happen if he had been wrong all along?

Chapter Thirty-two

I was sure that my real identity would be discovered at any moment. I had caught Rosie and another of the chambermaids whispering in the corridor and, as they lifted their heads to look at me, they blushed and hid their faces. As I passed through the hotel I felt, or at least imagined that I felt, a hundred pairs of eyes turn in my direction. Although I was hungry, I did not care to sit in the dining room for lunch – that would only mean a greater risk of exposure – and I needed to return to Flora's hotel to check on her. The few hours' extra rest, I was sure, would have done her good, but I was still concerned about Flora's increased pulse rate; that would need to be monitored and brought down if necessary.

As I was about to leave the hotel I heard someone call out my name, or rather my assumed name; each time I heard it I felt a dull ache in my heart, a conjoined pain brought about by Archie's betrayal and Kurs's cruelty.

'Mrs Neele? Mrs Neele?'

I turned to see one of the hotel guests – a small, birdlike woman I knew I had been introduced to but whose name eluded me – gesturing at a well-thumbed newspaper.

'Have you seen the latest? What do you think has happened? Do you have any idea?'

I shook my head.

'I was just saying to Mrs Robson at breakfast this morning that the disappearance of Mrs Christie is most peculiar. There's something very strange about it all.'

I did not know quite what to say.

'I wonder if she has been kidnapped and sold into the white slave trade. You may laugh, Mrs Neele, but it does happen more than one likes to think. Oh, to think of the things that the brutes could be doing to her now.'

As the woman continued to prattle on, I smiled politely, but then the lady stopped and stared at me, open-mouthed. As I turned to go, I felt the sharp peck of the woman's fingers on my arm. 'I say,' said the woman, glancing at the newspaper. 'Don't you look like her? Well, I never. You could be sisters, you could. Has anyone said that to you before? Have they?'

I did my best to react with indifference. 'A couple of people have mentioned it, yes, but I can't see it myself.'

'Have you been following the story in the papers?' the woman trilled. 'Aren't you gripped? Oh, the horror of it all. I mean, it's like something from one of her books, don't you think?'

'I'm sure this Mrs Christie is a very elusive woman, but I don't want to bother with her. I think the newspapers should let her get on with her life, don't you?'

'Ah, so you think she is alive then, do you? That is most interesting, as many of those consulted believe she is—'

I could endure it no longer. I turned on my heels and left the hotel. Really the woman was most insufferable; I would try to avoid her in future. As I made my way to the Cairn Hotel my pace quickened. I felt something was not quite right. Before I got to the room I had the key Flora had given me in my hand. I knocked gently, feeling the sweat prick the back of my neck and the sense of panic in my chest, before pushing the key into the door and turning the lock. The curtains were closed, the room was darkened, and Flora was nowhere to be seen. I pulled off the sheets, blankets and silk eiderdown, even checked underneath the bed and in the wardrobe, but there was no trace of her.

The dash across town, combined with the shock at not finding Flora in her room, had left me breathless. Perhaps a little water would help. I took a glass from the tray on the dressing table, walked over to the basin and reached out to turn on the cold tap. How could I be so stupid? Flora had told me, only a few hours before, that there was a problem with the water supply. As I recalled the scene from that morning, I turned the tap and cold water came gushing forth. A wave of nausea hit me. I had been out of the room for only a minute or so, but of course that would have given Flora enough time.

With my hands still dripping with water I ran across the room and grabbed my handbag. I started to search through its contents – here was my notebook, a compact, a handkerchief, a battered old address book – but I could not see the vial of poison. I lost patience and tipped the handbag upside down, spilling its innards onto the bed. My hands searched through the detritus, but it was obvious. Flora had taken the tetrodotoxin. I leant forwards, my head in my hands, and as I did so I noticed an envelope on the floor with my name written on it. It must have fallen onto the carpet as I stripped back the covers on the bed. I ripped it open and read:

My dear Agatha

I address you as a friend, if I may, even though we have known each other for only a few days. I do not have much time to spare, so please forgive the brevity of this letter.

When I saw you this morning, I realised that you had made up your mind to kill Patrick. I could not let you do this as I knew that such an action would result in your destruction. I knew that if you went through with this plan you would never be able to live with yourself, never free yourself from the dark spectre of murder.

You will know by now that I have decided to take my fate, and the fate of my husband, into

*my own hands. I should have done this at the
beginning, when you first came to me, as it was the
only possible solution to the heinous situation he
involved you in. I ask that you forgive me. I know
what I am about to do is a sin, but is there not such
a thing as the lesser of two evils?*

*I am going to take a train down south today.
I will make my way to Patrick's house in
Rickmansworth, where I intend to bring an end to
all of this. Please do not try to stop me. I realise
this may put you in a difficult position, but you
know in your heart of hearts that this is for the
best.*

Please say a prayer for me.
Yours truly
Flora Kurs

After reading the letter I let it drop into my lap. The
better part of me wanted to try to stop Flora, to telephone her and try to persuade her not to go through
with this. I could contact the police and alert them
to what was going to happen. Perhaps it was a rather
quaint idea, but I was worried about what would
happen to Flora's soul. But then I realised the contra-
dictions in my position; after all, I had been prepared
to carry out the very same act myself.

I stood up, walked across the room and studied
myself in the glass. Had my face always looked like
this or had I acquired the lines around my mouth and

the dark shadows underneath my eyes over the course of the last week or so? If Flora had not taken the lead would I really have gone on and murdered Kurs? Yes, I most probably would have done so. Since meeting the doctor my moral compass had been distorted and tested to its limits. First Kurs had asked me to kill Flora, which I had successfully resisted doing, but I had been forced into a position where I had had no choice but to consider murdering the doctor. I felt distinctly uncomfortable, like something had changed within me, as if a part of my innocence had been taken from me. I had to remind myself that neither I nor Flora had initiated any of this; the fault lay with Kurs and, as such, he would have to bear the consequences. I did not care one jot if Kurs died; my only sadness was for Flora. I thought of the last sentence in her letter. I bowed my head, and with tears rolling down my cheeks, said a silent prayer.

Chapter Thirty-three

She heard a key in the door and then the sound of footsteps in the hall. She felt ready for the encounter, perfectly composed. For years she had feared her husband and what he might do, not just to her but to those close to her. He may not have carried out the physical act of murder himself – he had his lackeys, his pack of degenerates to do that for him – but her conversations with Mrs Christie had shown her the true extent and depth of his evil. It was time to end that once and for all.

After taking the poison from Agatha's handbag, Flora had managed to dress herself and make her way down to the reception desk of the hotel. There, she had paid her bill and, under the guise of Dr Maxwell, had sent a telegram to Kurs, asking him to come and formally identify the body of his wife which would be waiting for him at the house in Leeds. She was sure that he would interpret this telegram as being a coded message sent from Mrs Christie, who could not risk associating herself with the crime. On receiving the telegram, Kurs would need to make sure that any loose ends were tied up. Her husband would want the dead body to be cremated so as to destroy any evidence of the poison within the system: even if Mrs Christie had committed the crime, and not he, there was a risk that she might have a breakdown and confess. Kurs must have left the house in Surrey at dawn and caught an early morning train to the north.

Of course, she had already sent messages to the servants to tell them to take the whole of the week off. She had kept the details vague, but had assured them that she was well and that she was going away for a few days. The break would give them, she hoped, time to do a spot of Christmas shopping, and serve as the perfect opportunity to see any relatives in distant parts of the countryside before the preparations for the festivities began. She said she was planning on having quite a few friends to stay over the period, which would entail a great deal of extra work. The least she could do, she said, was give them a little time off in advance.

A floorboard outside the room creaked and the handle of the door began to turn. Flora checked the tea things on the tray before her were just so and waited for Kurs to enter. In that moment she realised that this was one of the few occasions in recent years when she was actually looking forward to seeing his face. How would he react, she wondered, when he learnt that she had risen from the dead?

His entry into the room was slow and careful, like a cat ready to spring at the slightest threat of danger. Flora watched as the colour disappeared from his face and his black eyes burnt with a dark intensity that she had once found attractive but now only repelled her. He did not move, but stayed paralysed by the door. Then, in an instant, he recovered his senses and stepped towards her. As he came closer Flora noticed that he had a scratch on his face.

'I'm not surprised to find you here at all,' he said coldly.

'You're not?' said Flora, as lightly as if she were referring to his decision not to take marmalade with his breakfast toast.

'I suppose this is all Mrs Christie's work,' he said. 'I thought better of her, I really did.'

'You honestly thought she would go ahead and kill me?'

Kurs did not answer the question.

'I had to lie to her, to tell her that I was dying, in order for her to even consider taking the risk. She is a good woman, Patrick.'

'She's not as good as you think,' he hissed. 'Anyway, she will just have to take the blame for it.'

Flora knew what he was referring to, but she forced herself to ask the question. 'The blame for what?'

'For your death, of course. I can't let her get away

with this. But as far as I am aware, and please correct me if I am wrong, you have already been pronounced dead by a doctor, and your corpse has been seen by policemen. That's what I was told when the police came to my house.'

'Yes, that's right. But—'

'Well, so you see. All I need to do is to kill you, place you back in bed, and then when I am ready call the undertaker to cart you away. I would have thought whatever poison Mrs Christie gave you – I wonder what it was, you don't happen to know, do you?'

'No, no, I don't.'

'Never mind,' said Kurs, taking a seat opposite her. 'Well, whatever toxic substance she administered is likely to still be in your system. The pathologist will do a post-mortem, find the traces of the poison, and Mrs Christie will be arrested for your murder. I did tell her that this could be avoided, but she wouldn't listen. The public will be thrilled to learn the lurid details of how a detective novelist turned to murder. Now that will make for interesting reading.'

Flora looked at Kurs now not with hatred, but with a kind of deep sympathy. Tears formed in her eyes as she remembered their wedding day and the smell of the honeysuckle that lingered in the night air outside their window on their honeymoon at that sweet little hotel in Cornwall.

'And how do you expect to do it? To kill me, I mean?'

'I'm not sure yet. Do you have a preference?'

The coldness of the question leached the pity from her heart. She couldn't bear to look at him for one minute longer.

'Would you like some tea? You must have had a long journey.'

'To share one last cup of warming tea with my long-suffering wife. Yes, that would be nice.'

Flora glanced at the tray. 'Would you mind bringing some milk? I believe there is some in the pantry. As you can see I gave the servants some time off.'

Kurs's eyes narrowed with suspicion. He looked at the tea tray, with its fine china cups and saucers decorated with small pink flowers, set out on the table before him. He picked up a teacup carefully, examined it and rolled it about in his hands with a certain tenderness, before replacing it on the saucer and doing the same with the other.

'I think I will take my tea black, if you don't mind.'

Flora tried to swallow but her mouth felt parched and dry. 'Very well,' she said, failing to disguise the terror in her voice. As she poured the tea her hands shook and she spilled a little of the liquid onto the tray.

'I know what you are trying to do, Flora. I can see that you are nervous, and quite right, you should be. To think that you could fool me by asking me to go and get some milk from the pantry. As if I would fall for that, silly girl.' He made a series of slow tutting noises. 'Out of interest, you must tell me how she did it. She gave you some sleeping draught that made you look like you were dead? Extraordinary that she fooled the doctor, though. I wonder what she used. Are you sure you can't remember?'

Flora shook her head and passed a teacup to Kurs.

'It can't have been an ordinary opiate, I don't suppose. No, more likely to be something exotic. How intriguing. When I get back I must consult my dictionary of poisons. Or I suppose I could always visit Mrs Christie in jail before she is hanged.'

'Can I ask you something before, well before . . .?'

'Of course,' said Kurs, taking a sip of black tea. 'I don't believe there should be secrets between man and wife, especially at a moment such as this.'

'Am I right in thinking it was you who was behind the death of my parents in that car accident?'

'Yes, you are correct. It was easy enough to organise if you know the right kind of people. You must admit that they were getting on and I spared them a great deal of suffering and the indignities that inevitably come with serious illness.'

Flora stopped herself from lashing out at him, but she could not control the words that spat out of her mouth. 'But you've never actually carried out a murder yourself, you coward.'

'You are quite wrong, my dear. You see, only yesterday I disposed of a young lady who turned out to be quite troublesome, an aspiring journalist who was asking too many questions. She was sweet and rather bright, from a terribly grand family, and put up quite a fight at the end as you can see.' He pointed at the scratch on his cheek, but as he did so his hand stopped. It was, Flora thought, almost as if a sculptor had turned him into marble. 'What have you done?' His voice was quiet but full of fury. 'Flora?'

'Well, you wanted to know what Mrs Christie had given me. I thought I'd give you a taste of it so you could experience it for yourself. The poison in question is called tetrodotoxin – am I pronouncing that correctly? – and I believe it originates in tropical puffer fish. Quite an unusual poison in many respects. Mrs Christie told me about a very interesting case described in the log of Captain James Cook, but I don't believe you will live to be able to read about it.

'I can see that you are worried about the lack of feeling in your lips. That's the least troubling symptom, let me tell you. Soon you will begin to experience an excess of salivation, followed by – and listen carefully, as a medical man you will fully understand the implications of what I am going to tell you – perspiration, weakness, nausea, diarrhoea, paralysis, tremor, aphonia, dyspnoea, dysphagia, convulsions, bronchorrhoea, bronchospasm, respiratory failure, coma and, finally ... death.'

A silence settled over the room as the couple stared at one another. Kurs did not move – Flora wondered whether the paralysis had already begun to affect his body – but then suddenly he stood up, dashing his cup to the floor. A shard of shattered china whizzed across the room, slashing into her ankle. The liquid splashed onto the bottom of her dress and a dark bloom, a mix of blood and tea, began to spread across the white fabric. He came towards her with outstretched hands, knocking the contents of the tray and the teapot that contained the poison onto the floor. He grabbed her neck and started to squeeze.

'It – it doesn't matter,' she managed to whisper. 'I've taken it too. I know what to expect. I'm – I'm ready to die.'

Her words did not stop him from pressing harder around her neck. As she felt his hands dig deeper into her skin and tighten around her throat so as to constrict the flow of air to her brain she did not fight or struggle. After all, death by strangulation would be preferable to the terrible fate she would have to otherwise endure.

She had one last thing she wanted to tell him before it was all over, but she could not get the words out. She felt her eyes bulging in her face, and thought she might be swallowing her tongue. Surely it would be over any moment now. But then she felt Patrick's hands loosen and he collapsed backwards onto the floor. Through a haze of tears she saw her husband's body shake with a terrible force. She fell back onto the sofa with a mixture of relief and disappointment. The drug would kill him, she was certain of that, as the teapot had contained in excess of the fatal quantities of the poison. Yet she was sad that Patrick had not had the strength to finish her off quickly. She would have to die the same terrible death as him: long, painful, and conscious to the very, very end.

Chapter Thirty-four

My sleep was broken by nightmares, horrible visions of Flora and Kurs. In one dream she tried to poison him, only for Kurs to outwit her; after smashing the vial from her hand he grabbed her by the throat and squeezed every last breath from her. In another she succeeded in killing him, but was cast down to hell for her actions; as she felt the flames lick her ankles she called out my name, cursing me for what I had forced her to do. I awoke to feel the sting of my conscience spreading through my body like a nasty poison. Logically, I knew that Flora's plan had been the best one – there was little point trying to persuade her out of it and I knew that she did not have long to live – yet that did not make me feel any better. I felt sick, sick both in mind and in body.

When Rosie set down my breakfast tray I turned my face away to avoid the smell of the toast and butter.

When I raised my head to apologise for my lack of appetite she did not meet my eye, almost as if she were ashamed of something. Despite the shadow of guilt that was leaving its dark stain upon me I adopted a false, friendly manner and tried to engage her in light conversation. But her air of general joviality had been replaced by a hardened shell. The realisation came to me in an instant: it was obvious Rosie had finally told someone of the real identity of the woman in Room 105. As soon as the girl left the room I felt the familiar bird of panic flutter in my breast.

Last night I had seen two of the bandsmen looking at me in an odd manner. Later, after dinner, as I was on the way back to my room, I had caught a glimpse of the musicians talking to two other men who were obviously from the police but not in uniform. I could tell because one of them had the eyes of a man who had seen some terrible things and who clearly thought the worst of everyone. The other had a little pencil, the kind of thing constables used for the purpose of taking notes, poking out of the top of his trouser pocket.

I took up that morning's paper in a bid to try to distract myself from the inevitable, but there I was, my name spread across the pages like a nasty rash. The newspaper was full of lurid details of what was now being called 'The Great Sunday Hunt'. There was even some nonsense about how Arthur Conan Doyle had given one of my gloves to a medium in the hope that the spirit world could help pinpoint my whereabouts.

The whole thing made me quite angry – what was he doing with one of my gloves? – and I was just about to turn the page in disgust when my eye fell on a name that I recognised: Una Crowe, the girl I had met with Davison in London that day. The report stated that Miss Crowe, who was only twenty, had disappeared from her house in Chelsea on Saturday. The young woman had been suffering, or so the family said, from melancholia following her father's death and they were worried for her safety. There had been times, at my lowest moments following my mother's death, when I had been tempted to give in to the darkness. Had I not had Rosalind, and to some extent Peter, perhaps I might have chosen to end it all? Is that what poor Miss Crowe had done? I cut out the story and put it in the back of one of my notebooks.

I continued to turn the pages, pages that were thankfully free of any mention of me. I read about a police visit to the Kit-Cat Club; the recovery of a precious fourteenth-century manuscript that had been stolen by thieves in France; the imminent death of the Japanese Emperor, who had been critically ill for some time; and a police chase of two suspected cat burglars across the rooftops of central London. Then, as I turned the page, a familiar name jumped out at me.

DEATH OF DOCTOR AND WIFE

Couple found in Leeds

Police discovered the bodies of Dr Patrick Kurs, a medical practitioner from Rickmansworth, and his wife, Flora, in a house in Leeds yesterday. Detectives say that the bodies of the husband and wife were found in a house in Calverley Lane. Although the situation is far from clear some reports suggest that Flora Kurs died on Saturday and that Dr Kurs took his own life after learning of his wife's death.

Detectives suggest that the doctor arrived at the house yesterday and discovered his wife's body in bed. As the two bodies were found in the sitting room of the house it is thought that he must have moved his wife downstairs and killed himself yesterday in a fit of grief. The Leeds Constabulary are appealing for a lady thought to be in her thirties, a friend of the family who was believed to be with Flora Kurs at the time of her death, to contact them.

Initially, I read the story with a certain numbness, as if I had no personal connection with it whatsoever. Kurs was dead. The nightmarish ordeal was over. Instead of travelling south, as she had told me, Flora had simply returned to the house in Leeds. That had been my plan too – to meet Kurs at Flora's house, where he was due to inspect her body. There, I would have tried to poison him, most probably with something that would leave little trace. Flora had relieved me of that ghastly task; in many ways she had saved me. How could I have carried on being a woman, a mother, knowing that I had taken someone's life, even someone as vile as Kurs? I knew I should have felt elated at the news of Kurs's death – like I should shout it out from the window of my hotel room – but instead I only felt hollow and empty.

The truth was an innocent woman had died because of me. As I thought of dear Flora tears welled in my eyes and began to stream down my face. She had been so kind. And such an awful way to die. That damned *Roger Ackroyd*. If I had never written that book none of this would have happened. After all, Kurs had told me that it was that novel in particular, with its doctor narrator, that had sparked his sinister interest in me. Perhaps it would be better if I gave up writing altogether. The idea was laughable, I realised, as I might not have a choice; I had not been able to write anything half decent since my mother's death. My thoughts were interrupted by a knock at the door. It was Rosie who said that she had returned to collect the breakfast tray. I wiped the tears from my face. Now I was the one who could not meet her eye.

'Not so hungry today, ma'am?' she said as she picked up my tray. I sensed the embarrassment in her voice.

'No, not so much,' I said, trying not to sniff too loudly.

I did not know what to say and so we fell into silence. She slipped out of the room soon after. It was obvious that the game, as they say, was up. Perhaps later, when I went downstairs, I would find Archie waiting for me in the lounge. What on earth would I say to him? I could hardly tell him the truth. I could never associate myself with the death of Kurs and his wife in case I might be implicated. No, I would have to invent some kind of story that would explain my strange behaviour; whether people believed it or not was another thing altogether. I had once read somewhere of a woman who had gone missing after she had lost her memory. Yes, I could use that. I would maintain that I had suffered from an attack of amnesia. I would not be able to remember how I had disappeared nor how I had made my way from Berkshire to Harrogate. I would say and say again, until I was quite blue in the face, that I had been in a daze and at a loss to know what I had been doing in the northern spa town. But what of the letters that I had sent? I would deny all memory of them. Had I not read the stories of my disappearance in the newspapers? they would ask. I had seen them, yes, but I assumed that they were talking of some other lady. I would say that I had recognised the woman in the photographs, but when I stared at the newspapers it was as though I had been looking at a picture of an acquaintance, someone I knew vaguely or had met once or twice, a person I could not name.

I would maintain that I must have been suffering

332

from a terrible attack of nerves, brought on by my mother's death and the problems with my writing. After all, so much of this was true: I had been feeling terribly depressed about quite a few things. And what of the choice of name, Mrs Teresa Neele? Why had I chosen that? I would try to avoid that question, as the last thing I wanted was to bring scandal on the family, but if forced I would say that I must have heard the name mentioned somewhere, perhaps by my husband.

My one thought was for Rosalind, to make sure she was safe. I ached for her with a deep yearning, something more primitive and elemental than the need I had once felt for Archie. I just hoped the furore would soon be over. Part of me wanted to waltz downstairs and exclaim my identity, but I knew such a course of action would be unwise. No, it would be better to pretend that I was still suffering from amnesia until the authorities or the police or a stranger approached me. Until then, I would try to behave a little queerly when in public. That, I said to myself with a grimace, should come quite easily.

Chapter Thirty-five

Kenward was on the telephone to the man from the *Daily Mirror* when Sant walked into his office. He had spent the day trying to explain to a legion of journalists why Sunday's search had failed to unearth anything significant; the last thing he needed was another interrogation from his boss. He could see that Sant wanted him to bring the conversation to a close, but he had only just begun the interview. Kenward brought up his hand to signal that he would only be on the telephone for one minute more, a gesture that was met with a withering stare from Sant.

'You can take it from me that Mrs Christie will be found near Newlands Corner dead or alive,' Kenward said to the reporter. 'If she were in London or elsewhere undoubtedly she would have written, probably anonymously, to stop the search. We are so sure of ultimate success that from Wednesday an intensive, week-long search will be made over an area of forty miles.' Sant moved around Kenward's desk and came to stand behind him. Kenward could hear his superior breathing heavily, a noise that made him feel distinctly uncomfortable. 'Sorry, I've got to go. Can I telephone you back? Yes, good. Let's talk again in fifteen minutes. Goodbye.'

Kenward hardly had time to place the receiver back down on the telephone when Sant exploded.

'Another search? On Wednesday? Are you out of your mind?'

'But it's the only way forward, surely.'

'Forty miles? Which will take a week? What are you thinking?'

'Sir, let me explain the reasoning. If Mrs Christie was still alive then—'

'Yes, I heard you, then surely she would have contacted us. Perhaps, but not necessarily. What if she is dead, which is still open to question by the way, but her body is lying in some garage in Guildford or Camberley or God knows where? Have you thought of that?'

'If that is the case, sir, I am convinced that we will find some evidence that will lead us to that conclusion.'

'I don't think you realise the seriousness of the position. The future and reputation of the whole Surrey Constabulary is at stake here, don't you see?' Sant's voice had quietened now, but it had taken on an icy quality that chilled Kenward. 'I had another telephone call from the Home Office this morning. They had been assured that the resources we were expending were being put to good use and would guarantee a result. Now, am I to understand that not only did the so-called "Great Sunday Hunt" prove absolutely worthless, but also you intend to initiate another search, an even bigger search?'

'Yes, that's right, sir, but if you will let me explain—'

'I doubt there is anything you will say that will convince me of the rightness of your actions. Really, Kenward, this has got to stop. You're making yourself, and the force, a laughing stock.'

'But it won't cost that much more money. I have been pledged the help of eighty members of the Aldershot Motorcycle Club, and a London company has offered me the help of a diver to search the deeper pools around Newlands Corner. And we can draft in more volunteers, more people to help. You saw how The Hunt sparked the imagination of the general public. There were thousands who turned up yesterday. If we can just continue to tap into that then I am convinced we will find the clue that has so far eluded us. It would be foolish and short-sighted to give up now. What happens if we abandon the operation and then next week a dog walker stumbles across the body of Mrs Christie lying in some bracken or hanging from a tree? I can guarantee you then we will be the laughing stock of the nation.'

Sant hesitated for a moment while he considered the argument. 'I don't know whether to admire or pity your stubbornness, Kenward,' he said, mellowing a little. 'I must give you credit for determination, if nothing else. Very well, Wednesday it is then. But only for an operation that lasts another few days – a week is totally out of the question. And try and use as much volunteer force as possible. I don't want this to end with questions being asked in Parliament and I am certain you don't either.'

'Thank you, sir. You won't regret it.'

Captain Sant left the room without further comment. Kenward telephoned the reporter from the *Mirror* and halfway through the interview, just as he was detailing the specifics of the operation – which would focus on searching the Downs from Newlands Corner to Ranmore Common near Dorking and would also include areas such as Albury and Hurtwood – a constable placed a telegram on his desk. It was from his colleagues in the West Riding Police.

Kenward felt a shock run through him as he read that they had spotted Mrs Christie in Harrogate. She had been staying at the Swan Hydropathic Hotel there for the past ten days. What utter nonsense! He refused to believe it and pushed it to one side, firmly consigning it to the ever-increasing pile of miscellaneous sightings, mediumistic interventions and general crackpot theories. He wound down the conversation with the chap from the *Mirror*, hoping that the interview and others like them that he had done that day would go some way to avoid an impending public relations disaster. It was vitally important that he kept the people on his side. Out of habit his hand moved towards his desk drawer and although he was desperate for a drink, he managed to resist. With Sant on the warpath he needed to keep his wits about him.

Over dinner, Kenward regaled his wife with news of the meeting he had had with Sant.

'He's all bluster, that one,' she said. 'It's obvious he thinks very highly of you, but cannot bring himself to tell you. That's my opinion anyway.'

'Do you think so?' said Kenward in a self-satisfied manner. He was surprised, and more than a little pleased, with the way he had managed to turn the conversation round. 'You'll never guess the latest lunacy,' he laughed. 'I'm warning you, it's a good one.'

'What?' said Naomi.

'Just as I was finishing up the interview with the *Mirror*, Hughes knocked on my door and placed a wire on my desk. It said – wait for this – that Mrs Christie had been seen at a spa hotel in Harrogate!'

'Harrogate?'

'I know. It's so absurd it's laughable. As if she could have been swanning around a smart hotel in the north of England for the past ten days or so. At least it raised a chuckle.'

'I bet it did,' said Naomi, laughing. 'So what are you going to do?'

'Do? Why, nothing of course.'

'Quite right, dear,' said Naomi. 'Quite right.'

Chapter Thirty-six

When would it happen? When would I feel the soft touch of a stranger on my shoulder or hear a voice behind me whispering my name? I imagined that they would speak softly because they might be fearful that a forceful exclamation would cause greater distress. I could just imagine the kind of gibberish spouted by a psychiatrist, stuff and nonsense about the fragmentation of my personality and confusion of identity. Of course, I could play along with this very well indeed: a slightly neurotic, highly strung novelist with a propensity for losing herself in her characters who, after suffering a bereavement and the pain of infidelity, has a mental breakdown and experiences an episode of amnesia. Yes, that would do very nicely indeed.

I just hoped that there weren't any crime-fiction aficionados among the detectives who would soon interrogate me; after all, I had written about amnesia before, and the mysterious Jane Finn in *The Secret*

Adversary had pretended to suffer from memory loss in a bid to outwit her enemies.

I knew the moment of revelation would be soon, perhaps within a matter of hours. The night before, on returning to my room after dinner, I had realised that a few of my belongings had been moved. The change was hardly noticeable; certainly the man or men who had been in my room – the faint smell of tobacco lingered in the air – would not have been able to discern any difference. But the feminine eye picked up on these things. The police had altered, albeit ever so slightly, the position of my hairbrush on the dresser and the angle of the detective novel by my bedside. No doubt they would have been able to verify my identity from the small, framed photograph of Rosalind with her nickname 'Teddy' scrawled across it.

Of course, I had been careful to carry my notebook in my handbag; I didn't want anyone looking through that. At the first opportunity I would burn it. Not only did it contain detailed plans on how to poison Flora and kill Kurs – information which would lead to my arrest for the deaths of the couple – but I had used it as a repository for my thoughts on a number of other intimate subjects regarding my feelings for both Archie and Nancy Neele. It also contained my notes for *The Murder of Roger Ackroyd*; it would be desperately sad to see them go up in flames, but that could not be helped.

I spent the day in awful contemplation, reading *The Phantom Train*, a rather silly novel but perfect for taking my mind off the inevitable. I only ventured out of my room for meals and the occasional tour of the main rooms of the hotel where I kept my eyes open for suspicious individuals. After a rather late lunch, just as I was walking through the lounge to return to my room, I saw a man in a dark suit reading a newspaper. I thought I had gone some way to prepare myself mentally for the horrors of what was to come, but there was something so ghastly about seeing myself on the front page that I felt nauseous and weak and I had to steady myself by putting my hand on a brown leather armchair. MRS CHRISTIE SAID TO BE IN HARROGATE, then 'Husband of missing novelist leaves for the north to investigate', it read. So Archie was on his way. Would he be fooled by my story? Perhaps not; well, it hardly mattered now.

Back in my room, just as I was getting a little bored of *The Phantom Train*, I heard a quiet knock at my door. Surely Archie could not have arrived already?

'Hello?' I said as I moved towards the door.

'Mrs Christie,' a voice whispered. 'It's Davison – John Davison. I met you in London recently.'

What on earth was he doing here? 'Please open your door – I may not have much time,' he said.

Could I trust him? As my hand hesitated on the door handle I noticed my fingers were shaking.

'You aren't in trouble, I promise. I've got some bad news, I'm afraid.'

Oh no, had something happened to Archie or to Rosalind? Had Kurs put into action a grotesque plan from beyond the grave, a plan carried out by his associates, his degenerate friends? Please God, let my husband and daughter be safe. I opened the door to see a different Davison from the one I had met in London. All his vibrancy had been sucked out of him, his elegant sheen had disappeared, his eyes were bloodshot, and his skin seemed pale as if he had not slept for days.

'What's the matter? Please tell me it's not—'

'No, your family are quite safe,' he said, walking into the room.

'You're certain?'

'Yes, I am.'

'What on earth is the matter?' I searched my brain. Could it be Charlotte? Or had he come to tell me something that I already knew: Flora was dead? But why would he connect me with her?

'Could I trouble you for a glass of water? I'm sorry, it's just that I've just come from—'

At this his voice faltered. He placed a fist over his mouth to stifle a cry.

'Oh my, of course,' I said, fetching him some water. 'And please do sit down.'

Davison sat in the armchair by the window as he tried to compose himself. He took a sip of water and cleared his throat.

'I've just come from Leeds, you see. From the house where the bodies of Dr and Mrs Kurs were found.'

He waited for my reaction. Just what did he know? And why was he upset by the deaths of Patrick and

Flora Kurs? Surely he could not have known them? Was this the man that Kurs had mentioned to me? The one who was capable of doing those unutterable things?

'Yes, I read about the deaths in the newspaper,' I said, trying to make my statement as unemotional as possible. 'But I don't see how this has anything to do with me.'

Davison stared at me coldly. 'Do you remember Miss Crowe? The girl I was with that day I met you in London?'

'Yes, I read—'

'That she disappeared, yes. We've been searching for her everywhere, but to no avail. But now I'm afraid we fear the very worst.'

'What do you mean?'

'At first we thought she might have gone off and done something stupid. You know her father's death really did hit her very hard. That prospect was bad enough. But then the police contacted me to tell me that they had found a notebook of Una's in Kurs's possession.' He watched my face to gauge my reaction. 'It seems that the two were acquainted.'

'But how?'

'It was my fault, if only I hadn't encouraged her,' he said, his face colouring with anger. 'Why did I even suggest such a thing?'

'What do you mean?'

'When you went missing I suggested to Una that she look into your disappearance. She wanted to make her

343

name as a journalist, you see. And I thought this would take her mind off the death of her father. It was supposed to be a bit of light relief for her, a diversion,' he said, pronouncing the last word with contempt.

The sudden realisation was almost too much to bear. I felt my face stiffen into a horrifying mask, like something from a Greek tragedy. 'So she was on – on my trail?'

'Yes, yes, she was.'

'And you suspect Kurs of—'

'Murder.' The word seemed to infect the room with an airborne poison. 'She told me that she was going to see Miss Neele's doctor, but I thought nothing of it. Of course, I warned her not to take any risks, but ...' He paused and took a deep breath. 'From what I can gather it seems that Kurs lured her to Dorset with the prospect of introducing her to you – he promised her some kind of interview – and it's most probable that he killed her there. There is a search under way at the moment, but of course the sea may have carried her off and ...' His voice failed him.

The thought of that innocent young creature with that monster.

'My God, the evil of that man.' But how much did Davison know about my involvement with the doctor? 'It's all too wretched,' I said, trying to find a moment to think. I walked over and placed my hand on his shoulder. 'Were you very close?'

'Like brother and sister – or perhaps even closer,' said

Davison, spitting out the words and fighting back tears. 'I'm sorry – it's very unmanly of me, I know.'

'Not in the least,' I said. 'In fact, I think it shows strength rather than weakness.'

He bit his lip and swallowed. 'But what I don't understand is what kind of hold Kurs had over you.'

'I'm afraid I don't quite grasp what you are saying. I've – I've been suffering from nervous exhaustion.'

'I don't doubt it, but I am sure that Kurs played some part in all of this, in your so-called disappearance. It seems Una certainly thought so. Doing what you did – leaving your car like that near Newlands Corner and vanishing without a trace is completely out of character. It drove the police force to distraction and has ruined the reputation of one of Surrey's best men. Kenward will have to be gradually eased out, poor chap.'

I remained silent.

'You do realise that at some point I will need to know everything,' said Davison, clearing his throat. 'But I understand that here is hardly the time or the place, as I believe your husband is on his way to see you.' He looked at his watch, stood up and from his inside jacket pocket took out another card. It could join its partner in the inside pocket of my handbag. 'I am sure that with our help you will be able to keep this out of the press.'

I felt another wave of panic seize me. 'You don't mean that all of – of what happened will be reported in the newspapers?' I had seen the horrific coverage of my disappearance. What on earth would the papers make of the plot involving Kurs and his wife? I was not strong enough to think of the consequences.

'Don't worry. If you answer our questions and cooperate we can ensure this remains out of the public eye.'

'Are you quite certain?' It was too late to save my marriage, but I had to continue to protect my daughter. 'I could not risk any more scandal.'

'When you feel ready please do get in touch. We are still keen to bring you into the department, on something of an informal basis.'

'I see,' I said, beginning to realise that Davison was even cleverer than I thought. 'I'm terribly sorry about Miss Crowe, I really am.'

'So am I, more than I can say,' he said as he walked towards the door. He closed his eyes for a moment and regained his composure. 'Good luck with your re-entry into the world. Have you got your story straight?'

'I hope so,' I said, somewhat uncertainly. I knew, better than most, how stories were such troublesome things to get right.

Chapter Thirty-seven

I took longer than usual getting ready for dinner. I applied a spot of powder and a little blusher and lipstick – the news about Miss Crowe had left me feeling shaken and looking drawn – and dressed in that rather indecent georgette salmon-pink evening gown. When I had first set eyes on the dress on that damp day in Louis Cope I suspected that it would prove useful. Tonight I needed Archie to see me looking like a different woman.

On the way down to the lounge I bumped into Mrs Robson.

'Oh my,' said the lady, blushing.

'Is there anything the matter?'

'No, nothing at all,' she said, deliberately trying not to look at the way the dress clung to my curves. 'Are you all set for tonight?'

Had I been discovered already? 'Excuse me?'

'For the dance at the Prospect Hotel. I think it will be

fun. Even Arthur is looking forward to it, and he's not much of a dancer.'

'Oh dear, I'm so sorry. It completely slipped my mind.' What could I say to get out of it? 'I'm afraid I've just heard that my brother is going to join me at the hotel tonight. Will you forgive me?'

'Of course,' said Mrs Robson, moving closer to me. 'I'm pleased you've got some company at last. You've been so lonely for the past week or so, haven't you? Must have been terribly boring for you.'

'Yes, indeed,' I said quietly.

'Well, perhaps we can make it another day. I believe there's another on Thursday. Shall we make it a date?'

'Yes, good idea.' I knew that I would probably never see Mrs Robson ever again. Just as well really; I did not want to witness the look of disappointment and betrayal on the kind lady's face when she realised the truth.

'And try and have a little fun with your brother, for my sake, won't you? You deserve it.'

'Thank you, Janet.'

A dance around a big ballroom was exactly the kind of thing that would do me the world of good. I had a pocket of nervousness trapped in my stomach that would only disperse with a rush of vigorous exercise. Part of me felt like running around the grounds of the hotel and screaming my name to the wind, but while that would no doubt have cemented the image of myself as a rather queer individual I thought it best to restrain myself. Although I normally never touched alcohol – my favourite tipple was half a pint of double cream mixed with milk – on this occasion I would have liked to have been able to order a drink at the bar.

I wandered into the games room; yes, a spot of billiards might just do the trick. The exercise would help relieve my anxiety, while the sight of me in an evening gown brandishing a cue and striding around the table would convey just the right level of eccentricity. I began to play solo, enjoying the feel and the sound of the balls smashing around the cloth table, before I was joined for a game by a nice chap, Mr Pettleson, a wine merchant from London whose face was as ruddy as a fine port.

'I don't for the blazes know what is going on outside the hotel,' he said, as he pocketed one of the balls.

'What do you mean?' I said, although I knew very well what he would say.

'A commotion if ever I saw one. A number of cars. Men in suits hanging about. Photographers. If I'm not mistaken it looks as though the police are about to make an arrest.'

'An arrest?' I said, my voice breaking. Had they somehow linked my name to the deaths of Kurs and his wife? 'Are you sure?'

'Saw the same thing once down near Aldgate. The press had been tipped off by the police.' He looked up from his shot directly into my eyes. 'You never know, we might have a murderer in our midst, staying here at the hotel. What do you think to that, eh?'

'I'm sorry, Mr Pettleson, could you excuse me for a moment. I just need to return to my room.'

'Not feeling well? I hope my skill with the balls hasn't put you off. I'm normally an awfully poor player.'

'No, not at all. If you could just give me a few minutes.'

I walked as steadily as I could through the games room, past the lounge and up the stairs to my room. My windows overlooked the front of the hotel and, as I gently eased back the curtains, I could see the pack of reporters and photographers gathered in the grounds. There was something about their swagger and arrogance that reminded me of a hunting party I had seen on the trip to South Africa; on that occasion the men had been tracking a lion. I knew that I now was their quarry and that they would stop at nothing to secure if not my skin then at least a part of my soul.

From the crowd I thought I saw one of the men pointing up at my window and so I let the curtains drop and fell back from the window as if I were stepping away from a cliff edge. I poured myself a glass of water and sat in the armchair, my heartbeat rising with each roar of sound from the pack of men outside. A noise from the corridor startled me. Was there someone outside my room? Was it Archie? Had Davison returned? I looked at my watch: it was just after seven o'clock. Even though I was terrified I could not postpone it any longer. It was time to face the world not as Teresa Neele from South Africa but as Mrs Agatha Christie, if a rather damaged one.

I checked myself in the glass and applied a little fresh powder to my nose. As I did so I was conscious that I did not really need to put on that much of an act; the feelings of what psychiatrists would no doubt call disassociation were all too real. With a shaking hand and a quickness of breath, I opened the door and stepped out into the corridor; whoever had made the noise earlier had disappeared. I walked down the steps, making sure that I gripped the banister, and, taking a deep breath, stepped into the lounge. At first sight everything appeared to be in order. There was the usual gathering of couples, faces I recognised from my stay, and the quiet bubble of polite conversation. There was no sign of the reporters; obviously, they had been barred from entering the premises.

By a roaring fire there was a man whose face was obscured by his newspaper. As he lowered the paper, the man looked at me. It was a familiar face, a handsome face; it was Archie. On closer inspection I realised that he looked terrible. There was an unusual gauntness to his features, he had cut himself shaving and there were purple shadows under his eyes. Perhaps he had not been eating, perhaps he had been yearning for me. Could he still be in love with me? What utter nonsense, I told myself.

I opened my mouth to say something, but I could not bring myself to speak. Neither could Archie, who was looking at me as if I were some kind of stranger. His eyes darted around my dress, taking in the sheer delicate fabric, and a slight blush spread over his pale cheeks. What was he feeling? Regret? Longing? Desire? Shame? He opened his mouth to say something – I wanted him to say how nice I looked – but instead he gestured for me to sit in the armchair next to his. As I sat down I felt my old love for him resurfacing – had it really ever gone away? – and, for a split second, I considered blabbing out the whole sordid truth. He reached over and placed a hand on mine. His touch felt like the first real thing I had experienced in a long time.

'I say, are you feeling better? Mrs Neele?' The voice of Mr Pettleson destroyed the moment of tender intimacy between us. 'I waited for a good twenty minutes in the games room, but then I thought to myself that you weren't coming back. I hope I haven't put you off billiards for good?'

What could I say? 'Mr Pettleson, I'd like you to meet my – my brother,' I managed to mumble. 'Archie, this is Mr Alexander Pettleson, a wine merchant from London.'

'Good to meet you,' said Pettleson, shaking Archie's hand. 'Staying for long? First-rate establishment. I have no complaints.'

An awkward silence descended. What a grim business it all was. I could see Archie looking at me as if I were insane.

'Would you care to go into dinner, my dear?' said Archie in a rather formal manner, in an effort to move us away from Mr Pettleson.

'Yes, that would be very nice,' I said, equally stiffly.

On the way into dinner we met Mrs Robson again, who determinedly fixed herself to the spot so as to guarantee an introduction to this tall and handsome man. Again, I introduced my husband as my brother. As we walked to the table I kept up the charade with Archie; it was imperative that he thought I was unstable.

'That's the lady whose daughter had a baby just like I had, and her memory went,' I whispered. 'But you know, I shall get all right, because the lady staying in the Hydro says her daughter was like this when she had a baby, but she became all right.'

I saw tears welling in Archie's eyes. How awful to deceive him like this, but it was the only way.

'Don't worry, darling,' he said, talking to me not as a husband but as a concerned well-wisher. 'Everything will be all right. We will have dinner and then tomorrow we will leave here and get back to normal.' I knew that would never be the case.

After ordering steak for both of us, Archie took my hand again, and said in a low voice, 'You've been under a great deal of pressure, my dear. I can understand how difficult it has been for you. We're all so relieved to see you, you've no idea how terribly worried we were. And you'll never believe the police – what a hash they've made of all of this. But don't concern yourself with any of that now. The most important thing is to get you well again.'

'I don't understand. Have I not been well?' Archie

did not answer and we did not speak for what seemed like an eternity. After the food had been served Archie stared into my eyes and lowered his voice.

'Do you remember Rosalind?' he asked. 'She can't wait to see you.'

I couldn't prevent my eyes from lighting up. However, I did stop myself from asking the real questions I wanted to ask – how had she been, what drawings had she done, what new silliness had she dreamt up? – and continued to dissemble. 'Of course, dear Rosalind,' I said, cutting into the bloody meat. 'How is she enjoying married life? I hope it is to her advantage?'

'And Peter? You must remember him.'

'Yes, such a good friend of yours. How is his job in the City?' My heart ached for my dear dog. I could not wait to see him. Then a memory of that horrible package that Kurs had sent me, that bloodied paw, flashed into my mind. Suddenly the steak seemed inedible and I placed my knife and fork back down on the plate.

'Not hungry?'

'I thought I was, but I'm not now for some strange reason. And I'm feeling awfully tired and a little fuzzy in the head. Perhaps I have been ill, I can't remember. Do you mind if I go to bed soon?'

'No, not at all.'

After lapsing into silence once more Archie looked at me with concern and with pity, but not with love. No, that had gone. Yet I could tell that he was grateful to me, thankful that I had not made a scene about his affair. However, the state of my mind was unpredictable, or so I had led him to believe, and I suspect that he was relieved to retire early. He helped me from the chair and accompanied me up the stairs to my room. He told me that he had taken the room next to mine and that if I needed anything – anything at all – I should just knock on the interconnecting door. Otherwise, we would meet for breakfast at eight, after which a train would take us back home. My sister Madge and her husband Jimmy were on their way to Harrogate too, he said. They would travel with us the following day. Surely that would make me feel better.

Archie turned to me to say goodnight. 'Will you be able to sleep or do you need to see a doctor?' The word sent a shiver through me, and I felt my eyes darken. 'No, I can see that you are feeling tired,' he said, his voice breaking. 'A good night's rest will do the trick, I'm certain. There's time for a thorough medical examination when we get you home. We'll get the best man for the job, no expense spared.' I doubted that I would ever feel comfortable in the presence of a general practitioner again.

He kissed me lightly on the cheek, a limp and passionless gesture, and turned away, his eyes filling up with tears once more. I watched him as he walked, head bowed, along the corridor towards his room. His shoulders shook ever so slightly as he tried to hide his sobbing.

Chapter Thirty-eight

Breakfast was a miserable affair. The only sound at our table was the crunch of Archie eating his toast and the occasional ring of a teaspoon on a china cup. It looked as though he had not slept. The purple shadows under his eyes had darkened and his skin had taken on the appearance of thin parchment. Both of us knew that we would have to communicate, if only to talk about practical considerations – such as what time we were leaving – but Archie seemed so broken and defeated. Perhaps he had received some bad news. Had Miss Neele written a letter or sent a telegram severing relations with him? Certainly, the fact that her name had been linked with a married man – and for that friendship to be splashed all over the newspapers – would not have pleased her parents.

Finally, I could bear it no longer and I reached out and took hold of Archie's hand. He bit his lip and when he finally looked up his eyes were full of regret, sadness and guilt.

'I'm sorry,' he managed to say. 'I—'

'Don't be silly. There's nothing to be sorry for,' I said in a bright, artificial tone.

'I feel as though it was all my fault. If it hadn't had been for, well, you know ...' He hesitated, but finally, his face contorting in pain, he managed to say a name that now stood for many things: betrayal, the end of our marriage, private and public shame. 'Nancy.'

'Sh-sh,' I said, before we fell silent once more.

Archie took another sip of tea, and surprised by his tentative steps into the dangerous territory of emotions – a land that he regarded as suspicious and really only the preserve of the fairer sex – cleared his throat and started to talk of train times and suchlike. The certainty of facts soothed his troubled conscience and soon he reverted back to his old self.

'I'm not sure what time Madge and Jimmy will be down for breakfast,' he said, looking at his watch. 'They got in awfully late last night. They think it's best if you go and stay with them at Abney Hall rather than return to Styles. The press interest is just extraordinary. The *Daily Mail* offered £500 for an exclusive. Said they would even charter a special train for you! Vultures they are, but the police are no better. That damned Kenward. I've got a mind to sue the blasted daylights out of him. Sorry, darling. I didn't mean to alarm you. No, let's not talk about that. But I am afraid you will need to be aware that there is a large group of pressmen outside and they all want to get a word or a photograph or something out of you. Jimmy has come up with a super plan. He's got hold of a group of volunteers at the hotel to serve as decoys. Two couples are to leave the front entrance and get into a car in the hope that the reporters will follow them, while we all leave from the side entrance and slip away. What do you think of that? Also, we've spoken to the station master and he's arranged for us to have a special compartment on the train.'

He seemed so full of it now – a little life had come back into his eyes – happy that he could talk about solutions, not the problem that was his wife.

'Jimmy also said we should make the press believe that we are travelling to London, so we've put out word to that effect. By the time we change trains at Leeds we will have put the hounds off the scent.'

He ended his little speech on a note of triumph, like a small boy who had just solved what he thought was a particularly difficult puzzle.

'Very good,' I said. 'It seems you've thought of everything. Thank you.'

'Shall we go up and see them? Madge and Jimmy?'

'Oh yes, I can't wait,' I said. Archie's eyes looked encouraging, pleased that I seemed to be on the mend at last. 'Such handsome creatures.'

Archie hesitated as he nervously smoothed his hair with his right hand. 'You know Madge surely? Punkie?'

'Of course I do, silly, my favourite dog in the world.' When I thought about it Madge's nickname did have a canine ring to it. 'Closely followed by Jimmy.'

Archie looked down, embarrassed, almost as if he were in pain. How long would I have to carry on with this cruel farce? And how would I cope when I had to come face to face with Madge? Surely she would be able to see through me? At that moment my sister and her husband appeared at the entrance to the breakfast room. When she saw me Madge moved quickly across the room, but Archie bolted from his chair and went to talk to her and Jimmy. It was obvious he thought I was not ready to see them yet. I saw them whispering, followed by a few concerned looks in my direction. Madge shook her head and I think I heard her say something like, 'But I must see her, I must.' Archie became quite adamant over something and I saw the colour returning to his cheeks. Madge strained her head to look over in my direction once more, and so as not to meet her eye I concentrated on a palm tree in the distant corner of the room. 'If you are quite certain,' she said, taking her husband's arm and walking out of the room.

'Did you recognise them?' said Archie softly as he sat down at the table.

I shook my head and stared at the cup of cold tea in front of me.

'It will take a little time, that's all. Don't worry. It won't be long before you're back to your old self.'

The words had a hollow ring to them, as if he were just reading them from an over-rehearsed script. I, for one, did not want to return to my 'old self', whatever that was. Undoubtedly, part of me had been damaged, but another part had been set free.

'If we're going to make that train, we'd better get going. How is your packing? Need some help?'

'No, all ready,' I said blankly.

'Good, I'll get the boy to bring down the cases.'

As I waited for Archie to return I looked around me at the hotel that had been my home for the last week or more. When I had first arrived I had regarded the Hydro as something of a gilded prison, a place where I was being held against my will. Now that I was being told that I was free to leave I began to have fond feelings for the quaint, rather old-fashioned hotel. It had been here that I had danced to 'Yes! We Have No Bananas', something that still made me blush; here that I had shed my old identity and taken on another; it was here, too, that I had planned a murder.

'All taken care of,' said Archie, returning. 'Now, if you just take my arm, dear. We are going to go out of the side entrance, as I told you earlier. It will make things a little easier for us all.'

I could not bear to say goodbye to the acquaintances I had made at the Hydro, friends who were probably regarding me with a certain amount of suspicion. No doubt they felt foolish at being taken in so. Poor Mrs Robson, she had been so nice, and I had promised to go dancing with her. Archie led me down a corridor, then another, where Madge and Jimmy were waiting. I bowed my head as Archie opened the door. The chill

of the morning air took my breath away, the cold stinging my face just as it had done that night on Newlands
Corner when I had stepped out of my car to meet Kurs.
I pulled my cloche hat a little further down over my
head but at that instant a photographer, a mean-faced
little man in a cheap suit who said he was from the
Daily Mail, started snapping away at me. Archie at
first tried to plead with the man, but it was useless. I
could see Archie's face tightening with anger, his fists
beginning to clench, but the last thing we needed was
a scuffle.

'Please, Archie, just leave it be,' I said through
clenched teeth, leading him towards the taxi. 'Let's just
get the train.'

'Yes, the goods entrance of the station, if you please,'
said Archie in a slightly pompous voice to the taxi
driver. 'We have a private compartment waiting for us
reserved for Mr Parker and his party. That's the name
of the station master.'

By the time we arrived at the station the word had
got out. The London platform was crowded with a
swarm of journalists and photographers, all jostling for
position and shouting. The scene looked like something
from a painting I had once seen, a portrait of hell, full
of writhing beasts and people doing unutterable things.

I closed my eyes and gripped Madge's hand tightly
as she led me along the platform. At one moment
there was a surge of movement from behind, and I felt
something push my back, threatening to unsteady me.

Someone, I think a small boy, shouted, 'It's her. Mrs Christie! Look!' People strained their heads in different directions, but no one was quite sure where the small boy meant. A wave of motion passed through the crowd. I felt someone push against me again. I lost hold of Madge's hand and I saw myself being swept along the platform. I was back in the Underground with Kurs behind me, easing me towards my death. I screamed, and the sound of my own voice frightened me even more. The heat of steam burnt my face and I closed my eyes, darkness enveloping me. The energy drained from my body and I felt myself falling. Perhaps this was my punishment. This was how it was all supposed to end. At that moment, I felt someone take hold of me and lift me up and into the train.

Chapter Thirty-nine

I suppose I should have been happy. I had everything I could wish for. Rosalind was playing at my feet with darling Peter snuffling for a piece of broken biscuit near by. I could hear Carlo practising the piano in the drawing room. Madge had given me a supply of notebooks and pens galore. Abney Hall, her grand house in Cheshire, had a splendid library full of fascinating books and beautiful grounds in which I could walk. There was even a glass of delicious milk and cream on the table next to me. And yet I felt on edge, uncomfortable, decidedly ill at ease.

Perhaps I was still mourning the loss of Archie, who after rescuing me from that terrible throng on the platform and accompanying me to Cheshire had retreated back to Styles. Although we had not talked of divorce it was, I surmised, the next logical step. I knew that the public humiliation, the nasty gossip in the newspapers, the inference that he had had something to do with my disappearance, and my continuing mental instability had left him bruised and broken.

I suspected that he believed there was more to the story than a simple case of amnesia, but he probably didn't want to question me too closely because the truth – or his perception of it – would be too difficult to bear. In response to the coverage in the newspapers – claims that I had staged my disappearance as some kind of bizarre publicity stunt or as a way of enacting revenge on a straying husband – Archie had brought in a couple of doctors to examine me. They were kind enough men – nothing at all like Kurs – and, after asking me lots of questions, they had issued a statement to the effect that I had indeed suffered a serious case of memory loss. Still, there were certain elements of the press who did not believe that story.

Archie had written to me asking whether I would like to pursue the matter through the courts, but I wrote back telling him that I would prefer it if no further action was taken. I insisted that I never wanted to talk about the episode again.

Yet all these were superficial concerns when compared to the shadow that darkened my conscience: the deaths of Flora Kurs and Una Crowe. The girl's body had finally been found at the bottom of the cliffs off Ballard Point, Swanage. Although I had been preparing myself for the worst, seeing the news of the gruesome discovery in the paper had forced my stomach to lurch into my mouth. Apparently, her body had been spotted while a young woman had been out walking her dog. One report said that it had taken the police six hours to extricate the corpse from the jagged rocks. I had sent Davison a letter of condolence, but I had kept the correspondence brief and to the point. Since then I had often toyed with his card and thought about sending him a telegram. But I could hardly bring myself to recall, let alone talk about, the events that had taken me from the superficial comforts of my Sunningdale home to the wilds of Newlands Corner and then the horrors of Harrogate and Leeds.

No matter how hard I rationalised the situation, how often I told myself that none of what had happened had been my fault, it had all been initiated by Kurs, I still felt that I was to blame for their deaths. Would I be free of the guilt that ate away at me? Would I ever stop seeing their faces in my dreams? Perhaps my only release, if not salvation, would come through my writing. I had a great deal of work to do: I had to finish that blasted novel, *The Mystery of the Blue Train*, and then think about what to write next. There was only so long I could depend on Madge and Jimmy's kindness. I would need to earn my own living now.

As I took up my pen to scribble a fragment of an idea into my notebook my sister came into the room. We had not talked about those eleven days and I hoped we never would.

'Hello, darling. There's someone here to see you,' said Madge.

'Who is it?' I asked.

'Don't worry, it's not a beastly reporter or yet another doctor.' Madge knew that I was not keen on either profession but, of course, she would never be able to guess the real reason for my antipathy towards physicians. 'Nice-looking fellow, blond hair, lovely voice. Says he met you in London. You dark horse, you never told me about that.'

'What? Davison?'

'Yes, that's his name. I've told him to wait in the morning room. I tried to put him off, said you were still recovering, but he was quite insistent.'

I bolted up and walked quickly towards the door.

'Oh my, I thought you'd like a little distraction. But I didn't realise he meant that much to you. I've never seen you move so fast in all my life!'

'Madge, it's nothing like that, nothing of the sort,' I said somewhat irritably.

As I hurried down the long corridor, lined with paintings of horses and dogs and English landscapes, I felt my heart racing. What did he want? So far he had managed to keep my name out of the newspapers as he had promised. Was that all set to change? Was he coming to warn me that the blasted story was about to come out?

I stepped into the east-facing room to see him standing in the weak winter sun that filtered through the French doors. As he turned towards me he smiled, but his eyes looked haunted.

'Good morning, Mrs Christie,' he said, walking

towards me. As he approached I noticed the dark circles that still shadowed his eyes.

'Please sit down. Would you like tea, coffee?' I said somewhat stiffly.

'No, that's very kind, I'm not sure how long I can stay. I'm pleased to see you in better health. From some of the things in the newspapers—'

'Best not to believe everything you read in the newspapers,' I said, giving him a half-smile.

'Indeed.'

As we fell silent the sound of the ticking of the grandfather clock in the corner of the room filled the air.

'I'm – I'm sorry that our worst fears were finally realised,' I said. 'That poor girl.'

'Yes, it was most regrettable,' he said, deliberately choosing words to mask his real feelings. I suspected that if he allowed himself to articulate them he would break down completely.

'And what brings you north?'

'Actually, I'm on my way to London from Leeds.'

Would I always shiver when I heard the name of that northern city? 'What were you doing there?' I was not sure whether I really wanted to know.

'Just some background work into Dr Kurs and his unfortunate wife. It's only now that we are beginning to build up a portrait of just how unpleasant he really was.'

I wondered how much he already knew about my involvement. 'Have you discovered any more?'

'Yes, as a matter of fact I have. It seems Kurs had a hold on a good many people. We found, at his practice, a number of very interesting documents that could compromise a range of individuals, some of them in positions of power. His motive, however, was not financial. It seems as though he got a kind of thrill from being able to control people.'

'How intriguing,' I said, careful not to give anything away.

'The suggestion is that he saw himself as a kind of writer and the people around him as mere characters. We also found some manuscripts, or I should say fragments of manuscripts, but very interesting indeed. Detective fiction and the like.'

He watched me like a hawk. 'He was a great admirer of your work in particular,' he added. 'There are pages of notes devoted to his thoughts on *The Murder of Roger Ackroyd*. It seems that he was obsessed with the character of Dr James Sheppard. He regarded him as something of a hero.'

'That is most unfortunate,' I said.

'But of course there are certain gaps in the story,' he continued. 'To get the whole picture we will need to get the truth from you. A full account of what happened.'

I wasn't sure whether I could risk relating the whole sorry affair. I was afraid not only for my reputation, but for my sanity too.

'I can understand why you are hesitant, Mrs Christie,' said Davison, sensing my reluctance. 'For your information, the inquest into Una's death is due to be heard next week. Hartford, my colleague, and I have managed to keep your name out of it entirely. Kurs will not be mentioned either and the coroner will declare Una's death to be a suicide, the result of an unsound mind. Her father's death will be given as the main contributing factor in her breakdown. An expert will testify that Una tied her own feet together with tape and then – well, you know the rest of it.' He looked down as he swallowed. 'The press will never get hold of your involvement and to the public you will continue to be seen as the slightly eccentric lady novelist who suffered an attack of amnesia and, for eleven or so days, lost a grip on reality.'

'And in return?' I knew that all this would not come without a price.

'Do you remember what I mentioned to you that day on the steps of the Forum? And in Harrogate?'

I felt my heart begin to beat faster. 'Yes, yes, I do.'

'Well, I wondered if you had thought any more about my proposal. Something has come up and we wondered if—'

'I'm afraid the doctors have prescribed complete rest for the next couple of months. They say I really should take a holiday somewhere warm, but I don't know. I adore travel, but—'

'Well, that's something we may be able to help with.'

'In what regard?'

'The work would involve a trip to the Canary Islands.

There's a rather delicate matter that's cropped up, a very queer case, if you ask me. We wondered whether you'd be interested in helping us.'

I remained silent as I considered what to say.

'Of course,' said Davison in the manner of an aside, 'you do know that Flora Kurs was not dying?'

It was as if Davison was suddenly speaking in a foreign tongue. 'What? I don't understand.'

'Certainly, her health was delicate, but her medical records show that she did not have cancer, any kind of tumorous growth.'

'But she said . . .' I felt my face begin to drain of blood. I remembered the scene that day in her house, when she had told me about her illness. It all made sense now. Flora had made a greater sacrifice than I had thought. She had murdered her husband so that I did not have to. She had chosen to lie to me about her health to make it easier for me to accept her course of action. How could I ever repay her? How much did Davison know? Quite a lot by the sound of it. But why had Davison suddenly decided to tell me this? How astute of him to know that this was the final piece of information I needed in order to make up my mind.

It was too late now to think of regrets, of what I might have done; it was time to make plans for the future. Perhaps, if I went ahead with Davison's suggestion, I could go some way towards making reparation for the deaths of Flora and Miss Crowe.

'I will tell you everything, but only you and only

once,' I said somewhat sternly. 'After this, I will never speak of it again, do you hear? Never.'

'Yes, I understand.'

I felt a sense of excitement rising within me. I knew what I wanted to do.

'But before I begin, why don't you tell me a little more about the Canary Islands?' I said, my voice softening. 'It's funny, I've always wanted to go there. They say there is some spectacular scenery, and of course the climate is so very healing, especially at this time of year.'

The Facts

- Agatha Christie travelled to London on Wednesday, 1 December 1926 and stayed overnight at her club, the Forum. The next day she saw her agent, Edmund Cork, at 40 Fleet Street, and then returned to her house, Styles, in Sunningdale, Berkshire. On Friday, 3 December, Agatha and her husband Archie had a row and he told her he was going to spend the weekend at his friends' house, Hurtmore Cottage, near Godalming; the other guest was his mistress, Nancy Neele. Later that night, Agatha left Styles and drove to Newlands Corner, Surrey, where her Morris Cowley car was found abandoned the next day.

  Agatha checked herself into the Swan Hydropathic Hotel in Harrogate under the name of Mrs Teresa Neele on Saturday, 4 December. That night she was seen dancing to 'Yes! We Have No Bananas'. At some point during her stay she told a fellow guest, Mrs Robson, that she had suffered the loss of a baby daughter. She also told another guest, 'This Mrs Christie is a very elusive woman, but I don't want to bother with her.' On Tuesday, 7 December she took delivery of a parcel from London, which she said contained a ring that she had lost in Harrods. On Friday, 10 December she travelled to Leeds.

It's thought that her identity was discovered by chambermaid Rosie Asher, who told two bandsmen that the lady staying in Room 105 was the missing novelist. On Tuesday, 14 December, Archie Christie travelled to Harrogate and met his wife, who introduced him to a fellow guest as her brother.

The official statement released by the family was that Agatha had suffered a serious episode of amnesia. She rarely talked about the experience and omitted its mention entirely from her autobiography. Missing from her archive is the notebook she used to plot her masterpiece, *The Murder of Roger Ackroyd*. On Sunday, 23 January 1927, she left Southampton on the ship the SS *Gelria*, bound for Las Palmas.

Agatha and Archie Christie divorced in 1928 and he went on to marry Nancy Neele.

Agatha Christie is the best-selling novelist of all time.

- On Saturday, 4 December, Superintendent William Kenward of Surrey Police immediately launched an investigation to find the missing woman, a hunt that continued over the course of the next ten days. The failure to solve the case – he had believed that Agatha

Christie was dead – resulted in public humiliation. He retired from the Surrey Police Force in 1931 and died the following year, age fifty-six.

- Twenty-year-old Una Crowe, the daughter of Sir Eyre Crowe, was last seen by her family on Saturday, 11 December 1926. Her body was discovered at the bottom of cliffs near Ballard Point, outside Swanage, Dorset, on Sunday, 19 December. The inquest heard that her ankles had been tied together with green tape; the verdict was 'Suicide while of unsound mind'.

Acknowledgments

My first thank you must go to the Queen of Crime herself, who has been a source of entertainment, humour and wisdom since I first started to read her books at the age of eleven. In fact, one of my first creative efforts – a 'novel' written when I was twelve, for an extended exercise suggested by my English teacher – was inspired by her. This 46-page story, called *The German Mystery*, evolved from my admiration for two of Christie's masterpieces: *Death on the Nile,* and *The Murder of Roger Ackroyd*. I can still remember the relish with which I devoured these two books, my pulse racing, my jaw dropping as I tore my way through to the final pages.

I first had the idea for this book while on a train – none as grand as the Orient Express, I'm afraid, but one that journeys into the heart of the Christie world: the Great Western Railway line from London to Devon, where Agatha was born in 1890.

I moved to Devon in 2012 and one of the first things

I did was to visit Christie's holiday home, Greenway, which contains many of her possessions, including paintings, furniture and books from her parents' house, Ashfield in Torquay. I would like to thank the National Trust and its enthusiastic team of staff and volunteers for preserving a home that Christie quite rightly described as 'the loveliest place in the world'.

Although this is a novel, I wanted to try to make sure the facts surrounding Agatha's disappearance in 1926 were as accurate as possible. During the course of my research I consulted newspaper cuttings from the *Times*, *Daily Mail*, *Daily Express*, and *Daily Mirror*, as well as the two excellent biographies: *Agatha Christie: An English Mystery* by Laura Thompson (Headline, 2007) and Janet Morgan's *Agatha Christie* (Collins, 1984). The events of December 1926 are noticeably absent from Christie's autobiography, but Agatha's own story, first published by Collins in 1977, makes for compelling and absorbing reading. I also drew on this book to supply some of the details of Christie's life.

In addition to this, I also consulted Jared Cade's fascinating *Agatha Christie and the Eleven Missing Days* (Peter Owen, the revised and expanded edition published in 2011).

For information and photographs of William Kenward and the Surrey Constabulary, I would also like to thank Robert Bartlett. For an enjoyable day trip to Newlands Corner, the Silent Pool and the other sites relating to Agatha's disappearance, I would like to thank my partners in crime, Cherry and Martin Hughes. For tours and drives in and around Harrogate, I must thank my parents, David and Margaret Wilson.

I would also like to thank Dr Jamie Bernthal and Mia Dormer for organising the 2015 and 2016 Agatha Christie conferences at Exeter University. There, I met dozens of academics, writers and fans including Mike Linane and Sophie Hannah – thank you for extending the hand of friendship. I must also single out Dr John Curran, a world expert on Christie and author of the scholarly and detailed *Agatha Christie's Secret Notebooks*. He was kind enough to read *A Talent for Murder* in manuscript form and supplied me with a list of incredibly helpful suggestions and corrections. Christie's biographer Laura Thompson also took the trouble to read the book at this stage and I am grateful for her comments.

From the moment when I first conceived the idea for the novel, I have been supported at every stage by my wonderful agent, Clare Alexander. I cannot thank her enough for her enthusiasm, passion and continuing friendship. Also, at Aitken Alexander Associates I would like to thank the late Gillon Aitken, Sally Riley, Lisa Baker, Lesley Thorne, Leah Middleton, Nishta Hurry, Nicola Chang, and Ben Quarshie.

At Simon & Schuster I would like to thank my fabulous publishers, Suzanne Baboneau and Ian Chapman in the UK and Peter Borland in the US – it's an honour to work with you all – as well as Carla Josephson, Jo Dickinson,

Jessica Jackson, Justine Gold, Gill Richardson, and the rest of the fantastic team. Mary Tomlinson did a brilliantly thorough copy edit and I would also like to thank Mark Smith for the cover design.

Lastly, I would like to thank my parents and friends for their love and support. And, as always, Marcus Field, for too many things to mention.

Turn the page to read an exclusive extract from Andrew Wilson's
next Agatha Christie's adventure,

A DIFFERENT
KIND OF
EVIL

Chapter One

As I felt the ship tilt and roll I looked out of the port-hole to see a hidden horizon, the skyline obscured by a dirty smudge of a black storm cloud. I sat up and took a sip of water, trying to swallow down the feelings of nausea as well as wash away unpleasant memories of bad times at sea.

Perhaps a little fresh air would do me good, I thought, as I swung my legs over the edge of the bed. I checked myself in the looking glass, tidied my hair, quickly threw on some clothes and, as I knew it would be cold outside on deck, picked up the shawl that my friend Flora Kurs had given me and draped it across my shoulders.

I listened at the connecting door that led through to the cabin where Rosalind and Carlo were sleeping. All was quiet and so I decided not to disturb them. I knew from previous experience that if we were in for a rough crossing then it would be best if my daughter and my secretary were able to sleep through it.

I made my way down the corridor, but as I did so I had to place a hand on the wall to steady myself. Oh, please let this not be another Madeira. On that journey, the outward leg of the Empire Tour, the trip around the world that I had taken with Archie, I had suffered such terrible sea sickness that at one point I thought I would die. In fact, a fellow passenger, a lady who had caught a brief glimpse of me through the open door, had asked the stewardess, 'Is the lady in the cabin opposite dead yet?'

Although that made me smile now, at the time I had not found the observation amusing. I had had to be confined to the cabin for four days and, like a sick dog, had brought back anything I had swallowed. I had tried everything – dry biscuits, pickles, brandy, champagne – but nothing did any good. In the end, the doctor had given me what he said was liquid chloroform and after twenty-four hours without food Archie fed me with Brand's Essence of Beef directly from the jar. How fine that had tasted! I knew Archie hated illness of any kind and the sight of him offering me a spoon of the dark, viscous substance had made me love him all the more.

That love had gone for good now, at least on his part. The crisis at the end of the last year had finally squeezed the life out of our marriage. Archie had gone back to live at Styles, with a view to selling the house, while the new woman in his life, Nancy Neele, had left the country. Her parents had not wanted her to be caught up in the scandal I had caused with my 'disappearance' and had ordered her into temporary exile. I had heard, however, that on her return from her travels she and Archie planned to marry. The word divorce sounded so brutal, so ugly, and although I did not like the idea of it – with all the stigma and shame that accompanied it – I knew that it was something I would have to endure.

It was as inevitable as the force of the sea, I thought, as I opened the door and stepped onto the deck. The wind was beginning to whip up the water, sending its surface into a fury of white. A fine spray of sea mist left its moist trail on my face and, as I ran my tongue over my lips, I tasted salt. After leaving Southampton we had sailed through the English Channel heading for Portugal. Although I had been prepared for a spot of *mal de mer* as we sailed into the Bay of Biscay, the sea had actually been as calm as a duck pond. It was only after leaving Lisbon and travelling south that we encountered the bad weather.

I held onto the rail as I walked along the deck, straining my eyes towards the distance. Somewhere out there was my destination: Tenerife, one of the Canary Islands. John Davison, the man I had met at the end of the last year, had finally persuaded me to help him investigate the murder of one of his agents, a youngish chap called Douglas Greene. I had tried to resist his pleas to work with the Secret Intelligence Service – in fact, I remember to begin with I thought the whole thing had been nothing more than a silly joke – but after the deaths of

Flora Kurs and Davison's friend Una Crowe I felt duty bound to help. Neither woman would have died had it not been for me. How could I say no?

And there was something very queer about the circumstances surrounding the murder of Greene: Davison had told me that the agent's partly mummified body had been found in a cave on the island. At first sight, it appeared as though Greene's corpse had been covered in blood, but on further examination the glossy red sheen that covered his flesh was in fact the sap from the Dragon Tree, native to Tenerife. Bizarrely, all of his own blood had been drained from his system, but there was no trace of it on the dry earth in the cave or nearby.

When Davison had related this to me I could hardly believe it. But I knew, perhaps better than most people, that evil really did exist in this world. The way some people talked about crime astonished me – as if a sadistic murder or violent sexual attack could be blamed on a dreadfully unhappy childhood or an underprivileged background. No, I was certain that some people were born, not made, evil. Those that disagreed with me, I am afraid, were nothing more than blinkered idealists who could not face up to the brutal realities of human nature. I had stared wickedness in the face, in the form of Dr Kurs, and I would never forget it; one could literally smell the stench of evil emanating from him. His scheme to manipulate me into committing a murder had driven me to a point of utter distraction and despair. I doubted I would ever be the same again. Certainly, my dreams were still haunted by the horrors of those eleven days in December of the previous year. When I closed my eyes I still saw the faces of Una Crowe, that poor young girl who had been determined to follow my trail, and Flora Kurs, the woman who had sacrificed herself for me.

I looked out to sea once more and watched the sky blacken in the distance. As a child living in Devon, I would spend hours watching the shifting waters of Torquay Bay, the changing colour of the sea and sky, the reflection of the clouds upon the waves. I would imagine what lay over the horizon, the far-flung countries with their exotic climates and strange people, and try to picture my future. I don't think I ever dreamt that I would be a writer, much less get involved with working for a government agency. It all seemed so fantastical somehow, and yet it was true.

Davison had told me – what was it? – that I had a first-rate brain, or some such nonsense. I surmised that it had more to do with the fact that the division he worked for was extremely short on women. And surely no-one would ever suspect a socially inept, middle-aged lady of anything? I could move about in an almost invisible state, asking questions, listening to confidences. I could simply serve as an extra pair of eyes and ears. Before embarking on the journey Davison had stressed the importance of never placing myself in a dangerous situation. The murder of his friend Una still weighed heavily on him. He was taking no chances this time, and he had insisted on accompanying me on the journey to Tenerife. However, while on the S.S. *Gelria* – the ship that would take us from Southampton to Las Palmas, before it continued its journey – and also in Tenerife, he would travel under an assumed name: that of Alexander Blake. It would be simpler and more straightforward, he said, if we pretended to meet for the first time on the ship.

I had intended to leave my daughter Rosalind behind, under the care of my sister at Abney Hall, on the outskirts of Manchester, but when I mentioned to her that I might have to go away again she became terribly distressed. At eight, she was old enough to understand something of the miseries of the adult world and, no doubt, the thought of my absence brought back the horrors of the previous year: the sight of uniformed police, the strained atmosphere in the house, the look of worry and strain on servants' faces, the anxiety that she might see the front page of a newspaper or hear a newsboy's ghoulish call. Also, I don't think she had ever quite forgiven me for abandoning her for almost a year on my world tour in 1922. And so I had reluctantly accepted that my daughter would have to accompany me to the Canaries. She would be looked after by Carlo and I would make sure she did not come to any harm. It had taken me some time to persuade the family, and those fussing doctors, that a holiday would be beneficial – they worried about the difficulties of travel, the water, the foreign food – but finally they relented. A few weeks in a balmy climate would soothe my nerves and restore my spirits.

Just then a blast of icy wind forced me to hug the paisley shawl tighter across my shoulders. The fresh air had done me good, but the cold was getting too much. But then, just as I turned to return to my cabin, I heard what I first thought was the high-pitched cry of a gull. I stopped and gripped the rail. The sound split the air again: the unmistakable scream of a woman that seemed to be coming from the back of the ship. I ran from the front of the boat along the empty deck towards the stern. I looked around to enlist help, but there was no one to be seen. I heard my breathing – fast, shallow and full of panic – as I ran, but by the time I got to the stern the screams seemed to have stopped. Instead, I saw a heavily-set, dark-haired woman standing on the very back of the ship, staring into the sea. A few feet away from her stood another woman, a thin blonde, who on seeing me took a tentative step towards her companion.

'No, Gina, don't,' said the blonde-haired woman, stretching out a hand in the direction of her friend. 'I know you hate me, you hate us both probably, but really it's not worth it, *we're* not worth it.'

In response to this, the brunette climbed over the railings onto a narrow ledge, holding onto the wooden balustrade with both arms.

'Please, no,' I shouted into the wind, unsure whether the woman could hear my words. 'What's your name?'

I turned to her friend, the beautiful blonde whose face was wet with tears. 'Gina, did you say? Is that what she's called?'

'Yes, it's Gina all right,' she said. 'She somehow stowed away on the boat. She's been missing in England, no one knew she was here. She discovered, well, that her husband, Guy—'

I didn't hear the rest because at that moment a terrific gust of wind blasted in from the sea, forcing me to take a step back. Big fat drops of rain began to lash down from the ever-darkening sky.

'Have you tried to get help?' I shouted. 'Sorry, what is your name?'

'Miss Hart. No, I got up early to have a walk around the deck. I just chanced upon her and there was no one around. That's when I started to scream. I didn't know what else to do.'

'Are you close to her?'

'We were – once. But I'm sure she must hate me now. You see, Guy, that's Mr Trevelyn and I, well—'

I began to understand the sorry state of affairs. Guy had obviously been carrying on with Miss Hart behind his wife's back. Just like Archie had deceived me with Miss Neele.

I turned away from Miss Hart, as I tried to mask my contempt for her. 'Gina, listen to me,' I said, slowly moving towards her. 'Tomorrow, everything will seem very different, I can assure you. I found myself in just the same situation and at one point I even thought of doing, well, something stupid. But it is extraordinary what time, and a little perspective, can do. Of course, you feel like everything is worthless, but it is not the case. I'm sure you have a great deal left to live for. I'm sure you have friends, family, a favourite aunt or grandmother, a pet who adores you.' I thought of the feel of my dear dog Peter's soft head and the deliciously awful stench of his breath. 'Your life is precious, you may not think so now, but it is, especially to those close to you.'

She seemed to be on the point of turning around and looking at me and perhaps even climbing back over the railings. But then from behind me I heard Miss Hart scream once more. This time, the noise was low and guttural, primitive almost.

'Gina! No! Please don't!' she shouted, launching herself forwards. 'Not now. Not after everything!'

'Miss Hart, no!' I hissed. 'Please, stand back.'

I tried to stop Gina, attempted to calm her, but it was all so quick. She raised her arms and stood very still for a moment, before she started to sway ever so slightly as if she had given her body over to the force of the wind. And then, like an overweight ballerina, she moved as if she were about to fly, lifting her arms high above her head and then letting them drop to her side. Just as Miss Hart, in a panic, shunted forwards, a desperation in her eyes which reminded me of the look of an animal in the slaughterhouse, Gina raised her arms in the air once more and with a graceful movement she jumped off the ship. As I ran towards her I knew there was little point, that it was too late. But there was something inside of me – something which I was sure lives inside all people who count themselves decent and good – which propelled me to try and grab her. Instinctively, I thrust my hands out, but there was nothing to hold on to, only mist and rain and wind, the spray from an angry sea, and a darkening sky. I strained my neck to look over the railings, but there was no sign of Gina. She must have been dragged under in the wake of the ship.

'We need to see if we can rescue her,' I shouted, but to no response. I turned to see Miss Hart standing there, the life sucked out of her. 'Miss Hart. Quick. Go and get help. Find an officer.'

'Yes, of course, you're right,' she said, gradually coming back to her senses. 'Yes, it's worth a shot.'

As she turned and ran along the deck, I kept hoping to catch a glimpse of Gina in the water behind us. I called her name, even though I knew that the fierce roar of the wind and the sea would drown out my feeble voice. I was completely soaked through to my skin and my eyes were full of water, a mix of raindrops and tears. I imagined the poor girl in the water, gasping for air as her lungs filled up with salt water.

A memory came back to me from years ago when I had been swimming off the Ladies' Bathing Cove in

Torquay with my nephew Jack. I had set off with the little boy on my back – he was not yet old enough to swim by himself – towards the raft that lay anchored in the bay. As I swam I noticed that the sea had been possessed of a strange, queer sort of swell and, with the weight of Jack on my shoulders, I started to take in quite a bit of water. As I carried on – of course there was no option but to try to reach the safety of the raft – I became aware of not being able to breathe properly. Finally, realising that I was in grave danger, I told Jack to try and swim towards the raft. He said he did not want to, but as I went under he was washed off and had no choice but to swim. By this point, I had become so weak that I could not lift my head above the water; I suppose I must have taken in too much. As I began to drown I remember feeling cross that I wasn't having the sort of life-flashing-before-one's-eyes experience of popular lore. Neither did I hear strains of string instruments or soothing classical music. There was just a feeling of terrible emptiness, of utter blackness. The next thing I knew I was being tossed into a boat – which also rescued little Jack – and, on the shore, a man lay me out on the beach and started to work the water out of me.

Gina would not be so lucky, I was sure. But we had to try. Where was that woman? Why hadn't she managed to find help? Just then I saw Miss Hart come running with a man dressed in a smart blue uniform, who introduced himself as first officer William McMaster.

'Please, over here,' I said. 'A woman fell off just back here. Can you stop the ship?'

The officer lent over the stern and cast his expert eye over the surface of the water. As he turned to us the grim expression on his face said it all.

'Yes, we certainly will,' said McMaster. 'I'll go and tell the Captain now, but I'm afraid there is little hope. She would have been sucked down deep into the ocean. Even an Olympic-class swimmer wouldn't be able to survive that, I'm afraid.'

'I see,' I said, bristling at his pessimistic attitude. 'But we must do everything we can to make sure.'

'Of course. And if you could please go back inside. We're expecting some rather rough weather in the next few hours so we will be locking the doors that lead to the decks.'

'And if the poor girl did not survive,' I said, 'what are the chances of recovering her body? It seems only right we should give her a decent funeral.'

Miss Hart let out a quiet cry and bent her head forwards as she tried to stifle a sob.

'We'll do everything in our power to find her. But I am afraid that the weather and the sea are our enemies. We mustn't delay any longer. Please follow me inside.'

We trailed after McMaster like two mourners after a burial on a wet afternoon, our heads bent, our spirits low.

'Before I go and see the Captain, could you give me

your names?' said the officer, taking a small notebook from the inside pocket of his jacket.

'Mrs Agatha ... Christie,' I said, slightly hesitantly, fingering my wedding ring and wondering whether I would carry Archie's name for the rest of my life.

The officer raised an eyebrow. Perhaps he had read one of my books – or, more likely, he had seen something in the newspapers relating to the scandal surrounding my disappearance the year before. Would I ever be free of that? After noting my name he looked towards the beautiful blonde standing next to me.

'I'm Miss Helen Hart.'

The name sounded familiar.

'Thank you. I'm sure the Captain will want to talk to you later. And I'll let you know if we spot anything, anything at all.'

'Thank you, officer,' I said.

'How awful,' I said. 'What a dreadful thing to witness. You must be terribly shaken. Had your friend been standing there long?'

'I'm not sure,' said Miss Hart, brushing a strand of hair from her eyes. 'I'm absolutely soaking, aren't you?'

'Yes,' I said, looking down to see the water puddling on the carpet beneath our feet. 'Why don't we change into fresh clothes and perhaps we can have a talk in the library. I doubt there will be anybody there at this time of day.'

*

After agreeing to meet in half an hour, I returned to my cabin. Carlo and Rosalind were still sleeping. I ran a basin full of hot water and proceeded to wash. I dried my hair with a towel and brushed it, but it still looked a fright; it would have to be covered up with a hat. Just as I was dressing, Rosalind ran into the cabin, intent on telling me about a dream she had had: 'I lost Blue Teddy, mummy, I couldn't find him anywhere. It was horrible.'

'How upsetting for you, darling. But it was only a dream,' I said, stroking her hair.

'I know. Thank goodness. I should so hate to lose him. What on earth would he do without me?' She paused and looked at me as if she had seen me for the first time. 'What kind of dreams do you have, mummy? Do they make you sad?'

'Sometimes,' I said, remembering some of the horrific visions that had recently interrupted my sleep, often culminating in me sitting up in bed in a cold sweat. 'But then, I always tell myself not to be so silly as it's all make believe.'

'Dreams are such funny things, aren't they?'

'Indeed, they are,' I said, smiling. 'Oh look, here's Carlo.'

'Good morning,' said Carlo. 'I woke up because I felt the ship slow down. Did you feel it too? In fact—'

She broke off to walk over to the spray-streaked porthole. 'I'm sure the ship has stopped. Yes. Look – we aren't moving. And it's terrible weather too.'

I knelt down and kissed Rosalind. 'Darling, why don't you go and see if Blue Teddy is all right? I'll come and dress you in a moment.'

As I closed the connecting door I told Carlo of the events of the morning.

'How awful,' she said. 'And how awful too that you had to stand by and watch it all. Are you sure you don't need to rest? You know what the doctors said.'

'No, if I lie down I'll most likely start to feel seasick again. That's why I got up early, to have a breath of fresh air.'

Carlo looked pensive and serious before she said, 'She must have been driven to despair.'

'I suppose she must, yes.'

'And it seems as though this other woman, Miss Hart, was having an affair with the poor lady's husband?'

'Yes.'

'A familiar story.'

'Indeed,' I said, glancing at my watch. 'In fact, I'm due to talk to Miss Hart now.'

'Have we met him on board – the husband? What did you say his name was?'

'Guy Trevelyan. No, I don't believe we have.'

'Perhaps he was with that rather fast set we saw across the dining room last night. The ones making all that noise after dinner.'

I thought back to the previous night. As an ear-splitting guffaw cracked the air I remember looking askance at the group of young people in such high spirits at the far corner of the first-class dining room. Did they really have to be quite so loud? Perhaps it had been sourness or middle age or my own particular circumstances – whatever the reason I am sure I had not laughed like that in years – but I had cast a rather disapproving stare across the room and in the process I had met the amused eyes of a handsome, dark-haired man sitting next to an elegant blonde, who I now knew to be Helen Hart.

When I opened the door to the library Miss Hart was standing by the far shelves, with her back to me.

'I must say they've got a rather poor show of books. Not that I would read any of them if they had a better selection. Have you seen them?'

'No, I'm afraid—'

'Oh, I'm so sorry, I didn't hear you come in,' she said. 'I was talking to Mr Trevelyan.'

A tall, rugged-looking man stood up from one of the green leather armchairs. As he walked towards me I noticed that the mischievous glint in his eyes that I had seen last night had been extinguished; now his demeanour was serious and melancholic.

'Guy, this is Mrs Christie, the lady I told you about,' said Helen. 'She tried to help with—'

'I'm so grateful for everything you did this morning, I really am,' he said. 'Such a dreadful business.'

'I'm afraid I couldn't do more,' I said to Mr Trevelyan. 'Have you spoken to Mr McMaster?'

'Yes, he came to my cabin a little while ago. I'm

afraid there is no sign, no sign whatsoever,' he said. 'The Captain is going to hold the ship here for the next few hours to make sure, but I think that's more out of respect than anything else.' His handsome features, so dazzling at dinner the night before, looked a little worn around the edges and shadows had appeared beneath his eyes. 'Poor Gina. If only—'

'You can't continue to blame yourself, Guy,' said Helen. 'Yes, I know, well, we hardly behaved like saints, but Gina was always a bit unbalanced, wasn't she?'

'What do you mean?' I said gently.

'Please let's not go into all of that now, Helen,' said Guy. 'All I know is that I feel we've driven the poor woman to her death.' His dark eyes filled with tears and he bit into his knuckle to prevent himself from breaking down.

'Darling, you know that's not entirely accurate,' said Helen, placing a hand on his shoulder to comfort him. As she did so I noticed her large, strong looking hands. Her short nails were not painted and around the cuticles there lay a dark substance that looked like ingrained dirt.

I realised then how I knew her name: I had seen an exhibition of her sculpture – strange, primitive figures, fragmented naked torsos and the like – at a gallery in London. I recalled being quite shocked by some of the imagery, it was certainly powerful stuff, but one could not deny that Miss Hart had the ability to tap into the deepest parts of the human psyche. I also remembered feeling more than a little jealous of her talents. At one point I had had the very stupid idea of becoming a sculptress myself. I had even taken some lessons, but I had finally been forced to admit to myself that I was a hopeless case.

'I'm a great admirer of your work, Miss Hart,' I said, trying to lighten the mood.

'Really?' she said, her bright blue eyes shining.

'Yes, I saw your exhibition at the Pan Gallery early last year. I can't say I understood it all, but I certainly believe you have an extraordinary ability to capture the essence of things.'

'Well, isn't that lovely of you to say so. Isn't that wonderful, Guy?' she said. 'I recognise your name, but I'm afraid I haven't read any of your novels. Reading is not my forte. I can see things – forms, colours and such like – but I think I must be allergic to the written word. You must think me terribly stupid.'

'Not at all, Miss Hart,' I said, smiling. 'In fact, it's always something of a relief to talk to people who haven't read my books.'

'I know, why don't you join us for dinner tonight,' said Miss Hart. 'And by the way, please call me Helen.'

'Yes, of course,' Trevelyan said flatly. Helen looked at him sternly. 'Yes, please do,' he said, brighter and with more enthusiasm. 'I'm so sorry, Mrs Christie. I still can't quite believe it – that Gina is dead.'

'I know, a sudden loss is bad enough, but a death

of this nature something quite different,' I said. 'I'm sure she would not have suffered,' I added, not quite believing it myself. 'It would all have been over in an instant.'

'I suppose that is one thing we should be grateful for,' said Trevelyan. 'But I just can't understand it. The last thing I knew she had bolted from our house in Brook Street. She didn't leave a note or anything. I thought she would spend the night with one of her Mayfair girl-friends and the next day she would return. You see, it's a pattern I had seen on many occasions. Our marriage was far from a smooth one, you see.'

'And you say she was – well, she had a rather temper-amental nature?'

'That's putting it mildly,' said Helen.

'Please, Helen, you don't know the strain that Gina was under.'

Helen looked down, duly admonished, and let Trevelyan continue. 'Yes, it's true that Gina had a nerv-ous disposition. She seemed quite normal for a while, weeks at a time, and then, with no apparent reason, she would fall prey to an awful kind of mania. She would be up all night dancing or talking or walking the streets. She said she had the most extraordinary energy, creative energy. She once told me she had written a novel in the course of one night, but when I picked up the notebook I found it to be full of gibberish, nothing more than a few nonsensical phrases and obscenities. And then, with the same kind of suddenness, she would take to her bed, crying for no reason, threatening to harm herself, to do herself in. It was terrible, truly terrible to witness.'

'And when, may I ask, did your wife disappear?'

'It was on New Year's Day. We'd had quite a party at the London house. Too much drink, too much ... of everything. Perhaps Gina had seen something at the party, or suspected something. But the next thing I knew she'd gone. I contacted the police of course, and they issued a statement to the press – there were posters, searches, the lot. But nothing.'

'She didn't know about you and Miss Hart?'

'I don't know. Helen wanted me to tell her, but it never seemed the right time. Either Gina was in one of her periods of high-spirited ecstasy or she was in the grip of a terrible depression. There was never anything in between.'

Helen Hart sighed, an expression that spoke of a dozen unsaid sentences, a hundred suppressed wishes.

'There's no point sighing, Helen,' said Guy, his voice rising. 'What was I supposed to do? Tell my wife we'd been having an affair? Did you really want me to drive her to her death?' His eyes stretched wide with anger, and his voice cracked with fury. He strode purposefully across the library, opened the door and turned back. 'Is that what you wanted? Well, you've got your wish at last. I hope it makes you happy.'

With that he slammed the door and left us standing there looking at the elaborate patterns in the Turkish rug beneath our feet.

'As you can see, Mrs Christie, Guy has been left in a state of shock,' said Helen, the china white skin on her neck now a mass of red blotches.

'Grief does affect people in all sorts of different ways,' I said, trying to smooth over the acute embarrassment felt, no doubt, by both of us.

'Oh, please don't feel sorry for me,' she hissed. 'In fact, I'm pleased the bitch is dead.'

The statement – both the words and the way it was expressed – so shocked me that I was unable to utter a single word.

'I know it's a truly awful thing to say, but I am. She's out of our life for good now.'

The famous writer and amateur detective's adventures
continue in Andrew Wilson's gripping series . . .

**SIMON &
SCHUSTER**

A DIFFERENT KIND OF EVIL
Andrew Wilson

In January 1927 – and still recovering from the harrowing circumstances surrounding her disappearance a month earlier – **Agatha Christie** sets sail on an ocean liner bound for the Canary Islands.

She has been sent there by the British Secret Intelligence Service to investigate the death of one of its agents, whose partly mummified body has been found in a cave.

Early one morning, on the passage to Tenerife, **Agatha** witnesses a woman throw herself from the ship into the sea. At first, nobody connects the murder of the young man on Tenerife with the suicide of a mentally unstable heiress. Yet, soon after she checks into the glamorous Taoro Hotel situated in the lush Orotava Valley, **Agatha** uncovers a series of dark secrets.

The famous writer has to use her novelist's talent for plotting to outwit an enemy who possesses a very different kind of evil.

Available in print and eBook May 2018

**SIMON &
SCHUSTER**

DEATH IN A DESERT LAND
Andrew Wilson

Baghdad, 1928. Agatha leaves England for
the far-flung destination, determined to investigate an
unresolved mystery: two year ago, the explorer and writer
Gertrude Bell died there from a drugs overdose. At the time,
the authorities believed that Bell had taken her own life,
but a letter now unearthed reveals she was
afraid someone wanted to kill her...

In her letter, Bell suggests that if she were to die
the best place to look for her murderer would be Ur,
the archaeological site in ancient Mesopotamia
famous for its Great Death Pit.

But as **Agatha** stealthily begins to look into the
death of Gertrude Bell, she soon discovers the mission
is not without its risks. And she has to use all her skills
to try and outwit a killer who is determined to
stay hidden among the desert sands ...

Available in print and eBook May 2019

SIMON &
SCHUSTER

THE
DARK
PAGES

Visit The Dark Pages to discover a community of like-minded readers and crime fiction fans.

If you would like more news, exclusive content and the chance to receive advance reading copies of our books before they are published, find us on Facebook, Twitter (**@dark_pages**) or at **www.thedarkpages.co.uk**